WAITING FOR SPARKS

BOOKS 1-4

SPARKS IN TEXAS

MARI CARR

WAITING FOR US

SPARKS IN TEXAS, PREQUEL

WAITING FOR US

I Do is the easy part. *Happily ever after?* Not so much.

Evan and Annie are deeply in love, but that hasn't stopped tension from creating cracks in their relationship. Determined not to fail his wife, Evan takes action before those cracks become craters, damaging their marriage irreparably.

Over the Fourth of July weekend, he'll reignite Annie's passion with his own brand of fireworks. And this hot cop will pull out all the stops...and his cuffs.

Stand back and watch the sparks fly.

PROLOGUE

"Well, look what the cat dragged in. This is an unexpected surprise. Didn't know Maris' biggest, baddest lawman was planning to stop by tonight. Where's Annie?"

Lieutenant Evan Sparks claimed a seat at the counter and smiled at his cousin, Macie. He'd left work a little later than normal and had almost been home when he found his cop car making an illegal U-turn in the middle of Sagebrush Lane to come to Sparks Barbeque instead. The restaurant had been in his family for three generations and it felt more like home sometimes than his actual house.

He'd been depressed all day and he needed some advice. He could count on straight-shooting Macie to lay it all out for him.

Evan shrugged. "She's at home, I guess."

Macie narrowed her eyes. "You guess?"

He glanced at his watch. It was almost six-thirty. Quitting time at the bank, where his wife Annie was a loan officer, was at five o'clock. "Yeah. She'll be home by now."

Macie reached into the cooler and pulled out a Heineken. She popped the cap and slid it across the counter to him. "And you're *here.* Looking like someone shot your dog. Did you two have a fight or something?"

He shook his head. He and Annie rarely fought. At least, not with words. Instead, there was a tension hovering in the air so thickly these days that sometimes Evan thought it would almost be a relief to break it up with some screaming. However, they couldn't do that because they'd both be yelling at the wrong person. No one was to blame for what was making their lives together so unbearable.

Macie looked around the restaurant. Their cousins, Jeannette and Sydney, would be in the kitchen cooking, while Macie's mom Stella and their Uncle TJ were serving dinner and chatting with a large table of patrons in the corner.

The general consensus in Maris, Texas, was that the Sparks family made the greatest barbeque in the world. Countless entrepreneurs and food critics had found their way to Maris in he hopes of bottling the sauce or creating a chain of Sparks restaurants. The family had turned down every offer, dedicated to maintaining quality over mass-producing something that wouldn't live up to their standards.

Macie always manned the bar, since she was damn easy to talk to and made one hell of a Bloody Mary. She had a bubbly personality and an incredible memory. Evan suspected she knew the drink of choice of every single person who had ever walked into the restaurant.

Once Macie was sure they could chat relatively undisturbed, she leaned over the counter and lowered her voice. "Okay, spill. What's wrong, Evan?"

He hesitated, though he wasn't sure why. He'd come here because he needed someone to talk to and he trusted Macie. Evan wondered if it was embarrassment or pride holding him back.

"You know, Mace, there's only one thing I've ever been sure of in my life. One thing I've known about myself since I was young."

"What's that?"

"That I want to be a father. That's the life I've always wanted to live. The feeling's always been there."

Macie sighed softly, her eyes filled with compassion. "Still no luck?"

He shook his head miserably. Evan and Annie had married when they were in their early thirties, both well established in their careers. They'd planned to start a family immediately, hoping for a honeymoon baby. Everyone in town knew they were anxious to become parents and in those early days, very few weeks passed when someone hadn't asked if they were expecting yet. Then the months turned into a year and that year extended into another. With the passage of time, people stopped inquiring, and actually tried to avoid making eye contact with him and Annie anytime the subject of babies came up.

"I know the doctor said there was nothing medically wrong, but have you and Annie considered talking to someone else?"

"We have."

Macie seemed surprised by Evan's admission. He didn't blame her. She'd been his confidant for most of his life. Maybe it was strange for him to be so close to a female cousin who was several years older than him, but even when they were younger, Macie had felt like a kindred spirit. "When?"

"We drove to Austin a few months ago to see a specialist."

"And?"

"And Dr. Bryan was right. There's no medical reason why we can't conceive, so the specialist gave us some tricks to try. None of them are working."

"So adopt." It was an answer Macie had offered countless time in the past two years.

"You know I'd do that in a New York minute, but Annie really wants to have a baby. She doesn't want to stop trying yet."

Macie smiled sadly. "None of this is news, Evan. What's wrong? Why are you here, sweet pea?"

He took a drink of his beer, then he stared at the bottle, unable to hold Macie's gaze. Then he heard the words that had been trapped inside him for well over a year falling out.

"I'm fucking done in, Mace. I'm tired. Sex is completely regimented. We're on this schedule. I'm all but punching a goddamn time clock in the bedroom. It's hurting my marriage. I love Annie. Really love her, but we're just so tense. Every month when we find out she's still not pregnant, I hold her while she cries and tell her it will be okay. But what if it's not? What if those words are a lie and it's just another way I'm failing her?"

Macie reached out and took his hand, waiting until he raised his eyes to look at her. "You aren't failing her. Don't say that. Don't even think it."

"I don't know what to do."

Macie squeezed his hand. "Everything happens for a purpose and in its own time. Can I make a suggestion?"

Evan nodded. Her advice was the reason he'd come. He was out of ideas and running on empty. He needed someone to point him in the right direction.

"Stop trying."

He frowned. Hadn't she been listening? He and Annie wanted to be parents. They wanted to have a baby of their own. "Macie—"

"It's time to put the baby thing aside and focus on your marriage, Evan. I'm not saying you and Annie should stop trying to get pregnant, but don't schedule sex or read charts about ovulation times or have Annie stand on her head for twenty minutes afterward or whatever other voodoo shit y'all have been trying."

Evan laughed. "You think the standing on her head thing would work?"

Macie shook her head and snorted. "I'll bet you twenty dollars Annie is sitting at home feeling like *she's* failing *you*."

The thought bothered Evan more than he cared to admit. "That's ridiculous."

"She'd say the same thing to you, and you're both right. It is. You and Annie are a solid couple. You always have been. Don't fuck that up. So here's my solution. It's a holiday weekend. Y'all should put it to good use."

"I think you're forgetting I'm a cop and the words 'Fourth of July' in this town are synonymous with 'party 'til you're stupid'. I'll be patrolling the streets, arresting drunk drivers."

Macie frowned. "Maris isn't that big a town and most of the drunks know to stay put once they got a snoot full. Besides, everybody and their brother will be down by the lake, dancing on the beach then passing out in tents and cabins. You've got some seniority at the department. Take the early shift. Give the rookies the later one. It'll be good experience for them."

Evan admitted she had a good point. He'd been with the Maris police force for eight years. And though the Fourth typically included lots of heavy partying, he could count on one hand the number of drunken arrests he'd made during the holiday weekend—be it driving under the influence, idiots picking fights, or one fella pissing in the fountain in the middle of town.

"Well..." He couldn't think of a good reason not to ask for some time off, except lately, work had been his escape from the stress at home.

Macie must have sensed she was wearing him down. "We're closing the restaurant tomorrow and taking our meat on the road, setting up a big spread like we always do. You and Annie need to come eat, drink, listen to Tyson's band and then watch the fireworks with all of us. Let's face it. One night with our crazy family is sure to make you forget your worries. Kick up your heels and shake the rest of this crap off for a little while. The two of you need to give yourselves a break."

It was good advice. His thoughts had been consumed with worry and fear of what the future held for so long, he couldn't remember the last time he'd relaxed and simply lived in the moment. Macie was right. If he and Annie didn't take a big step back, they were in danger of destroying a good marriage. He loved his wife more than anything and the idea of losing her felt like a hard punch to his gut.

It was time to reignite the romance, time for them to remember what it felt like to be in love, without a care in the world. It was time to make the sparks fly again.

CHAPTER ONE

Evan glanced at the clock on the dashboard of his car and sighed. He only had a few more minutes left on his shift. Traffic had been steady most of the day as revelers headed to the lake to celebrate the Fourth, but it had slowed down in the last hour or so. He figured most everyone had already gathered by the lake and had started digging into the barbeque ribs Sparks laid out every year. His mouth watered just thinking about them.

He'd taken Macie's advice and managed to talk his captain into letting him get off early. He had made plans to meet Annie at the lake around six for some barbeque and dancing.

For the first time in months, he was actually looking forward to seeing Annie, rather than worrying about heading home to find her either waiting to rush him into the bedroom because it was a good time for sex, or upset because she'd gotten her period again.

It was date night, and he was determined they were going to have fun. They were going to turn things around this weekend. Get back on track.

He was just about to pull onto the road when he saw a familiar car speeding by, going way faster than the forty-five mph limit. He turned on his lights and followed, grinning at the chase.

His wife had always had a lead foot. They'd actually met when he pulled her over for speeding.

Evan caught up with her car on the outskirts of town. She had the top down on the convertible, enjoying the last of the day's sunshine. The weather was surprisingly mild for July in Texas, the temperature not creeping much above eighty-five all day. In Maris, any summer day that didn't touch a hundred was a cool one.

She waved when she spotted him, not bothering to pull over or slow down. Obviously she thought his pursuit was a joke. They were only a few miles away from the turn off to Harper's Lake, where they'd planned to meet up.

Annie's family owned a cabin on the lake that they used on weekends and holidays. However, her parents were out of town, visiting Annie's brother in Seattle this Fourth of July, so he and Annie had decided to take advantage of the empty cabin, packing overnight bags and staying there after the fireworks. It saved them driving back into town later and added to the element of romance. They could almost pretend they were away on vacation if they weren't in their own bedroom.

As Annie continued to fly down the road, a wicked plan began to play out in Evan's mind. It would mean missing the barbeque, but it would be worth it. The more road they ate up, the more Evan was convinced he'd discovered the perfect way to rejuvenate and reignite the passion in his marriage.

He and Annie were going to recreate the first night they met—only this time, Evan intended to put a sexy spin on it. A *very* sexy spin.

He sped up, not bothering to turn off the lights or siren. The road was clear, so he began to overtake her. Once he pulled even to her car, he used the loudspeaker.

"Follow me," he commanded before continuing past, enjoying the confusion on her face.

When he made the turn for the lake, Annie was right behind him. This was the same road he'd pulled her over on nearly five years earlier. She'd been on her way to the cabin to spend a long weekend with her parents when he'd stopped her for driving way past the legal limit. They'd struck up a conversation as he studied her license and registration. He hadn't been fooled by her obvious attempts to charm her way out of the ticket, but he'd pretended to fall for them just the same. She'd been flirtatious and funny and he'd tried hard to find ways to keep talking to her. Plus, she'd been wearing a bikini beneath a low-cut cover-up and it had been difficult for him to concentrate on much of anything besides her sexy tits.

Luckily, it had been late and, just like now, he'd been at the end of his shift. Somehow, they'd wound up taking their conversation down to the lake, the two of them sitting on the sandy beach, dipping their toes in the cool water. They'd talked all night. Then, somewhere around four a.m., he'd gotten his courage up enough to lean over to kiss her. He hadn't kissed another woman since.

Unfortunately tonight, the public beach by the lake would be packed with people celebrating the Fourth of July. What he had in mind required more privacy. A hell of a lot more privacy. He took the left that would lead them down the long, meandering dirt road to her parents' cabin. It was isolated and perfect for what he planned.

His phone beeped. Glancing at the screen, he spotted a text from Annie. It was simply a question mark, but it made him chuckle. She was probably wondering why he'd gone the wrong way, driving away from their destination.

Texting while driving. Another violation to add to his growing list. She was making things too easy for him. He didn't bother to reply. Instead he tossed his phone onto the passenger seat and continued. After several minutes, they reached the cabin. It was on a slight incline with a path that led to the lake and a large dock he and her father had built a year earlier after a flood had wiped out the old one.

Maybe they'd make it down to the water eventually. But first, he had some punishments to mete out. His wife had been a very naughty girl.

She started to park her car behind his, but he gestured out his open window for her to go around him. If all went according to plan, he intended to make use of his police car's spotlights later on.

Annie followed his directions. He stepped out of his car slowly, letting her curiosity build. She started to open her car door, but he said, "Don't get out of the car," in his most authoritative policeman's voice.

She hesitated, glancing over her shoulder, and he wondered if she'd obey. Then she leaned back against her seat and waited for him.

As he approached, she gave him an exasperated look. "Were the siren and lights really necessary the whole way here?"

"License and registration."

She laughed, making no move to reach for either thing.

He crossed his arms. "License and registration, ma'am."

Her laughter died at his stern expression. "What are you doing, Evan?"

Evan refused to break character. He had plans for the evening. Back in the early days of their relationship, they'd taken a few walks on the wild side, incorporating role-play into their sexual exploits, blowing vanilla sex out of the water as they experimented with bondage, domination and submission.

The fact that she still hadn't picked up on his intent proved to just how far they'd let their relationship fall to the wayside.

"Evan—"

"You have ten seconds to produce the paperwork I've requested or I'm citing you for not complying with a policeman's orders—in *addition* to the speeding and failure to pull over. There are stiff fines attached to evading arrest." He made sure to emphasize the word *stiff*, but she missed the sexual innuendo attached to it.

Her eyes narrowed at his haughty tone and he saw a spark of anger flash in her eyes. It had been too long since he'd seen any expression other than sadness or disappointment there. The fury was a welcome sight. It meant the lively, opinionated girl he'd fallen in love with was still there.

She dragged her wallet from her purse, muttering curses that sounded a lot like "jackass" and "arrogant prick," as she produced her driver's license.

Annie handed it to him with an annoyed smirk. "Having fun? You realize we share a bank account, so you may want to think about that before slapping too many fines on that ticket. Go too far overboard and our trip to New Orleans this fall is out." Her tone was pure sarcasm, but he didn't take the bait. He knew what part he was playing tonight and he fully intended to see her assume her character as well.

He looked at the license. "Annabel Iser." He purposely left off her married name. "Do you have any idea how fast you were driving, Ms. Iser?"

Her anger was wiped away, replaced once more by confusion. "Um...sixty?"

"Sixty-one. In a forty-five."

"You know as well as I do that speed limit is set too low. You've said so yourself, Evan, so why—"

"My name is Lieutenant Sparks. You can call me Lieutenant. Nothing else."

She was taken aback by his firm voice, his quick correction. "You're joking?"

He frowned. "Do I look like I'm joking?" He moved away from her door. "Step out of the vehicle, Ms. Iser."

Annie opened her door, still leery of his strange behavior. He hoped his next move would help clear things up for her.

He pointed toward the front of the car. "Stand facing the vehicle and put your hands on the hood."

She moved as he directed, taking her time. No doubt she was waiting for him to call the game to a halt with a laugh. Once she was in position, he stepped behind her. "If you'd been driving four miles per hour faster, I could have charged you with reckless."

"It's an obvious speed trap. Proven by the fact you were sitting there. Like a spider on his web capturing poor, unsuspecting flies."

He leaned closer, letting her feel the erection in his pants as he brushed it along her ass. "And you flew right into it."

Annie started to step back, intent on rubbing against him, but he moved away, patting her down. At first the touch was cursory, no nonsense. Then he repeated the motions, letting his hands linger on her sides, the tips of his fingers stroking her breasts.

"Are you searching for something special, officer?"

The breathless quality of her voice let him know she'd finally caught up with him.

"I need to be sure you aren't carrying any concealed weapons."

She looked over her shoulder and gave him a flirty smile. "Oh, I'm packing heat. But you aren't looking in the right place."

He fought to restrain a groan. Annie was a master at dirty talk. Then it occurred to him that this fantasy—the cop and his criminal—was one they'd never played out. Which was strange considering his occupation and the fact he had all the right toys.

"Face forward, Ms. Iser. I don't think you understand the seriousness of this situation."

Annie held his gaze a few seconds longer before looking away. Her hips wiggled seductively as he moved his "search" lower. He didn't take the bait. He had a definite strategy for how the night would unfold and it had everything to do with his pretty criminal submitting to his authority.

"Have you been drinking, Ms. Iser?"

She lifted her shoulders casually, unconcerned, unrepentant. "I may have had a glass of wine earlier. It is a holiday, you know."

Annie wasn't much of a drinker, even on the holidays, so he wondered about the wine. Was she feeling the same pressure he was? Had she been looking for a way to relax before seeing him again? That thought made his chest ache. He pushed it away. Hopefully, tonight would help them mend the rifts they'd unconsciously let grow.

He reached for her upper arm, dragging her upright and turning her until she faced him. "Drinking and driving?"

"You don't really expect me to confess to that, do you, officer?"

"Lieutenant." The mischief in her eyes told him she was

purposely refusing to acknowledge his rank. "And I don't need your confession. I have a breathalyzer."

She didn't pretend to be worried. He loved her spunk, the challenge in her posture. She crossed her arms, allowing them to push up her breasts. The move drew his attention to her hard nipples. His mouth watered for a taste of them, but it was far too early for that. If he started taking off her clothes, the game would end too fast.

For months, he'd viewed sex as a chore, the two of them going through the motions with very little passion or foreplay. As he looked at her flushed face, as he watched her chest rise and fall with breathless expectation, he wanted to kick his own ass for forgetting how good it could be between them.

"Don't I have to consent to the breathalyzer?"

He shook his head. "I'm not giving you a choice." He cupped her face in his hands, pulling her closer. "Are you ready?"

He didn't give her a chance to respond before placing his lips on hers. He pressed them open, touching his tongue to hers. He couldn't detect even the faintest hint of wine on her breath. Regardless, he kept kissing her, tasting and breathing her air. Evan didn't need alcohol. He could get drunk on Annie.

Finally, after several minutes, he forced himself to release her, working overtime to maintain control, to stay in character. "You realize you're in quite a bit of trouble, Ms. Iser."

She feigned a contrite smile that didn't fool him for a minute. "Maybe there's some way I can convince you to forget all this and let me off with a warning?"

He narrowed his eyes. "Are you attempting to bribe a police officer?"

She reached out to run her hand along his chest, toying suggestively with his badge. "I didn't say anything about a bribe."

He moved so quickly she didn't have time to counter or retreat. Evan turned her toward the car, grasping her wrists and tugging them behind her back. She had just begun to struggle when he slapped on the handcuffs. Then he bent over her, pressing her against the hood of the car, letting her helplessness sink in.

"What did you have in mind?" he murmured in her ear.

He'd taken her off-guard. It took her a few moments to regroup.

"I..." She swallowed heavily when he ground his cock more firmly against her ass. "I..." She paused again. Finally she said, "What do you want?"

Evan chuckled. Annie was rarely at a loss for words. It felt good to shake up the self-assured woman. "I want it all, Ms. Iser. Your total submission. For the entire night."

"Submission?" Annie repeated the word with the same tone some women used when they mentioned chocolate or wine. She wanted the same thing he did. Badly.

"I'm taking you into custody. You will be punished for every single crime you committed tonight—speeding, failure to yield to a policeman, resisting arrest, drinking and driving, carrying a concealed weapon—"

"Hey. You never found that," she argued.

"Oh, don't worry, Ms. Iser. I'm definitely going to uncover that heat." Then he finished his list. "And texting while driving. You've been a very naughty woman. So do you agree to my demand or should I read you your rights and take you to lockup now?"

Annie bit her lower lip, pretending to consider her options. He was transported back in time, to the days when sex was playful and fun and so goddamn hot, he went to bed most nights with a cock sore from fucking.

"I don't want to go to jail," she said at last.

"Then you're mine." Evan made sure to evoke as much menace into his voice as he could. He fully intended to test Annie's limits tonight. He'd lost his way, so overwhelmed by guilt for letting her down that he'd forgotten what they could truly give each other.

They'd let their disappointment and sadness beat them down until they were mere shadows of their former selves. Somewhere along the line, they had relinquished their desires and given up on their relationship. Tonight, he was reclaiming it...and then he would demand even more.

He lifted the hem of her white sundress, pleased to find her wearing his favorite thong. Annie had dressed for the holiday, adding bright red flip-flops to her outfit and tying her hair in a ponytail with a thick blue ribbon adorned with stars. She'd been ready for an evening spent sitting on the sandy beach by the lake. He ran his hand over the bare cheeks of her ass.

"You were driving sixteen miles over the legal limit," he said as he continued to stroke.

Annie began to move sensually, soaking up his soft touches. Her chest was still pressed to the hood, her hands constrained behind her back. She was truly his captive. There was little she could do to resist his advances. Evan didn't think she'd realized that yet. But she would. Soon.

"I'm going to punish you for that, Ms. Iser. Now...count."

He lifted his hand, striking her firmly on the ass. Annie started to rear up, but without the use of her arms, it took very little for him to hold her against the car. They'd experimented with spanking in the past—only a couple of times—but they hadn't gone much beyond him taking her over his lap and placing a few taps on her bottom before they gave in to the heat of the moment. Tonight was all about practicing restraint—his and hers.

"Evan—" she said with a gasp.

"You will call me *Lieutenant*. And you will count."

He spanked her again, his hand landing on the opposite cheek with the same amount of force.

"Two," Annie said, still struggling to escape.

He cupped one globe of her ass in his hand as he bent over her back. "No. That was one. The count will start over every time you forget."

She shot him a dirty look over her shoulder and started to protest. Evan didn't give her the opportunity. He lifted his hand and struck again.

"Two," she repeated through gritted teeth and with a look that promised retribution.

He wasn't worried. He knew how to distract her from her anger. He placed three lighter blows on her upper thighs as she counted. Then he caressed her heated skin. Annie sighed at his softer touch. Unable to resist, Evan ran his finger along her slit, amazed by how incredibly wet she was, her thong drenched.

The last few weeks, they had actually started using lubrication during sex. The fact Evan hadn't considered that abnormal or wrong drove home just how low he'd sunk. He hadn't been wrong when he'd told Macie he was letting Annie down—he'd just mistaken the reason.

Never again, he vowed silently. He loved this woman and she deserved all his attention and care...in the bedroom as well as out.

Annie opened her legs, silently urging him to touch her more deeply. He resisted the temptation. The punishment wasn't over yet.

He lifted his hand and struck her harder on her left cheek. The sudden roughness caught Annie unaware and she nearly forgot to count. He was just about to tell her to start over when she quickly said, "Six!"

He repeated the motion a half-dozen more times—varying the placement and strength.

Annie was gasping for breath as she said "thirteen." He stopped once more. He didn't even need to touch her to feel the fire radiating from her body. She wasn't complaining about the pain. Instead, the spanking had morphed into something that was clearly pushing her arousal higher. She quietly pleaded for more. He wondered if she meant for him to continue the spanking or if she wanted a different sort of more.

He shoved the string of her thong aside and pushed two fingers inside her pussy, marveling at the pressure of her inner muscles as they clenched around him. Damn. How good would that heat, those strong contractions feel on his cock?

He thrust shallowly a few times before pulling out.

Annie cursed him loudly, demanding he continue. He

silenced her with the final three slaps, letting that action remind her who was in control.

She pressed her forehead against the hood of the car. "Please. I need you." The words fell out on a whisper. It took all the strength in his body to refuse her. He couldn't recall the last time he'd brought her to this place, to the moment where she wanted him with such a fierce hunger.

"That's right, Ms. Iser. I want you to beg me. Plead for me to fuck you."

The use of her maiden name seemed to draw Annie back into the game, to remind her of where they were and what he wanted from her.

"I won't beg you, Officer," she taunted.

God, he loved her. He lifted her from the car, letting her sundress fall back into place. She challenged him with a gaze that said she was ready for more, that she was capable of handling everything he dished out. He couldn't wait to prove her wrong. He was going to demand more than he'd ever asked for before.

He lifted his hand to her face, cupping her cheek. Then he let his gaze slide down to her lips. He touched them. "Such a pretty mouth."

She licked her lips. "Evan."

He placed his finger on her mouth to keep her from saying more, his expression stern. "Before the night is over, you *will* call me Lieutenant."

She didn't deny it with words, but the fire in her eyes let him know she would resist until the bitter end.

He opened the driver's side door and urged her to sit sideways on the seat. He didn't miss her slight wince when she landed on her sore bottom. The alpha male he'd kept locked away for too long felt like beating his chest. He was marking this beautiful woman as his. There was something heady about making sure she'd remember this night every time she sat down for the next few days.

His cocky grin must have revealed his pride because she

narrowed her eyes in a way that said she'd get her revenge eventually.

Her hands were still cuffed behind her back. Though he wanted to challenge her, to keep her on edge, the part of him that had always stood as her protector came to the forefront. "Are the cuffs too tight? Are they hurting you?"

She shook her head.

"Then they stay on." Bending forward, he lifted her slightly so he could raise her dress, the material gathering around her waist. Then he tugged her thong off, tossing it aside.

"Open your legs, Ms. Iser."

He loved the way her eyes went heavy every time he used her maiden name. It continued to fuel the fantasy, to keep her on edge. And hot.

She spread her thighs a few inches. She wasn't finished fighting him yet. Annie intended to make him work for everything. He stepped between her legs, using his knees to open her as wide as the confines of the car would allow. The height of her sitting on the seat, with him standing in the open door, was perfect for what he had in mind next.

Evan unhooked his gun belt, laying it on the backseat of the convertible. Annie's gaze never left his hands as he unzipped his pants, then reached in to draw out his cock. He held back the groan of relief he felt as he freed his erection. He'd reached critical mass the moment she'd stepped out of the car and the tightness of his pants had become painful.

Annie moved forward slightly, but he halted her.

"I haven't told you what to do."

She looked up. "I hardly think I need instructions."

Her sassy smile faded when he pulled the ribbon out of her hair, her auburn waves falling over her shoulders. He wrapped a handful of tresses around his fingers, tugging it roughly.

Annie flushed, her breathing becoming rapid.

"You will do exactly as I say and nothing more." He stroked his cock with one hand as she watched, the other still gripping her hair, holding her captive.

Annie didn't resist his tight hold or try to take control. Slowly, the submissive part she kept at bay ninety-nine percent of the time started to emerge. They'd only scratched the surface on her desire to yield to him during their previous sexual games, but Evan had recognized her needs.

"Open your mouth, Ms. Iser."

She complied so quickly, Evan failed to hide his smile as he directed his cock toward her pretty lips. Even without the use of her hands, Annie was more than able to test the limits of his control. She drew her tongue along the sensitive underside of his cock, humming as she dipped the tip of it into the slit at the head of his dick.

He took several deep breaths, forcing himself to calm down, to resist. "Did I tell you to do anything more than open your mouth?"

Annie stilled, raising her eyes to his face. He didn't withdraw from her mouth, didn't wait for an answer.

"I told you to do exactly what I say. Nothing more. Understand?"

He fought a wave of lightheadedness when she nodded, his cock still deep inside her mouth.

"I'm not interested in a blowjob, Ms. Iser. You're mine this weekend. You're here for my pleasure. And what I want right now is to fuck your mouth." His words were deliberately crude. They'd spent the past year tiptoeing around each other in the bedroom, playing nice until Evan thought he'd go mad. The kid gloves were off. His wife was going to see the man he longed to be.

She nodded once more, her eyes telling him she wanted the same thing. He used his grip on her hair to direct her motion. Pushing his hips toward her, he pulled her forward. His cock brushed the back of her throat. She gagged slightly, trying to fight against his hold. He didn't relinquish, didn't release her.

He continued to thrust in, pushing her farther than he'd ever dared. On the fifth pass, her throat opened and his cock slid deeper. Annie groaned, the sound triggering something primal inside him.

Evan moved faster, took her with more force. She was with

him. Her mouth opened wider and soon it wasn't his hand moving her toward him, it was Annie increasing the pace, the depth. She was wild, unrestrained. Beautiful.

Evan closed his eyes as his balls drew tight. Then he held Annie still, his cock exploding, sending jet after jet of come down her throat. She swallowed, and as he started to withdraw, she followed him, licking him clean with her tongue, sucking lightly on his now flaccid cock.

He pulled free, reaching down to pull her up. He held her face as he kissed her. When they parted, it was on the tip of his tongue to tell her how much he loved her, but he wasn't ready to leave the game yet. There were still fences to mend.

He turned her away from him gently, releasing her from the cuffs. She started to rub her wrists, but he stopped her, massaging them himself.

Annie was uncharacteristically quiet. One look at her face told him she had fallen deep into the fantasy. Time to take it up a notch.

"Don't get used to your freedom, Ms. Iser. You're still in custody."

He led her to a tree nearby. The sun had set as day gave way to dusk. When it grew darker, he'd move them back to the convertible and make use of the spotlights on his police car. His cock—though sated—twitched as he considered his plans for the rest of the evening.

"Take off that dress."

Annie didn't hesitate as she reached for the hem, tugging the lightweight cotton over her head in one quick motion. She made no move to undress further. His little submissive was learning her lessons well.

"Kick off your flip-flops."

Again, she complied instantly.

He stepped closer and reached into the cups of her lacy bra. Evan drew her breasts over the stretchy material, so they were pushed up, her nipples tempting him to take a taste.

Bending his head, he sucked one turgid tip roughly into his

mouth. She gasped, her hands flying to his hair. He stood rapidly, stripping the bra off. He needed to see every bare inch of her.

Then Evan tugged out the handcuffs he'd stuffed into his back pocket. His pants were still open, though he'd tucked his cock inside his boxers. It wouldn't stay there for long. Just the image of her naked had the blood rushing south once more.

He grasped her hands, lifting them above her head. He'd picked his spot well. It was perfect for what he had in mind. Evan tossed the cuffs over a branch then secured her wrists once more. The branch was low enough to allow her to bend her elbows slightly while still standing with her feet flat on the ground. He studied her face, checking to make sure she was comfortable.

Saucy little thing winked at him.

He schooled his features, though it was hard. Annie always knew how to make him laugh. "Apparently I'm going too easy on you. After all, this is punishment, Ms. Iser."

She didn't bother to hide her pleasure. She clearly loved being bound, at his mercy. They would definitely have to expand on this concept in the future. He wasn't going to be a fool again, wasn't going to lose sight of what they could do to and for each other.

Evan recalled the way she'd taken his cock into her mouth, the pleasure she'd given him. Now it was her turn. He knelt before her, grasping her ankle to guide one leg over his shoulder. It left her pussy level with his mouth and open, his for the taking.

He drew his tongue along her slit, tasting her sweet juices, soaking in the sound of her startled but aroused, "Oh!"

Evan cupped her ass as he held her pussy to his mouth. He used his teeth to tease her clit before dipping his tongue inside her. Annie jerked, so he tightened his grip, holding her still for his sensual assault.

"God, Evan."

He savored her cries as he moved his hands, using them to separate the globes of her ass. He continued to fuck her with his tongue as his fingers drifted toward her anus. She was gyrating wildly and oh so close to coming. He knew her tells. Years spent as lovers had made him an expert on Annie's orgasms. Not that he'd been utilizing that knowledge the way he should have lately.

He ran one fingertip around the rim of her anus. She gasped then closed her eyes.

"Please." The word escaped on a hungry whisper.

Anal play was one area they hadn't explored in the past. Annie has always pulled away whenever he made the suggestion and he respected her boundaries. Given her response to his touch, he regretted giving up so easily.

Evan shifted away for a moment. It took only a few seconds for Annie to realize he didn't intend to return to her pussy.

Her eyes opened, finding his. "Don't stop."

"Don't tell me what to do." He deliberating kept his voice low, the tone rife with warning. He pressed one finger into her pussy, letting the juices of her arousal coat it. Then he dragged it back and pushed it into her ass.

Annie's gaze never left his. He waited for her to struggle, to try to escape, to refuse the touch, but she didn't. Instead, she watched him. Let him expose her to the new experience.

He didn't move quickly, careful to read her expressions, looking for any sign of discomfort. He saw none. Once his finger was buried to the hilt, he paused. He knew what he wanted, but he also knew now wasn't the place or time. He'd need to prepare her for the experience. And they needed lube.

Even so, he wanted to ramp up her anticipation, play with her mind as much as her body to enhance the experience. The dominant Lieutenant who'd taken her into custody with the intention of using her wouldn't care about her comfort.

"I'm going to fuck you here." *Eventually*.

She blinked rapidly, her brows creasing. Evan schooled his features, careful not to grin at her obvious uncertainty. The sensual threat increased his desire when he realized something— she wanted to say no, but she also wanted to say yes.

She wants to say yes?

He took a deep breath, cataloging that information for later. He may have impulsively jumped on board the kinky train, but he sure as hell wasn't getting off at the next stop. Evan fully planned to ride this thing all the way to the end of the line. They would need years to indulge all the sexy ways he wanted to take his wife. And anal sex had just jumped to the top of the list.

"Stop thinking, Ms. Iser. I wasn't asking your permission. Merely telling you what's going to happen."

Annie digested that information quickly, then like the sun emerging through dark clouds after a storm, her face cleared, her confusion passed.

Evan slowly pulled his finger out before thrusting it back in—once, twice—before removing it completely. She was gasping once more, her arousal fired to full blast within seconds.

Then he stood and stepped away from her.

Annie frowned, the anger he'd seen when he'd first pulled her over reemerging. "Wait, I was close."

She was damn close. Which was why he'd stopped.

"And you're going to get closer still, but you're forgetting why you're here. This night is about your punishment and my pleasure." That wasn't entirely true—he had no intention of leaving her unsatisfied—but the way her body flushed and her nipples tightened every time he spoke of her incarceration told him she liked that fantasy. One of her favorite roles whenever they used to play was that of the captive. She loved the thrill of the chase, the exhilaration as she tried to escape. She never failed to put up a fight. Her aggression and failure to submit triggered the Dom in him and those nights—the rough fucking, the explosive passion—had been the most incredible of his life.

How had they traveled so far from there to here?

"Evan, please, I need—"

He stood quickly, grasping her hair roughly. "You will call me Lieutenant. Continue to forget and you won't enjoy the consequences."

A soft moan escaped her lips. Annie tried to take a step closer to him, fighting the bondage to rub against him. She was sex and sin rolled into one. It would be far too easy for him to uncuff her, toss her to the ground and pound into her sweet body all night.

He tightened his grip, holding her away from him. "Say 'yes sir'."

She resisted his demand a heartbeat too long.

"Say it, Ms. Iser. Now. Or I'll make damn sure you don't come tonight."

"Yes sir," she whispered.

Evan tugged the key to the handcuffs out of his pocket, reaching above her head to unhook her. He put the keys and cuffs away. They'd used them enough this evening and he didn't want to hurt her, keeping her bound for too long.

Annie's arms fell to her sides and he was there, ready to stroke the blood back into them. He massaged her shoulders, working his way down before clasping her smaller hands in his.

He leaned forward, unable to stand being even a few inches away from her. He squeezed her hands. "Ready to continue?"

CHAPTER TWO

Annie nodded, and then added, "Yes sir," to her response. Evan's eyes darkened with lust. She couldn't recall the last time he'd looked at her with so much hunger, so much need. Her heart ached with the beauty of it. And the relief. And the excitement.

Annie wasn't sure what the hell had gotten into her husband, but she wasn't going to look this gift horse in the mouth. She'd had a glass of wine earlier in the day, hoping it would relax her because she'd been nervous about tonight. Lately the tension between her and Evan had grown so thick, she feared she'd need a sledgehammer to break through it.

She'd been so scared these past few months. Evan had slipped further and further away from her with each passing day and she hadn't had a clue how to pull him back. Now he was standing in front of her, bringing all her wildest fantasies to life.

He reached for her and before she realized his intent, he'd lifted her into his arms. She resisted the hold, insisting he put her down. She had gained some weight since they'd married and part of her was embarrassed for him to realize how much.

"Be still." His voice was gruff, powerful. The timbre sent shivers of excitement through her.

Even so, she tried to escape his grip. "Put me down. I'm too heavy."

His eyes narrowed, the slightest trace of anger creeping in. "No. You're not." He'd been walking toward the car, but he stopped at her protestation. She ceased her struggles when it became apparent he wouldn't move again until she obeyed him.

"Are you ready to behave?"

She stopped squirming. Then reluctantly nodded, hoping it would encourage him to hurry up and get where he was going.

He raised one eyebrow until she added, "Yes sir."

Annie wasn't sure what it was about her that loved it when Evan turned into this commanding alpha male. She certainly didn't want him trying to call the shots in their daily lives; she enjoyed the true partnership they shared when establishing a budget or dividing the household chores. But in moments like this, there was something about being taken over by a powerful, sexy man that made her panties melt and her heart race.

Evan continued to hold her for several moments longer, letting his lesson sink in, before starting toward her car. He walked to the trunk of the convertible and lowered her slowly to the ground.

Patting the metal, he said, "Hop up there."

Night had fallen. While the sky was clear and the moon was shining, most of the light it offered was hidden behind the thick overhang of leaves from the trees. She was grateful for the darkness.

Though she was used to walking around in front of her husband naked, it was slightly unnerving to be so revealed outside, regardless of the remoteness of the area.

She reached behind her, using her hands to hoist herself up. Evan stood before her, waiting until she was seated. Then he grasped her knees, pulling them apart.

"Don't move," he commanded.

She was startled when he stepped away from her, turning and walking to his car. She wanted to call out, ask him where the hell he was going. He'd left her hanging—literally and figuratively—at the tree. Her body hadn't forgotten the orgasm he'd denied her. However, she managed to bite her tongue, certain the dominant man her husband had become would add that to her list of punishable offenses. She smiled at the thought, sorely tempted to do it simply for that reason.

Her grin died when Evan reached into his car, turning on spotlights that cast her center stage. She reached up to shield her eyes, unconsciously closing her legs.

"Hold the position I put you in."

She froze, wariness creeping in. Annie knew there was no one else around. That Evan was the only one who could see her—and he'd seen her naked at least a thousand times in the past. But that didn't make exposing herself like this any easier.

"Ms. Iser."

She repressed a shiver at his use of her maiden name. It was all he'd called her tonight and damn, if it didn't make her a little bit wetter every time he uttered it.

Slowly, she opened her legs. Her cheeks flushed, her skin growing hot. Evan walked to the front of his car and leaned against the hood. She lost sight of his features as the bright lights overwhelmed her vision, making him appear as nothing more than a silhouette.

Less than ten feet separated them, but he felt much farther away. Without a clear view of him or the sound of his breathing, it seemed as if she was completely alone. It was unnerving...and exciting.

It was quiet except for the natural sounds surrounding them—crickets chirping, a slight breeze rustling the leaves, the more distant lapping of the lake against the dock. Evan didn't speak for several moments, which left her even more in the dark.

What was he doing? Thinking? Typically she could tell from his tone or expression if he was tired, stressed-out, hungry or amused.

Now, he'd hidden from her, leaving her exposed under the lights. It forced her to focus not on him, but on herself, on her own feelings. As the minutes stretched, Annie was lulled into a state of relaxation by the gentle rhythm of the water in the distance. The heat produced by the police car's lights made her almost sluggish, sleepy. She stopped worrying about her nudity or Evan's impression of her.

She was pleasantly warm, fuzzy, horny. Her arousal hadn't waned. In fact, it had grown.

"Touch yourself."

She jumped slightly when he finally broke the silence. Had she somehow given herself away? Revealed her need?

It took her a moment to process his command. By then, he'd lost patience.

"I'm not going to repeat myself, Ms. Iser."

Her hands moved to her breasts—seemingly of their own accord—and she cupped them, letting their plumpness fill her palms. The women in her family had a history of being rather well endowed. Most of the time she cursed her large boobs, wishing she didn't have to lug the ungainly things around all day.

Evan, however, loved her breasts. It wasn't unusual for the two of them to fall asleep, him spooning her from behind with one of her breasts in the hand he'd wrapped around her.

She squeezed the globes harder, intending to use the action to arouse him. He was still hidden in the shadows.

Was he watching? Was her sexy peepshow working?

Annie moved her fingers to her nipples, sucking in a shallow breath when she stroked the sensitive tips. How long had it been since she'd felt like this—her body on fire, her pussy clenching with a gut-aching need?

She pinched her nipples tightly, pushing the sensation just beyond pleasure to pain. She winced, not because it hurt, but because the rough touch sent shards of electrical currents directly to her clit. She started to close her legs, hoping to find some relief, but she recalled Evan's order.

He wanted her legs open, wanted her completely exposed. After the magical wickedness of the evening, she couldn't think of anything she wouldn't give him right now. She'd fallen in love with the man five years earlier that first night by the lake, and she'd fallen just a bit deeper every single day since then.

Evan didn't speak as she played with her breasts, didn't offer commands or try to direct her actions. If not for his silhouette leaning against the car, she could almost forget he was there.

Almost.

Annie moved one hand lower, drawing it over her stomach to her pussy. She wondered if Evan would stop her. He didn't move, so she took the freedom he offered.

She needed to come. Like yesterday. The need had built up until she'd reached the point of no return. He'd told her to touch herself and that was exactly what she was going to do.

She caressed the firm bud of her clit, going straight for the kill. She was no stranger to masturbation, to finding her own pleasure. She'd spent too many single years before meeting and marrying her hot cop. Too many lonely nights.

As she increased the speed and pressure, she was overcome with gratefulness that she had met Evan. Though her touch was doing the trick, she realized whatever climax she gave herself would be lukewarm compared to the explosive sparks Evan provoked.

Or at least, the ones he *used to* provoke. Before she became obsessed with getting pregnant and having babies.

Guilt crept in and Annie hesitated, her fingers pausing mid-stroke. She didn't want to come without him. Didn't want to keep feeling alone in a house where she wasn't alone. Annie spent every single night with Evan and yet, she'd missed him.

Now he was there, with her, and she needed this time to make things right between them.

"Don't stop," he commanded.

She wanted to submit, wanted to give him what he asked for, but first...

"I'm sorry."

Evan didn't reply immediately and she suspected her apology confused him. After all, how was he supposed to know what she was sorry for?

"I'm so sorry, Evan. For everything. I know I haven't been the easiest person to live with lately, but—"

She didn't get another word out of her mouth. Evan was there, crossing the distance between them in three long strides.

"Hush," he urged, pressing his lips firmly to hers. She clung to him as he deepened the kiss. Their tongues tangled as tears sprung to her eyes.

She'd missed this closeness, this passion. She gripped his hair more tightly when she sensed him trying to pull away. She wasn't finished yet. She needed more. So much more.

Evan reached behind her, tugging her ass toward him, dragging her to the edge of the trunk of the car. She reached down, drawing his cock from his still-open pants. It occurred to her they'd spent the last couple of hours with her in some state of nakedness while he was fully dressed. They'd address that issue later.

For now...

She directed his cock to her wet opening, groaning as he pressed deep, thrusting inside with one relentless, powerful motion.

Annie wrapped her legs around his waist, trying to pull him even closer. The incredible restraint her husband had shown all night appeared to be lost.

He grasped her hips, keeping her in place as he took her. Neither of them held back anything as he pounded harder, Annie urging him on.

"More! God, more," she demanded.

Evan pressed on her shoulder, directing her to recline on the trunk, tugging her ass closer to the edge. He slowed his motions, thrusting shallowly, stoking the fire but controlling the blaze. Evan's gaze traveled along her body, the admiration reflected there making her feel beautiful, cherished.

Then his hands followed the path of his eyes. He ran his fingers along her neck and down her chest. The delicate stroking provoked a strong shiver. She was a woman on the edge.

"I need—"

"Shhh," Evan admonished. "I know what you need, Annie."

He cupped her breasts in his hands as he slowed his thrusting even more. She started to tell him it was clear he didn't have a damn clue what she needed.

Then he pinched her nipples.

Annie's back arched, her pussy clenching greedily on his cock. Stars flew behind her closed eyelids.

He pinched again.

She pressed her hands flat against the car, wishing she had something to grab on to. She was in serious danger of flying away.

Evan bent forward to kiss away the little pangs of pain, his mouth gently sucking one of her nipples in. With his tongue, he soothed and stroked. Annie balled her hands into fists as she fought for the strength to hold on.

She'd been on the verge of coming for hours, yet she didn't want to give into it yet. Something told her that the pressure building would explode white-hot, and it would be magnificent. She wanted Evan with her for that.

So she sucked in some much-needed air then bit her lip, hoping to distract herself with the pain.

Evan rose once more. She instantly missed the heat of his body on her chest, his departure reminding her once again that they were outside.

Though night had fallen, the temperature hadn't. Instead, the humid July air, the heat produced from the bright spotlights and the fire raging in her body left her in danger of suffocating. And the worst part was she welcomed that intensity.

Evan didn't seek to increase his pace. Instead, he drew his hand away from her breast, lightly teasing the skin of her stomach before drifting even lower. He found her clit instantly. The man was an expert on her body, though she'd sort of forgotten that fact.

She was ashamed of herself for taking the joy out of their bedroom, for making Evan feel like nothing more than a stud to her broodmare. She'd stopped treating him like a man, like her lover. Instead, she'd become a slave to ovulation charts and optimum body temperatures, snapping her fingers whenever she needed him and turning her back on nights when she didn't.

Another apology rose, but Evan wiped it away, distracted her from the words when he pressed her clit harder, stroking it faster. He'd begun to move once more, his thick cock traveling deep, touching every hot spot. With his fingers on her clit and his dick inside her, he slowly, steadily drove her to the brink of paradise.

"Come with me, Annie."

She didn't need to be told twice. Her head fell back against the car as her climax flashed. For a moment, she panicked it was stronger than she was and she wouldn't survive the tremors, the sizzling electricity flowing through her veins.

She was overwhelmed, overcome. Undone.

Evan briefly stiffened as her inner muscles clenched his cock, his fingers tightening where they now gripped her hips. "Fuck," he muttered. "Shit. Yeah. God, baby!"

Annie had only just started to come down, had only found one second of reprieve before Evan's hard thrusts triggered another climax. Her cries were drowned out when sparks of red, white and blue began to light the darkened sky, a loud explosion—matching the one inside her head—disrupted the quiet night.

Evan joined her, filling her with hot jets of come. He slowly leaned forward, holding himself above her on his elbows. He kissed her as more fireworks flashed. Neither of them sought to separate, too wrapped up in the wonder and magic of the moment.

He kissed her softly, matching her smile. Then he studied her face and the somberness she'd grown too used to returned.

"I'm the one who's sorry, Annie."

She shook her head, unwilling to hear him take even the slightest bit of blame. "No."

He pressed a quick kiss to her lips to silence her. "I love you."

She swallowed heavily, trying to dislodge the lump in her throat. "I know, Evan. I've never doubted it. I hope you realize that. But I'm sure I've made you question my feelings for you."

"No. You haven't. God, Annie. I've failed you in so many ways."

She scowled. "Don't say that. Don't think it. It's ridiculous and wrong."

He gave her a crooked grin. "Macie said the same thing to me."

She didn't return his smile, too upset by his words. "You've never let me down. Never. Not once."

He lifted one eyebrow and she suddenly understood exactly how he felt like he was failing her. She repeated her previous assertion. "Never, Evan."

He reached up to cup her cheek. "How did we forget this? How good it was between us?"

She chuckled softly. "I have no idea. Pure insanity."

"It won't happen again. You have my word."

"And you have mine." No matter what life threw at them, Annie refused to let stress or disappointment or fear drive them apart again. As long as she had him in her life, they could handle all the rest together.

Evan stood slowly, provoking a slight shiver as he withdrew. She pressed her legs together, trying to hold on to the memory of his possession, to trap the heat for as long as she could.

She was surprised when he walked away from her, back toward the tree. She sat up, giving him a questioning look when he returned with her flip-flops.

"Here. Slip these on."

She did as he asked as Evan went to his car, turning off the spotlights and grabbing a blanket from the trunk. "Grab those beach towels from your bag."

Annie reached into the backseat, procuring the towels. Then she took the hand he proffered, letting Evan lead her to the trail that meandered to the lake.

As they got closer to the water, she could see the light of a big bonfire in the direction of the public beach. The fireworks display still lit up the sky. If she listened very closely, she could hear faint strains of music. Evan's cousin, Tyson, had formed a band last winter—the talented group blowing most people in Maris away with their rockabilly sound.

When they reached the dock, Evan released her hand and began to disrobe. She watched him in silence, enjoying the sexy striptease and the way the moonlight and brightly colored flashes of fireworks lit his skin.

Once he was naked, he walked toward the ladder at the end of the dock. "Feel like skinny dipping?"

She giggled. "I'd love to. I'm so hot right now."

He winked at her. "You're always hot, Annie. But yeah, I swear the temperature is rising tonight. You gotta love Texas in July."

Evan climbed down the ladder, sliding into the water with a loud sigh. Annie was right behind him. The cool water felt like heaven against her overheated skin.

Evan was waiting for her a few feet from the dock. She swam straight into his open arms, loving the strength in his hold.

They'd spent countless summer days—and nights—in this lake together, playing or floating or just diving in to cool off before getting right back out again. They had gone swimming that first night he'd pulled her over. The sun had been coming up, adding to the heat that hadn't waned a bit. She'd been wearing a cover-up over her bathing suit, so she'd suggested they take a morning swim to cool off.

Evan had accepted her invitation, stripping off his uniform until he was left in only boxers. Then he'd joined her in the cool water. And just like now, she'd swum into his arms, the two of them kissing and floating, content to cling to each other, swaying with the water.

The fireworks display ended, allowing them to hear the sounds from the beach more clearly.

"Orange Blossom Special?" Annie asked, picking up on the tune of one of her favorite songs.

Evan smiled, nodding. "Do you want to get dressed and head down to the beach? I suspect the party still has a few more good hours in it."

She shook her head. "No. I'm happy here. With you."

They kissed once again. Then a thousand more times. Annie

wasn't sure how long they stayed in the water, but by the time Evan suggested they get out, she noticed the party had quieted and the moon had shifted a bit farther along the sky.

Grasping a towel, Evan dried her, wrapping her in the soft terrycloth before retrieving the other for himself. He spread the blanket over the grass at the edge of the shore. They lay down together, both falling to their backs to stare at the night sky.

Evan reached out, clasping her hand. They didn't talk for a long time. Annie was lost in her thoughts—reliving the wonder of the night.

Then she recalled his fears. Evan had truly thought he'd been failing her. Just the idea of it caused her heart to break. She'd been so wrapped up in her own sadness and self-pity, she'd let those hurts affect her marriage and upset Evan.

She shifted to her side, facing him. "Evan—"

He looked at her. The expression on his face told her he knew what she was going to say. "No. Not tonight."

"But—"

"We need to talk about it, Annie. And we will. I promise. I mean, God only knows what I'd be without you." He rolled toward her, pulling her beneath him. "But for tonight, can we just focus on Annie and Evan?"

His request required no thought. She understood what he wanted and she knew how important this time was. They had some rebuilding to do. Some trust to reestablish. There was plenty of time for them to talk about the future—about children, conception, adoption. None of that mattered if they didn't fix what they'd broken in their search for those things.

She reached up to touch his face, careful to school her features. "No. We can't."

Evan frowned at her refusal.

"We can't be Evan and Annie tonight." She gave him what she hoped was a sultry smile. "But I *would* like to spend some more time with that sexy lieutenant. Damn if he doesn't know how to make sparks fly."

Evan chuckled.

And then, before her very eyes, her dominant, sexy, amazing husband transformed himself into the man of her dirtiest fantasies. He stripped the towel from her body, and then parted her legs with his.

She closed her eyes, sighing when his thick erection parted her sensitive folds, thrusting deep.

"Open your eyes, Ms. Iser. Look at me."

She obeyed, giving him a sexy smile. "Yes, Lieutenant."

EPILOGUE

Evan walked into Sparks Barbeque after his shift ended. He'd promised Annie he'd pick up their dinner—nothing like barbeque to go—on his way home. Macie was in her usual place behind the bar.

"Jeannette is just finishing up your order. Good thing you called ahead. This place is packed. Lots of people looking to kick off the long Labor Day weekend with beer and barbeque."

Evan grinned. "That's my plan too. Only I'm doing my celebrating at home."

Macie gave him a funny look. "You're a cop. Didn't think you guys found much pleasure in three-day holiday weekends, between the traffic and the drunks."

"Didn't say I was celebrating Labor Day. Or at least...not the kind of labor you're thinking of."

Macie tilted her head, confused. "Have you already started drinking? What the hell are you talking about?"

"I'm saying that I'll be celebrating a different sort of labor day in about seven months. Right around the fourth of April."

Evan watched the light go on.

"Shut the front door!" Macie exclaimed so loudly most of the patrons in the restaurant turned to look at her.

He and Annie had kept her pregnancy a secret until they'd seen a doctor and eight weeks had passed, and they were more confident everything was okay. They'd broken the news to their parents earlier in the week, but they'd asked them to keep it quiet for a little while. This morning he had asked Annie if he could tell Macie, since it was her good advice that had led to this moment.

What he'd failed to realize was that telling Macie in a public place was the equivalent of telling everyone. The woman had no poker face, her emotions—whether it be anger, sadness, or absolute joy—radiating from every part of her.

She jumped up and down several times before coming around the bar to tackle hug him. Luckily he'd seen her coming and had time to plant his feet. She leapt at Evan, hugging him tightly as she laughed and cried.

Macie's crazy response drew a crowd, and soon Evan found himself embraced by three more cousins and two aunts who happened to be there. Then several men—friends and family—slapped him on the back, adding their congratulations.

"I see you told Macie."

Evan turned to find Annie standing close. He gave her a sheepish grin. "I'd intended to tell *just* her."

Annie laughed. "That's why I stopped by. It occurred to me when I left work that breaking the news in Sparks Barbeque would pretty much open the floodgate."

Macie offered Annie the same exuberant hug as Jeannette unpacked their take-home boxes, insisting they stick around to eat so everyone could celebrate.

He and Annie claimed two stools at the bar, enjoying the buzz as Macie proclaimed Annie was having a son and Jeannette and Sydney began making a list of baby names for them.

Soon, his family drifted away to wait on the other customers. Annie ignored his teasing when she ordered an extra helping of coleslaw for her barbeque, insisting it was fine since she was eating for two.

Evan watched her, soaking up her smiles and laughing at her exuberance as she ate. He'd counted at least three throaty "mmms," two "oh my God, that's good" moans, and a "wow" that was accompanied by a sexy lick of her fingers.

Evan shifted on the stool, trying to coax his ever-growing erection down. He was getting seriously turned on by his wife's enjoyment of her dinner. He wrapped his arm around her shoulder after they finished the meal. "What do you say we head home, Ms. Iser? I have a hankering to hear you make all those delicious noises again. In bed."

Annie was off the stool before he'd added the last bit. "You'll have to catch me first, Lieutenant."

And with that she jiggled her car keys with a giggle and left.

Evan threw some money on the counter to pay for their dinner then said good night to Macie. As he pulled his police car onto the road, he switched on the lights and siren with a grin.

Life was good.

It was very, very good.

WAITING FOR YOU

SPARKS IN TEXAS, BOOK 1

WAITING FOR YOU

How do you protect the woman you love...when the greatest danger is sleeping in her bed?

Sydney can't remember a time when Chas wasn't part of her life—from childhood playmates, to high-school sweethearts, to long-distance friends. Now, Chas is leaving the Marines and coming home.

Together again, it feels as if they were never apart, the love they'd shared as innocent teens now vastly more intense as adults—with a sexual hunger to match.

However, Chas can't shake the memories of his tours in the Middle East and struggles to hide his increasing lack of control, terrified of losing everything he'd just regained--including Sydney.

CHAPTER ONE

"Good morning, Gran. What brings you here so early? We usually don't see you until lunchtime." Sydney Sparks put a clean coffee cup down in front of Mrs. Parsons, her grandmother through self-appointed adoption, and filled it for her.

"I actually stopped by because I wanted to see you."

Sydney rested her arms on the counter and grinned. She'd known Mrs. Parsons, Chas' grandmother, for most of her life. Chas and Sydney had grown up together, best friends since the first day of kindergarten. His grandmother and uncle had raised Chas, so Sydney had spent a lot of time in Gran's kitchen after school or on hot summer afternoons as she and Chas mooched homemade chocolate chip cookies or ice-cold lemonade.

"Well, that's nice of you. But I just saw you the day before yesterday in the grocery store."

Gran took a sip of her coffee. "Yes, but that was before I got this." Gran slid an envelope across the counter.

Sydney recognized the handwriting instantly and her blood went cold. She'd been anticipating this moment for several weeks now. Chas had enlisted in the Marines fresh out of high school, shipping off for basic training just two weeks after graduation. Since then, he'd re-upped twice.

The time had run out on his third term of service and Sydney expected—feared—he'd continue his tour for a fourth.

Chas had spent the majority of the past decade in the Middle East. A fact that had cost Sydney—and she suspected Gran as well—countless nights of sleep. His unit had been deployed to Iraq once and he was currently finishing up a third tour in Afghanistan. He'd been shot twice, lost several friends in skirmishes with militant forces and seen horrors Sydney couldn't even begin to imagine. Not that Chas talked about it much. Usually whenever he was home for too-brief, too-infrequent visits, he purposely didn't discuss his experiences overseas. And Sydney didn't press because she understood his desire to put it all away, to forget about it for a little while.

But she'd seen the truth in his eyes. They weren't the same twinkling, mischievous sky blue they'd been when they were kids. Instead, they were now serious, haunted and she'd swear they had faded to slate gray, though she wasn't sure if it was possible for eyes to actually change color.

Sydney looked at the envelope, but made no move to pick it up.

"Aren't you going to read it?" Gran asked.

Sydney shook her head. "Not much point. I know what it says."

Gran seemed surprised. "You do? He told you his plans?"

Sydney lifted one shoulder casually, hoping she could hide her disappointment but suspecting Gran wouldn't be fooled. "I know Chas. He'll do another four years."

Gran grinned. "Maybe you don't know him as well as you think."

Sydney wasn't sure how to respond as hope flared. "He didn't sign on for another stint?"

Gran shook her head. "No. He's coming home, Sydney. To stay."

Sydney struggled to take a breath, certain she'd heard Gran

wrong, that her mind was playing tricks on her and letting her hear what she wanted to hear because it simply couldn't accept the truth.

"Home?" she whispered.

Gran rose from her stool slowly and reached out to clasp Sydney's hand in hers, squeezing it gently. "Our boy is coming back to us."

"But I thought..."

Gran patted Sydney's cheek. "I thought the same. Thought he'd keep going back until he got too old. Figured he'd work until it was time to retire." Lifting the letter, Gran slipped it into Sydney's hand. "He'll be back a week from Monday. He's begged me not to plan a welcome-home party, says he doesn't want it."

Sydney smiled. "That sounds like Chas. He hates to be the center of attention."

"Only kid I ever knew who pitched a fit if someone threw him a birthday party. Even so, I was hoping you'd come to the airport with Julian and me to pick him up. I think he'd be right pleased to see you there when he gets off that plane."

Julian was Chas' uncle, though Sydney swore the man could have been Chas' father. She'd never seen two men look more alike. They were both tall—nearly six-five—and broad, muscular. Their size should, and did, make them intimidating...until they opened their mouths to speak. Two kinder, funnier men have never lived. Gran called them her giant teddy bears. It was an apt description.

"I'd love to come to the airport, if you're sure you don't mind. I don't want to intrude on a family reunion."

Gran waved her concern away. "You *are* family, Sydney. You have been since you were knee high to a grasshopper."

The fact that Chas was coming home—really coming home—was finally starting to sink in. Sydney couldn't have stopped smiling if her life depended on it.

"I'll make a sign," Sydney said. "A huge welcome home banner. And I'll make him his favorite—red velvet cake with cream cheese frosting."

Gran stepped away from the counter. "Well, I best be going.

I'll call you later in the week with the details for our trip to the airport."

Sydney started to hand the letter back, but Gran refused to take it. "No. That's for you."

Sydney couldn't understand why Gran wanted her to have the letter, but she kept it, tucking it in the pocket of her apron as she walked around the counter to hug the woman. As big as her boys were, that's as small as Gran was. Barely touching five feet, she was fairly petite. Sydney had noticed Gran seemed to be shrinking, but that fact didn't diminish the woman's strength. When Gran hugged her, Sydney felt it all the way to her bones and it made her feel warm, cherished.

"Thank you for being such a good friend to my boy. I'm glad he's had you in his life all these years."

Sydney felt tears form in the corners of her eyes, though she tried to hold them back. Gran was a kind woman, but she didn't hand out a lot of compliments, nor did she talk about her feelings much. She showed her love for Chas and Julian, and by extension, Sydney, through her actions...and food. So her words felt like a precious gift to Sydney. Something she'd never forget.

Gran didn't wait for her to respond. Instead, she released Sydney, gave her a quick wink and left. Sydney walked back to the counter, claiming the seat Gran had just vacated. Pulling the letter out of her pocket, Sydney unfolded the single sheet of paper, amazed how so few words could change so much in her life.

It simply said, *Gran, I'm finished with the Marines. It's time for me to take Uncle Julian up on that offer of a job. I'll be home in a couple of weeks to stay. Warn Sydney. Much love and see you soon, Chas.*

Warn Sydney. What the hell was that supposed to mean?

Sydney laughed and rolled her eyes. Who knew with Chas? They'd gone from rough-and-tumble friends—climbing trees, swimming in the river, and building forts in her backyard—to very brief childhood sweethearts. Chas had been her date to the senior prom when both of them found themselves faced with that option or going stag. Neither of them had dated much in high school.

Chas worked after school and during the summer at his uncle Julian's construction company, while Sydney spent a great deal of time working in the family restaurant, Sparks Barbeque.

Between work and school, the two of them typically chose to spend their down time simply hanging out watching TV or eating cheeseburgers at the local diner with a handful of Sydney's cousins—she had a gazillion—and a few other friends.

Then prom had come along. Sydney suspected Chas had issued his invitation because Gran had either threatened or bribed him. He'd been content to skip the whole affair. Dancing wasn't Chas' thing. Hell, it wasn't hers either, but she'd still desperately wanted to go to the prom. She'd been relieved when Chas asked her because she hadn't liked the idea of showing up alone.

Sydney had actually laughed and called him James Bond, hoping to dispel some of the nervousness she'd felt when he'd shown up at her house in his uncle's fancy sports car and dressed in a tuxedo. She'd expected him to punch her in the arm and tell her to shut up for teasing him, but instead he'd taken one look at her and said, "You're beautiful." His tone had been the perfect blend of awe and astonishment. Friend Sydney had wanted to call him to task for acting so freaking surprised, but the teenaged girl who'd never had a boyfriend, never had a boy tell her she was pretty, was too touched to respond.

"You look great too," she'd said at last, hating how lame her compliment seemed when compared to his, and sorry she had laughed when she'd first seen him. The truth was he had looked incredibly hot in his tuxedo.

Then the night had gone the complete opposite of how Sydney had expected. She'd been perfectly prepared for them to find their usual crowd of friends and fast dance in a pack all night, while taking bathroom or water breaks during the slow songs. Chas clearly had different plans. He'd drawn them away from the others, his focus solely on her. It almost felt as if he couldn't take his eyes off her. It was a heady, wonderful feeling.

When a slow song played, he pulled her into his arms and for the first time, Sydney felt that spark she'd heard other girls allude to and she was overcome with unfamiliar feelings of desire and need. She wanted him...wanted Chas.

She'd never understood what the fuss was about, never worried or wondered much about sex. Sometimes she feared that part of her was broken. Sydney had always been too practical to fall for a bunch of romantic bullshit and she was more tomboy than girly.

Chas had proven to her that she was just as capable of feeling lust as the next horny teenager. When his lips brushed her cheek, all bets were off.

They'd spent the rest of the evening sneaking seductive touches, the heat building steadily between them until midnight. They'd planned to go out for a midnight breakfast with some friends. Instead, Chas took her to a secluded spot by the lake. It was the same place they'd come to a million times as kids, swimming and diving off the rocks and dunking each other during the lazy days of summer that seemed endless and too brief all at the same time.

He grabbed a blanket from the trunk of the car, took her hand and led her down to the small, sandy cove. The place was deserted, and for a moment, Sydney could imagine they were the only two people on the planet.

He laid the blanket out and then reached for her. Sydney walked into his arms as if she belonged there, as if she'd spent a lifetime in his embrace. Neither of them spoke. She knew why they were here. It was where she wanted to be.

Chas kissed her then. Their first true kiss. His lips touched hers without hesitation. She marveled at his confidence. She knew all about Chas' experience with kissing and other sexual things. They were best friends. They had no secrets from each other.

His knowledge was only slightly less limited than hers. He was a virgin too. Most guys wouldn't have admitted to such a thing, but Chas didn't seem to care. He'd always claimed there weren't any girls in Maris, Texas, he wanted to be with and none of the other boys in their group ever gave him shit for it as far as Sydney knew. Who would? There was no one of their acquaintance who was willing to risk Chas' wrath. He was huge and could kick all of their asses...at the same time.

Besides, Chas had always sort of been wise beyond his years. He didn't fall victim to peer pressure or the typical teenage bullying tactics that bothered so many other kids in school. He knew who he was and what he wanted from life and everyone understood it.

The kiss went on for what had felt like ages to Sydney at the time. However, when she looked back, she cursed how quickly it had passed. Chas had unzipped her dress, carefully placing it on the blanket, then taken off his jacket and shirt. Sydney had seen him in his bathing suit more than his regular clothes over the years, but she'd never opened her eyes and really *looked*. He'd taken her breath away that night. And then the rest of their clothes fell away—shoes were kicked off, then her bra and panties, and his boxers were tossed onto the pile.

Sydney marveled over how free and comfortable she'd felt in that moment. There had been no shyness between them, only wonder. That younger version of herself had been much more confident in her appearance than the woman she'd become since. Sydney realized she'd never be able to stand in front of Chas these days completely naked with such ease. Not that she planned to be naked with Chas again.

Of course, she hadn't planned it that night, either.

Chas had laid her down on the blanket, fished a condom out of his pants and then just like that, he was inside her. She'd expected pain, but there hadn't been any. Just this amazing sensation of being filled, being whole. Chas had kissed her throughout and Sydney ran her fingers through his dark hair. She'd gripped it tightly as she wrapped her legs around his waist. She'd never wanted the night to end.

But time stops for no one, not even young lovers. Chas had held her afterwards, his gaze never leaving her face. She wasn't sure what he'd been looking for. Regret, pain, fear? He wouldn't have seen any of those things. The only thing she'd felt was love. Blinding, breathtaking, soul-stealing love.

Maybe *that* was what Chas had been looking for, because he'd kissed her and just before his lips left hers, he'd whispered, "I love you too." She'd started to say she hadn't uttered those words, but didn't bother. The *too* was accurate.

They didn't say anything else that night. They had remained there, staring at the sky and then, after some time had passed, Chas had taken her again. After that, they'd fallen asleep, a brief respite before Chas nudged her awake and told her they needed to go home.

For one don't-blink-or-you'll-miss-it month, Chas had been hers. All hers. They'd been inseparable for four perfect weeks. And then he'd left, gone to the Marines. He'd told her he would always love her and that she would always be his best friend. Then he'd instructed her not to wait.

Sydney had started to protest, but Chas made her promise not to. He knew her too well, knew she'd never be happy living anywhere besides Maris. She'd known the ending to their story the night she had walked down to that beach with him and given him her virginity.

And if she were placed in that spot a million times over, she'd make the same choice. Every. Single. Time.

Sydney hadn't waited for him. At least, not intentionally. The first time Chas had come home after basic training ended, she'd wondered how it would be between them. But Chas had remained true to his word. Instead of the sweet, attentive boyfriend he'd been when he'd left, her fun-loving, nothing-serious friend had returned. She'd been grateful to him for keeping things casual, for helping her make the break.

Until he'd informed her on the last night of his trip home that he was being deployed to Iraq.

Then she'd been angry and sad and terrified. He'd taken her to the lake to tell her about his placement. She'd punched him in the stomach—hurting her fist more than him—and railed at him for wasting their time together. All she could think was that he could die.

He'd taken her cursing and her punch in stride. The man was

a solid wall of muscle and so emotionally stable that sometimes when they'd been younger, she'd tried to push his buttons just to get a rise out of him. It had never worked. She suspected his steady attitude would make him a wonderful Marine. He could think and react without emotions gumming up the works.

He'd let her persist with her tirade—tantrum, actually—for several minutes, then he'd gripped her upper arms and tugged her against his chest, holding her so tightly she feared she'd break.

He had kissed her forehead and tried to explain again why it was better this way. Better for her to move on without him. The words had made sense, but they hadn't changed her feelings, hadn't taken away the unbearable ache in her chest, the pain slicing through her heart.

Instead of telling him it was okay, she'd been cruel. Told him it only made things easier for *him*. Now he could fuck his way across the world without feeling any guilt.

Of all the things she'd said and done in her life, her actions on that night were still on the top of her list of regrets. Chas didn't return home for a year after that confrontation. When he had, he was distantly polite—a favor she'd returned because she'd been too ashamed of herself and uncertain how to fix what she'd done.

It had taken two more years before they'd broken through the chill and found their way back to the friendship they'd always enjoyed. Since then, she'd written him a letter a month, and whenever he made his way back to the States, they hung out just like they had when they were kids. They'd never crossed the line into a physical relationship again and if anyone asked, Sydney assured them what she and Chas had shared had been nothing more than a high-school-sweethearts phase, then she swore it was over.

Warn Sydney.

Chas' words kept returning to her. While she was grateful he was returning home, she didn't fool herself into believing it would be easy for her to maintain a friendship without longing for more. She tried to tell herself she'd built up that first time, that she could only recall that night of the prom with a starry-eyed teenaged girl's too-whimsical, too-romantic memory. It couldn't have been as perfect as she remembered.

So did he want his gran to warn her of his pending return so that she could gird her loins, strengthen her resolve and find a way to maintain the status quo?

She sighed, and then decided she'd managed to get through the last twelve years' worth of days without him, though the fact he'd been on another continent had certainly made that simpler.

Surely she could handle a few dozen more years alone, even with him nearby.

Maybe.

CHAPTER TWO

Sydney stood next to Gran, who was flanked by Julian on the right. The three of them were standing at the international arrivals gate, grinning like fools as they held the banner Sydney had made. Chas' flight had landed and her heart was racing a million miles an hour. She'd seen him just a few months earlier over the holidays. They'd exchanged small gifts and consumed a bottle of eggnog together. Chas had even told her a little bit about two friends he'd lost in combat, the story breaking her heart.

Chas had ended up sleeping on her couch that night, while she'd tossed and turned in her bedroom, fighting the urge to go out and comfort him. However, there had been something in his eyes —some dark, unfamiliar sadness—that had stopped her, that had told her to keep her distance.

Several more people walked through the gate. Sydney watched as relatives reunited with hugs, laughter and sometimes tears. She loved coming to the airport, loved the energy and the atmosphere, the hustle and bustle. It was a hotbed of emotions unlike any other place.

Gran captured her attention with a nudge of the elbow. "There he is."

Chas strolled through the doors in jeans and a t-shirt. It would seem so weird to see him dressed in civilian clothing rather than his fatigues from now on, and she wondered if he'd give up the crew cut he'd kept for so many years and return to the longer style of his youth. He looked around the area, searching for them. Sydney smiled and waved when his eyes met hers.

Chas walked faster then, laughing when he read their banner. Sydney took it from Julian and Gran, stepping back so that Chas could greet his family.

She was shocked when he bypassed both of them and walked right up to her. He tugged the banner out of her hands and dropped it to the floor a split second before he grabbed her in his embrace and kissed her.

His mouth was demanding, forcing her lips apart so he could stroke her tongue with his. Sydney fought off a wave of dizziness and disbelief. Even a bit of embarrassment when she recalled his grandmother was standing less than five feet away from them. She put her hands on his shoulders, intent on pushing him away, but Chas only gripped her tighter, one of his hands rising to cup the back of her neck, his fingers lightly stroking the sensitive skin there.

She was a goner. Sydney stopped giving a shit who was there and what they were seeing. Chas was home. And he was kissing her.

Twelve years melted away into a haze of nothingness. He was home. Finally.

After several very long, heated minutes, Chas released her, giving her a wicked smile and a suggestive wink.

"Sorry Gran," he said as he turned, offering his grandmother the big bear hug she'd been waiting for.

Gran laughed, wrapping her arms around his waist and squeezing tightly. "Oh boy, it's so good to have you back home. Safe and sound."

Sydney detected just the slightest crack in Gran's voice, the only indication she'd ever seen that told her exactly how much Chas' grandmother had worried about him.

Julian stepped closer as he and Chas did the man-hug thing, slapping each other on the back. "It's about time you got your ass back to Texas."

Chas laughed, but nodded in agreement. "You're right. It was time." He looked at Gran and then Sydney before adding, "Past time."

Sydney's head whirled as she struggled to put two and two together. She'd spent the last week since she'd heard Chas was returning trying to talk herself into resuming and maintaining a casual friendship with him. Not once had she anticipated that kiss.

Chas bent down to retrieve her banner, handing it back to her. "Sorry. I think I ripped it."

She glanced at the paper stupidly, spotting the large tear near the middle. "It doesn't matter. Served its purpose."

He gave his gran a quick kiss on the cheek, then looked at Julian. "Swear to me there's no one waiting at the house to surprise me."

Julian raised his hand, making the solemn promise. Sydney fought to keep a straight face. The truth was there were at least two dozen friends gathered at Sparks Barbeque waiting to welcome their Marine home. But that wasn't what Chas had asked, so Julian made the vow without hesitation.

Gran had considered respecting Chas' request for no party for about three minutes, then as word spread he was coming home, she'd decided to heck with it. Chas was well liked in the community, his name mentioned nearly every single Sunday in the prayer at church. Maris wasn't exactly a small town, but it was one that had grown slowly over time as people moved into the area. As a result, everybody pretty much knew everybody else. There were a lot of people sighing with relief that Chas was returning safe and sound and they felt the need to celebrate.

Chas threw his duffel over his shoulder and then—to Sydney's surprise—he wrapped his arm around her shoulders possessively and tugged her close as the four of them walked to the parking lot.

Sydney was tempted to ask him what the hell he was doing,

but his grandmother was next to him, chatting a mile a minute as she told him about the renovations she'd had Julian do to the house. Chas had moved his bedroom from upstairs to the mostly finished basement when he was in high school, claiming he needed more space to chill with his friends.

When Gran heard he was coming home to stay, she'd had Julian and his construction crew build him a proper apartment downstairs, complete with a full bath, living area, kitchenette and personal entrance.

"Gran. You didn't have to do that."

She shrugged as Chas threw his duffel into the trunk of Julian's car. "I didn't do it for you. I did it for me. I want you to stay with me, but I could hardly ask a grown man to move in and be roomies with his old grandmother."

Chas chuckled. "Hate to break it to you, but you were going to be stuck with me for a while regardless. You could have saved yourself some money and effort. My old room was just fine with me."

Chas opened the back door and gestured for Sydney to climb in. She did so, grinning when Chas claimed the backseat next to her.

"And by the way," Chas added, leaning toward the front seat as Julian sat behind the steering wheel and Gran grabbed shotgun. "You aren't old."

Sydney joined the conversation as she, Julian and Gran caught Chas up on all the gossip from home. She forced herself to keep her tone casual despite the fact that Chas' hand had somehow found its way to her knee. He was lightly stroking it, almost absentmindedly as they chatted.

Then, when she looked at his face and saw his gaze glued to the bare bit of leg revealed by her dress, she realized Chas knew exactly what he was doing.

She'd worn a short sundress and strappy sandals to the airport. Her cousin, Macie, had wolf-whistled when she'd seen her this morning, then given her a suspicious look. Sydney had tried to play off the outfit, pretending she hadn't gone out of her way to look her best, and maybe even a wee bit sexy.

He looked disappointed when they pulled into the parking lot at Sparks Barbeque. "Are we dropping you off, Syd? I was hoping you'd come back to the house with us for a little while." Then he leaned closer and whispered, "Or for the night."

What the hell was going on with him? For twelve years, he'd never broken the friend code, never let on that he wanted anything more from her.

She was equal parts thrilled and annoyed.

Before she could answer, Gran turned around. "I was trying to decide what to make for your first meal home, then realized your favorite dinner wasn't anything I make." Gran pointed to Sydney. "It's what *she* makes."

Chas' eyes widened in delight. "Pulled-pork barbeque with your special sauce and homemade coleslaw on a sesame seed bun?"

Sydney laughed. The more things changed, the more they stayed the same. "Would I serve you anything else?"

Chas rubbed his stomach. "Great plan. I'm starving. On that last damn leg of my flight, they only gave us peanuts and a lousy cup of Coke. Mine was more ice than drink. Wouldn't mind an ice-cold beer."

Sydney wondered if he'd feel quite as happy with this plan when he realized his meal came with a lot of company. The four of them got out of the car. Mercifully, Macie had remembered to take down the sign on the door that said they were closed for a private party. That would have given them away too early and Sydney couldn't be sure Chas wouldn't turn tail and run.

Julian opened the door, holding it for them. Gran and Sydney entered first, trying to block Chas' view until the last minute, which was a futile task. He topped them both by at least a foot.

No sooner had Julian closed the door and blocked the entrance than the huge crowd of people yelled, "Surprise!"

There were at least fifty people in the restaurant—way more than Sydney had expected—though she shouldn't have been shocked. There weren't too many folks in Maris who didn't like a good party.

The restaurant was decorated in red, white and blue streamers with small American flags serving as centerpieces on every table. She and Gran had spent most of the morning setting up. It had been a great way to pass the hours until it was time to go to the airport. However, even being busy, the morning had lasted an eternity.

Sydney held her breath as she waited for Chas' response. She was delighted when she heard his booming laughter, then he turned to look at his grandmother with narrowed eyes.

"Is this what you call no party?"

Gran was ready for his complaint. She played the innocent, claiming it must be a coincidence that everyone just happened to be there. "It is a restaurant, after all, my boy. I can't tell everyone in town to stay away just because you want to eat here."

Chas bent down to kiss Gran on the cheek, thanking her for her efforts. Sydney watched the older lady quickly bat away a tear. Sydney understood the feeling. She was teetering on the edge of so many emotions. Overwhelmed by absolute joy while struggling not to dissolve into a puddle of tears. And in the midst of it, all she kept saying over and over in her head was *thank God he's home.*

Then Chas turned to her, his hands on his hips. "I suspect you played a part in this too."

Sydney gave him an unrepentant grin. "*I* didn't promise not to throw you a party."

Chas took a step closer. "Payback's a bitch."

"I love parties, so it's totally worth it," she teased. "Do your worst."

"Okay. I will."

And with that, Chas bent down and kissed her just as he had in the airport. Right there in the restaurant in front of her family, God and everybody. His intention to claim her affections couldn't have been clearer if he'd had it painted on the wall in bright neon letters.

This time when Sydney pushed away, he let her go.

"What the hell are you up to?" she muttered.

He tugged her hair playfully. "I kind of thought that was obvious."

"We're having a long talk later."

"I look forward to it."

That was all the conversation the crowd allowed them before the shock of Chas' kiss wore off and everyone moved forward to hug him.

Sydney found herself pushed farther and farther away from him as the crowd around him grew. She tried to will away the heat that suffused her cheeks when he'd kissed her so publicly. She could feel Macie's gaze on her, but she pointedly ignored it. The last thing she wanted was to deal with her cousin's questions. Mainly because Sydney didn't have the answers.

She'd been ready to play the friend role. She didn't have a clue what to do with this guy. This sexy, not-taking-no-for-an-answer, kissing-her-senseless-every-time-she-turned-around guy.

Shit.

She'd told him they would talk later and they would. It was pointless to worry about it now. There were too many people around and Chas was already making the rounds, reconnecting with old friends, accepting a beer and the cheers that came with it.

She marveled at how at ease he seemed. There was definitely something different about Chas. Her old friend would never have kissed her in public or been such a gracious guest at a party in his honor. She'd watched him storm out of two birthday parties—the only two his gran had ever held for him—when he was younger. One when he was just seven and the other on his thirteenth. He'd been too embarrassed and uncomfortable to remain at either for long.

At his seventh birthday, he and Sydney had retreated to his tree house in the backyard, neither of them coming out until all the guests had departed. At his thirteenth—a picnic at the lake—he'd snuck away to a hidden cove and it had taken Sydney nearly an hour to find him. When she did, he begged her not to rat him out. So...again...she'd stayed with him until nearly dark, then they'd returned to face his grandmother's disappointment together.

This time he appeared to be enjoying himself and he gave no indication of trying to escape. Or at least, that was how it appeared on the surface. After a half hour or so, Sydney noticed tight lines by his eyes and mouth. She wasn't sure if his enthusiasm was waning or if his ability to pretend he was okay with the party was.

Sydney watched as Julian slowly left his post by the front door and moved closer to Chas. Apparently, his uncle had noticed the same thing. Chas and his uncle had always been close. In truth, Julian was more father than uncle to Chas. She caught Julian's eye then pointed to the kitchen, and he gave her a discreet nod, letting her know he'd keep watch over Chas.

Reassured, Sydney left the dining area and headed to the back of the restaurant to help her cousin Jeannette fill the serving dishes. They had made all of Chas' favorites, hoping to win his forgiveness for having the party with food.

Fortunately Jeannette had been in the kitchen when Chas planted that kiss on her, so Sydney wasn't subjected to any questions. Together, they began to carry the large bowls to the dining room. Macie was behind the bar, serving up the drinks, she and Chas trying to outdo one other, each telling old high school stories meant to embarrass, much to the amusement of everyone there.

Chas was told to fill his plate first as he was the guest of honor. He gave her a hungry smile as she loaded a pork barbeque sandwich for him. However, it didn't take a brain surgeon to tell her the smile had nothing to do with wanting food. His sexy gaze was hot and sent shivers of desire down her spine. The room was suddenly muggy, the air thick, and her body started to ache with need. This wasn't good. There were too many damn people around, most of them her relatives. Hell, the preacher was third in line for the meal.

Sydney narrowed her eyes, warning him to cut it out, but Chas was relentless. When she placed the sandwich on his plate, he reached for her hand and pulled it to his mouth to suck off the tiny bit of sauce on her fingers.

Her pussy clenched and she began to suffer her own unbearable cravings. God. At this rate, she wouldn't have to worry about Chas slipping away from his own party. She'd drag him away. Straight to her bedroom.

Which would be foolish. And wonderful. And stupid. And...

Dammit. She'd spent twelve years getting over the bastard, resigning herself to the fact she'd never be more than just his friend.

Now, in just one short hour, he'd shaken her to the core and shone a spotlight on the irrefutable truth. She'd never stopped loving him.

She tugged her hand out of his, but not before they'd caught the attention of too many people around them. She wasn't getting out of the restaurant tonight without being asked a lot of unwanted questions. Her family wasn't the type to let anything pass by unnoticed or without comment.

She left the serving to Jeannette while pretending to go to the kitchen to get something she'd forgotten. She really just needed a breather, a chance to get away from the curious stares and compose herself.

She leaned against the kitchen counter, grateful for a few minutes of quiet. Unfortunately it was short-lived. She should have realized Chas would notice her absence.

"Syd?"

She glanced toward the doorway. "I'm here."

This time, she noticed with some satisfaction, his smile was rueful, almost apologetic. "Thanks for the party."

She scowled. "You hate parties."

He shrugged. "I know. Still not crazy about them, but they don't bother me as much anymore."

"Why not?"

He crossed the room until he was standing next to her. She stiffened her spine, anticipating a touch or perhaps another of his unexpected embraces or kisses. She was almost disappointed when he did neither.

Well, not almost. She was *completely* disappointed.

"I know I'm lucky to be here, Syd. I had a couple good friends die over in Iraq. I can't help but think how much it would have meant to their families to be able to throw them a welcome home party like this."

The same haunted look she'd seen in his eyes too much over the past few years reappeared. His words went through her like a knife, reminding her once more that she could have lost him. She didn't realize she was crying until she felt his fingers on her cheeks, wiping away the tears.

"Hey now, pretty girl. I didn't mean to make you sad."

She couldn't speak through the lump in her throat. Instead, she reached out and wrapped her arms around his waist, clinging to him, wondering if she'd ever find the courage to let go. She wouldn't mind spending the next decade or so standing right here, just like this. Because at least it would mean he was with her and safe.

"It's okay, Sydney. I'm not going back."

Until he spoke, she didn't realize she'd verbalized her fears, didn't hear herself saying over and over, "Don't leave me again."

He pressed a gentle kiss on the top of her head and let her hang on. He kept his arms around her, giving her the time she needed to compose herself once more.

"I hated every single minute you were gone."

"I know you did," he whispered. "I'm sorry."

She shook her head. "Not your fault. You told me in kindergarten you were going to be a Marine. It's not like you didn't give me plenty of warning." She tried to laugh, but the sound that came out was mixed with a sob.

He slowly extracted himself from her grip, his hands still supporting her, firmly holding her upper arms. "I told you not to wait for me."

She frowned, confused. "I didn't."

He gave her an amused grin. "You are the most stubborn woman I've ever known."

"What's that supposed to mean? I *didn't* wait for you."

"Fine. If you say so."

His tone told her he didn't believe her, but her pride wouldn't let her back down. Mainly because she was starting to think he was right. "I mean it, Chas. I haven't been sitting here pining away. I've gone out on dates."

Chas' smile faded briefly and for a second Sydney thought he looked almost jealous. "I know about the dates. You could've done a lot better than Mac Mitchell."

Sydney laughed. "We only went out three times. Who told you about that?"

He shrugged. "I have my sources."

"So you've been spying on me."

He ran his fingers along her face in a way that made her skin warm and her heart flutter. "I prefer to call it keeping tabs on my best friend. Making sure she was staying out of trouble."

"You never expressed much interest in my love life when you came home for visits. Why now?"

"I didn't want to know who you were sleeping with, Syd, because it would have killed me. Or made me want to kill the guy."

She wasn't sure what to do with that confession. His dark expression told her he was telling her the truth. She'd thought Chas had managed to walk away from their relationship without a backwards glance. He'd never seemed to suffer the same sense of loss she'd felt. Finding out he had threw her for a loop.

She took a deep breath. "All I'm saying is, I didn't wait. I just didn't find anyone else."

She expected her comment to make him laugh or open the door for him to tease her about her bad taste in guys. With the exception of him, she'd dated a very long list of dogs in the past dozen years.

However, he never cracked a smile. Instead, he muttered, "Thank God."

"Chas—" she started.

Before she could nail him down on his current intentions, ask him about all these kisses, Gran appeared in the doorway.

"There you two are. Everyone's looking for the guest of honor. And Sydney, Jeannette wanted me to ask you to bring some more buns. We've got a hungry crowd out there."

She and Chas stepped apart, he to follow his gran, while she went to the storage closet for more sandwich rolls. His voice caused her to turn and she realized he'd hung back by the doorway.

"I'm home to stay, Sydney. And all that stuff I said when we were eighteen doesn't apply anymore. You understand?"

She nodded slowly.

Chas studied her face, then appeared satisfied that she really did get it. "Good. We'll talk more later."

He left her alone in the kitchen as she struggled to catch her bearings.

Chas intended for them to pick up where they'd left off twelve years ago.

Holy shit.

And thank God.

CHAPTER THREE

Sydney stood in front of the griddle at Sparks Barbeque, absentmindedly flipping a couple of hamburgers. After the party for Chas, she'd gone home alone. Not that Chas hadn't tried to persuade her to spend the night with him. However, she'd demurred, insisting he spend the evening with his family. His uncle and Gran had worked hard on his apartment in the basement. He needed to give them a chance to catch up with him alone and he'd agreed she was right.

Of course, right or not, that didn't mean she hadn't sort of expected to see him waiting at the door to the restaurant this morning. She was disappointed when he wasn't there. Her phone had been out in plain view all day and she'd glanced at the screen no less than a million times, in addition to flipping it on countless times to make sure the battery was still charged. He'd never called.

She had told him last night that she hadn't waited for him. At the time she had believed it. However, in the hours since then, she'd questioned the accuracy of that statement. Perhaps she *had* subconsciously been waiting for Chas' return. She'd been devastated each time he'd signed on for four more years with the Marines, going into a funk for weeks afterwards. And she hadn't exactly chosen stellar guys to date. Her cousin, Jeannette, claimed she had some weird affinity for assholes, but Sydney wondered if she'd gravitated toward those men because they weren't a threat. She'd never dated anyone more than a handful of times.

Sydney blew out an exasperated breath. Chas had been home one day and he'd managed to throw her boring, predictable life into complete turmoil. He had her questioning every choice she had made since he'd left and those damn kisses of his had fired up her libido to dangerous levels. She'd pulled out her vibrator three times last night. Three times!

"Why are you still here?" Jeannette asked as she carried a gallon of milk from the walk-in refrigerator. "I'm the dinner shift. And it's not like we're that busy. Go on home and relax, or better yet, call up Chas and burn off some of this lust you're obviously suffering from."

Sydney scowled, but didn't bother to argue with her cousin. She and Jeannette had spent several hours a day for years in this kitchen together. It had begun to feel as if they shared a hive mind. There was very little about Jeannette that Sydney didn't know and vice versa.

Jeannette chuckled at her irate expression. "Damn. You *do* have it bad. And I don't blame you. Chas has filled out in all the right places over the years. The Marines were very good for that man's physique. It's like he's chiseled out of stone."

Sydney didn't need the description. She'd fantasized about those muscles for hours last night, imagined herself licking each and every single curve. However, before she could tell her cousin to shut up because she was just making things worse, Macie bebopped into the kitchen with a shit-eating grin on her face.

She stopped short when she saw Sydney at the griddle. "What are you still doing here? Your shift ended an hour ago."

"That's what I told her," Jeannette added.

Macie turned to Jeannette, mischief twinkling in her eyes. "Hey, Jeannette, Luc and Diego are sitting at the counter out there. They want to know when you're going to go out with them."

Jeannette was the mildest of souls and her temper had a very long fuse. Except for when it came to two of Maris' firefighters, the sexy-as-sin Diego and Luc. The mere mention of their names more often than not flipped her lid.

Jeannette slammed her spatula down on the counter. "Oh my God. Those two will not catch a clue."

"They like you," Macie said with a wicked grin, provoking Jeannette's irritation even more.

"They. Do you hear what you're saying, Mace? *They* like me. The rest of Maris may turn a blind eye to their exploits, may pat them on the back for their dating habits, but I have no issue calling them out for it. It's not normal for two grown-assed men to date women together. When did threesomes become an acceptable practice around here?"

"When Diego and Luc started doing it," Sydney said, covertly winking at Macie. It was fun pushing Jeannette's buttons on this subject. She couldn't understand what it was about those two men that got to her cousin so much, especially considering she was the most accepting of souls when it came to everything else in the world, but there was something about the firefighters and their dating practices that provoked Jeannette like nothing else.

Jeannette took the bait, spinning angrily to face Sydney. "Seriously, Syd? That's your argument? Two good-looking guys invite a woman out for dinner, drinks and God knows what else, and we're supposed to turn a blind eye and act like it's no big deal. Since when did we hand the keys to the city over to those two?"

Macie flipped her hair over her shoulder. "I don't know about the keys to the city, but I'd sure as hell give them the keys to my bedroom."

Sydney leaned against the counter, giggling. "You have to admit it, Nettie, those two are hot with a capital H. Besides, they're not from here. They're from Dallas."

Jeannette shook her head. "You act like that explains everything."

Sydney lifted one shoulder casually. "People play by different rules in a big city. And I'm not saying it's not unusual, but heck, I don't see too many women saying no. I think half the female population of Maris would love to go out with them."

"And the other half is married. Although let's face it, they want to too," Macie added with a laugh.

Sydney loved working in the restaurant with her family. Her cousins were her dearest friends—the sisters of her heart—and she couldn't imagine spending a day where she didn't talk to one or most of them. In addition to Macie and Jeannette, she was also close to her other cousins, Evan, Paige, Lacy, Gia, Tyson, and Adele. Chas had once claimed he couldn't turn around twice in Maris without bumping into one of her relatives. The statement was probably true, and Sydney loved it.

She'd started dragging Chas, Gran and Uncle Julian to her family's Christmas celebration when she and Chas were in ninth grade because she simply couldn't fathom a holiday spent with just three people. The Sparks' family Christmases were huge events with no less than sixty people squeezed into her Uncle George's house, armed with enough food to feed an army. Sydney's ears usually rang for hours afterwards because of the noise from so many people talking at the same time.

It was chaos.

And it was home.

It was also one of the reasons Chas had given for breaking up with her after graduation, when she'd suggested they throw caution to the wind and elope. He'd insisted he could never take her away from her family. She'd argued with true teenage bravado, claiming she could leave Maris just fine. But Chas had been right, had known she never would have been happy anywhere else.

Jeannette returned to the coleslaw she was making, stirring it with a vengeance. "Macie, you can give Luc and Diego my standard answer."

Macie rolled her eyes. "Gotcha. I'll inform them that hell hasn't frozen over yet."

Sydney shook her head. "Wasted opportunity, Nettie."

Macie stopped in the doorway, nodding her head in agreement. "I think so too. Besides, they're not going to stop asking until you agree. Why not surprise them with a yes? Then treat yourself —if the rumors are to be believed—to the best sex of your life."

Jeannette didn't bother to look up from the slaw. "No thanks. Not interested. Why don't *you* girls go out with them, if you think it sounds like such a peachy deal?"

"They aren't asking us," Sydney replied, though she didn't admit she wouldn't accept a date with Luc and Diego either.

Not that she wouldn't have been tempted. They really *were* hot. She just wasn't attracted to them like that. They were fun, nice, crazy guys who were a blast to go out for a few beers with—as friends—but she simply didn't want any more from them than that. The same didn't hold true for Jeannette. In fact, the louder Jeannette protested, the more Sydney was convinced her cousin had it bad for the sexy firefighters.

Macie sighed. "If they did, I wouldn't be a fool and say no."

Now *that* Sydney believed. Macie didn't waste much time on thinking, like Sydney and Jeannette did. Macie tended to grab life by the horns and hold on for the ride. Sydney wished she could be a little more like that. She was too cautious and practical. While she thought the idea of a threesome was hot, she'd never indulge in such a thing.

Jeannette had calmed back down. "Just tell them my answer is still no, Mace."

"Fine." Macie left the kitchen.

"And *you* need to go home," Jeannette added.

"I don't mind hanging out here. It's not like there's anything waiting for me at home."

"What about Chas?"

Sydney didn't pretend to misunderstand the question. Chas wasn't at her house, but that didn't mean he didn't want to be. "He wants me. Said he wants to pick up where we left off in high school."

Jeannette put her spoon down and walked over to Sydney. "Seriously? I mean, I figured as much after all those kisses he was giving you last night, but wow. That's really cool."

Sydney bit her lower lip. "You think so?"

"You two were great together, Syd. I can't tell you how many times I've heard someone wonder where you and Chas would be if he hadn't joined the Marines."

"But he did join. And he was gone for a long time."

"He's back now."

Sydney sighed. "He hasn't called."

"So what?" Jeannette asked. "Call him."

"I don't know how I'm supposed to respond to any of this. Am I supposed to just jump right back in with both feet?"

"You never stopped loving him, so why should it be hard? Take what he's offering and run with it. If you'd stop overanalyzing and thinking it to death, you'd see it's exactly what you want. What you've been waiting for since high school."

"I didn't wait." Even as Sydney spoke the same words she'd said to Chas the previous evening, she knew for a fact that was exactly what she'd done.

Dammit.

Jeannette didn't bother to answer. Instead she just laughed, the sound saying it all.

Sydney's back went up. "Nettie."

Jeannette raised her hand. "Don't waste your breath. You've spent most of your adult life waiting for Chas to come home to you. He's here now. Don't blow it."

Sydney didn't know how to respond to that. Simply because it was true. She had always been in love with him, was *still* in love with Chas.

Maybe that was why this was so difficult. She'd been in love with him before and he'd broken her heart. She thought she'd forgiven him for that. Hell, she'd even managed to justify his reasons, tell herself he was right to walk away. However, there was a small part inside that was still hurt. Still afraid.

He wasn't the same boy he'd been when he left. They'd spent more time apart than together. Jeannette had said it herself. Sydney had been alone her entire adult life, clearly clinging to the man Chas had been when he'd left. And while shades of that boy were still there, this Chas was different.

She wasn't the same person either. While she hadn't seen as much of the world as he had, she'd lost a lot of her young, starry-eyed take on life in general. She was older, more serious, maybe less fun. What if he didn't like the woman she'd become?

What if they tried again only to discover the spark wasn't there anymore? Did she really want to set herself up for all that hurt again?

Twelve years had passed. Chas had grown harder—and not just in a physical sense. There was an edge to him she didn't recognize or understand. He'd seen more than his share of fighting during his stint in the Middle East. He'd watched two friends die in a firefight, one of them bleeding to death in his arms. While Chas hadn't shared many of the details with her, he hadn't been the same since. Obviously a traumatic event like that would change a person.

When Sydney failed to respond, Jeannette picked up Sydney's cell and handed it to her. "Call him, Syd."

Frustration hit hard. "And say what, Nettie? Hey Chas. What's up? Want to get together tonight for dinner or to fuck like rabbits or to get married?"

"I'd be up for any of those."

Sydney whirled at the sound of Chas' voice in the doorway. Macie stood next to him with an expression that was equal parts horrified and amused.

"Oops," Macie mouthed. Then she pointed to Chas. "He was asking where you were. I didn't think you'd mind me bringing him back here."

Sydney didn't need a mirror to know she was bright red. Her face was flaming and she wished the ground would open and swallow her. "I was just..."

Chas walked in. "I'm sorry I didn't call earlier, Sydney. My uncle had me up at the ass crack of dawn to go to the construction site. I didn't realize when he said he wanted to retire and hand the reins of the business over to me, that he meant immediately. Apparently Julian has his sights set on some retirement community in Florida."

"We were talking about that on the way to the airport yesterday. It sounds like a cool place." She was grateful that Chas had brushed over her comment as though she hadn't even said it.

"We drove to his current site, which is near Amarillo. It was an hour-long drive and then I was thrust into a meeting with the group that hired him to do the project. I swear to you, I didn't have one damn minute to myself today as Julian introduced me to every single guy on his crew and discussed every detail of the company. I think my head's about to explode."

Sydney laughed. "You don't have to apologize, Chas."

"I think I do." He reached out and took her hand. "I sort of dropped a bomb on you last night, then walked away. I wouldn't mind taking you up on the dinner part of that invitation you just blurted out."

She scowled. "You weren't supposed to hear that."

Chas leaned forward to place a soft kiss on her cheek. While there, he whispered, "I'm glad I did. Sounds like we're on the same page."

"Confused and horny?"

He laughed and she turned her head slightly so that her cheek was pressed to his. She soaked up the smell of him—soap and coffee. He'd showered before coming here.

"Dinner sounds good. My place?" Sydney wanted—needed—to spend some time alone with Chas. They'd only managed to have one very brief, very serious conversation out of earshot of others since his return. Even now, she could feel Jeannette and Macie hanging on their every word, though they were both pretending to be busy.

"Yeah. But you've been cooking all day. What do you say we pick up a pizza and a six-pack on our way there?"

She nodded. "Sounds perfect."

"We can take my truck and I'll bring you back here tomorrow for work."

She crossed her arms. "Tomorrow?"

He gave her a wicked grin. "I'm not settling for just the dinner part of your invitation. I also heard something about fucking like rabbits."

"You're pretty sure of yourself, aren't you?"

Chas chuckled. "I like to consider myself an optimist." He glanced around at Macie and Jeannette. Sydney knew he wanted to say more, but wouldn't in front of her cousins.

"Shouldn't you be manning the bar, Macie?" Sydney asked.

Macie nodded. "Of course, I should, but it's way more interesting back here."

Sydney pointed to the doorway. "Go away."

Macie laughed as she left. Jeannette turned to look at them, then sighed. "I need to grab some stuff from the storage closet. But you two are going to have to wrap up this mating dance pretty quickly. I have four orders to fill."

Jeannette stepped out of the kitchen as well.

"Chas. I'm not sure where this is going, but I think we should take it slowly."

He shook his head. "Twelve years is about as slow as two people can go. If I've learned anything since I've been away, it's that life goes by too fast. Maybe you weren't waiting for me, Syd, but you're here now and I'm not going to let this opportunity slip away again."

"I'm not the same woman I was. God, I wasn't even a woman when we were together last time. I was a girl."

"And I was boy. I'm different too. But we're ahead of the dating curve. Maybe we haven't seen a lot of each other these past few years—"

"Twelve years," she interjected.

Chas ignored her interruption. "But the friendship never wavered, never died."

She wanted to debate that, but she held her tongue.

Chas grasped her waist and pulled her lower body to his. There was no denying the desire was still there. She could feel his erection beneath his jeans. "I want you, Syd. I want you so bad, it hurts."

His admission pierced her heart, touched a part of her she

thought she had lost forever. She had told everyone that same lie, even herself. The truth was, she *had* waited for him. And now that he was here, she'd fight the devil himself to keep him.

Sydney ran her hand over his cock, squeezing slightly. "The feeling is mutual."

He gripped her wrist, tugging her hand away. "We better get out of here now or no one in this restaurant is getting fed tonight."

She started to laugh, but something feral, unleashed in his gaze, sent flashes of electricity through her. She thought she understood some of that painful desire he'd mentioned, but last night's lukewarm horniness was nothing compared to this scorching hunger.

Chas held firmly to her hand. "What do you need to grab before we go?"

She pointed to a cabinet in the corner. "My purse. My keys."

He led her to the cabinet, opened the door and picked up her bag. "Yours?"

She nodded.

"You good?"

She nodded again.

"Then let's do this."

Sydney didn't have a chance to say goodbye to anyone. Instead, she followed in Chas' wake, sharing the same sense of urgency he seemed to feel. He opened the door to his pickup truck, helping her inside, then buckling her seat belt. She started to tell him she was perfectly capable of doing that herself, but something in his expression stopped her.

He'd warned her that he wasn't the same. She was only beginning to understand exactly what that meant. Chas climbed into the driver's seat and started the engine.

They drove to her house in silence, but that quiet didn't mean they weren't communicating. Chas' large hand rested on her knee as they traveled through town, distracting her so much she didn't realize he'd bypassed the pizza place. Once they hit the divided highway that led to the little cabin she lived in near the lake, his fingers began to inch along her thigh.

She opened her legs slightly as he reached higher, silently asking for a more compelling touch. She cursed her jeans, wishing she'd worn something with easier access.

As if reading her mind, Chas ran his finger along the seam at her pussy. "I liked yesterday's sundress. You have more?"

She shook her head. "Just that one."

"Do you own skirts?"

She nodded. "A couple." She wasn't exactly the queen of fashion or femininity. Give her a pair of loose jeans and a t-shirt and she was a happy camper.

"Would you start wearing them for me?"

She licked her lips. She'd walk around naked for him at this point. "Yes."

He glanced at her. "You're the most beautiful woman I've ever known."

She blushed, wanting to contradict him, call him out for something that couldn't be true. She wanted to tell him she was nothing special. But she didn't. Because she could see in his eyes, she *was* beautiful. That idea touched a place inside her that had been cold and dark for so damn long.

"Chas."

His finger stroked along the vee between her thighs once again. "We're almost to your place. You keep looking at me like that and I'll say to hell with it, pull over here and fuck you where you sit. If we do that, Evan is sure to catch us."

Her cousin, Evan, was part of the Maris police force and he patrolled this highway quite a bit.

Despite his warning, Chas stroked again, pressing harder.

She opened her mouth to tell him doing it on the side of the road was fine with her, that she didn't give a shit about Evan, but he shushed her, then lifted her shirt slightly, his fingers dipping beneath the waistband of her jeans.

His touch tickled against her stomach. She tried to suck it in to allow him better access. Then, with his thumb and forefinger, he slipped the button free and drew the zipper down.

Sydney was impressed with his skills. Even with one hand and his eyes on the road, he was doing a better job at getting her out of her pants than most of the yahoos she'd dated in recent years.

Once the denim was parted, Chas lost no time burrowing his fingers deeper, diving under her lace panties until he struck pay dirt.

She gasped when he found her clit on the first pass. He hadn't lied. This older, more mature Chas sure as shit knew his way around a woman's body. While their first time had been magical, romantic and sweet, they'd both been too innocent, their touches exploration rather than experience.

She much preferred the latter. Sydney's head flew back against the headrest when he pressed her clit more firmly. She'd been a woman on the edge since last night and though the vibrator had relieved some of the pressure building between her legs, it hadn't fired her up as much as Chas' single finger on her clit.

Her eyes drifted closed as Chas made the turn onto the road that would lead to her cabin. They were so close, yet it felt as if they'd never reach it. Her body was feverish and her head fuzzy. Chas pushed his finger lower until just the tip breached her opening.

She shifted on the seat, spreading her legs more as she tilted her hips. She was coming at him like a cat in heat, but no force of nature could stop her from responding.

She was surprised when the car stopped. Opening her eyes, she discovered they were at her cabin. Thank God.

She'd expected Chas to take his hand out of her pants and drag her inside. Instead, he pushed his finger a bit farther, not stopping until he was two knuckles deep in her pussy.

Sydney moaned. "That feels so good."

Chas unfastened his seat belt and hers, then he tugged her closer, turning her to face him. He twisted his hand around and pressed his finger into the hilt as he leaned closer, his lips against her ear. "I want to hear you scream before tonight is over."

Her lips lifted in a grin that died when she realized he was serious. "I've never screamed in bed, Chas."

He didn't seem concerned by that admission. If anything he

looked even more determined. "That's a shame, Syd. A woman like you should be screaming in bed every night. Guess I'm going to have to make up for some lost time."

Chas pulled his finger out slowly and—again—she thought they were going to go inside. But he surprised her when he pushed it back in faster. He added another finger to the first, fucking her with a strength and speed that would have been frightening if it hadn't felt so freaking good.

"Pull your pants down," Chas demanded as his fingers continued to stroke her pussy.

She lifted her hips, gasping as the movement allowed him to dive even deeper. She shoved her jeans and panties to her knees as Chas continued to fuck her with his fingers.

"You're not getting out of this truck until you come twice."

She didn't think that was going to be a problem. She was damn close already. Chas added another finger to the dance as he pinched her clit with his other hand.

Sydney jerked. "Oh! Oh my God!" She'd never been taken so roughly, and she liked it. She *really* liked it.

Chas didn't relent or give up his pounding pace. Instead, he continued to pump his fingers inside her as her inner muscles clenched and her body trembled.

She reached for his shoulders, digging her fingers into his shirt. She needed something to hold on to. He was fucking her into oblivion with just his hand.

"God. Please." She had no idea what she was asking for, but Chas seemed to understand.

"That's right, Syd. Beg me. Beg me to fuck you harder."

"Harder." The word came out on a gasp and Chas responded. He gripped her hips and pulled them closer to him until she was sprawled out on her back on the seat. His fingers returned, moving faster, deeper. She lifted her hips toward him on each inward thrust.

He used his free hand to stroke her clit, alternating between firm caresses and pinches.

Sydney gave up all hope of holding on to her sanity. Chas

played with her body, twisting and moving her in different positions—each one pushing her closer to a place she'd never been before. She felt like she was on fire one moment, the next she was floating, whirling, spinning. She writhed and cried out. She scratched Chas' upper arms, pinched, even punched when the pressure built too much.

Chas took it all, then he gave her even more. When he bent his head and took her clit into his mouth, she was a goner. He sucked roughly on the sensitive flesh, then bit her.

She screamed as her body flew apart.

She'd heard people talk about out-of-body experiences—usually in relation to terrifying, life-threatening situations—and Sydney suddenly understood the concept. However, rather than terror, she felt nothing but bone-shattering bliss.

As her strength slowly returned, she opened her eyes, her gaze meeting Chas'. He was back behind the driver's seat, fully dressed and looking completely normal. On the flipside, she was sprawled on the seat, her clothing in disarray and feeling like she'd just spent eight seconds on the meanest bull in the rodeo.

Part of her expected him to give her a cocky grin. After all, he'd earned the right. He'd promised to make her scream before the night was out. It had taken him less than ten minutes to achieve that goal.

However, his expression was more pensive than arrogant, more concerned than pleased.

She slowly tried to push herself up. Chas gripped her upper arms and helped her.

"You okay?" he asked.

She nodded. "Jesus. Yeah. Way okay."

Her response prompted a small smile. "Good."

"Where the hell did you learn to do all of that?"

He ran his fingers through her hair in what she assumed was a way to push it out of her eyes and fix it. No doubt she looked a mess.

"The past doesn't matter anymore, Syd. All I want from now on is a present. A future."

His words fired off her curiosity about his time in the Middle East. She could only imagine the horrors he'd witnessed that he longed to forget. Sydney had brought up the subject a few times when he'd been home for visits, but he'd always brushed off her questions, told her he was home to forget, not to rehash.

Only once, this past Christmas, had he offered her a crumb, shared a bit about the night his two friends had died. And she knew he'd only done that because he'd consumed too much eggnog.

His silence had hurt her feelings the first few times he'd come home for visits because they'd been each other's confidantes in school, sharing every secret.

Then she'd accepted and respected his need for privacy. The secrets of teenagers could hardly compare to the hardships Chas had seen while away.

She leaned close to him, offering a kiss. It was the first one she'd initiated, that fact lost on neither of them. This time, Chas did give her a cocky smile.

When they pulled apart, she glanced over her shoulder at her beloved little cabin. She'd moved in several years earlier after scrimping and saving for the down payment. Chas had only been there a few times, usually over the holidays when he was home on leave.

"You want to come inside?"

"I promised you two orgasms in the truck."

She shivered in response, her body still weak, exhausted from the first. "Can I get a rain check on the second? I'm still trying to recover."

He grinned. "I like the idea of a rain check. Means you owe me one. Just so you know, I *will* collect on that." He opened his door. She was just climbing out of the truck when he reached her. He helped her down, but this time she didn't hold her tongue.

"I can get in and out of your truck on my own. It's not that high off the ground."

He shrugged, unrepentant. "I'm going to take every opportunity I have to touch you. You might want to get used to that."

She graced him with a sassy smile. "That won't be a hardship."

He wrapped his arm around her waist as they walked toward the front porch. She was glad for his support as her legs felt a wee bit wobbly after her orgasm. Her pussy still tingled and she felt the slightest twinges from unused muscles that had gotten one hell of a workout.

They hadn't even gotten undressed or in bed and she was already feeling well used. Once she unlocked her door, Chas led them inside. He didn't bother to look around. Instead, he kept a firm hold on her hand as he directed her straight to her bedroom. She wished she'd taken a few minutes to tidy up this morning. Instead, she'd been so distracted with thoughts of him she hadn't even bothered to make her bed.

Then she realized her vibrator was lying on the nightstand.

She crossed the room quickly, hoping she could block his view. Unfortunately, Chas was too observant, his all-seeing eyes noticing it immediately.

"Rough night?" he teased.

"Screw you." Her tone held more bravado than she felt as she reached for the sex toy, planning to stuff it in a drawer.

She was startled when Chas came up behind her and grasped her wrist. "Give it to me."

Sydney turned to face him, intent on arguing, but her words died when she caught sight of his dark, demanding expression. Something about this new Chas sent tremors of excitement through her. She was finding it impossible to resist. She relinquished the vibrator to him.

"Take off your clothes, Syd."

CHAPTER FOUR

Sydney hesitated for only a moment. Chas narrowed his eyes, which prompted her to respond. She tugged her t-shirt over her head. Chas had seen her naked before, too many years and more than a few pounds earlier. Time had changed her looks. She started to lift her shirt to cover her breasts, but he was waiting for her, his hand stripping the cotton away from her grasp.

"Keep going."

She reached behind her back, unfastening her bra. Again, she felt a strong urge to resist, to hide behind the clothing. Chas' gaze was relentless, all his focus on her body. Taking a deep breath, she dragged the bra away, dropping it to the floor.

Her nipples budded in the cooler air. Or maybe it was Chas' hungry look that fueled the reaction. She'd just come, but her body acted like she hadn't had sex in years. It was revved up, ready for more. And something told her Chas had plenty more to give. He was exposing her to a sexual being she didn't realize lurked beneath her skin.

There was something about his dominant stance, his commanding tone, and his intense focus that left her off-balance in a very good way. Sex had never felt this exciting, this dangerous.

Chas captured her attention as he crossed his arms, his face darker. "I'm not going to keep prodding you, Syd. Take off everything. Now."

While he didn't add "or else," it definitely felt implied. She wondered what he'd do if she continued to stall. He took one step toward her and she sprang into action, not sure she wanted to know.

She tackled the button and zipper on the jeans she'd only just done up in the truck. Then she tugged down her pants and panties, kicking off her sandals as well. Within seconds, she stood before him completely naked.

And he was fully dressed.

There was something very arousing about standing in front of him like this. The way his gaze traveled along her body made her feel as if she were on display. Most shocking of all was the realization that she didn't want to shield herself from him. Her modesty in the face of his genuine admiration had faded. Once again, he made her feel like the most beautiful woman alive simply with a look. She could get used to this.

When he lifted his finger, indicating he wanted her to turn around, she was in motion before she could consider her actions. She didn't worry about him seeing what she considered her flabby ass or that she was jumping through his hoops without question. He asked and she gave. It felt as natural as breathing.

Once her back was turned, she glanced over her shoulder at him. He was staring at her ass. And she suddenly didn't hate it as much as she always had.

When his eyes met hers again, she saw something she hadn't seen since he'd left. Something she was beginning to think she'd never see again.

Love.

He loved her. Suddenly she remembered what it had felt like to be loved by him all those years ago. She'd locked the memory away because it had hurt too badly. He'd been away so long.

He stepped closer and she turned, accepting his embrace,

falling into his arms. "I love you too," she said against his chest, her voice breaking slightly.

"I'm sorry I worried you," he whispered against the top of her head.

Sydney swallowed back the tears. She refused to cry, to ruin this moment with weakness. "I was so afraid you'd be killed, so afraid every time you left that you'd never come back, that I'd never see you again."

"I know."

There was nothing else to say. Instead, they just stood there, clinging tightly as twelve years of emotions—fear, anger, regret, sadness, loneliness—ebbed and flowed between them.

And then, just like that, Sydney let it go. She was in love with this man and he was right. The past was over. It was time to move forward. She could waste a bunch of time fighting the inevitable or she could admit that right here, right now, with him was exactly where she wanted to be.

Chas must've noticed the change in her. He released her, his hands reaching out to cup her face. He kissed her, the touch gentle at first—in direct opposition to the hard kisses he'd been giving her since he stepped off the plane—then it became deeper, more forceful.

He twisted her face this way and that, his tongue stroking hers then exploring her mouth. She struggled to catch a breath, then decided breathing was overrated when his hands moved to her hair, his fingers tangling and tugging until her scalp tingled.

Her breasts rubbed against the soft cotton of his t-shirt and she became greedy. She reached for the hem, raising it until they were forced to break the kiss—just for a split second—to pull the shirt off. Then he was kissing her again as she savored the feeling of skin against skin, the hair of his chest tickling her sensitive nipples.

She ran her fingers over his back, teasing him with light scratches. She'd never felt the need to mark a man, but she couldn't resist leaving evidence on Chas' body. She wanted him to remember this moment when he said goodbye tomorrow morning and headed off to work.

He hissed when she scratched harder, but he didn't move away from her, didn't tug free of her arms. Instead, he pulled her hair harder, bending her head back so he could devour her mouth. He took full possession of her lips, her air, *her*.

She groaned when he cupped her breast with one hand, firmly pinching her nipple.

"Harder," she urged.

Chas didn't hesitate to give her what she wanted. In some ways, she thought her arousal, her need for roughness, was feeding his own desire.

After so many years of going through the motions, of feeling numb, she felt as if Chas' strong touch was bringing her back to life.

When he bent his head to suck on her nipple, she threw her head back, her fingers digging into his hard, muscular shoulders.

"God, Chas."

He didn't speak. He didn't need to. He told her exactly what he was feeling through his actions, his harder sucking, the way his teeth nipped the sensitive bud, sending sparks to every erogenous zone in her body.

"Need you. Now."

Her vocabulary had shrunk until she struggled to form complete sentences. Too much more of this and she'd forget her own damn name. She reached for his jeans, intent on stripping him out of the denim that was keeping her from her treasure.

He pushed her hands away as she fought with the button. "Let me."

It was probably a smart call on his part. With her shaking hands, she'd likely injure the thick erection pressing against the stiff denim.

Chas quickly and efficiently toed off his shoes, then tugged off his jeans. He went commando. Something she liked very, very much.

Sydney reached for him but again he gripped her wrist, holding her at bay.

"Lay on the bed, Syd. I'm going to fuck you seven ways to Sunday. I'm going to take your mouth, your pussy and maybe even your ass before this night is over. But if you touch me right now, I'm a goner. I've wanted you too badly for too long. So you're going to have to let me run the show this time. Okay?"

She nodded and started to tell him he'd been running the show since he got off the plane. Instead, she lay down on the center of the bed, and then reached for him.

He straddled her, covering her with his big, hard body. He made her feel tiny, delicate. Dropping to his elbows, he kissed her once more.

His chest rubbed against her breasts, his cock nudged her stomach. She wanted him inside her. She tried to grasp his cock, determined to guide him where she wanted, but Chas was far stronger and determined to remain in control.

He gripped both her wrists and dragged them above her head. Shifting so that he could hold both with one of his hands, he pressed them firmly against the mattress. "Do that again and I'll tie you up."

It was the most delicious threat she'd ever heard. And one she was sorely tempted to take him up on. Her face must have given her away because Chas' expression darkened.

"Not this time, Syd. Rest assured, one night very soon, I'm going to strap you spread eagle to this bed and I'm going to take you hard. You'll be my captive, mine to control, to use however I want."

She licked her lips. "If you're trying to scare me, you're failing miserably."

For the first time in a long time, he grinned and she saw shades of the safe, "just friends" Chas she'd always known. Then, as quick as that, he disappeared once again and she was left with this dominant stranger who seemed to understand her desires better than she did.

"Are you on the Pill?"

She nodded. "I don't want anything between us. I don't need it. If you don't."

He ran one finger along her neck, the delicate touch making her shiver. "I'm clean. Just had a physical last month."

She knew he wouldn't even ask to forgo the condom if there was a concern. "Chas." It was all she could say. Her body ached. He wasn't the only one who needed this badly.

He kissed her cheek, then shifted, pressing her legs apart as he knelt between them. He ran his finger along her slit, lifting the juices he'd gathered there to his lips to taste.

She flushed, amazed by the sheer sensuality, the unbridled passion in him. He wasn't holding anything back. It made her want to give him the same.

Then he grasped his cock, ran his hand along the thick flesh twice before placing the head at her entrance. They'd been here before, so many years ago. He'd been her first. But that had been a different Chas and a younger Sydney, another lifetime.

Tonight felt like her first time again. Everything new, unfamiliar, exciting.

He pressed in slowly, giving her time to adjust to every delicious inch. He felt bigger, harder than she remembered. When he was seated to the hilt, he immediately started the retreat, then the return.

His thrusts were slow and steady at first, the lines on his face betraying how hard that was for him. He was trying to make it good for her. She cupped his cheek.

"Don't hold back, Chas. I'm close. I swear. We have all night to make it last."

She hoped her words would comfort him, allow him to relax, but she felt him struggling to remain in control. Apparently this dominant streak of his ran deep.

Pity for him. She didn't always feel the need to play fair.

She reached down and found his balls, letting them fill her palm.

Chas hissed and narrowed his eyes. "Move your hand, Sydney."

She pretended to misunderstand. "Okay." She stroked his balls, then added the slightest bit of pressure.

His jaw was clenched tight and for just a moment, he stopped moving. Then he bent down and took her earlobe between his teeth, biting at the tiny bit of flesh. It was a quick, sharp pain that he soothed with his tongue.

"I'm going to make you pay for this," he said through gritted teeth when she squeezed his balls a little tighter.

"I can't wait."

He grabbed her wrist, dragging it and the other above her head once more. He used his grip there to steady him as he relinquished all semblance of control. He pounded inside her pussy in a motion that was rough and deep. She didn't shy away from the almost-brutal thrusting. She couldn't. It felt too good. She lifted her hips to add her own friction to the fucking.

"So close," she said. "So close." Stars started to flash, almost blinding her, though her eyes were wide open.

Chas groaned and she felt him straining to hold back. The stubborn man wouldn't come until she did.

She was almost there, but she knew he was closer. Pulling away from his grip, she reached down and touched her clit, determined to put her considerate lover out of his misery. She rubbed her clit firmly, matching the pace of his cock as it thrust in and out.

Her pussy clenched and her back arched with her orgasm a second before she felt Chas' cock explode, hot jets of come filling her.

He collapsed next to her, and then wrapped his arm around her shoulders to pull her against his chest.

"Never again," he said once their breathing had returned to normal.

She frowned. "What?" Surely she hadn't pissed him off that much. So much that he wouldn't have sex with her again?

"You're never going to have to find your own pleasure again. I swear it."

She lifted her head, grinning. "That's a pretty big promise to make. You sure you're up to it?"

He pushed her onto her back. She was amazed by his stamina. She felt like rubber, certain she could sleep for the next twelve hours straight without moving a muscle. Meanwhile, Chas was there, his cock still soft but definitely starting to make a comeback.

"I think it's time for you to see what you've signed on for, Syd." He reached for the vibrator he'd tossed to the mattress earlier.

She lifted her hands defensively. "Wait. I was kidding."

"I know you were. But I'm not. I'm not going to be an easy lover. I'm going to ask you for things I'm sure you've never done before. I'm going to take what I want and then I'm going to demand more."

"And what makes you so sure I'm going to agree to all that?"

Chas' face softened, his blue eyes twinkling, reminding her that deep down inside, he was still her sweet, considerate friend. "You're not going to give it to me. You're going to beg *me* to give it to you."

"Arrogant much?"

He gave her a platonic kiss that was in direct contrast to the situation. After all, he was straddling her naked body wielding her largest—and favorite—vibrator.

"The military is very good at instilling confidence."

"It would appear you learned that lesson well."

"I'm a very good student. And an even better teacher. Open your legs."

Sydney knew for a fact her personal record for orgasms in a single night was three. And Chas set that record. No one had come close to breaking it. Ever.

It looked like tonight was the night.

She gave him a sexy smile that he returned. Then she parted her thighs, ready for another trip to paradise.

Chas ran his fingers along her slit, then stopped to toy with her clit. He knew just how to touch her, how to fire off a whole new round of arousal and need.

She was squirming within seconds. Her heart raced in anticipation of what he would do when he held up the vibrator. It was no small toy, though Chas certainly didn't need to worry about any comparisons.

Even so, he said, "Takes a lot to satisfy you these days, doesn't it?"

She laughed. "If you're waiting for me to say you ruined me for all other men—"

Her joke died on her lips when he pressed the vibrator inside her. He didn't hesitate, didn't tease her. Just pushed the toy straight to the hilt in one glorious thrust.

She gasped, trying to suck in some much-needed air.

"I'm pretty sure I didn't ruin you for anything back then, but I'm definitely going to make sure you never want to look at another man after tonight."

Sydney wasn't sure how to respond. The truth was she'd been about to tell Chas he *had* ruined her that very first night they were together.

He didn't wait for a response. He didn't seem to want one. Instead, he turned the vibrator on low and started moving it in and out of her pussy. It was a gentle rocking motion that was nowhere near enough for her. If anything, it was almost an annoyance.

She made a few grateful sounds, not wanting him to think she didn't appreciate his efforts, but soon, when he continued the slow pace, she found her mind wandering to other things—like what she had in her refrigerator to make them for a late dinner. They'd said they would pick up a pizza and beer, but that plan had been forgotten when Chas started fondling her in the truck.

She gave another fake moan, then tried to recall if she had a frozen pizza in the freezer. Or maybe she had enough leftovers from the pork barbeque she'd brought home from the restaurant last night.

"Yes," she murmured, dismissing the barbeque idea. She was out of sandwich rolls.

Her thoughts were interrupted when Chas stopped moving.

Sydney's gaze lifted to his.

"How long were you going to pretend you liked that?"

She wasn't sure how to respond to his question. "Um..."

Chas pulled the vibrator out and tossed it to the mattress. "You failed the test."

"That was a test?"

"I'm not here for some one-night stand with you, Sydney. I'm in this for the long haul. Which means I expect you to always be honest with me about your feelings and your needs. What were you thinking about just then?"

She bit her lower lip, debated lying. It would be pointless. Chas knew her too well. "Dinner," she answered at last.

"What are we having?" His question was sardonic.

"I haven't decided yet."

"Let me know when you figure it out."

Sydney struggled to decide if Chas was pissed off. She didn't think he was, but his brows were furrowed, his expression far-too-serious.

"In the meantime..." He gripped her arm and tugged her to a sitting position.

"Chas?"

He didn't offer any explanation, just kept moving her where he wanted her. He was as strong as an ox.

Before she knew what was happening, he was perched at the edge of the mattress and she was facedown over his lap. She reared up just as he placed the first smack on her bare ass.

"Are you freaking kidding me?" Her temper flared. What the hell did he think he was doing?

"Don't ever lie about what you want from me, Sydney." He spanked her again. They were no more than taps, so pain wasn't an issue. Given his strength, he wasn't spanking her nearly as hard as he could.

She continued to try to escape, but he had a firm grip on her shoulder, pressing her head down as he peppered her ass with his light blows. When it became obvious she wouldn't be able to rise, she struck out with her fingernails, scratching his leg.

He simply added more of the annoying swats to her ass.

Bending forward as much as she was able, she tried to bite

him, reaching out for whatever she could grab to sink her teeth into.

Chas anticipated her intent, wrapping his hand in her hair to hold her mouth away from his leg. The damn tug on her hair sent a different sort of heat through her. She never realized how hot it was to have her hair pulled. Sensation shot through her, her arousal becoming painful once more.

She stilled, trying to take deep breaths, hoping to find some way to shake off her sudden desire. God, she was annoyed as hell at his heavy-handedness, but so hot for him she could hardly see straight.

He was fucking with her head. And she couldn't decide if she liked that idea or hated it.

Once she was calmer, he released her hair, his hand returning to her upper back. He had no intention of allowing her to rise, even though he'd stopped spanking her—if she could even call his light swats a spanking.

"You hold all the cards here, Syd."

"Not from where I'm standing...or should I say sprawled out?"

He stroked her back and from his soft touch, she sensed he was amused though she couldn't see his face.

"I want to make you happy—in bed and out. But you have to meet me halfway. By being honest. And open-minded."

"I don't have a problem with honesty."

Chas ran one finger along her spine, the delicate stroke causing her to shiver. "Then why didn't you tell me you didn't like the way I was using the vibrator on you? Why did you make all those fake 'oohs' and 'ahhs' like you just couldn't get enough?"

She'd spent too many years faking orgasms simply because that seemed like the easier and more expedient way to get rid of the inept jackasses she'd foolishly taken to bed. But she didn't want Chas to leave.

"I didn't want you to think I didn't appreciate your efforts."

He snorted. "Jesus. I don't think my ego is that fragile."

"I'm sorry."

She really was. The man had been back a day and a half and

she'd felt tipsy and off-balance every moment since he'd walked off that plane. She just couldn't quite get her head wrapped around everything that was happening.

She started to push up, but Chas still held her down. She'd thought her apology would help.

"Chas."

"Not so fast. We haven't had a chance to really explore all our options for this position."

She shot him a dirty look over her shoulder. "I think you've explored plenty."

He shook his head. "I didn't really spank you and you know it."

Sydney did, but her pride wouldn't let her admit it. She hadn't liked what he'd done. Like the too-slow fucking with the vibrator, his light swats were just an irritation.

"What are you saying?"

He gave her a wicked grin. "I want to do it for real."

She wasn't sure how to reply to that. "But it will hurt."

"Do you like it when I pull your hair?"

She nodded. There was no sense denying it. They both knew the truth.

"I think you'll like this too."

"What if I don't?"

He tugged her up until she was sitting on his lap. She curled against his chest, soaking up the warmth of his embrace. "You only have to tell me to stop, Syd, and I will. I never want to hurt you. You know that, right?"

She did. No one in her life had ever made her feel more protected and cherished than Chas. Even during the years when they were just friends, he'd always kept her safe from any perceived danger. Holding her hand whenever they were walking after dark, putting himself between her and the busy street when they were on the sidewalk together, offering his jacket when she was cold. They were all small things that added up to making her feel cared for.

"I do."

"Then you say, 'Chas, stop', and it all ends. But I was serious about the open mind, Sydney. You and I have some similar needs, things I don't think you've considered trying before. I'd like you to try them with me."

Her curiosity was piqued. "Like what?"

"One thing at a time. I want to spank you. I think you might like it more than you expect."

She wanted to press him for more details about their shared desires, but she let the question go unanswered. She wouldn't have thought she'd like having her hair pulled and he'd proven to her several times tonight exactly how much she did. Maybe he would be right about this as well.

"Fine." She sort of expected him to strong-arm her back into position, but instead he simply waved his hand, indicating he wanted her to assume her spot over his lap on her own.

She moved slowly, questioning her sanity. Was she really going to let Chas spank her as if she were some naughty child?

Once she was facedown over his lap again, she held her breath, anticipating and fearing the pain.

When his hand landed on her ass, not to spank, but to caress it, she jerked.

He chuckled. "Easy, kitten. Let's ease into this."

He stroked her sensitive skin over and over. Sydney felt herself begin to relax, her body going limp.

Her eyes had just drifted shut when his hand struck, the pain and the loud smack jarring her back to awareness. She forgot her resolve to keep an open mind as she fought to find a way off his lap. Chas resumed his previous grip, his large hand holding her head down, keeping her from rising.

"Chas," she cried out when he struck her again.

Tears formed in her eyes. He was wrong. She didn't like this. Twice more he struck. Unlike the first time, her sweet lover wasn't pulling his punches, wasn't holding anything back.

She'd just opened her mouth to call it quits, to beg him to stop, when his hand slipped to the slit between her legs, finding the opening to her body. Two fingers slid inside her easily, her pussy soaking wet with arousal.

A tremor shook her entire body as he stroked inside her a half dozen times. Then, just like that, his wicked fingers were gone and she felt the flat of his palm on her ass and upper thighs once more.

He never struck her in the same place, never hit with the same amount of force. Sometimes it was a light tap, other times flames erupted where his hand landed. She couldn't anticipate what he would do next, but she kept trying. Somewhere in the midst of it all, she realized she wasn't asking him to stop because she didn't want him to.

He pressed three fingers deep inside her pussy again as she groaned. Her voice was thick with unshed tears. His spanking hurt—more than she'd expected—but the pain was morphing into something else, something better.

She lifted her hips as much as her position would allow, encouraging him to thrust deeper. He accepted the invitation, increasing his pace. A girl could get used to Chas' talented fingers. He knew where all the hot spots inside her were and he used that knowledge to her benefit.

She was mere seconds from her climax when he withdrew his fingers again.

"Dammit, no. Don't stop."

He spanked her, this blow harder than all the rest. "You're not calling the shots, Syd. If you want me to stop, say so. Otherwise, I make the decisions."

Her feminist side wanted to tell him to take his cocky assertion and stick it where the sun didn't shine, but she was too close. She didn't dare say anything to make him stop because if he did, she'd expire on the spot.

"Please," she said at last, her voice breathless with need and exhaustion. How long had they been at this? She'd been on the razor's edge of one climax after another since she'd left work. It was dark outside, so she could only assume a few hours had passed.

He didn't respond, didn't even give any indication he'd heard her. Instead, he continued his spanking. Sydney gasped and found herself floating on that lovely cloud again. How could he keep doing this? Keep pushing her outside of herself into such a wonderful place?

His fingers returned to her pussy. He'd no more than pushed two to the hilt, than her inner muscles contracted, clenched, seized. She gasped for breath and her orgasm flowed almost painfully, blinding her to everything except brilliant white light.

As Sydney returned to consciousness, she was surprised to find herself back in the center of the bed. Chas lay next to her. It took several moments before she realized the vibrator was back in his hand.

"Oh God. I don't think I can take any more."

He grinned, but didn't take her complaint seriously. "Let's test that theory."

"You're an asshole."

He laughed, the deep, rich sound filling the quiet room when the vibrator started to slide in. He hadn't turned it on, which left her on edge. She'd learned not to underestimate him. She'd failed his initial test. That wouldn't happen again.

Once the toy was lodged to the hilt, he paused to look at her. "Slow or fast?"

She eyed him suspiciously. "You're giving me a choice?"

Chas winked at her. "I'm letting you state a preference. Then I'll decide if I agree with it."

She scowled, though there wasn't a bit of anger in her. She was equal parts nervous anticipation and blissful lethargy. Sydney had no idea how those two things fit together, but they were the only words she could think of to describe her current state.

"Fast."

He kissed her on the cheek. "Good answer."

With that, he flipped the switch, firing the toy to high. She jerked in surprised, then groaned when he gave her exactly what she asked for. For a guy, he sure as hell knew how to make good use of a vibrator.

She panted, her fingers white-knuckle clenching the sheets

below her within seconds. Sydney started lifting up on her heels, trying to capture even more of the vibrator, the sensations.

In and out, Chas kept up a relentless pace for what could have been minutes or hours. Sydney constantly lost track of place and time with him. He rubbed her clit as her climax approached. Then, just before it hit, he withdrew the toy and tossed it to the floor. She didn't have time to complain before Chas was there, inside her, fucking her so much better than the vibrator.

She wrapped her arms around his shoulders, her legs around his waist and held on for dear life. Chas thrust inside, deep and sure, stroking every nerve ending and hitting her G-spot every time.

"Come, kitten," he urged, though she fought to hold off her orgasm. She wanted to wait for him, but there was simply no way.

With his permission, she gave herself over to it. She was going to be so sore tomorrow. And she didn't give a good goddamn.

As her orgasm waned, Chas slowed his thrusts, moving inside her more seductively. She'd thought she preferred his rough, hard fucking, but there was definitely something to be said for this gentle wooing of the senses. He kissed her lips, her cheeks, her shoulders. His tongue teased her earlobe and found the light sheen of sweat at her brow. She didn't work out this hard at the gym.

"Salty," he murmured. "You're salty *and* sweet."

She cupped his cheek and lifted her face, ready and waiting as he kissed her once more, his tongue dancing with hers.

They continued to rock together, neither of them in a hurry to see the night end. Finally, Chas hit the brink and she was surprised to realize he'd brought her with him. She didn't expect the orgasm. She and Chas clung together, each of them groaning softly as he filled her once more.

They parted slowly, Sydney wincing slightly as he withdrew.

"Sorry," he said, though his too-pleased grin told her he wasn't feeling much guilt.

She rolled her eyes, and then accepted his embrace when he held his arms out, cuddling her.

"We never got dinner," she said after a few minutes.

"It's okay. We'll get there. Might take a few months or years for us to feed *this* hunger, but eventually our stomachs will get a turn."

She giggled. "God help me if it's months or years. Every muscle in my body hurts."

"Sorry," he repeated, wiggling his eyebrows.

"I keep wondering if this is real. If you're really here."

"It's real, Syd. I'm here. And I'm not going anywhere. Promise."

Sydney closed her eyes, certain she'd never slept on any pillow more comfortable than his chest. His breathing deepened after a few minutes, the easy rise and fall a sure sign he'd fallen asleep. Her rest came slower. While her body was miles beyond the state line of exhaustion, her brain wasn't finding it as easy to shut down.

Oh, the difference seven days could make. A week ago, she was planning a surprise welcome home party for a friend, depressed over her still-single state and suffering from unending loneliness. Now, she was wrapped up in the arms of the man she loved and looking at a future filled with happiness, security and incredible sex.

What a week!

CHAPTER FIVE

Chas stood at the edge of the construction site, his eyes not seeing a bit of what was going on in front of him. Instead, his mind was replaying last night.

He'd spent nearly every night for the past month in bed with Sydney, neither of them able to get enough of each other.

He'd walk in from work and within minutes, they'd be horizontal on the floor or the couch or occasionally, they'd make it to her bed.

And every time Chas thought he'd hit that point where he was satiated and able to make it without touching her until bedtime, Sydney would walk by and he'd catch a sniff of her floral perfume, or she'd bend over to get something out of the oven, and the next thing he knew, his cock was rock-hard and he had her pressed up against the wall with her panties around her ankles.

The sex was incredible. Not that he was surprised. He'd never forgotten their too-brief time together that summer after graduation. Though they'd both been young and inexperienced, there had been a physical connection. Something Chas had never found with any other woman since. If he mentioned it to Gran, no doubt she would give him the same advice she always used to when he said he hadn't found the right woman yet.

"Friends first, Chas," Gran would say. "That's the secret to a happy relationship that lasts. You young people are always so anxious to hop between the sheets. You forget to build a solid foundation before you start laying the bricks."

Her comments about laying bricks always made him laugh, but when he considered her guidance now, he could see the truth in it. He and Sydney were solid. They'd grown up together, knew each other inside and out. She'd been there when Gran had told him that his mother—though long estranged—had ODed. She was the first one he'd told after he'd signed up to join the Marines. And she was the one whose letters had kept him going when homesickness or boredom or depression threatened to take him down during his years away.

Sydney had given him her trust, her loyalty, and her virginity. She'd always been standing nearby, ready to offer him whatever he needed.

She'd offered him comfort even when she hadn't realized she was doing so.

He'd come home on leave four years earlier, staying in Maris longer than he had since leaving home at eighteen. For a full month, he'd visited with his gran, done a bit of part-time work with his uncle, and spent the rest of the time hanging out with Sydney—either at the counter of Sparks Barbeque or by the lake. They'd taken long walks, talking about a whole lot of nothing. He'd listened as she filled him in on all the local gossip.

He'd come home hoping to find some semblance of peace after losing two of his closest friends. He hadn't told Sydney—or Gran —the reason for his visit at the time, though he had confided in his uncle. Chas hadn't wanted to answer a lot of questions or to see the fear in his gran's and Sydney's eyes when he returned to his unit. So, he'd come home and let Sydney sweep him back into his old life.

It had been just the cure. During that month, he'd wrestled his demons alone at night, worn out and on edge. Then he'd go find Sydney and for a few hours, he was able to forget about Iraq, blood, pain, war. He could see the world through her beautiful eyes and escape.

It had taken him every bit of those four weeks to find his sea legs, until he felt strong enough to return. He'd considered telling Sydney how much she'd helped him, but he preferred to keep his life at home separate from the years he'd spent overseas. Chas wasn't ready to meld the two. He wasn't sure he'd ever be ready to, though he'd started to build a small bridge this past Christmas. He'd overindulged in the holiday eggnog and found himself telling her about Scott and Jeremy. He had shared stories about the trouble they'd gotten into pulling pranks on the other guys, the time they'd gone joyriding in a general's jeep. Then before he could stop himself, he revealed how Scott had died in his arms; Jeremy alone, his body lying in a pool of blood in the middle of a dirt road as bullets continued to whiz through the air.

Chas ended the story when he'd realized Sydney was crying. He hadn't meant to tell her so much. Hell, he hadn't meant to tell her any of it. It had taken him four years to beat down the nightmares, to keep them at bay. Every now and then, the memories came back, catching him unaware.

He'd meant what he'd said to Sydney. He wanted to forget about the past. Talking about Iraq here felt like rolling around in mud while wearing all white. He didn't want to soil this world with reminisces of the other.

Sydney had asked him about his time in the Middle East the first few nights they were together. He'd hold her after they'd made love, the quiet closeness calling to her, making her long to know about all the years they'd been apart. He'd put her off, changed the subject, filled those hours instead with funny little stories about mishaps on the construction site or recalling silly things they'd done in high school.

Lately, she'd stopped asking about his time in the service completely.

His uncle walked over and put a hand on his shoulder.

Chas jumped, spinning and raising his fists defensively.

Julian put his hands up. "Whoa! Sorry about that. Didn't mean to sneak up on you. Just noticed that you're drifting again."

Chas tried to laugh off his overreaction, tried to still his suddenly racing heart. "Yeah. I guess I was."

Julian studied his face, concern in his gaze. "Good thoughts or bad memories?"

It had been a bit of both, but Chas simply replied, "Sydney."

His uncle chucked. "Oh to be young and in love."

Chas took the opening, the opportunity to deflect comment on his jumpiness. It wasn't the first time he'd reacted badly around the site. A pickup truck backfired a few days ago and Chas had hit the dirt. He'd felt like a jackass when all the other men had looked at him in surprise. He supposed his edginess was to be expected. It had been twelve years since he'd lived in a civilian world, but lately his reactions to normal, non-threatening things was getting worse, not better. And his ability to hide his freaked-out responses or joke them off was getting harder, especially with Julian, who could read him too easily.

He grinned at his uncle. "Syd's amazing."

Julian nodded, agreeing. "Yeah. She is. I'm happy for you, Chas. And I'm damn glad you're home again. I've been worried about you the last few years."

Julian knew about the gunfight that had killed his two friends. "I'm doing good."

Julian studied his face. Chas tried to give him a confident look, something to reassure his uncle. Julian wasn't easily fooled, however, and Chas wasn't doing a very convincing job.

The flashbacks had started a few days earlier—right after the truck backfired. They appeared out of the blue, and since then, Chas couldn't seem to stop replaying the same scene. Over and over. It always started with images of him with his friends, the three of them cutting up like always. Jeremy was doing some asinine walk as he crossed the street, making Chas and Scott laugh.

And then, just like that, half his head was gone.

Bright flashes of light and the sound of gunfire erupted around them. Chas had hit the ground a split second faster than Scott. It had saved his life. Scott hadn't moved quickly enough and had fallen in front of him, a tiny speck of red forming on his chest. Chas had watched in horror as the circle of color expanded, grew. He'd grabbed his friend and dragged him inside a nearby building, then he'd held him as Scott slowly bled out.

Chas shook his head, trying to drive the memory away. Julian was watching him, his eyes too knowing.

Dammit. He needed to get control of this. He thought things would be better at home. It was one of the reasons he'd chosen not to re-enlist. The ache in his chest was too familiar as it pressed down on his lungs, threatening to suffocate him.

"You know...if you ever need to talk or..."

Chas cut off his uncle's offer. "I'm fine, Julian. Honest." It wasn't that he didn't appreciate his uncle's concerns. It was just that Chas didn't see much point in drudging up painful memories. He'd worked hard to put Scott and Jeremy's deaths behind him. He'd only been moderately successful at it while he was still in the service, which was why he'd packed it in and come home. He'd felt certain the change of scenery, the peaceful lifestyle, would do the trick. The sudden reappearance of these flashbacks was confusing.

Julian clearly wasn't convinced, but he cut Chas some slack. Another reason he loved his uncle so much. He knew when to apply pressure and when to back off.

Julian changed the subject, discussing the next move in their construction project. For nearly thirty minutes, they discussed timelines and debated whether or not to consider adding overtime to a few of the men's hours in order to hit their deadline. A couple of nasty thunderstorms had blown through Maris earlier in the week and set them back a bit.

"Well," Julian said, looking at his watch, "it's quitting time. You spending the night at Sydney's again?"

Chas shrugged. "She's working late at the restaurant tonight. I was actually thinking I should take Gran out for dinner and spend a little time with her."

Chas felt guilty about how little time he'd actually spent with Gran since his return. Between work and Sydney, he was starting to think he'd seen more of his grandmother when he was in the Marines.

Julian nodded. "She'd like that. She was thrilled when she found out you were coming home to stay."

"Yeah. I missed her. She's a tough old bird."

Julian gave him a lopsided grin. "That she is. Though I'll admit I've noticed she moves a bit slower these days and she struggles with the porch stairs. I offered to build her a ramp, but you know her, she acted like I'd insulted her with the suggestion."

"She doesn't like to show any weakness."

Julian crossed his arms. "That trait seems to run in our family."

Chas caught his uncle's drift, but still didn't take the bait. "Yeah. I guess it does."

They were all pretty good at playing their cards close to their chests, keeping their aches, pains and anxieties to themselves.

Sydney had pointed that out to him more than a few times over the years. She seemed to consider it a character flaw, insisting it wasn't healthy to keep stuff bottled up inside.

She'd obviously inherited that belief from her relatives. The Sparks family were famous for wearing their hearts on their sleeves. When they fell in love, they fell hard. When they had disagreements, they didn't bother being quiet about it. If they had a thought, they shared it—with anyone in listening distance.

"You want to join me and Gran for a bite to eat?"

Julian dug in his front pocket, pulling his truck keys out. "No. Thanks for the invitation, but I'm going home. I got a hot date with my recliner, a couple of cold beers, and the baseball game. I'll see you in the morning."

Chas waved as his uncle climbed into his truck, then he said goodbye to the fellas on the crew. As he drove into town, he considered stopping by Sparks Barbeque to try to talk Sydney into a quickie in the back storeroom.

The idea was tempting, but he decided he'd better head on

home. He needed a shower before he took Gran out to eat and she didn't like to have her dinner too late. As he pulled into the driveway, he was surprised to find Sydney standing there.

"I thought you had to work," he said as he climbed out of the truck.

"I was just about to call you."

Her quiet tone alarmed him. "What's wrong?" He glanced at his grandmother's house. "Is Gran alright?"

Sydney raised her hands quickly. "She's fine. Honest. She just took a small tumble in the bathroom when she was getting out of the shower. Her cell phone was in her bedroom, so she had to crawl to get it because she was having trouble standing."

"Jesus."

"It's okay, Chas. Honest."

"She called you?"

Sydney nodded.

"Why? Why didn't she call me or Julian?"

Sydney gave him a comforting smile. "I was closer and she knew it. Plus I don't think she liked the idea of her son or grandson seeing her naked on the floor."

Chas took the porch steps two at a time, rushing by Sydney and into the house. "Does she need to go to the hospital?"

Sydney followed him. "No. I phoned Tyson and he swung by on his way home from the office."

Tyson Sparks was Sydney's cousin and a well-respected physician in Maris. Most of the people in town managed to find their way into his family practice at one time or another.

"What did he say?"

"He actually just left a few minutes ago. She has a little bump on the head and a few bruises. She's lying on the couch, resting. He said there wasn't anything wrong with her a couple ibuprofens couldn't fix. So, I gave her some Advil and a Diet Coke and she's happy as a lark watching *Judge Judy* on TV."

Chas headed to the living room, his heart still racing. He'd come home to help care for his aging grandmother and so far he'd only spent a handful of nights in her house—usually only when

Sydney worked the late shift at the restaurant. Hell, even then, he'd more often than not hung out at Sydney's place, waiting until she got off.

He was an asshole, thinking with his cock. He'd have to talk to Sydney about possibly splitting their overnights between her place and here.

Gran looked up when he entered the room. She raised a finger to stop him from speaking. "Don't say one word, Chas. And get that panicked look off your face. I'm absolutely fine. I'm just a clumsy old woman who slipped in the tub. This isn't a reason to declare a state of emergency."

Chas sank onto the coffee table next to her. "Even so, you're going to humor me. First thing tomorrow, I'm ordering you one of those showers with a door so you don't have to step over the rim of the tub. And I want you to promise me you'll take your cell phone with you whenever you're in the bathroom. Otherwise, I'm getting you one of those necklace, Life Alert thingies."

Gran rolled her eyes. "Help, I've fallen and I can't get up?"

Chas wasn't amused. "Joke about it all you like. I'm dead serious."

Gran reached out to pat his hand. "I know you are, sweetheart. I'm sorry I didn't call you. I have too much pride for my own good. I'd appreciate the new shower. And I will keep my cell on hand from now on."

Chas flipped his hand over to capture his grandmother's. In his eyes, she'd always been indomitable, a powerhouse. She'd taken him in when he was only three years old, driving six hundred miles to get him away from his drug-addicted mother. She'd tried unsuccessfully for nearly a decade to get Mom into rehab, but the heroin she loved so much refused to relinquish her. Her death by overdose had been no surprise to anyone, and Chas couldn't recall feeling much remorse. At the time he'd felt guilty for his lack of emotion. It was Sydney who'd comforted him, had pointed out he hadn't even really known his mother. She was virtually a stranger and it was Gran who was his true mom.

Chas owed Gran everything.

And he couldn't keep his dick in his pants long enough to spend any quality time with the dear woman. Dammit. He owed her a huge apology.

"I'm sorry I haven't been around much."

Gran winked at him. "You've been busy." Gran looked up at Sydney, who stood nearby. "And with good reason."

"Even so, I'm going to start spending more nights here."

Gran shook her head. "Only if Sydney agrees to stay as well. You're not going to screw up the best thing that's ever happened to you just because I took one tiny tumble."

Sydney laughed. "Sort of a sad testament to his life if I'm the best thing."

Chas was used to Sydney's self-deprecating comments. It wasn't that she had low self-esteem. It was simply that compliments embarrassed her.

"I've had two very good things in my life and they're both in this room with me." Chas glanced over at Sydney. "I thought you were working tonight."

"I was. Or I am. Jeannette is covering for me until I can get there." Sydney glanced at the clock on the mantel. "I should really go. She's been in that kitchen close to twelve hours now."

Chas released his grandmother's hand and stood. "Let me walk Sydney out, Gran, and then we'll figure out dinner. I'll find something in the kitchen to cook."

Gran smiled, her eyes betraying that she was tired and still in a bit of pain. Chas' chest tightened at the thought of how badly today could have gone if not for Sydney's help.

He placed his arm around Sydney's waist as they walked to the front porch together. "Thanks, Syd. For everything."

"There's nothing I wouldn't do for that lady, Chas. She's wonderful."

Chas pressed a kiss to Sydney's cheek. "So are you."

"I guess I'll see you tomorrow?"

He shook his head and pulled his keychain from his pocket. "No. Tonight." He pulled the key to his basement entrance off and placed it in her palm. "Come here right after work."

She laughed at his insistent tone. "It wouldn't kill either one of us to abstain for a day."

"You're wrong. It would. My bedroom. Around midnight?"

She nodded. "Okay. But no hanky-panky. Just sleeping. Not quite sure how I feel about having sex in your grandmother's house."

He cupped the back of her neck, pulling her closer until his lips touched the shell of her ear. "You didn't mind back in high school."

"That was different. It was the middle of the afternoon and she was at work."

He kissed her ear, then turned her face until her lips met his. "I don't want to sleep alone. I've gotten used to you stealing all the covers."

She didn't bother to argue. Instead, she accepted his kiss, her tongue meeting his. This touch had become familiar, but it still had the power to set his heart racing and send blood rushing to fill his cock.

When his hands drifted along her back to grip her ass, she broke away. "I really have to go to work," she said with a laugh.

He sighed and silently tried to will his hard-on away or Gran would be sure to notice it. "Okay. I'll see you later."

She was obviously struggling with her own arousal issues. She took a deep breath that did nothing to dim her flushed cheeks or the faraway look in her eyes that told him work was the last place she wanted to be.

"Midnight. Maybe earlier if I can kick everyone out," she said as she turned and walked toward her car.

Chas stood on the porch for a few minutes after she left, soaking in some much needed fresh air and trying to clear his head. Julie Wilkins, the little girl who lived across the street, was riding her bike up and down her family's driveway. She was singing a silly made-up song, the words making sense only to a small child.

But the tune and her voice triggered a memory.

Unwanted images appeared, blinding him to his surroundings, changing the scenery.

He was standing beside a dirt road in Afghanistan as the sound of gunshots filled the air. He was crouched down behind a car when he saw a toddler dart away from her mother's arms, running toward the road.

Chas started to move toward the child, but his commanding officer put a strong hand on his shoulder, holding him in place.

"You'll give away our position," his sergeant whispered angrily.

Chas didn't bother to acknowledge him. Instead he watched as the mother dashed after her baby, calling for the little girl to come back. The child was singing—not words, just some high-pitched little noise.

More gunshots fired and Chas watched the mother fall. The child turned and raced to her mother as Chas shook off his sergeant's grip and took off toward the pair. Bullets flew, but Chas kept his focus on the little girl, willing her to get down.

Get the fuck down!

He was yelling at her, he realized, as she looked at him, crying, fearful. When he reached her and her mother, he was relieved to see the woman had only been grazed in the leg. He reached beneath her arms and dragged the young mother toward the house, the child running along beside them. His sergeant continued to yell his name.

"Chas! Goddammit, Chas!"

"Chas."

Chas startled at the sound of his name, spinning quickly, his hands raised defensively, fists clenched.

"Chas? Sweetheart? Do you mind helping me to the kitchen? I want to get a drink of water."

It was Gran calling out from the house. Chas glanced around, genuinely surprised to realize he was home. He was back in the States, not on some desolate street in the middle of Hell. He swiped at his brow, wiping away a bead of perspiration trickling along his face. He tried to ignore that the night was almost chilly.

He shouldn't be this damn hot and sweaty. Chas worked hard to calm his breathing, to stop gasping like he'd just run a marathon.

"Chas? Are you there?"

"Yeah, Gran." He fought to make his voice as natural as possible. "Just a minute."

Chas closed his eyes, hoping to block out the memory, but all he saw behind his lowered lids was the face of the terrified child, her mother's blood smeared on her hands, the horror in her eyes. Something in the little girl's expression told him she wouldn't be singing again. At two years old, her innocence about the world around her had been stripped away and that wasn't something Chas could ever give her back.

He rubbed his face, forcing it all away, pushing it down into that place where he kept things hidden. Chas couldn't understand why it was all coming back now, but he refused to let any of it resurface. It was over—the past was dead and gone. He was moving on.

Chas returned to the living room and spent the rest of the evening successfully forgetting. Gran made it easy. They had soup and grilled cheese sandwiches for dinner—the limit of his culinary abilities—then they settled on the couch to watch *Jeopardy*. They laughed as they pretended to compete. Chas knew going in he would lose because he always lost to her. Gran's brain was a damn encyclopedia and he'd been telling her for years she should try out for the show.

Then they found an old movie on TV, but Gran was asleep before it was halfway over, so he carefully helped her upstairs to her bedroom, tucking her in as she had for him when he was a child.

Chas considered watching the rest of the movie, then gave in to his own exhaustion. Taking the stairs down to his small apartment in the basement, he settled in to wait for Sydney.

Unfortunately, the quietness of the house gave him too much time to think. Too many images of his tours with the Marines kept crashing in on him. Some of the memories were good, others bad.

Clearly downtime was his enemy. In the service, he kept busy, worked hard. When he had some time off, he filled it by working out at the gym with buddies or blowing off steam between the sheets with a willing woman. As his experience in the bedroom grew, his sexual needs focused more and more on power exchanges. He stopped resisting his dominant urges, seeking out partners with submissive qualities. None of his past lovers had come close to satiating those needs, not like Sydney did. In sex, as in so many other aspects of their lives, she was his perfect complement.

He flipped open his laptop and looked up the website for the local gym. It was time to establish a routine, get back to what would now be the new normal. Chas simply needed a pattern, something that would keep his mind so occupied all the past bull-shit would fade away.

He found a number for the gym. He'd call first thing in the morning for an appointment to sign-up. He would continue learning everything he could about Julian's construction business so he would be ready to take over the reins when his uncle retired. And he would talk to Sydney about their relationship and where they were headed.

While he'd only been home a month, and he suspected she'd call him crazy for his desire to do some long-term planning, he intended to prove to her that he was in this for the long haul. He wouldn't have kissed her at the airport if he hadn't known she was the one he wanted to spend the rest of his life with.

He'd always known that, but the two of them had very different ideas of what they'd wanted when they were eighteen. Chas had planned to join the military since he was just a young boy, determined to serve his country. Meanwhile, Sydney was a Maris girl through and through, devoted to her family and the restaurant.

He may have longed to see the world, but Sydney would have been miserable being dragged from one military base to another. Most of the time, she would have been living alone while he was stationed overseas. Better that she live her life where she was happy, surrounded by those she loved, than tied down to a man who may or may not return home.

So, he'd done what he'd thought was best for her at the time. He'd let her go and asked her not to wait. It had killed him to leave her, but he'd actually intended his military commitment to be a lifelong one, envisioning himself retiring from the branch when he was much older.

However, after the deaths of his friends, something had broken inside him. He'd signed up for one more stint thinking time would heal that wound, but it hadn't. So when the time came to re-up again, he'd walked away instead.

Chas had come home in search of peace. The first person he'd seen was Sydney and he knew he'd made the right choice. He'd known from the second he'd told the Marines he was leaving that he would come home to her. That he'd do whatever it took to win her heart, to claim her. He'd been in love with her forever.

What he *hadn't* anticipated was the unbridled passion that didn't merely simmer between them. They spent every night leaping into the fire, consumed by the flames. It was the most powerful affair of his life. Though he'd experimented with his need to dominate in the bedroom, he'd never found anyone whose complete submission he wanted more.

For the first couple of weeks after his return, she'd helped him forget. Hell, he'd been too exhausted from their marathon sex to think about anything.

But some memories don't stay buried. No matter how much soil you cover them with.

He closed his eyes and rubbed them wearily.

When he opened them again, Sydney was standing there, staring at him curiously. How had he missed the sound of the key in the door?

Glancing at the clock, he was surprised to discover it was already midnight. He rose from his chair.

"Hey," she said, her eyes concerned. "You okay?"

He nodded, trying to shake off the heavy thoughts that consumed him. "Yeah. I'm fine."

"You looked a little upset when I walked in."

Chas shook his head. "No. Just impatient."

She laughed softly. "I was afraid I might wake you."

"No, Sydney," he said, lifting his arms. "I'm not tired. I've been waiting for you."

CHAPTER SIX

Sydney walked into his embrace, accepting the soft kiss he offered. Chas was such a contradiction—sometimes a gentle, sweet lover, other times a rough, demanding sex god who made her body quiver with his deep-voiced commands.

"How was work?" he asked as they pulled apart.

"Same old, same old."

Chas grinned. "And you loved every minute of it."

She laughed. "Yeah. I think I must be the most boring woman on the planet, but the truth is I love my little piece of the world."

"I know you do. And it doesn't make you boring. It means you're lucky. You've found genuine happiness in your career, you have an incredible family and you have that rare ability to appreciate the little things in life. I'm sort of jealous of that."

Sydney tilted her head, a slight unease forming. "Are you unhappy with your decision to come back home?"

He quickly shook his head, setting her worries to rest quickly. "Oh no. That's not what I meant. I'm glad to be back in Maris. I'm just sorry I didn't appreciate how much it had to offer a long time ago."

She blushed when his eyes drifted from her face to her breasts, the bold man letting her know exactly what he was appreciating these days. She rolled her eyes, then changed the subject. "How's your gran?"

"Fine. Even so, I think I'm going to stay close to home for the next week or so just to be sure. Are you okay with that?"

"Of course I am. Though I'll admit I'll be a bit sorry to curtail our nighttime fun. I swear I think you're turning me into a sex addict."

Chas narrowed his eyes. "What do you mean curtail?"

Sydney put her hands on her hips. "I meant what I said earlier, Chas. I'm not having sex with your grandmother in the house."

Chas raised his hand and Sydney braced herself as he began ticking off all the reasons why they would indeed be having sex. "Hate to disagree with you, Sydney. However, *I* am because, number one, my grandmother's bedroom is on the second floor. We're in the basement. Secondly, she sleeps with the TV on and she's slightly hard of hearing. And lastly, there's no way you're coming to bed with me without coming. Period."

"Chas—" She knew the second she said his name she was wasting her breath.

He grasped her hand and led her to his bed. They sat down side by side. He'd gotten the king-size bed when he was in high school as he continued to outgrow every mattress his grandmother bought for him.

Sydney placed her hand on his cheek, unable to shake the feeling that he hadn't been happy when she'd walked in. For one thing, he'd been so deep in thought he hadn't even heard her open the door and his face had looked so sad. "Are you sure you're okay?"

He nodded too quickly. "I'm fine.

She decided to take him at his word. Even if something was bothering him, she knew exactly how to distract him. She rose up, tossing one leg over his thighs until she straddled his lap. Since his return, Chas had taken the lead in all their bedroom play, issuing sexy commands that made her blood run hotter than molten lava.

He placed a loose grip on her waist and she wondered how

long he'd let her hold the upper hand before pushing her away. She ran her fingers through his hair, delighted that he was letting it grow out. While the shorter military style had been hot on him, she liked having something to stroke, to grab on to when they kissed.

Her gaze drifted to his lips at the thought and she moved the few inches forward until her mouth touched his. Chas let her lead the kiss, molding his lips to hers but not seeking to take over.

She wrapped her arms around his shoulders, digging her fingers into the powerful muscles there until she heard his soft intake of breath. She didn't mean to hurt him, yet she did. So many times she found herself touching him roughly, sort of the equivalent of pinching him to make sure he was really there.

Of course, the kiss wasn't much gentler. Her touches were demanding, powerful. A dare. Sydney wanted to force his hand. Challenge him to take control. Something in the way he held himself so stiffly now, the way he'd looked so lost when she'd entered the room told her he needed this.

She gave an internal eye roll.

Yeah.

That's why she was doing this. For purely unselfish reasons. She barely resisted the urge to snort. They'd spent every night since his return exploring the dynamics of their sexual relationship. She clearly had submissive qualities as well as a taste for pain. It was news to her, but she wasn't going to deny it, wasn't going to pretend it wasn't there.

Why would she, when her desires were the perfect counterpart to his? To his dominant streak, his need to be in control. Chas was clearly suffering from some unpleasant memories, but not when he was with her. Not when they were like this.

While she couldn't read his mind, she knew with utter certainty that when they came together like this, when they gave themselves to each other, it was just the two of them in the room— no past, no future. Just the here and the now.

Perhaps that explained his unquenchable need for her. Maybe their time together helped him forget. Sydney wanted to make him forget, wanted to wipe away every painful moment he'd suffered in the Middle East. She loved him. With everything she had, everything she was. This man had claimed her heart and she had no intention of making him relinquish it.

She tightened her grip, pushing the envelope. It had the desired effect. Chas gripped her wrists and tugged them behind her back. The action pressed her breasts forward, something he took time to acknowledge and appreciate with a long, heated look.

"Had your fun?" he asked.

She gave him a seductive smile. "I was just getting started."

He released her hands with a stern, "Behave, Sydney."

Her smile grew. So far she'd obeyed his requests without question, without resistance. Obviously he expected her to comply tonight as well. Thought he could use that deep, sensual voice that sent every sexual electric current she possessed straight to her pussy and she'd fall in line.

Not this time.

She moved quickly, taking him off guard as she kissed him once more. Before he could push her away again, she nipped at his lower lip, slowly biting down until he jerked away from the pain. He reached up to swipe at the wounded area when he tasted blood.

"You bit me."

She grinned unrepentantly. "So what are you going to do about it?"

Sydney was purposely trying to provoke him, to see what he'd do next. While he'd introduced her to a much rougher, much stronger type of sex, instinctively she knew there was so much more. He'd been holding back, going slowly. The master teacher taking his time to instruct his apprentice with patience, methodically.

She wanted more, thirsted to learn it all.

"Be very sure, Sydney."

She tilted her head. "Of what?"

"That this is the road you want to go down. Once we start,

there's no stopping. You'll belong to me in ways you can't even begin to imagine."

How could such ominous words sound so inviting, delicious?

"Show me."

Chas cupped her face and she sensed he was still holding back.

She offered another tweak. She knew how to get a response out of her brave Marine. "What are you afraid of?"

His expression darkened, but not with anger. It was as if he'd held tightly to some invisible reins and he'd just opened his hand to let them fall.

He twisted, one smooth action that put her on her back on his bed with Chas on top, caging her under his large, hard body.

"You just poked the bear."

She laughed. Despite his domineering ways, underneath it all, he never stopped being Chas, her dearest friend, the man who could always make her laugh. Even when her heart was racing with anticipation and the slightest bit of aroused fear.

"That's a shame," she said, the breathy quality of her voice betraying her, giving away the tiny sliver of nervousness residing there.

"Why is that?"

She reached down and cupped Chas' cock in her hand, giving the thick flesh a firm squeeze. "I was hoping he'd poke *me*."

Sydney was surprised when Chas rose, leaving her feeling oddly exposed and cold. She much preferred being under him, buried in all that rock-hard muscle.

"Chas—" She was ready to put up a fight if he tried to protect her from this again. Now that she knew he'd been holding back, she felt almost resentful.

Before she could say more, he yanked her from the bed, taking her place on the mattress. "Take off your clothes."

Her hands flew to the button on her jeans instantly. She was used to Chas' gaze on her, the way he ate her alive with his eyes as she bared more and more skin. It was easy being naked in front of him because he never made her feel anything less than completely beautiful. The flaws she faced daily whenever she looked at herself in the mirror seemed to vanish before him.

"I'm going to take you over my knee and spank you, Sydney."

"Finally. I was afraid I was going to have to throw a temper tantrum and start breaking stuff."

He barked out a loud, boisterous laugh that reminded Sydney of where they were. She glanced upwards. Chas recognized her concern.

"If you're uncomfortable having sex here, we could put this on the back burner and just go to sleep."

She shook her head quickly. "No. I believe you when you say she can't hear us. Besides, I have a feeling after her fall today you're not going to leave her alone very often. I either have to adapt or buy a bigger vibrator."

He scowled. "No more vibrators. I'm already intimidated by your current one."

Sydney laughed, but the sound was cut short when he reached for her hand, tugging her until she was facedown over his lap.

She wished he'd taken off his own clothing; the fact he was still completely covered while she was naked as the day she was born was not lost on her.

He ran his hand over her bare ass. She'd expected firm slaps, something painful. This touch was sweet, warm. Pure comfort.

It wasn't nearly enough. The damn hesitance was back. She pushed up and Chas offered no resistance. She sat on his lap, wrapping her arms around his neck. "Tell me."

"Sydney. I can't...I won't... What I need from you won't be easy. There's too much inside me right now, fighting to get out."

It was the closest he'd come to admitting what she'd seen in his face upon her arrival had really been there. Something bad was rattling around in Chas' head. Maybe one day he'd find a way to talk to her about it, to confide in her.

Until then...she could feel how much he needed this moment. His emotions lay bare, his body tense. He wasn't hiding anything from her.

"Do it."

"Sydney—" His tone was one of warning.

She didn't want it.

"You already said it, Chas. I belong to you. Do it. Do whatever it is you need to make these demons disappear."

"I don't want to hurt you. You're still new to…" He seemed to struggle for the word to describe their sexual desires.

"I think it's called BDSM."

His brows creased.

She lifted one shoulder casually. "I Googled it."

He smiled, though she didn't sense any true happiness behind it. He was still worried, still the protector. Even if what he was trying to save her from was him.

She didn't feel threatened or scared. For the first time in her life, Sydney felt as if she was truly home, even though she'd never left the damn place.

He didn't appear convinced, so she took control once more. Hopefully for the last time tonight. One last nudge…

She walked to a small dining table his gran had placed in his galley kitchen and bent over it. She rose up on her elbows and looked over her shoulder at him.

He was standing now, his gaze glued to her bare ass. She added fuel to the fire, parting her legs, displaying far more. Everything.

"I know what you want, Chas. I want the same thing. I'm not afraid. I trust you and I know you'd never intentionally hurt me. Take what you need from me. There's nothing I won't give you."

His hands clenched as he continued to resist. He was still trying to find the power to walk away. She wouldn't let him. "Please," she whispered.

Then, the clouds cleared and she knew she'd won. She smiled as Chas approached her, reaching out to stroke her bare ass.

He chuckled when Sydney jerked at the first touch. "Nervous?"

Now that he was all in, she'd expected something stronger. She shook her head.

His gaze narrowed. "Don't lie to me, Syd. Not here. Not now."

"I'm fucking terrified. And I love it."

"I love you."

Those sweet words should feel wrong at a time like this. After all, she was naked and bent over a table as he loomed over her, fully dressed, clearly intent on doing all sorts of unspeakable things to her. And yet, no time had ever felt more right.

Before she could return the sentiment, Chas lifted his hand and struck.

Damn. Suddenly she was reconsidering those kid gloves. The blow hurt. She only had a moment to consider that pain before he delivered another smack and then another.

Those muscles she'd admired since his return didn't seem so sexy anymore. He was putting his strength to good use and though he'd spanked her once before—their first night together—it was obvious he'd been holding back then.

"Wait," she cried out when he lifted his hand once more.

Chas bent over her prostrate form, his lips tickling her ear. "Three minutes. Give me three more minutes. If you want to stop after that, we will."

She nodded, trying not to think of how much pain he could evoke in a mere one hundred and eighty seconds.

Another blow landed and Sydney squeezed her eyes closed, forced herself to concentrate on her breathing, to find somewhere else to be.

Chas, the clever bastard, didn't allow her that retreat. With his toe, he nudged at her ankle, indicating he wanted her to open her legs farther. She hesitated only a second and then gave him what he desired.

Her ass was on fire and those flames didn't abate even when he began to gently caress her bottom. She squirmed when those soft touches sparked yet another inferno—this one inside her pussy.

She gasped, struggling to breathe, to understand. How could something that had hurt so bad feel so freaking good?

"Chas..." Her tone revealed her wonder, her surprise.

He pressed one finger inside her oh-so-wet opening. "Still want me to wait?"

She shook her head quickly. "Stop and I'll kill you."

She'd expected her words to evoke a laugh, but instead he leaned over her once more. "You hesitated when I asked you to open your legs."

Observant man. "I'm sorry."

"Don't do it again."

Chas didn't wait for her to reply. He removed his finger and ran his hand along her slit. She was drenched, hot, trembling with need.

He dragged some of her body's juices to her anus. She'd never experimented with anal play and Chas knew it.

He'd taken his time, slowly exposing her to the act. He hadn't fucked her there yet. Instead, he had let her get used to his fingers —one, then two, then three. Each time he ramped up the exploration, the experience, allowing her body to adjust to the new sensation.

Tonight, he wouldn't hold off. He'd made no secret of his desire to take her this way and through patient play and exposure, he'd made very sure she wanted it as well.

She groaned softly when he pushed one finger inside her ass, straight to the hilt. Her body was relaxed, the fact not lost on her, considering how tense she'd been only a few moments early.

"I'm going to test your limits tonight, Sydney." She couldn't help but wonder if he wouldn't be testing a few of his own as well.

"I'm ready."

He kept his finger buried as he caged her beneath him. "I'm fucking you here." Her back stiffened despite her desires. Chas wasn't a small man and regardless of his attempts to prepare her, she wasn't foolish enough to believe there wouldn't be some pain. Then she considered his spanking. It had hurt like hell. And yet here she was. Gasping, clamoring for more, dying to come.

Chas added more fuel to the fire. "I'm going to bury my cock as deep as it will go and take you hard."

Sydney didn't balk, didn't protest. The words would only be a lie. Instead, she gave him the truth. "Yes."

"But not yet. You've been a bad girl."

Rising, he wasted no time in pulling his finger from her ass, his hand striking her powerfully.

Sydney rose up on her toes and for a moment, she tried to decide if she should move closer or get the hell away.

It didn't matter. He didn't give her a chance to escape. He brought his hand down on her ass and upper thighs over and over. Tears formed behind her closed eyes, then began to stream down her face. Tears of pain mingled with cries of need. Her empty pussy clenched, desperate to be filled.

Sydney didn't shy away from his spanking, didn't resist or ask him to stop. She shuddered and begged, pleading for more. More of everything. She was so close. So close to coming.

Chas must have recognized it because he pressed two fingers into her pussy, driving them in with one hard thrust. Then he curved them, finding her G-spot.

Sydney gripped the table, her knuckles going white as she held on. Held her breath. Fought like the devil to resist.

"Sydney—" He was going to command her to come.

"Please. No. Not like this."

He stopped instantly. She'd said it wrong. He started to withdraw his fingers, but she closed her legs around his hand tightly. "No! Don't leave me."

"I don't understand. What do you—"

"Gag me."

"What?"

"Goddammit, Chas. I'm going to scream. There's no way I can do this quietly. Your gran..."

He didn't question her further. She watched him walk to his dresser, his image fuzzy due to the tears and pulsing throb between her legs.

Pulling out a clean cotton t-shirt, Chas ripped it into a long strip. Tying a knot in the middle, he returned to her and wrapped it around her head. Sydney shook her head slightly to test it, but she couldn't dislodge it. He moved around the table and knelt so that she could see his face.

"If you want me to stop, hold up two fingers, like this." He imitated the gesture. "That's how I know you're scared or hurting. Understand?"

She nodded, though she wasn't concerned with sign language. She was too close to coming to give a shit about anything. God, she'd never considered herself a particularly passionate woman. At best she would have said she was slightly better than frigid. Now she realized just how poorly she'd chosen her lovers.

"Jesus, Sydney. If I'd known this all those years ago, I never would have been able to walk away from you."

Returning to his spot behind her, he pushed her legs apart, shoving the same two fingers inside her pussy. She jerked and resumed her grip on the table. The gag in her mouth muffled her cries, so she stopped holding them back.

He thrust in a dozen or so times, then used his free hand to reach around her chest. She pushed away from the table so he could find what he wanted. Chas pinched her nipple tightly between his forefinger and thumb. Last week, he'd introduced her to nipple clamps. The tight pinch of the toy had set her off like a firecracker. He imitated the same pressure now and it had the same result.

Sydney shook, the table sliding a few inches across the floor as her orgasm overtook her. She was glad she'd asked for the gag because there was no way his gran would have mistaken the sounds coming out of her mouth.

This time she wasn't holding back.

Chas didn't acknowledge her orgasm; rather, he continued to stroke her with his fingers. He kept the sparks flashing, giving her no time to recover, to regain her wits. "I love the way your inner muscles clench against my fingers. I can't wait until it's my cock you're squeezing like that. Should we see if we can make you scream again?"

Suddenly the gag didn't seem like such a great idea. Chas was teasing her, toying with her body, dragging her back to the precipice. She was barely clinging to her sanity. And then he slowed his fingers, holding her back from what she needed most. If she'd had her voice, Sydney would have cussed him out, demanded that second climax.

"I want you to come, Sydney. Want you to know that I'm going to push you to the edge, watch you fall apart, then let you pull yourself together so I can do it all over again. How many times can you come in a night? Three, four, ten? How many times can I bring you here?"

She shivered at the thought as she pressed her forehead against the cool table and silently willed him to do it. Mentally, she screamed, "Bring it on!"

And then, he did.

Chas pressed his fingers deep, hard, and her orgasm hit her like a freight train, rattling her bones. She clenched her teeth into the gag in her mouth as she let the overpowering sensations consume her.

Chas held still after this orgasm. She felt his eyes on her, knew he was studying her reactions. He was using her responses against her. It was heady, beautiful. Exhausting. Her eyes drifted closed, but opened once more when she heard Chas chuckle.

"Oh no, you don't. The night is still young."

Sydney whimpered when he slowly pulled his fingers out of her pussy. She started to close her legs, intent on trapping him, but he was wise to that trick. He pressed his legs against the inside of hers, holding her open.

His large palm encircled her upper arm as he helped her stand on weak legs. "Time to move to the bed."

She let him half lead, half drag her to the large mattress. She dropped onto it with the grace of a tipsy elephant.

She started to lift her hands to the gag, to remove it, but Chas shook his head. "No. Leave it. You're not finished screaming."

She shifted in the bed until she lay on her back in the center of it. Chas made no move to join her.

He reached for the buttons on his jeans, tugging the denim down.

For a moment, she was surprised to realize he was still dressed. Then he pulled his t-shirt over his head and gave Sydney a moment to study his naked form. Had he lived in the Renaissance, the great artists would have fought to sculpt him and women would have swooned. As it was, he already appeared to be chiseled from stone, the poster child for male perfection. From his six-pack to his broad muscles to his firm ass to his thick, long cock, everything about him appealed to her.

She let her eyes fall on the tattoos on his upper arms. He'd gotten them shortly after joining the Marines, during the time when they'd been apart, their friendship in tatters. She remembered the first time she'd seen them. Gran had invited Sydney along on a small family picnic by the lake. Chas had pulled his shirt off, tossing it to his towel on the sandy beach. He'd turned to face her when she'd gasped, realizing she had spotted the U.S.M.C initials, flanked by the Corp's motto of Semper Fidelis on his upper right arm and an eagle on the left arm with the word Strength. Since then, he'd added a smaller tattoo to his upper right pec. It simply said Never Forget, with a cross containing the initials of the two friends he'd lost.

Chas walked to his closet and pulled out a bag. Sydney watched as he removed a tube of lubrication. She knew what he intended to do with it. She was ready.

Once he returned to the bed, he opened the nightstand drawer and grabbed a condom. "Hands and knees. Now."

Sydney complied instantly. After a month together, she no longer paused to consider his requests. He asked and she gave. The mattress shifted under Chas' weight as he forced her knees apart so he could kneel between her legs. He stroked her ass, the skin still sensitive from the spanking he'd given her. She hissed in a breath.

"Looks sore. Suspect sitting won't be comfortable for you tomorrow."

She glanced over her shoulder and narrowed her eyes. He grinned, and then reached for the gag. "I hate not hearing your smartass replies."

Sydney gave him a saucy grin. "All I was going to say was, lucky for me I have a job that requires I stand all day."

He leaned forward and placed a soft kiss on each cheek of her ass. "You're perfect for me, Syd. You always have been."

She raised one eyebrow. "Took you long enough to figure that out."

Chas ran one finger along her spine, his eyes following the path until he stopped just at the edge of the slit between her legs. "You're right. It took me too long. What do you say we make up for all that lost time?"

She smiled, her breathy reply showing how much his gentle touches were affecting her. "Sounds good to me."

He captured her gaze, his face growing stern. "Eyes forward. And keep them there."

Her pussy clenched with need at his command. Shit. Her body's responses to his dominance seemed to grow stronger with each experience. It was exciting, but a little bit frightening as well.

How far would he take her? How far would she follow? She genuinely didn't know and when Chas tugged her ass cheeks apart, she stopped caring.

Chas reached forward with one hand and pressed at the nape of her neck, pushing her head down. "Rest on your elbows."

She dropped lower. When he touched her anus, she sucked in a breath and held it. Once again, she was overwhelmed by emotions—excitement, fear, arousal, hunger. Chas was adept at pulling each feeling out. Like a musician with his guitar, he knew how to strum the chords, how to pluck each string to find the perfect sound.

The breath she'd been holding burst out when he placed the tube at her anus and squeezed some of the cold gel inside. He worked the lubrication deep with one, then two fingers. Like sex, he found a rhythm and she responded to it. Her fears quickly faded as she began to anticipate his thrusts. She moved in time with him, trying to draw him deeper into her body.

She hadn't anticipated enjoying anal sex. After all, the sensations were definitely different, not as pronounced as when Chas fucked her pussy. She certainly didn't expect to become this aroused.

Once he'd insured her body was slick enough to accept him, he withdrew his fingers. She rested her forehead on the pillow beneath her and fought to calm her breathing as the sound of him opening the condom drifted to her ears.

Chas didn't keep her waiting for long. Within seconds, he had the condom on and his cock was there, nudging against her anus, seeking entrance.

Sydney held perfectly still. Despite the three fingers he'd stretched her with, his cock was going to be a much tighter fit. She closed her eyes, her body tense once more.

"Relax, Sydney. And breathe."

"I'm trying."

He ran his hand through her hair, the touch soothing, sweet. "Try harder. If it hurts, if you don't like it, you only have to say stop."

She didn't need to hear the words, though she appreciated his reassurances. "I know."

"Then breathe."

She did as he asked and was surprised when more of his cock slid in, easier. She took another deep breath and again, he was able to move deeper. Chas never sought to speed things up, didn't push her to accept more than she was able. He took his time, entering her slowly.

And then...he was there. Buried to the hilt. Her ass felt full, but it wasn't painful. He held still for several moments, allowing her to adjust, and she was amazed by his restraint. His patience.

She tended to want to rush them straight to the good part, night after night, racing toward him like a kid on Christmas morning, tearing through the wrapping paper, not bothering to enjoy the hidden treasure before rushing on to the next gift.

Tonight, she'd taken heedlessly, reaching for climax after climax while continually grabbing for more. It was Chas who'd forced her to slow down, to appreciate the beauty of them. He was doing the same now.

Most incredible was, he hadn't come yet. Not once.

"Chas," she whispered.

He responded to the unanswered request, not with words, but with action. He withdrew until just the head of his cock remained buried and then he thrust back in. Sydney cried out at the force, the impact. He repeated the motion, over and over, as stars flew before her eyes.

She lifted up to her hands, needing more friction. More.

She met him thrust for thrust, her back arching in pure animalistic need. Chas gripped her waist firmly, used his hold to pull her ass against him, to drive him even deeper.

The room became unbearably hot, muggy, sweaty. The only sounds were those of their quiet moans as his flesh pounded against hers. Chas' fingers tightened, telling her he was close.

She wanted them to get there together. Reaching down, she stroked her clit with her fingers, just once. Chas reached around her and tugged her hand away. "No. That's mine." He'd promised she'd never have to find her own pleasure again and he'd held true to that promise. He stroked her clit again. And again.

And then, she was there. She dropped her face into the pillow, her loud "Ahhh!" muffled by the soft down.

Chas stiffened behind her as his own climax erupted in a vast array of curse words and sweet nothings. "Fuck" was followed by "perfect". "Jesus Christ" came on the heels of "God, I love you".

He withdrew slowly, tugging the condom off and dropping it to the floor by the bed.

She chuckled. "Such a guy."

"Why?"

"That's gross."

He lifted his shoulders nonchalantly. "I'll clean it up tomorrow."

She didn't bother to reprimand him further because God knew she wasn't getting up anytime soon. Every muscle in her body ached and she was fairly certain she could sleep until noon...the day *after* tomorrow, without rousing.

They lay together in quiet contentment, neither saying a

word, content to simply hold hands, until they both gave in to sleep.

SYDNEY STARTLED awake some time later. It was still dark outside, the room dimly lit by a thin stream of light provided from the bathroom, the door slightly ajar.

Chas sat with his back to her, his head in his hands. His shoulders rose and fell as if he'd run a race.

"Chas?"

He jerked at the sound of her voice and for a moment she got the impression he didn't remember she was there. She sat up and placed her hand on his bare back, shocked to find his skin slick with a cold sweat.

"Are you sick?"

He shook his head, but the hollow sound in his voice gave her no comfort. "No. I'm okay, Syd. Go back to sleep."

She wasn't satisfied by his answer. "Bad dream?"

He didn't reply.

"Want to talk about it?"

"No. It's nothing. Really."

Sydney wanted to press him further, but his tone told her he wouldn't say anything more. Which meant he was clearly remembering something bad.

She wished he would confide in her. Every now and then, a shadow seemed to fall over him and she sensed he was in some dark place. But no amount of prodding on her part could convince him to share his fears or his pain with her.

So the silence drove a wedge between them. Sydney wondered how much distance their relationship could withstand. She wasn't the type of woman to let things like this lie, but Chas was reluctant to let her in. That hurt. A lot.

"You don't have to do this alone."

Chas turned, the light hitting his face. She sucked in a breath at the pure anguish in his expression. She only got that tiny glimpse of how deeply his pain ran before he shuttered the emotions and shut her out. Again.

"I don't know what you're talking about. I'm not doing anything. Just sitting here."

She swallowed heavily. A trace of anger laced his words and she decided to let the subject drop. She didn't want to start an argument, didn't want to put any more stress on him. It was clear he was fighting some pretty big demons on his own.

"Okay." She leaned forward and placed a soft kiss on his cheek. He didn't pull away from her, but she could feel how tensely he was holding himself, his jaw rigid as if he were clenching his teeth together.

Sydney looked at him for a few moments, trying to figure out what she should do next. Chas made the decision for her.

"Go back to sleep, Syd."

She lay down, waiting for him to join her. Instead, he rose and walked to the bathroom.

She listened as he turned on the shower. Sydney picked her cell up from the nightstand and glanced at the time. Four a.m.

She sighed. It would appear neither one of them would be getting any more sleep tonight.

CHAPTER SEVEN

Sydney stood outside the door to Tyson's office two weeks later. Chas' bad dreams and sleeplessness had gotten worse as Sydney woke up every morning to find herself alone in bed, Chas sitting in a chair, his face haunted. He continued to proclaim it was nothing, dismissing her concerns out of hand, offering her no insight to what was bothering him.

She'd hit her limit this morning and decided to talk to Tyson before heading in to work the afternoon shift at the restaurant. His nurse waved her on when she walked in, telling her Tyson was taking lunch at his desk. Sydney didn't stop by often when he was at work, but Tyson's door had always been open to her when she did. She took a deep breath and knocked.

"Come in."

Sydney walked in and had only just closed the door behind her when Tyson saw her and scowled. The man had a sixth sense when it came to family. They used to joke about it at family occasions, how eerie it was that Tyson could take one look at someone he loved and know exactly what they were feeling.

"What's wrong?" Tyson asked as she approached him.

"How do you know anything's wrong?"

"Because you have dark circles under your eyes that tell me

you haven't been sleeping. And you never visit me out of the blue. So what's going on?"

Sydney plopped down into the seat opposite him, his desk separating them. "Sorry. About not visiting you for social reasons. Makes me feel sort of rude about dropping in now."

Tyson laughed. "I love when you drop in, even if it is because you want something. I'm one of the few males in a family that is predominantly female. I'm used to needy women."

Sydney picked up a pen from his desk and lobbed it at him as Tyson chuckled and dodged. "Asshole," she said, affectionately.

"Trouble in paradise with Chas? Because if so, I really think you picked the wrong cousin to talk to. My dating track record sucks...as you well know."

"Chas and I are doing great." Even as she said it, Sydney felt her throat close up on the lie.

Tyson recognized the fib immediately. "Apparently not. Are you fighting?"

"No. No. It's nothing like that. I'm worried about him."

"Chas?" Tyson, Evan and Chas had been friends growing up, the three of them playing on the same little league team for years. "I'll admit I haven't seen much of him since his welcome home party, but he seemed okay there. What's going on? Is he sick?"

"He's sort of been having these bad dreams."

Tyson leaned back in his chair and Sydney thought she saw a dawn of understanding in his face. "Oh. Every now and then or a lot?"

"Lately, it's been every night. He won't talk to me about them."

"Is it just dreams? Anything else different about him?"

She nodded. She'd called Julian before coming here to ask his opinion about whether or not she should talk to Tyson. He'd thought she was smart to come here and he'd mentioned some small things he'd noticed about Chas as well.

"Not at all at first, but lately, something's changed in him. We'll be in the middle of a conversation and he'll sort of drift away for a moment. According to his uncle, there have been some incidents on the worksite. A truck backfiring and Chas hitting the ground. They were doing some blasting yesterday. Apparently Chas went missing and when Julian found him, he was in his truck, sweating profusely, pale as a ghost."

"You've heard of post-traumatic stress, right?"

Sydney nodded. "Yes. I wondered about that, but Julian suggested maybe it's survivor's guilt. Is that even a thing?"

Tyson frowned. "It is. He lost friends in battle?"

"Yes."

"And Chas was there? He saw it all?"

Sydney nodded, uncertain how many details she should divulge. She trusted her cousin implicitly, but this wasn't her story to tell. It was Chas' and he didn't seem to want to talk to anyone about it. She knew he'd only told her because his inhibitions had been lowered by the rum in the eggnog at Christmas. She'd wondered ever since his return home, and his pointed refusal to talk about the past, if he would have confided in her at all if he hadn't been tipsy.

Once again, her chest tightened, her feelings hurt by his determination to hold her at arm's length in regards to his personal pain. If they stood a chance at making this relationship work, they needed honesty and trust. She wanted to be there for him, but if he wouldn't let her in...she wasn't sure how long she could remain without his distance driving a wedge between them.

Tyson turned to his computer monitor, tapping a few keys. "I know you, so I'm sure you've gotten on Google and done a web search."

Sydney laughed. She had a reputation in her family as queen of the Internet. She was constantly looking up random facts on Google whenever her curiosity was piqued. At the last family dinner, Evan had secretly kept count, informing everyone at the end of the evening that Sydney had consulted her smartphone and shared interesting facts regarding their discussions twenty-seven times. Everyone had laughed, while Sydney simply replied they were now all twenty-seven times smarter than they were at the beginning of the night.

"I may have done a little bit of research."

Tyson winked at her. "Here's some information that may be more detailed. I'm not saying this is what Chas is suffering from, but it wouldn't hurt for him to speak to someone—me if he wants —and describe his symptoms before we take it any further."

"Okay. I'll tell him that."

Tyson pulled the printed papers off the printer but before he handed them to her, he wrote something on the bottom. "I'm including the name of a colleague, a psychiatrist I know who has dealt extensively with PTSD. I can make a call if you want. Get Chas in to see him if you think he'd be more comfortable talking to a stranger rather than an old friend."

"Let me talk to Chas first before you call. I'm not sure how he'll feel about counseling."

Tyson frowned. "If it is PTSD, this isn't something that goes away on its own, Sydney."

"I know."

"It is, however, treatable."

She nodded, then stood. She was suddenly feeling guilty for doing so much of this behind Chas' back. She hadn't even told him her suspicions, but she was nervous about broaching the subject. She'd thought perhaps it would be easier if she was armed with some facts, some answers.

But now that she was armed with information, she knew that wasn't the case. This was going to be a hard conversation to have regardless of how much she'd learned.

CHAS REACHED up and cut off another tall piece of the bush. His gran had apparently been after Julian to trim the hedge for months, but his uncle—not much for yard work—had found excuses to get out of it. When he heard her mentioning it to Julian on the phone this morning, he'd offered to do the chore, grateful for something to do to pass the time between dinner and Sydney's arrival at midnight.

His gran had taken off for a long weekend with a couple of the old gals in her bridge club. They'd gotten cheap flights and were probably just landing in Vegas. Chas grinned when he considered his grandmother and her friends hitting the slot machines and shows. Gran had done nothing but talk about the trip for days.

Chas turned off the trimmers and bent down to load the clippings in a lawn bag. He'd only just started when the sound of rapid gunfire erupted in the street behind him.

Chas leapt into the hedge, barely feeling the sharp branches as they scratched his arms and legs. Twisting, he crouched, preparing to face his enemy, weaponless.

He barely breathed as he scanned the nearly empty street. Then he watched Mrs. Michaels come out onto her porch and yell at her two teenage sons for making so much racket. The boys apologized, then begrudgingly handed over the rest of their firecrackers. The three entered their house, none of them aware of what the boys' simple fun had done to him.

Chas remained crouched in the hedge for a very long time, fighting to catch his breath. When his legs began to cramp, he rose slowly and carefully picked his way out of the hedge, grateful no one had seen his reaction to the firecrackers. He grabbed the trimmers, but left the clippings and the bag in the yard. His hands were still shaking, so trying to do any more work this evening would be pointless.

A glance at the clock told him it was nearly eight. Still too many hours until Sydney came. He paced the floor of his bedroom, wishing she wasn't working the late shift tonight. His head pounded as he tried to get a grip.

Rifling through the medicine cabinet in his bathroom, he found some Advil. He popped three of them and lay down, hoping a quick nap would take care of his headache and loosen the tightness in his chest. He'd been sleeping like shit lately, so it was probably just exhaustion that had caused his overblown response. He'd been too tired. And caught unaware.

Chas had gotten better at controlling his reactions on the construction site, holding himself tightly, mentally preparing himself for the jackhammers and other loud noises that sounded too much like war. While it was exhausting, he hadn't lost his shit again at work, diving to the ground, looking like an idiot in front of the other guys. If something was scheduled that he thought would bother him, he separated himself from the group until he got a handle on his anxiety.

He just needed sleep. Unfortunately, Chas had no sooner closed his eyes than the memories returned.

Chas held a finger to his lips as he and Scott stood near the back door of the house. They'd received intelligence that insurgents were holed up inside. Their job was to wait in the back until hearing the signal, then enter from the rear door.

If all went well, they could catch the men by surprise and capture them without gunfire. At least Chas hoped so. Peering in a dirty window, Chas tried to make out what they were up against. From the sound of the voices inside, it appeared most of the occupants of the house were in the front room. Which meant he and Scott would have to move through the back rooms fast in order to help their team coming in from the other side of the house.

There was no movement in the room, or so Chas thought. He was just about to look away, to signal the all clear, when he spotted him. A young boy—no more than ten years old—lay on a cot on the floor near the corner, his left foot bandaged. Chas stilled when he saw the AK-47 lying next to him. He shouldn't be surprised to see the child armed. He was in a house with known members of the Taliban and child soldiers weren't an unknown enemy. Chas didn't doubt for a moment that the boy would fire if they entered the house. Which meant Chas would have to fire back.

The thought of killing a child didn't rest easy on him. He felt Scott move closer beside him. Glancing to his left, he saw his friend peering through the window.

"Kid," Scott whispered.

Chas nodded, understanding any speaking at all was dangerous, that it could alert someone to their presence. There were patrols in the area. One misstep and they'd be in deep shit.

He and Scott had been in this position enough that they didn't need to talk. Chas could see his friend found no more pleasure in this assignment than he did. Neither of them wanted to fire on the small boy.

The sound of footsteps behind him caught Chas unaware. Scott's eyes widened as he saw something coming and started to lift his gun.

The scene changed from the house to the street, and once more, Chas watched the bullet hit Scott's chest. He shouted, no longer concerned about remaining silent.

"No! Scott! No!" His friend lay bleeding on the ground.

They were right behind him. Chas lifted his weapon, prepared to fire, when someone gripped his shoulders, shaking him roughly.

Chas jerked at the touch. He wouldn't go down without a fight. "No!"

The gun fell from his hands at the unexpected attack, so Chas raised his fist, striking out. He'd kill the bastards with his bare hands. Make them pay for Scott. For Jeremy.

The sound of a woman crying out roused him from his dream. Chas opened his eyes, blinking against the bright light from a bedside lamp.

Where the fuck was he?

When his vision cleared, he saw Sydney on the floor, her hand pressed to her cheek.

There were tears streaming down her face—and he realized he'd hit her.

Jesus.

He leapt from the bed, his heart shattering when Sydney's eyes widened with fear.

"Jesus Christ, Syd. Oh my God, baby." He knelt next to her. "I'm sorry. I'm so fucking sorry."

Her stiff posture relaxed when he reached for her and he was surprised when she lifted her arms, accepting his embrace. He couldn't breathe, his chest felt as if it was being squeezed in a vise, all air cut off.

He'd just punched Sydney. He'd never forgive himself. *Never.*

Over and over he murmured his apology, stroking her back, regretting that he'd ever thrust himself back into her life. Clearly he was damaged goods.

"It's not your fault," she said, her voice finally permeating through the roaring in his ears.

He gripped her upper arms and pulled her face away from his chest, forcing himself to see the damage he'd wrought. The entire left cheek was flaming red and she'd be lucky if she didn't have a black eye.

Remorse coursed through him. "Fuck. Jesus. Fuck!"

She cupped his face in her hands. "Stop it, Chas. It wasn't your fault."

He frowned. "The fuck it wasn't. I hit you."

"I shouldn't have come up to you like that. You were having a nightmare and I thought I could wake you. That was stupid. You didn't know what you were doing."

"That doesn't matter. I hit you." Chas kept repeating the words, wishing there was some way he could take it back.

"Please. Please don't do this. Don't blame yourself. It doesn't even hurt anymore."

She was lying to him. There was definite pain in her eyes. She was still crying, sniffling.

He rose from the floor. "Don't move. I'm going to get some ice." He put together a makeshift ice pack with a Ziploc and a soft washcloth, something Gran had done for him many times when he was growing up.

When he returned from the kitchen, he found Sydney standing in front of his dresser, looking at her reflection in the mirror.

She smiled when he stepped up behind her. He couldn't understand why she wasn't running out of this room as fast as her feet would take her.

"It's not that bad."

"I'm not blind, Sydney. You're going to have a black eye and a bruise on that whole side of your face."

She bit her lip, not bothering to deny the truth. He lifted the ice pack to her cheek, feeling a sharp, piercing pain in his gut as she winced when the cloth touched her. "I'm sorry."

He'd said the words a hundred times, yet they didn't make up for what he'd done. They never would.

"Chas. It was an accident. It's over."

But it wasn't. It was never going to be over. Not for him. For twelve years, he'd lived on the front stoop of death, his life in constant danger. Yet he'd never felt helpless or out of control. Not like he did now.

In Afghanistan, he'd had a gun and he'd had his training. He knew how to fight the enemy. He didn't have a chance against this one. No matter how many times he tried to ward off the memories, they kept coming, fucking with his head, scaring the shit out of him.

She took his hand and led him to the bed. He stood, still as a statue, as she sat on the end. She patted the mattress but he couldn't make himself move, couldn't be that close to her. He didn't trust himself. What if another flashback came? He wouldn't keep putting her in danger.

"What was the dream about?" she asked.

He shook his head. "It doesn't matter."

"It matters a lot, Chas. You think I haven't noticed, haven't seen the way you drift away every now and then? The way you jerk at loud noises? And you can't sleep. Not soundly. What are you thinking about?"

When he didn't answer, she asked, "Afghanistan?"

He swallowed heavily. His jaw was clenched so tightly, it hurt. "I'm not going to talk about it."

"I think you need too."

He shook his head, his headache returning with a vengeance. "It's all in the past. It doesn't matter anymore."

"If that were true, you wouldn't be having these bad dreams. Tyson knows the name of a doctor—"

"You talked to Tyson about this?"

Sydney winced at his sharp tone. "I was worried. He thought if you talked to a psychiatrist, you might—"

"A shrink? You think I need a shrink?" The walls of the room seemed to close in on him and he fought for air.

"Chas. Please. I just want to help."

"Talking to someone isn't going to help. I'm not weak! I can control this, Sydney. I just need some time!"

Sydney fell silent. He hadn't meant for his tone to sound so harsh. He'd hit her because he'd thought she was an enemy coming to attack him. She was absolutely right to suggest he get help. He just wasn't sure what a doctor could do for him. It wasn't as if there was a drug to wipe out bad memories. Nothing any shrink could do would bring Jeremy and Scott back.

"Time?" she asked when the silence drifted too long.

"Alone."

Chas forced himself to face her, to recognize the pain he was causing. Another blow. It needed to be done. She was in danger.

"I think you should leave, Sydney."

She scowled. "What? No. Hell no."

"Please, baby. Be reasonable. You said this was an accident, but the truth is I can't promise it won't happen again. That dream..."

He knew her. Knew she wouldn't leave unless he made her.

"Chas. The last thing you need is to be alone. I love you. I want to help you."

"You can't help. And I don't want you here."

Tears streamed down her face, but Chas didn't back down. Not when the evidence of what could happen to her was written so clearly on her cheek.

He should have left her alone. Kept the status quo and never kissed her in that airport. If he'd known then...

"Please," she whispered.

"Just go, Sydney." When she didn't move, he shouted. "Now!"

She jumped, and for the first time, she seemed to genuinely fear him. The idea sickened him, but he didn't reach out to her. Didn't try to call her back when she turned to leave.

The door had only just closed behind her when Chas sprinted for the bathroom. He fell to his knees before the toilet and threw up. Reaching for a towel, he wiped his mouth, then his ass hit the tiled floor, his back pressed against the wall as tears streamed down his face.

The same words repeated themselves like a mantra in his head.

I hit her.

I hit her.

Dear God, I hit her.

CHAPTER EIGHT

Sydney sat in a booth at Sparks Barbeque and watched the early morning crowd start to roll in. That crowd consisted of just a couple of retired guys who sat at the counter, drinking their coffees and gossiping like old women. They nodded to her as they claimed their usual seats, but the look on her weary face must have told them she wasn't up for conversation.

After leaving Chas last night, she'd driven here in a fog, not wanting to go home. The restaurant was much closer to Chas' place and she felt the need to remain nearby. She'd been terrified when she'd left. Not of him, but of what he might do. He'd been consumed with guilt over hitting her. She knew him, knew he wouldn't forgive himself for what was nothing more than an accident.

At first light, she'd called Julian and asked if he'd meet her for breakfast. He'd promised to get there as soon as he could.

Jeannette had arrived at dawn, surprised to find Sydney there, still wearing the same clothes she'd had on the night before. Mercifully, her cousin had honored Sydney's request that she not ask her any questions. Sydney was exhausted, numb and one second away from a complete meltdown. Jeannette had clearly recognized all of that.

Jeannette had agreed and headed toward the kitchen to start getting ready for the breakfast shift. Just before she left Sydney alone in the dining room, she'd turned to look at her. "I'm giving you a reprieve, Syd, but you might not want to hang out too long. Tyson and Evan come in every Thursday at eight for coffee before work. If they see that..."

Sydney's hand had unconsciously risen to her injured face. Evan was one of Sydney's favorite cousins. Jeannette had been right to issue the warning. He wouldn't stand idly by if he thought anyone had physically harmed her. He'd go to Chas' house and arrest him for assault, Tyson tagging along to make sure he got the job done right. "I'll be gone before then." She'd make sure of it.

"You and I are going to have a long talk about what happened tomorrow."

"Tomorrow," Sydney had whispered, wondering how she'd find the words to explain the sheer terror and devastation on Chas' face last night. She'd remained in her car outside his house for nearly an hour before she'd managed to convince herself to leave. Even then, she couldn't go farther away than the restaurant. If he'd called, if he'd needed her, she had wanted to be there in an instant.

He hadn't called.

The bell above the front door tinkled. Sydney blew out a long sigh of relief when Julian entered. He made a beeline for her table after a brief wave to the two old guys at the counter.

As he sank into the booth across from her, his gaze landed on her face and his expression turned dark. "What happened?"

"It's not what you think."

Julian didn't appear appeased. "I hope to God it's not, because what I'm thinking is making me sick to my stomach."

Jeannette had heard the bell and came from the kitchen with a coffeepot in hand. The early morning crowd was small enough that only one of them worked the first hour. She started toward their table, but something in Julian's face must have warned her to stay away. Instead, she walked over to refill the other customers' cups, then returned to the kitchen.

"He was having a nightmare. A really bad one. I tried to wake him up. I shouldn't have done that."

Julian's anger faded into something Sydney considered even worse—helplessness.

"He was fighting someone in his dream. When I shook him, he struck out. He was still asleep, Julian. And so fucking scared. I've never heard his voice like that."

"Then what?"

"He woke up and saw me on the floor. I tried to tell him it was an accident. That it was okay, but he wouldn't listen. He was devastated."

Julian studied her face and though she tried to stem the tears, they fell anyway. "Looks like he wasn't the only one."

"It wasn't his fault."

Julian ran a weary hand over his stubbled jaw. Clearly he'd skipped his morning shave in order to get here faster. "Maybe it wasn't, but he's not going to see it that way. He'll never forgive himself for this."

Sydney closed her eyes tightly, trying to stop the tears. Julian wasn't telling her anything she didn't know, but that didn't make it hurt less. "I shouldn't have touched him. I could see how distraught he was."

Julian reached across the table and clasped her hand tightly in his large calloused one. "It wasn't your fault either."

Sydney smiled tremulously. "I don't know what to do."

Julian released her hand and leaned back. "Chas is different. I've noticed subtle changes in him these past few years, but he was never home long enough for me to pick up on anything that rang alarm bells in my head. I chalked up his newfound reserved nature to stress on the job. He was deported four times in twelve years to countries most of us wouldn't dare to step a toe in."

"And now?"

"I think you were right. It's post-traumatic stress."

Sydney's tears dried, replaced by a chill that racked her body. "Yeah. That's what I think too."

"We're going to have to get him some help, Syd."

"I talked to my cousin, Tyson. He's knows a psychiatrist with experience in this area. He's offered to call and set up an appointment for Chas."

Julian nodded. "That's good."

"Not really. Getting the name of the doctor was the easy part."

Julian ran a hand through his hair. "You told Chas about it?"

"Yeah. He freaked out."

"Did you have this conversation before or after the hit?"

She bit her lower lip to keep it from trembling. "After."

"It wasn't the idea of going to the doctor that freaked him out. It's going to take him some time to come to grips with that." Julian lifted his hand and pointed to the bruise on her cheek. "That will be hard enough for him to deal with right now."

While Julian's words broke her heart, it was a relief to speak to someone who truly understood the situation, who appreciated what she was up against. "It was an accident."

"It's not me you have to convince."

"What do I do? He was so upset last night. He asked me to leave and when I wouldn't, he yelled for me to get out."

"He yelled?"

Sydney nodded. Chas never lost his temper, never raised his voice.

"He was afraid he'd hurt you again."

"That's stupid. Chas would never hurt me intentionally. Never raise his fist to me in anger. We all know that."

Julian sighed. "Chas was a confident young man when he left here. I never saw an eighteen-year-old guy with a stronger sense of self, of right and wrong. The Marines were a perfect fit for him. But he's seen things, dealt with hardships that would break a lesser man, and he's prided himself on that strength. Hitting a woman falls in the *wrong* category. He'll never see that any other way. And he'll think going to a psychiatrist will be admitting he's powerless, that he's not in control. He'll see that as a sign of weakness."

"So what do I do?"

"Sydney—"

She cut him off, spoke her biggest fear aloud. "Am I making it worse for him somehow? These memories?"

Julian raised his hand. "Hell no. You're perfect for him, Sydney. I figure if anything, you've helped him ward off the demons haunting him as much as possible. I'm starting to think Chas has been dealing with this since before his return home. This isn't a new problem. You've been providing a pretty nice distraction, but I'm afraid that's not really a cure for what ails him."

"Like treating cancer with aspirin?"

He nodded sadly. "Yeah. Doesn't mean you don't help ease his pain though. He needs you. Now more than ever."

The bell rang over the door to the restaurant, distracting her. Sydney winced when Tyson walked in. He was early.

Tyson smiled when he saw her, but that expression quickly faded. He walked over to the table, his anger clearly growing with each step. He didn't even spare a sideways glance at Julian, all his attention focused on her face. "What happened?"

"It was an accident."

"What sort of accident?"

Sydney glanced around Tyson, noticed they'd caught the interest of the two old guys at the counter. The last thing she needed was for the rumor mill to catch wind of this. "Sit down, Tyson. And lower your voice."

Tyson didn't move immediately, her sharp tone catching him off-guard. Then, he pulled a chair over from a nearby table and sat at the end of the booth. When he spoke again, his voice was quieter, but just as furious. "Tell me."

For a moment, Sydney wasn't sure how to respond. Tyson was the most mild-mannered of all her cousins. She wasn't accustomed to his temper.

"I went over to Chas' last night after work. I have a key. When I got there, he was asleep. In the middle of a really bad nightmare."

"Shit." The light of understanding in Tyson's eyes encouraged her to continue.

"I tried to wake him up."

"Oh Sydney—"

"I know. It was stupid. The wrong thing to do. He lashed out in his sleep, fighting some enemy behind his closed eyes."

"And then he woke up and the nightmare got worse."

She nodded. "He was upset when he realized what he'd done. He wouldn't listen to me, didn't care when I said it was an accident. That's what it was, Tyson. You have to believe me."

"I do. But Chas isn't going to see it that way. So the dreams are getting worse?"

"Yes."

"Did you give him Dr. Jennings' phone number?"

"I tried."

"When? Last night?"

Julian had already mentioned how poor her timing was. She didn't have the strength to hear it from Tyson too. "I'll try again."

"No." It was the first time Julian had spoken since Tyson's arrival. "I'll talk to him."

Sydney wanted to argue, but wasn't sure she should. Chas and Julian had a very special bond. Maybe what needed to be said would be better coming from his uncle. "What am I supposed to do?"

Julian gave Sydney a sympathetic look that immediately sent her back up, and she knew without a doubt she wasn't going to like what he was about to say. "I think you need to give him some space, Sydney. Some time."

Time. It was the same thing Chas had asked for last night, but she wasn't willing to give it. She shook her head. "No way. You can't seriously expect me to leave him alone to deal with this?"

Julian's gaze drifted to her face. "Right now, you're going to be a painful reminder. Given what you've said, his emotions are riding very close to the skin. He needs time to get them under control, to come to grips with what happened. Seeing you..."

"I'll cover it with makeup."

Tyson reached for her hand. "I think Julian is right, Syd. Chas is one of the good guys. He doesn't hit women. In fact, he beats up guys who hit women. Remember Jessica Martinique senior year?"

She nodded. Jessica had taken up with a college boy from a neighboring town. Chas had come upon Jessica and her new beau one night. The guy was manhandling her, calling her stupid, then he slapped her. Chas had lost it and shoved the guy. A scuffle ensued that ended with the guy bleeding and apologizing profusely to Jessica just so Chas would let him leave.

"I remember."

"Let your uncle talk to him. And me."

Sydney narrowed her eyes. "Why you?"

Tyson shrugged. "It's a guy thing. Trust me."

"Does it involve a fistfight?"

Tyson grinned. "I don't like to rule things out."

Julian chuckled. "Tyson should talk to Chas."

Sydney noticed the meaning*ful* look—that meant nothing to her—the men exchanged. "Tyson—"

"If he sees you, Syd, sees that bruise, it will only send him deeper into depression. I know you don't want to leave him alone and I'm not saying you should dump the guy and move on. Just give us a week."

"A whole week?"

Julian laughed at her loud exclamation. "Oh to be young and in love." He'd made that same observation several times in her presence. Pretty much every time she and Chas were together.

"Fine. One week, but I'm texting him."

Tyson held up a finger. "One text. Tell him you're giving him some time, but that the two of you need to talk. Even though I'm pretty sure he's beating himself up right now and determined to keep you at arm's length, somewhere in that thick skull of his, he'll appreciate knowing you haven't given up on him completely."

She was only slightly reassured by Tyson's beliefs. He hadn't seen Chas last night. Hadn't seen the utter devastation in his eyes. But the truth remained. She didn't have an answer, while Tyson and Julian seemed to have a plan. She'd take the week away to gather her thoughts and come up with her own scheme. Because there was no way she was giving up on what she and Chas had.

The war he was fighting in his head was nothing compared to the one she planned to wage.

CHAPTER NINE

Chas sat on the couch in his grandmother's living room and stared at the television. Some kid's show was playing, but he didn't bother to turn the channel.

Yesterday, he'd remained in bed, not bothering to rise. Chas had skipped every meal, tossing and turning restlessly as he replayed scene after brutal scene in his mind—Sydney, Scott, Jeremy.

Then he'd woken up this morning to find a text from Sydney, telling him she was giving him one week and then she was coming to talk.

Talk.

What the hell was he going to say to her? What words could he offer that would make amends for what he'd done?

When no answer appeared, he had thrown on workout clothes, choked down a bowl of cereal and spent the better part of the morning laying waste to the heavy bag. The punishing workout had done nothing to calm the fear, the anguish that had eaten at him like a cancer since he'd woken from that nightmare to find Sydney sprawled out on the floor.

He'd fucking hit her. Hurt her.

A knock sounded on the door. He ignored it. There was no one he wanted to talk to.

The person persisted, the knock turning to a bang, but Chas made no move to answer. They'd go away soon enough.

"Open the door, Chas. I know you're in there. You and I need to have a little talk. Man to man."

Tyson.

Chas should have known one of Sydney's cousins would arrive, seeking justice. He was surprised it was Tyson and not Evan standing on the porch, looking for retribution.

He stood slowly and walked to the front door. Tyson had every right to be there. If anyone had hurt someone Chas loved, he'd be setting the record straight as well.

He opened the door and braced himself. Though Evan definitely would have punched first and asked questions later, Tyson was more unpredictable. Either way, Chas prepared himself for the fist that was sure to fly sooner or later.

Tyson stood there, arms crossed, his eyes flashing fire. "You going to invite me in?"

Chas shrugged. "Depends. How bloody are you planning for this to get? My gran wouldn't appreciate stains on the carpet or busted furniture."

For a moment, Chas thought Tyson was fighting a grin, but soon his scowl obliterated any expression other than pure anger. "Maybe you should join me on the porch then."

Tyson stepped aside as Chas let the screen door slam behind him.

Tyson wasted no time getting to the point. "You want to explain that bruise on my cousin's face?"

Chas swallowed down the bile that Tyson's heated question pulled up. His punch had left a mark. "I hit her."

He'd expected his words to wave the flag, give Tyson the green light to swing, but the man still didn't move.

"Why did you hit her?"

Chas felt his own fury begin to spark. He was standing there with his hands down. He wasn't going to put up a fight or resist what he had coming to him. Even so, he didn't appreciate Tyson toying with him like a fucking mouse. "Does it matter? I fucking hit her."

"Yeah," Tyson said. "It does matter. Tell me why you hit my cousin."

Chas' jaw tightened. "We both know why you're here. Stop stalling and do it." Chas held his hands out by his side. "I'm not going to stop you."

"I'm still waiting for my answer."

Chas' temper blew. "I'm not going to fucking answer you! So hit me or get off my porch!"

Tyson threw a quick jab, a hard right that glanced off Chas' jaw. It didn't do as much damage as Chas knew Tyson was capable of.

"That one wasn't for Sydney. It was for you. For not answering. So I'm going to ask again. Why did you hit my cousin?"

Chas ran a hand over his jaw. The blow, though unexpected, hadn't come with much force. It probably wouldn't even leave a bruise. Then he realized he wasn't going to get the fight he wanted until he came clean.

"I was having a bad dream. Sydney tried to wake me up."

Tyson nodded slowly. "So you were pissed off that she tried to wake you and slugged her."

Chas scowled. "Of course not, you jackass. I was asleep. I wasn't hitting *her*."

"Who were you hitting?"

Chas shut up fast, annoyed at how quickly Tyson had backed him into a corner and gotten him to say stuff he didn't want to say. "No one," he grumbled.

"Someone from your time in the Marines?"

Chas looked away. "I'm not talking about this."

"The enemy?"

"I'm not talking about this!"

"What was the dream about?"

Chas threw up his hands. "None of your fucking business!"

Tyson took a step closer to him. "You're dating my cousin.

That makes this my business. So I'll ask one more time. Why did you hit Sydney?"

Chas spoke through clenched teeth. "It was an accident. I thought she was someone else."

"Fine."

"Fine?" It wasn't the answer Chas wanted. He hit Sydney. It was only right that Tyson kick the shit out of him. He deserved it.

"Yeah. It's fine. You said the same thing she did. It was an accident." Tyson repeated his words back to him.

"So that makes it okay?" Not in Chas' mind. He'd hurt her. Left a mark on her face. He couldn't erase that. Ever.

"It does to me."

Chas ran a frustrated hand through his hair. "Are you fucking kidding me? That's it? That's what you came for? Where's Evan?"

Tyson barked out a loud laugh. "He doesn't know about this. Why? You sorry you got the peaceful cousin?"

"I think you'd be well within your rights to beat the shit out of me for what I did to Sydney. I know it's what I'd do if I were you."

"Would you?" Tyson asked. "If a friend told you he'd come back from the war and started suffering terrible flashbacks, that he'd accidentally hurt someone he loved because of that and had obviously been kicking his own ass every second since then, would you hit him? Because that doesn't really sound like you, Chas."

Chas took the two steps necessary and dropped into his gran's rocking chair. He leaned his head back, tired beyond reason. "I really wish you'd hit me, Tyson."

Tyson claimed a spot on the porch swing and gave him a rueful grin. "Yeah. I know. But it wouldn't change things, man. It wouldn't make you feel any better."

"I'm willing to give it a try if you are."

Tyson chuckled. "Sorry. I'm a peaceful guy at heart."

"Do me a favor. Send Evan next time."

"You got it."

They sat in silence for a few minutes. Chas knew there was more Tyson wanted to say, so he waited for it. He'd hurt the man's cousin. As uncomfortable as this was, he owed it to him to hear him out.

"I've called you a few times for happy hour. You've never come. Why not?"

Chas frowned, surprised by the change of subject. "I've been busy." Tyson gave him a knowing grin and Chas rolled his eyes. "I'm not discussing my sex life with Sydney."

Tyson laughed. "I appreciate that. Otherwise, I *would* have to kick your ass. She's working tomorrow night."

Chas shrugged lightly. "Okay. Thanks for the update."

"So come to happy hour with me and the guys."

Chas shook his head quickly. "No, I—"

Tyson blew out an exasperated breath. "We were really good friends before you left, Chas. I'd sort of like to get back to that."

Chas wanted it too. More than he cared to admit. But something he couldn't quite define was holding him back. Maybe it was the former camaraderie? He hadn't been able to form any real male friendships since Jeremy and Scott died.

"I'll get back to you about it," Chas said at last, hoping Tyson would let him off the hook.

Tyson, mercifully, didn't press the issue. "Okay. But if you bail, I'm going to invite you the next time. And the time after that. And the time—"

Chas raised his hand to cut him off. "I think I got the pattern."

"Good." Tyson stood and Chas resisted the urge to release a sigh of relief. He didn't want to hurt his friend's feelings, but he was struggling to hold his shit together. His head hurt, his chest ached and it was taking all his strength to keep his hands from shaking. He needed a drink.

He rose and took the hand Tyson proffered for a shake. "Stop beating yourself up, man."

It was on the tip of Chas' tongue to say he wasn't the one who'd been beaten, but he held it in. He appreciated Tyson's visit, understood that he was trying to help. Hell, for all Chas knew, maybe Sydney had sent him.

He got all of that, but none of it changed what had happened. Or how he felt about it.

Tyson walked back to his car and pulled away. Chas stood on the porch for a few minutes more before walking inside and pouring himself a bourbon.

NEARLY A WEEK after he'd sent Sydney out of his place, her cheek red from his blow, Chas returned home from two hours at the gym to find Julian sitting on the front porch swing.

Despite the shower he'd taken in the locker room, he was still overheated and every muscle in his body ached. He wasn't in the mood to socialize, but Julian's determined look told Chas he wasn't being given an option.

Chas climbed the three stairs on the porch, then leaned against the railing. "You didn't tell me you were coming by tonight."

"Yeah. I know. Figured the element of surprise would work in my favor."

Chas frowned. "We're together all day everyday, Julian. This wasn't something you could say at work?"

"Nope."

Chas' chest constricted. He'd been waiting for this talk. Maris wasn't that big a town. It was bound to get back to his uncle that he'd hit Sydney. He'd actually expected this conversation to happen much sooner.

"You over it yet?" Julian asked.

Chas shook his head, not bothering to ask for an explanation.

"Well, get over it. I've had enough."

This wasn't the conversation Chas had been expecting. He'd thought his uncle would call him to task, give him hell for hitting a woman. "What are you talking about?"

"I know you, Chas. I changed your dirty diapers, taught you how to drive, gave you the damn sex talk. I can tell when something is wrong. I've been patient, but it's time for you to stop burying your head in the sand, pretending nothing's bothering you when I know the truth."

Chas fought to get some air in his lungs. Then he opened his mouth and said the three hardest words he'd ever spoken. "I hit Sydney."

"I know you did and I know it was an accident."

"God!" Chas yelled. "You sound like her and Tyson. Do you really think that matters?"

"Yes. I do."

Chas turned his back to Julian. "Well, I don't."

"Who did you think you were hitting?"

Chas closed his eyes, wished his uncle would leave him alone. He couldn't deal with this right now. He'd gone to the gym hoping to work himself into an exhaustion that would let him sleep. He was so fucking tired, but he couldn't seem to fall asleep anymore.

"Chas," Julian pressed. His uncle wasn't going to let this go.

Tyson had asked him the same question. The problem was, Chas didn't know who he was hitting. Some faceless enemy. The only faces he could see when he closed his eyes were those of the victims. The red mark on Sydney's face, the blood on Scott's chest, and Jeremy facedown in the middle of the road. "I don't know. I never see a face. I just feel the danger."

"How long has it been going on? And don't say it just started. I won't fall for that bullshit."

Chas swallowed heavily. "Since they died."

"Your friends? Jeremy and Scott?"

Chas nodded. "I came home right after. I thought I'd managed to put it behind me and move on. And for a while, I had."

"What happened?"

The little girl escaping her mother's grasp had happened. From that point on, Chas had felt trapped in a never-ending free fall. However, he'd found ways to compensate, to overcome the panic attacks, the bad dreams. He was a Marine. He wouldn't accept weakness. It was his duty to prevail.

The silence between them stretched too long.

"How much do you remember about living with your mom?" Julian asked.

Chas was so startled by the abrupt change of subject, he turned, facing his uncle once more. "None of it."

"Really?" Julian said, more to himself than as an actual question. "I always wondered. Worried."

"Worried?"

"You never asked about her, Chas. Not once. I thought you must've remembered what it was like with her."

Chas hadn't wanted to know about his mother. As far as Chas was concerned, Gran and Julian were his parents. "I don't remember anything."

Julian nodded slowly. "I'm glad. And sad that you don't have any memories of her. You know, your mom was the sweetest little girl who ever lived. Before the drugs changed that."

Chas glanced away, part of him wanting to cut his uncle off, to tell him he didn't want to hear any of this. But there was a larger part of him dying to know it all. It was that curiosity that made him stay on the porch.

"Jenny was a sweet girl. And she loved you, Chas. I really believe that."

Chas resisted the urge to deny it. He'd never felt as though his mother cared about him. Not once. He'd painted her as the drug addict who gave birth to him, then pawned him off on someone else. He wasn't sure why that picture was easier to accept than the idea that he had a mother who'd loved him.

"She got into drugs in high school, smoking pot. I knew she was doing it, but she assured me it wasn't any worse than the beer I drank at the bar. When she got a job in Dallas, she fell in with a rougher crowd. I swear that girl was a bum magnet. If there was a sketchy, jobless, no-morals guy within five miles of her, she could sniff him out and start dating him."

"Great. So I can assume one of those guys is my father?"

Julian grimaced. "Shit, Chas. I didn't mean—"

Chas cut him off. "It's okay. I'm not upset about that. Go on with your story." Now that Julian had opened the vault, Chas wanted to know more.

"She started doing the harder stuff after she left Maris. Coke, ecstasy. We didn't realize it. Then, one day, she showed up here and asked Gran if she could move back in for a little while. Turned out she was pregnant."

"She lived here when she was pregnant with me?" All Chas had heard was the story of Gran coming to pick him up in Dallas when he was three and bringing him home to live with her.

Julian nodded. "She told me she didn't trust herself not to use drugs. Knew she wouldn't touch them here in Maris, not with Gran around. She didn't want you to be a crack baby. Said she couldn't do that to you. That you deserved the best start to life she could give you."

Chas swallowed, trying to dislodge the lump in his throat.

"You were born here. And when you were six months old, Jenny took you to Dallas with her. She promised me she could handle things. She had her addictions under control. I believed her, Chas. I swear to God, I did. I watched her with you, saw the way she looked at you, and I honestly believed her love for you would pull her through, keep her clean."

Chas glanced down and said the most painful words he'd ever uttered. "It didn't."

Julian shook his head. "Someone introduced her to heroin and that was it. Maybe her love didn't save her, but it did save you."

Chas scowled. "How? She left me."

"No. She called your gran. Told her she was in trouble and asked her to come to Dallas. We didn't know she was using again. Not until Jenny called. She was always very good at hiding her problem. So Gran drove to Dallas and found Jenny in a bad way. Your mother handed you to Gran and she asked her to take care of you until she could get off the stuff."

"I guess we know how that ended."

Julian shrugged. "Yeah. But I know she tried. And I know she did the best she could by you. Maybe her best wasn't all that great, but..."

Julian's voice faded. Chas realized this conversation couldn't have been easy for his uncle. Chas had no memories of his mother—good or bad. Julian had them all. He felt the pain over the loss of a little sister he'd clearly adored, despite her flaws.

Then Chas considered the memories he *did* have. Of Gran kissing every boo-boo, baking every birthday cake, of packing him his favorite sandwich for lunch every day. And of Julian moving in to help Gran take care of him, teaching him how to fish and shoot and reading to him on nights when Gran worked the late shift at the hospital.

His mother *had* saved him. Had given him the best she'd had to offer.

"I'm glad you told me that."

Julian looked at him, held his gaze. "Nobody's perfect, Chas. We all just do the best we can. When we make mistakes, we admit them, learn from them, ask forgiveness and move on."

Chas sensed the tide on the conversation was returning to the original subject. "I apologized to Sydney."

"And she forgave you?"

Chas nodded. "It still isn't enough."

"That's because you haven't forgiven yourself. But it's time to. It's also time to stop using that accident as a smoke shield."

"What's that supposed to mean?"

Julian leaned forward, rested his elbows on his knees. "What do you know about post-traumatic stress?"

Chas laughed, no mirth in the sound. "God. Plenty. I heard all the lectures about it after Jeremy and Scott died, got the complete rundown."

"Then you know the symptoms.

Chas faced his uncle. "I can handle it."

Julian shook his head. "No, you can't. Not alone."

"I've got it under control."

Julian rose, stood right in front of him. "Do you? Why is it so hard for you to ask for help?"

Chas' temper flared. "Because I don't want to forget them!

Don't want to move past it! *They* sure as fuck can't. Jeremy and Scott…where's their second chance?"

Julian didn't speak for several moments, though he didn't look away, didn't give Chas the option of lowering his eyes or avoiding what he'd just said.

"Every year you pull away more and more, Chas. It's like you're purposely cutting yourself off from everyone."

"That's not true."

"It is. You had a bunch of friends in high school. Guys who are still here and who'd love to go out for a beer with you. I've run into Evan, who's asked about you, who's mentioned that you've never returned his calls. You and Tyson used to be really tight and I know he's invited you out too. Why are you avoiding them?"

Chas shrugged. "I've been busy. Work, the gym, and—" He started to say Sydney, then stopped himself. Her absence in his life the past week had been felt profoundly. His gut had ached nonstop since he'd lost his temper, driven her away.

His uncle knew what he'd left out. "Sydney *was* the only exception. And it appears you've pushed her away as well."

"I had to."

"All I can figure is you feel some deep-seated guilt. Something that says you don't deserve a life, that you can't have friends or love because Jeremy and Scott can't have it. That sound about right?"

Chas didn't respond, wouldn't allow himself to even blink. It was hard hearing his guilt laid bare before him.

"None of that is true. You weren't to blame for your friends' deaths. It's time you stop thinking you were. It's time to get some help, son."

Chas shook his head, but Julian wouldn't allow him to refuse. "I'm not taking no for an answer. You feel bad about what you did to Sydney?"

"You know I do," Chas averred.

"Then prove it. Fix it so it doesn't happen again. Pushing her away doesn't make the nightmares stop. Given the dark circles under your eyes, I'd venture to say they've gotten worse without her in your bed. You're a Marine, for God's sake. It's time to buckle up the boots and fight the enemy, son."

Chas only knew how to fight foes with guns. In this, he was weaponless with no one to aim at. Even so, he knew his uncle was right.

"What do I do?"

"You go see that doctor friend of Tyson's. You stop pushing the people you love away. You find Sydney, apologize again—even though those words will be for you, not her—and then you propose to the girl. She's waited a hell of a long time for you."

Chas chuckled. "According to her, she didn't wait at all."

"She's a damn liar."

At that, Chas' laughed, hard. For the first time in a long time, he actually felt a spark of hope. And he owed so much to the man standing in front of him. "I've always known who my father is."

Julian reared back, surprised. "You have?"

"You're my dad. Always have been."

Julian smiled, though Chas could see the sheen of tears in his uncle's eyes. He'd never told Julian how much he loved him, how much he appreciated the sacrifices of a twenty-seven-year-old man, who'd given up his apartment and bachelor lifestyle to move back in with his mother to help raise a toddler. He owed Julian so much.

"I couldn't love you more, Chas, if you'd been my real son. Now go do what you've always done. Make me proud."

Julian's belief that Chas could overcome his problems strengthened Chas' resolve. "I will."

CHAPTER TEN

Chas hung up the phone and sighed. It had taken him all day yesterday to find the courage to call Tyson to get the doctor's number, and then most of this morning to work up the nerve to call the psychiatrist. Chas had done foot patrol in Afghanistan with less anxiety.

He'd spent years trying to suppress the memories he was now going to be expected to drag out and relive.

But he realized he'd been reliving them every moment since they happened. The doctor had spoken to him personally on the phone, gotten some basic information, then set up an appointment for the day after tomorrow.

Chas wasn't as nervous about the visit now that he'd talked to the guy. He seemed pretty cool. Said he was a poker buddy of Tyson's. Maybe this wouldn't be as hard as he feared.

Sydney had texted him earlier that morning. A very sweet, short message that said she missed him and wanted to see him.

He hadn't responded. He wasn't sure what to say. He wanted to see her too, but he wondered if it would be better to wait until after he'd spoken with the psychiatrist.

He dismissed that idea. It was time he stop hiding from his problems, avoiding her.

He loved Sydney and he owed her his honesty, his stories. All of them.

He'd just picked up his cell to text her when voices drifted down from upstairs.

"Chas," Gran called from the top of the basement stairs. "You have a visitor." Since her return from Vegas, Gran had noticed his depression. And Sydney's absence. He hadn't known how to explain anything, so he'd brushed aside her concerns using tiredness as an excuse.

He walked upstairs, hoping Sydney was the visitor. As soon as he turned the corner, she was there, picnic basket in hand.

"I was hoping to drag you away for a late lunch," she said with a sunny smile, as if the last time they'd seen each other hadn't ended with her leaving in tears.

"I'd like that, Syd." Though he didn't want to, he forced himself to look at her cheek. Either the bruise had faded or she'd done a good job with her makeup because he couldn't see anything.

"Great."

Chas turned to his grandmother. "You going to be okay on your own for a little while?"

Gran narrowed her eyes. "I'll be fine on my own *all* night. Stop hovering around me like I'm an old woman. Been living alone for the past dozen years or so and having a fine time doing it. I'm headed over to Sparks to meet a couple of the girls for a barbeque sandwich and then we thought we might go see a movie. I was actually worried about leaving *you* alone. Good thing Sydney showed up. Saves me finding a babysitter."

Chas chuckled, then bent closer to kiss his grandmother on the cheek. She looked at him in surprise. He wasn't usually very affectionate, but after talking to his uncle, he realized he'd let too many things go unsaid between him and the family that raised him. "Love you, Gran. Don't stay out too late," he teased.

She smiled, clearly moved by his kiss. "You kids have fun."

Chas started to reach for the picnic basket, but Sydney turned quickly, refusing to relinquish it. He followed her to the driveway.

"I'll drive," she offered.

"Okay. Where are we going?"

"It's a surprise."

They climbed into the car.

"Sydney—" he started.

"Don't."

He frowned. "Don't what?"

"Don't apologize. In fact, don't ever mention it to me again."

Chas' lips curled up in a grin. "Ever? That's kind of a long time."

She glanced his way, sensing the change in his demeanor. She'd clearly been expecting the distraught, out-of-his-mind man she'd left last week. Mercifully, she picked up his teasing tone. "Ever," she repeated.

"Tell you what. I'll agree to that on one condition."

"What's that?"

"You let me apologize one last time."

"Chas, it was an accident. Seriously, I—"

"That's not what I want to say I'm sorry for. Well, I mean I'm sorry for that too, but mainly I want to apologize for afterwards. I shouldn't have yelled, shouldn't have told you to leave. I won't push you away again, Sydney. I've missed you like crazy this past week."

Her smile blossomed, a full-blown beauty that lit her entire face. "I'm going to hold you to that."

She turned her attention back to the road, and then fiddled with the radio. She stopped when she found the Zac Brown Band and started singing along to "Knee Deep". He let the upbeat music and Sydney's infectious happiness soak in and soothe all his dark places. For the first time in a long time, he felt as if he were turning a corner.

He rolled down his window and let the fresh warm air wash over him, his toe tapping in time with the music. For a moment, he was taken back to high school, the two of them riding around with no particular aim, just happy to listen to the music, feel the wind in their faces and be together.

He was surprised when Sydney took the turn to her house.

"Thought this was a picnic."

She grinned. "It is." She pulled into her own driveway and turned off the car.

Chas looked at her suspiciously, then lifted the lid to the picnic basket. "It's empty."

"The food is in there." She pointed to her house.

"Why do I get the feeling you're trying to lure me into your house, Miss Sparks?"

Sydney feigned shocked innocence. "What? I have no idea what you could be talking about." She pulled the keys from the ignition and dropped them down her bra. "Should we go inside?"

Chas laughed. "If I decide I want to escape, do you really think I won't go for them?"

She gave him a flirty wink. "I'm hoping you will. Because the only way you're getting my car key is if you take it yourself."

His eyes drifted to her blouse, but it certainly wasn't a car key he was looking for. Sydney had worn a tight t-shirt that was cut just low enough to display a mouthwatering amount of cleavage. Clearly she wasn't above using *the girls* to get what she wanted.

And—hallelujah—it appeared she still wanted him.

Sydney got out of the car and walked into her house. Chas couldn't help but notice her relieved look when she turned and found him following. Did she really think he didn't want this?

He glanced at her empty dining room table as they walked inside, his grin growing. "Picnic in the kitchen?"

She shook her head and continued on toward her bedroom. "Nope. Back here."

"Dammit, Sydney." He loved where she was headed, but he really wanted to talk to her first. They had a lot to discuss, resolve, set straight. That would be impossible in a room that contained her and a bed. His cock was already thick, erect. It had been since the second he'd climbed the stairs at his house to find her there.

As they entered her room, he looked around and joked, "No food here either."

"Maybe not," she said with a seductive smile, "but this is still my favorite place to assuage my hunger."

He crossed his arms and shook his head, though it was impossible to hide his grin. "You damn Sparkses never act like you're supposed to. You never do what normal people would do."

"Careful, Chas. You and Gran and Julian have been honorary members of the family ever since you started coming to Christmas dinner. That means you're lumping yourself in with that putdown."

"I didn't mean it as an insult."

She laughed loudly. "Oh good. Because I didn't take it as one."

He sighed, his hands falling to his sides in defeat. "I was hoping we could talk first."

"I don't want to talk. We have the rest of our lives to talk."

He considered pointing out they had the rest of their lives to have sex too, but he wasn't an idiot. He'd offered as much resistance as he could muster. So what if it was token at best? He wanted her.

"Fine. Then I'm just going to say this for now. I called the psychiatrist Tyson suggested. I have an appointment set up."

She tilted her head, pleasure suffusing her face. "I'm glad."

"Take off your clothes, Sydney."

Her hands went to the button on her jean shorts and without hesitation, her clothing began to fall away. They laughed when she removed her bra and her keys jangled to the floor.

He made no effort to join her. He wasn't going to miss one second of this show. Besides, if his pants came off, it was game over. It had been a long fucking week.

But he still had something to make up to her. If she wouldn't let him do it with words, he would do it with his hands...and lips... and tongue.

"Lay down on the middle of the bed. Hands above your head."

Sydney licked her lips as she complied. She was made for him. As she climbed onto the bed, he went to her dresser and opened the top drawer. He'd been in her bedroom enough to know where she kept her things. The drawer yielded exactly what he wanted.

Tugging four scarves from the piles—Sydney owned an ungodly number of scarves—he approached the bed.

"Chas." She spoke his name softly, a plea in her voice. But not for him to stop...it was an invitation. Her chest rose and fell rapidly, drawing his attention to her full breasts, her hard nipples betraying her arousal. She started to press her legs together, but he gripped her ankle.

"No. Wait for me." He didn't release her ankle. Instead he tied it to the corner post of her bed. Then he secured her other ankle to the opposite post, leaving her spread eagle, open. "I think I promised to tie you up."

Her breathing came even more rapidly and she started to lower her hands. He narrowed his eyes, shaking his head in warning, and she placed them over her head once more.

"I don't think I can take too much foreplay," she admitted, her grin rueful. "I swear to God, I feel like I'm going to explode already."

He chuckled. She never held back her feelings in bed, but her confession didn't help her. It only made him want to push her higher, further than she'd ever gone before.

Chas walked to the side of the bed and secured her wrists to the posts, same as he'd done to her ankles. She was stretched out on the mattress, a goddess, his to claim.

"You're not going to play nice, are you?" she asked when he returned to the foot of the bed.

He gave her a wicked grin. "Of course I am." He climbed onto the mattress, kneeling between her outstretched thighs. "I'm going to play very, *very* nice." Leaning over, he caged her beneath him, kissing her softly at first. When he felt her begin to relax, he nipped her lower lip. She jerked, her closed eyes flying open.

He captured her gaze, held it for just a moment, and then he kissed her once more. This time, he took her mouth hungrily, his tongue delving into hers, tasting...chocolate?

"You're sweet. Delicious."

She sighed. "Hot chocolate."

Sydney had a sweet tooth. "I should have known."

He gave her one more quick buss, then his lips traveled along her cheek, her jaw, before drifting lower. He took his time, exploring all the soft, hidden hot spots around her neck, below her ear. He soaked in her quiet moans and sighs.

Once again, he let her lose herself in the moment, her body becoming pliant beneath him, before he yanked her back to the present. He closed his lips around one of her nipples, sucking softly, then building the pressure until Sydney cried out, her back arching.

She didn't close her eyes again. Instead her gaze locked on his face, watching every move he made, trying to steel herself for whatever surprises lay in store. He made sure to keep her on her toes. Licking a long line between the valley of her breasts, he turned his head to her other nipple. He didn't suck on this one; rather, he pressed his teeth into the sensitive flesh, tightening them slowly as if he were attaching a vise. He waited for the tell-tale sound—her loud cry—that told him he'd hit the mark. Sydney didn't disappoint.

"Oh my God." Her voice was breathless, but she was nowhere near the place he wanted to take her.

He spent several minutes playing with her breast, using his hands, lips and teeth to tantalize, tease, even to provoke tiny pricks of pleasurable pain. She responded to the soft touches with sweet sighs; the rougher ones were met with louder cries and hungry pleas for more.

Chas' cock pulsed, too full, too ready. He'd been smart to keep it confined in his pants.

When Sydney began to writhe beneath him, her words a continual litany of *please* and *oh my God* and—his personal favorite—*if you don't fuck me now, I'll kill you*, he moved away from her breasts, traveling lower.

Sydney sucked in a loud breath and held it. She was waiting to see what he would do and—no doubt—hoping for a reprieve. She'd have to keep waiting.

He lowered his head and sucked her clit into his mouth.

She reared up. "Yes."

She'd shown her hand too soon. She was close. Damn close.

He released her clit and looked up, waited until her eyes met his.

"Do that again." Her voice was strong, demanding, her gaze filled with the perfect combination of rage and desire.

He shook his head. "No."

She swallowed heavily. "Chas—"

"You don't give the orders, Sydney. I do. Your job is to obey."

"Fuck that! I need to come!"

He scowled, though he felt far from angry. He was elated, horny, and working overtime for the patience required to tame his wildcat. "I know what you need, but you'll get it when I give it to you. And not a second before."

She opened her mouth to continue to berate him, but he cut her off with a stern look. "Say another word and I'll leave the room. Leave you tied up in here alone to cool your heels."

He watched an internal battle wage behind her beautiful brown eyes. She wasn't a woman who would be easily commanded. In fact, he'd never try to assert this kind of power over her outside the bedroom. She'd emasculate him.

But here...she wanted it. Hell, she needed it. Badly. Even if it was hard for her to accept.

She remained silent, so he rewarded her restraint. "Good girl," he murmured as he stroked her clit with his tongue. Just like that, she was on fire once more. Unable to resist adding more fuel to the blaze, he pressed two fingers inside her pussy. Her inner muscles clenched down on them tightly. She was so wet, so fucking hot.

Chas forced a deep breath through his nose, hoping to calm his own overwrought needs. Unfortunately, the air was filled with the sweet scent of her arousal and it worked against him. He never had trouble remaining in control of his body before Sydney. He'd prided himself on his ability to play with his lovers for hours before slaking his own needs. It was impossible with her.

One touch, one taste, one smell and it was as if she were a Siren leading him to his doom. He was helpless to resist the draw.

Pressing his lips against her clit once more, he sucked on the distended flesh as he pressed his fingers deep inside her.

"God," she cried. "Please."

Chas repeated the motion three more times, then he added another finger to her pussy. "Come for me, Sydney."

She flew apart beautifully. Her back arched, her eyes closed, her pussy pressing hard against his fingers.

He let her ride out the storm, then he began the game again. He continued to stroke inside her as he alternated between sucking and biting her clit.

Her second orgasm came mere minutes behind the first. She trembled, a slight sheen of sweat coating her skin. Little beads of sweat hung on her long chestnut hair.

Sydney was gasping for air, but still managed to make the request he was helpless to deny. "Make love to me, Chas."

He released the scarves at her wrists and ankles as he rose from the bed to undress. She watched him in silence, then lifted her arms to draw him back over her body once he was naked.

She parted her legs, moaning softly as he pushed his cock to the hilt in one quick thrust.

He gritted his teeth and fought the instinct to come immediately. "God, Syd. I don't think this is going to last long."

She giggled. "Thank God. If I was a bigger bitch or had even an ounce of control, I'd make you suffer. As it is..." Her words faded away with a gasp when he hit her G-spot with a hard thrust.

She was just as close as he was. Sydney wrapped her arms around his neck, her legs encircling his waist. The new position allowed him to go deeper, a fact lost on neither of them as they groaned in unison.

Chas decided to hell with it. He'd make it up to her next time. Moving his hips faster, he thrust over and over, stars flying behind his eyes.

"Sydney. Jesus. Baby."

Mercifully her climax hit a split second before his. His control completely gone. They came together as Chas fell to his elbows, kissing Sydney. Then he pulled back just so he could see her beautiful face.

She smiled. "I love you too," she whispered.

As he fell to his side, Sydney was there, curling into his arms, her cheek pressed against his still rapidly thudding heart. She fell asleep almost instantly, but Chas didn't dare close his eyes, didn't give in to the exhaustion trying to tug him into slumber.

He still lay there, staring at her ceiling, when Sydney stirred an hour later.

She lifted her head to look at him, her smile fading when she looked at his face. "You didn't sleep."

He shook his head even though her words weren't a question. "No."

She didn't ask why. She didn't have to. Sydney knew him inside and out. A lifetime of friendship had allowed them both time to build an arsenal of knowledge about each other.

She licked her lips nervously, then asked the question she'd asked so many times before. "Do you want to talk about it?"

He understood her hesitance, her fear. He'd always rejected this offer, driving a wedge between them. Chas couldn't do that anymore. Not if he hoped to keep Sydney in his life.

"Yeah. I do."

She seemed surprised by the request. And pleased. She pushed herself up to a seated position. Chas followed suit, propping a pillow against the headboard to lean against it. Once he was settled, he drew her closer, feeling the need to have her in his arms.

Then he told her all of it. Sharing everything and holding back nothing. He told her about Scott and Jeremy, the way the three of them had met in boot camp and become inseparable.

And while he'd previously shared a bit about the day they'd died, this time he held nothing back, sharing the sheer terror he felt, the devastation afterwards when he realized they were really gone. He tightened his embrace when Sydney cried on his shoulder and he didn't bother to hide his own tears from her.

Then he talked about the little girl and her mother and the

child soldiers. He shared every pain, all the anger and fear. It all came out in a rush of words and tears. Through it all, Sydney held on.

As the words ran out, so did his energy, and he drifted to sleep, unable to stop it from taking him.

He was home now. He'd wanted to protect Sydney, but it turned out he was the one who needed safety, security. And he'd found it at last.

In her arms.

WHEN HE AWOKE, Sydney was lying next to him, still holding him tightly, her gaze on his face.

Chas was surprised to glance at the clock and discover hours had passed. He hadn't slept so deeply, so peacefully in years.

"You were out cold. Put a mirror under your nose a few times to make sure you were still breathing." He appreciated the humor in Sydney's tone. After the heaviness of the past few hours, he loved how she always found a way to drag him back into something lighthearted, fun. "Feel better?"

He nodded. He felt great. Amazing. "Yeah. I do."

"Shower?" Sydney asked.

He shook his head. "How would you feel about taking that picnic down to the lake? I sort of like the idea of skinny-dipping with you. It's one of the things we never did when we were in high school."

"I love that idea." Sydney hopped out of bed and started rifling through her drawers, then pulling on her bathing suit. She seemed surprised once she'd put it on to find him still lying on the bed.

"What are you doing?" she asked.

"Enjoying the show."

"You realize that just gives me a head start to the lake. Race you!" she yelled as she sprinted for the bedroom door.

Chas laughed as he hopped out of bed and reached for his

shorts. He was jumping around on one leg trying to put them on hurriedly when he called out to her, "Wait for me!"

She stopped and turned at his request, grinning wildly at his none-too-sophisticated attempts to tug on his shorts while rushing toward her.

She put her hand out when he reached her and he took it, allowing her to pull him close enough that she could reach up on her tiptoes to kiss his cheek.

"Always," she whispered.

WAITING FOR HER

SPARKS IN TEXAS, BOOK 2

WAITING FOR HER

Jeannette is determined to stay single, however not only are lovers Luc and Diego a danger to her libido, but also her heart.

Firefighters Luc and Diego have had a hunger for Jeannette since they rolled into town, but everyone knows she doesn't date.

That changes quickly when an arsonist throws Jeannette in harm's way, forcing her to find security and comfort in Luc and Diego's arms. When the men learn Jeannette has a dark secret, it presents them with a challenge unlike any they've ever had to face.

CHAPTER ONE

"Hey, Jeannette. Where's my side of fries for this order?"

"Sorry, Paige. Coming right up." Jeannette Sparks closed her eyes, wishing she could wake up a bit, find some energy.

She'd been dragging her weary ass through the last seven hours of work, listless and bored. Both feelings were fairly new to her. She usually loved her job and had a blast working with her family to keep Sparks Barbeque one of the top-ranked restaurants in Texas. For years, they'd placed number one in the travel guides as countless tourists were told to plan a stop at Sparks. Jeannette was proud of the role she'd played in putting her hometown of Maris, Texas, and her family's business there.

However, lately, the bloom was fading on that rose. She'd had to force herself to climb out of bed and come to work this morning, and then she had basically phoned it in, slapping sandwiches and ribs on plates all damn day.

"You okay?" Sydney asked when Jeannette returned to the kitchen to grab the fries she'd just forgotten. "You've been quiet all day."

"I had some trouble sleeping last night," Jeannette lied. That was the complete opposite of her trouble. In fact, Jeannette had been falling into bed as soon as she got home every day and sleeping the sleep of the dead for ten hours—twelve on her days off—without even rolling over.

She considered paying a visit to Tyson, her cousin and the town's resident doctor, to see if she'd caught mono somehow. Though she couldn't imagine how she'd catch that disease. God knew she hadn't kissed anyone in a freakishly long time. Years.

She picked up the fries and took a steadying breath. She was one hour away from quitting time. She just had to get through the lunch rush and then she was free to go home and hit the couch. She and Paige had worked the morning and lunch shifts and her cousins Sydney, Macie and Adele were covering the dinner crowd.

"One hour," she murmured as she pressed open the swinging door between the kitchen and the main dining area.

As she turned, she caught sight of three new patrons sitting at the bar chatting with Macie—who'd come in early and taken up the reins as Mistress of Happy Hour. Two were familiar faces. Diego Rodriguez and Luc Kovach made up the sum equivalent of the Maris fire department, the only full-timers. The rest of the department was made up of volunteers.

The two dark-haired men were sexy as sin, shameless flirts, and well known around town for their propensity for threesomes. She'd heard countless rumors about Diego, Luc and whatever flavor of the month they'd managed to ensnare in their web. Not that there were many flies trying to avoid that trap. Too many of the single women in town were casting themselves upon it.

Ordinarily, Diego and Luc went out of their way to annoy her, flirting and asking her out just to make her blush and get under her skin. They knew she didn't approve of their dating style, though apparently she was the only person in town who felt it wasn't normal. She'd even heard her Aunt Louise and Aunt Beverly tittering about the firefighters one morning over coffee, Aunt Beverly wishing she were thirty years younger.

However, it was the third face that caught Jeannette's attention.

"Look what the cat dragged in," Macie said with a huge grin, pointing to the man.

Jeannette had heard Billy Mathers was back in town. For the first month or two, she had expected him to stop by to see her. Mercifully, he hadn't. Three months had passed and she had foolishly begun to feel safe, thinking he was avoiding her, which suited her just fine.

So much for that small bit of luck. As if her life didn't suck enough nowadays.

"Hey, Billy." Jeannette inwardly winced at the bitterness in her tone. She'd had time to practice her response to him. She needed to do better than this.

Billy smiled at her, the same sweet smile he'd graced her with all those years ago when he'd won her heart in the tenth grade. "Hi, Nettie. Good to see you again." Though his face had aged and his middle had widened, she could still see the boy he'd been underneath the man he had become. Unfortunately, the kind tone and greeting did nothing to calm her nerves.

"You too." She choked out the lie awkwardly. The fact was it *wasn't* good to see him. She had hoped to never see him again. Coming face-to-face with him now after all these years brought up a host of memories she'd thought were buried deep enough they would never see the light of day again. Apparently she'd been wrong about that too.

She didn't have the energy for this. She really didn't.

"You two know each other?" Diego asked.

Jeannette didn't bother to answer. She didn't need to. Macie was there, and when her vivacious cousin was in the room, it was unnecessary for Jeannette to speak. Which never really bothered Jeannette. She had always suffered from shyness, so Macie had assumed the role as her mouthpiece.

Sometimes that worked in Jeannette's favor, allowing her to be a part of the conversation without having to put in much effort. Sometimes—like now—it wasn't a great thing.

"Jeannette and Billy were quite the item back in high school. Dated for all of...how long was it, Nettie? Eight months? Nine?"

Jeannette shrugged. She'd dated Billy ten months, three weeks and four days. He'd been her first love. Hell, he'd been her only love.

"Quite a long run for teenagers," Macie declared.

Jeannette could feel Billy's eyes on her face, but she didn't look in his direction. Instead, she focused all her attention on Macie, while trying to beat down the red flames heating her face. If she didn't get out of here soon, she'd give herself a sunburn from the inside out.

Luc perked up and turned to Billy. "Her boyfriend, huh? Got any pointers for us sad saps she keeps refusing to go out with?"

The words were spoken in jest. Like they always were whenever Luc and Diego tried to convince her to date them. Usually, she'd just give them a warning look and walk away as they laughed, but hearing him make the joke in front of Billy made her stomach clench nervously.

"Here are your fries, Paige." Jeannette handed them to her. "I need to clear some tables," she announced to no one in particular as she walked away hastily, pointedly ignoring the surprised look on Macie's face. As far as her cousin knew, Billy had been the love of Jeannette's life, the boy who'd broken her heart, the one Jeannette had never gotten over. Clearly Macie had anticipated some conversation.

There were some parts of what her cousin believed that were true, but it was the stuff Macie *didn't* know that had pretty much fucked Jeannette up.

She'd spent a lot of nights wondering how her life might have turned out differently if not for two things—the death of her parents, and Billy Mathers. While she had always suffered from shyness, she'd begun to shed some of that awkwardness in tenth grade, coming out of her shell. That was why Billy had noticed her. Jeannette had started taking more care with her looks, wearing makeup, trying to feminize the pixie cut her mother had insisted looked good on her, choosing outfits that didn't scream *convent*.

That year had been the best of her life. She was gaining confidence, friends, and had gotten herself a boyfriend. She'd been on top of the world.

Then the bottom fell out. Her parents were killed in a car accident. Their deaths knocked her down hard, but not completely out. That final blow came from Billy. She had still been staggering to her feet when he'd delivered the knockout punch.

After that, she didn't bother to stand up. She'd crawled into her shell and stayed there.

Which would be fine, if the fucking casing didn't chafe so much.

She hoped no one was watching her as she began to clear away dirty dishes from a booth against the wall. If they were, they'd see her hands trembling.

Her Uncle TJ had been hanging out at the center table with a bunch of his cronies. As he was never one to let an awkward silence hover, he joined the conversation. "What brings you back to Maris, Billy?"

Jeannette eavesdropped as Billy explained the reason for his return. "My Uncle Roy's been having some health issues lately, so Scott and I came back to help him keep the farm running."

So Scott was back too. Jeannette had never been overly fond of Billy's older brother. He'd been the poster child for bullying in school, using his larger size to intimidate anyone who was younger or smaller than he was. However, she'd never mentioned her dislike to Billy, who seemed to think his big brother hung the moon.

Everyone knew Billy and Scott would inherit Roy's land when he passed away. The grumpy old man had never married, never had kids of his own. Like Scott, Roy was a mean son of a bitch.

Even so, Billy had been gone fifteen years. Part of Jeannette had hoped he'd simply sell his uncle's land and split the profit with his brother, remaining far away from Maris. After all, it wasn't like the boys had any long-standing ties to the community. They'd lived here a year and a half when they were teens after their mother had split up with stepfather number three, moving them again when she married bachelor number four.

"We moved around a lot when we were kids. I have to admit, Maris was the only place that ever felt like home," Billy explained.

Jeannette caught a glimpse of Macie staring at her and she quickly looked away. This wasn't good. No doubt the matchmaking wheels were already spinning madly in her cousin's head. It wouldn't be the first time Macie had tried to set her up with someone. Hell, it wouldn't be the fiftieth time. Macie was relentless when it came Jeannette's love life—or lack thereof.

"That's great. I suspect there are a lot of folks around here who will be tickled to death to hear you're planning to stick around," Macie said, looking pointedly at Jeannette.

Jeannette's chest tightened and her stomach roiled. She wouldn't go out with Billy again. Not ever. But she couldn't tell her cousin why. That was a secret she'd buried right along with herself a long time ago.

Billy demurred and Jeannette feared he would follow Macie's gaze to her. She turned her back on them and forced herself to concentrate on the table, tossing the cups and dirty napkins in the bin, while returning the salt, pepper, ketchup and vinegar to the little basket that remained there.

"It's good to see you again."

Billy's voice right behind her caught her unaware and she jumped, nearly dropping the tub of dirty dishes.

He reached out and helped her steady the load, his arm grazing hers. She recoiled at the touch as if he were a venomous snake, taking a quick step away from him.

Billy frowned as he studied her face, and then slowly nodded. "I should go."

"Okay," she said too hastily, too loudly.

"Goodbye, Nettie." Billy turned to leave.

Jeannette gritted her teeth. She fucking hated that nickname. Her sister, Gia, had started calling her that when she was learning to talk, "Jeannette" clearly too big a mouthful for a little kid. It had been a sweet thing she'd shared with just her baby sister. Until she'd started dating Billy and he had picked it up as well, calling her Nettie at school. The name had stuck until everyone—her entire family included—began using the cursed moniker.

"I'll walk out with you, Billy," Uncle TJ said. "Need to check on my wife."

Macie laughed and called out, "You need to check on Mom, or on those oatmeal raisin cookies she was baking earlier?"

TJ gave her a guilty grin. "Can't I do both?"

Macie's mom, Louise, and Aunt Beverly worked next door at Sparks Bakery. They made most of the desserts they served in the restaurant as well as the rolls for the sandwiches.

Macie didn't appear to notice Jeannette's unease when she walked behind the bar and set down the bin of dirty dishes.

"How about that?" Macie exclaimed. "Billy Mathers. Back in Maris."

Diego glanced at Jeannette—and she realized that while *Macie* had been oblivious to the undercurrents flowing between her and Billy, Luc and Diego had not.

"Seems like a decent enough guy," Diego said, fishing.

Macie grinned. "He's a great guy. Nettie's only boyfriend."

Jeannette wanted to crawl under the counter as Diego and Luc digested that information. Unlike most everyone else in town, Diego and Luc were relative newcomers. They'd only been in Maris a few years, so they weren't in possession of her long, sad life history. It set them apart because they didn't know better than not to joke with Nervous Nettie. Rather than treating her like the leper every other guy in town gave a wide berth, Luc and Diego acted like she was a normal person.

If she really thought about it, she'd have to admit she liked that.

So she didn't think about it.

Macie kept talking. "She was devastated when his family moved away."

Jeannette was tempted to defend the *devastated* comment, but realized she couldn't. No doubt her actions back then had resembled those of a heartbroken teenaged girl. If she objected, she'd have no way to explain her behavior, so she remained quiet.

"Roy Mathers is his uncle?" Diego asked.

Macie nodded.

Luc toyed with the label on his beer bottle. "Didn't know Roy had any family. Seems too mean to have any real life ties. Sort of had him pegged as Satan, vacationing in Maris, tormenting people as recreation until he returned to Hell."

Jeannette snorted, the sound escaping before she could stop it.

Luc gave her a pleased grin and winked. She quickly recovered as she narrowed her eyes in annoyance and looked away, her typical response to any and all of his attempts at charming her.

Diego and Luc were regulars in Sparks Barbeque. Hell, sometimes she thought they were there as much as she was. Neither man cooked, so it wasn't unusual for them to eat a couple of their daily meals at the counter.

They were there often enough that the title of acquaintances had given way to that of friends. Not that they were close or anything. In fact, the only people she really considered friends were her relatives.

However, Diego and Luc were in the restaurant enough that Jeannette felt as if she had come to understand their moods. She could tell when one of them was in a foul temper, which was rare, or when they were exhausted due to a middle-of-the-night call. And she could identify those smug expressions that told her they'd had a particularly fun evening with someone of the opposite sex.

"Roy has a sister and she had Billy and Scott. They only lived here a couple of years," Macie explained before she walked to the cash register to ring out a couple of patrons who'd risen to leave.

Jeannette tossed the dirty napkins into the trashcan, aware that Luc and Diego were looking at her a little too closely for her liking.

"Old boyfriend, huh?" Luc asked.

"It was high school. Ancient history." She wished everyone would let the subject die.

"You know," Macie said, once the customers had paid, "now that Billy is back—"

"No." Jeannette raised her hand to stop anything else Macie might say. She knew exactly what her cousin was thinking and she was determined to put the brakes on before the key even hit the ignition. "I'm not interested in Billy. Period. End of sentence. Don't even think about trying to fix us up."

Macie opened her mouth to persist, but Jeannette shook her head vehemently. "I mean it, Macie. Absolutely not. Under no circumstances."

Her cousin's shoulders fell. "It's not normal for a woman to never date."

Jeannette grimaced, sick of this continual argument. "Why can't you just believe me when I say I'm happy with my life as it is?"

Macie frowned. "You're thirty-one, but you'd think you were *eighty-one*, the way you carry on. Don't you think you're a bit young to accept such a lonely life?"

Diego and Luc were listening, but neither man sought to interrupt them or interject their own opinions into the conversation. Jeannette was grateful for that. She was also slightly mortified.

"I'm not lonely, Mace. God, how could I be lonely in Maris? I can't spit without hitting a relative, and I have Penny."

Macie closed her eyes, a sure sign she was frustrated and perilously close to losing it. "Penny hardly counts as a life partner. It's a damn cat!"

"She's not an *it*. And I love that cat."

Diego chucked. "How is dear Penny? Climb any trees lately?"

He was throwing her a life preserver, changing the subject to something safe.

Jeannette grabbed it. "I'd always thought that cat-stuck-in-a-tree thing was just a running joke in cartoons and old sitcoms."

Luc rubbed the top of his hand. "Yeah, well, I got a scar from your wildcat that proves it's not a very funny one."

Jeannette felt compelled to defend her cat. "She was only a tiny thing. How badly could she have hurt you?"

Luc lifted his hand and, sure enough, there was a thin white line cutting across it.

"You move too fast, Luc. It's always the same." Diego turned his gaze to Jeannette, a wicked gleam in his eyes. "I'm forever telling him he needs to go slow, to stroke the pussy nice and easy until it's purring."

Macie laughed loudly at Diego's off-color joke, but there was something in Diego's expression and the tone of his voice that sent a different type of reaction through Jeannette. She frowned as she considered her unusual, somewhat aroused physical response. Sex wasn't something she ever thought about or wanted. Just another way she was completely abnormal.

She'd always rejected Diego and Luc's invitations for a date, then gone about her merry way without a regret. After all, they *both* wanted to date her. Both of them. She couldn't manage to successfully spend time alone with one guy, let alone two. But for a moment, she let herself consider what that might be like.

She dismissed the thought the second she imagined being alone with Diego and Luc, because her stomach tightened and a cold sweat broke out on the back of her neck.

Yep. This was why she lived alone with a cat.

Macie called her uptight and constantly begged Jeannette to lighten up and relax, but that wasn't something that came naturally to her. According to her grandmother, Jeannette had come out of the womb fretting and worrying and she hadn't stopped since. Jeannette didn't necessarily like that about herself, but she'd long ago accepted this was who she was and it didn't seem likely to change. No matter how much she wanted it to.

"Hey, Nettie," Rebecca called out from the corner booth. "Can I get a top up on this coffee?"

She nodded, grabbing the pot and walking over to pour. Then she returned to the bar, prepared for more of Macie's attempted persuasion.

Four more regulars walked in, followed by Billy's older

brother, Scott. The bell over the door jingled to announce their arrival.

Wow. This day just kept getting better and better.

They were all guys Jeannette had gone to school with and, with the exception of Scott, were currently working for Sydney's boyfriend Chas' construction company. Something told her they were employing the five-o'clock-somewhere work ethic today, and Sparks wasn't their first stop. She could smell beer on their breath as soon as they grabbed chairs at a table.

"Uh-oh," Jeremiah Rogers said. "Nettie's here, fellas. Keep all movements slow and easy. Don't want to spook the poor little thing."

She frowned. "Very funny, Jeremiah."

The man was harmless, but he'd been teasing her since middle school about her shyness and tendency to jump at her own shadow. He certainly didn't help matters, considering it was his habit to sneak up behind her and yell, "What are you doing?" loudly in her ear.

He gave her an affable grin. "You got anything good on the menu today? Boss gave us a half-day since we finished the last job on time. Thought we'd do some celebrating."

Colby Markum leaned his elbows on the table in an attempt to steady his swaying. "Shoulda had lunch first," he slurred.

All she'd had was one more freaking hour of work. Any other day, the lunch crowd in the restaurant would have thinned out and she could have coasted to quitting time. Today, sans energy, she was faced with two flirting firefighters, an ex-boyfriend and a bunch of drunken construction workers.

Macie offered them all coffee, but they opted for beer instead. Her cousin studied their faces, then decided they were likely more tipsy than drunk. She gave them the beer. Colby was the exception. He got the coffee. Of course, the added alcohol meant the men would only continue to get louder and more obnoxious.

She glanced at the clock. Thirty minutes left. Unfortunately, Adele wasn't there yet, and who knew when TJ would saunter back in. Jeannette didn't want to leave Sydney, Paige and Macie here alone to deal with the guys. It looked like she would have to clock some overtime.

So much for her nap on the couch.

She took the men's orders, and then went back to the kitchen to warn Sydney they had their hands full.

Sydney shrugged lightly. "Those guys are all bluster and hot air. I'll put the food together and if they start to get out of line, I'll call Chas to come over."

Jeannette hadn't considered that. It was a good plan. "Oh, okay. Cool."

Sydney studied her more closely, her eyes reflecting her concern. "Why don't you take off, Nettie? Macie, Paige and I can handle things here. TJ's just next door if we need him."

The suggestion was inviting. However, despite her exhaustion, the thought of going home was suddenly no more appealing than staying here. The quiet of her house was almost as miserable as the noise in the restaurant.

Jesus, she was fucked-up. She wanted to cry, scream, sleep and punch someone all at the same time. Maybe it wasn't Tyson she needed to see. Given her current state, she might be better off checking herself into a rubber room.

Loud laughter drifted from the dining room. Normal people having normal conversations. Having fun. Jeannette understood the concept even though the ability to have any of that herself seemed impossible. She tried to remember the last time she'd laughed. Really let go and gave in to a belly laugh, one that made her stomach hurt and tears flow.

She couldn't recall, but she knew it had been years. She needed to get out of here.

"I think I'll take you up on the offer." Jeannette grabbed her purse, and then headed back to the dining room. Her car was parked out front on the street. She stepped behind the counter quickly to say goodbye to Macie.

"I'm going to sneak out a few minutes early. You okay here?"

Macie nodded. "Oh yeah. Sure. But will you at least consider going out with Billy? You really liked him back in school."

Jeremiah perked up at Macie's comment. "You and Mathers hooking up again? Damn, Nettie. I thought you'd given up on all men. You mean I might've had a shot all these years if I'd asked?"

She shook her head, fighting back tears. The man meant no harm, so her reaction was overblown, ridiculous. Even so, she turned away from them and simply threw out a haughty, "Not in a million years, Jeremiah."

The rest of the guys laughed and she was forgotten before she'd taken two steps away from them. Or at least, she was forgotten by most.

Before she could make her escape, Scott rose from his chair and blocked her way. "Well, if it isn't little Nettie, all grown up."

She ignored the sneer in his voice, anxious to make her escape. "Hi, Scott."

His gaze traveled over her in a way that made her skin crawl. "You haven't changed much."

He didn't mean his words as a compliment. He'd never been particularly kind to her, teasing her when they were younger about her glasses and braces. She was used to guys ignoring her, but Scott was looking at her too closely and not bothering to hide his disdain.

"Neither have you," she said, hating the thin, weak sound.

Macie stepped from behind the bar, clearly intent on rescuing her, but Diego and Luc beat her there.

"This guy bothering you?" Diego asked.

She shook her head, wishing Scott would just go back to his beer and leave her alone. Their little scene had caught the attention of everyone in the place, the conversations around them dying.

Scott wasn't easily intimidated, even though he was clearly outmatched. "Just catching up with my brother's old girlfriend."

Belatedly, Jeannette realized Scott wasn't merely tipsy like the other guys. He *was* drunk. Wasted. And it didn't improve his personality.

"Never did understand what he s-saw in you," Scott slurred.

"Scared little mouse. All I can figure is you must've been one hell of a lay."

Macie flew by her, but Jeannette had anticipated the response. She grabbed her cousin's arm, holding her back before Macie could slap the asshole.

However, it wasn't her cousin who needed restraint.

Diego and Luc were on the guy like white on rice. Luc twisted Scott's arm behind his back, while Diego leaned forward, his face furious. "Apologize to her."

Scott's inebriated state became even more obvious as he clumsily stumbled, unable to break free of Luc's grip.

"*Now*," Diego stressed.

Scott gave her a sideways glance and spat out the least sincere "sorry" in the history of the world. Then Luc dragged him to the door.

Macie followed, yelling, "Don't even try to show your ugly face in here again!"

"Jesus, Nettie. I'm so sorry," Jeremiah said. "Met up with Scott at the last bar. We started reminiscing about school days and he seemed okay. I never would have invited him here with us if I'd known he would—"

"It's okay, Jeremiah. It's not your fault. He never was a very nice guy."

Jeremiah seemed relieved by her easy forgiveness. "Fruit doesn't fall far from the tree, I guess. His uncle is a Grade-A son of a bitch too."

She nodded but didn't reply. She needed to get the hell out of here.

Diego and Luc were settling up their tab with Macie.

"Hold up, Jeannette," Diego said, raising his hand. "We'll walk out with you."

She didn't want to wait, but didn't know how to say no thanks after they'd just defended her. She paused as Macie gave them their change, then said goodbye.

Her car was at the end of the block, so she sped up her pace. If she could just get there, they wouldn't have time to—

"You okay?" Diego asked.

Shit. So much for that.

Jeannette nodded. "I'm fine."

Luc reached for her hand, pulling her to a stop. She jerked when his hand touched hers, tugging it out of his clasp. Regardless, he'd managed to turn her to face him. "Are you crying?"

His question must've caught Diego's attention as the other man stepped in front of her. They were huge guys, both well over six feet tall. The height difference was rarely apparent, as her usual association with them was at the restaurant and they were sitting while she stood. Now she felt like David facing two Goliaths.

It also didn't help that their chosen career path required they be physically strong. Their workouts at the gym added width to the height. They had broad shoulders, huge pecs and firm biceps.

In the past, big guys had always scared her, gave off this air of danger. But as she'd gotten to know Luc and Diego better, it wasn't fear that kept her eyes averted. It was the funny feeling in her stomach she got whenever she looked at them. Attraction wasn't normal...or particularly comfortable for her.

Diego had black hair and eyes that betrayed his Latino heritage. She'd never asked about his family, never wanted to invite that sort of closeness, but she'd heard him mention that his mother was originally from Brazil, while his father was born and bred in Jersey. Luc bore a slight resemblance to his best friend, but his hair was dark brown compared to the black of Diego's.

Luc's hazel eyes were framed by thick lashes that accentuated his emotions, making his laugh lines more prominent, his scowls darker, and his sadness deeper. She felt as if she could read everything he felt simply by gazing into his beautiful eyes.

Beautiful? Jesus. Get a grip, Jeannette. They're just eyes.

Then she recalled Luc's question and realized they were still waiting for an answer. "No, I'm not crying. It's the pollen in the air. I have allergies." Sometimes she was amazed at her ability to spin lies so quickly. If anyone ever asked her to list her talents, lying would be second only to cooking.

Diego frowned. "I don't think we've hit that season yet. It's only early March and still pretty chilly."

She shrugged but didn't respond. She'd learned that silence was also an effective way of avoiding the truth.

Diego ran one finger along her cheek. It was a friendly gesture, but it sent a spark of electricity gliding along her skin. "Don't let that guy get to you, Jeannette. He's a drunk prick."

"I know that."

"And as for those other goofballs," Luc added, "they're harmless, if a bit stupid."

She grinned. "I know that too." Jeremiah had always been the class clown, but underneath it all, he was a decent person who wouldn't hurt her feelings for anything.

"I really am fine," she repeated, because it was the only thing she could think of to say. In polite society, most people accepted those words at face value and walked on.

Diego didn't seem to have a working knowledge of the concept. "Are you sure? You've been pretty quiet lately."

She snorted, the sound pure derision. "How the hell can you tell that? I'm always quiet."

Both men were taken aback by her sudden burst of anger.

"Jeannette..." Diego reached for her hand, but pulled up short as she visibly stiffened. Their gazes connected for a moment, his black eyes going dark with something that looked too much like recognition. She broke the link quickly, looking down at the sidewalk.

He knows.

Fear accompanied that thought before she dismissed it. She was being silly. Paranoid.

"I'm sorry," she spat out, desperate to escape. Her bad mood certainly wasn't their fault and she felt terrible taking it out on them. But part of her *was* angry. At them and herself. As always, she'd been the victim in her own life story, letting others defend her, save her.

She was tired of being so weak, but when faced with standing up, she'd always found it easier to retreat.

Speaking of which, she needed to get out of here. "I'm just feeling out of sorts. I'll sleep it off and hopefully tomorrow I'll wake up on the right side of the bed."

"Or," Luc said, leaning closer, "you could consider going out with us tonight. Line dancing at Cruisers? And if it goes well, you could wake up in the wrong bed instead."

"You're relentless." There was no heat behind her complaint.

She'd always been annoyed by their constant flirting, but lately she was starting to like it. It made her feel good. Which was bad.

Most of the guys in town were born and bred in Maris, which meant they didn't bother to flirt with her. They all remembered the awkward, shy girl she'd been growing up, the buckteeth it had taken four years of braces to correct and the big-framed glasses she was forever pushing up. The boys from town knew that, besides Billy Mathers, she'd never dated anyone and didn't want to.

She'd even caught wind once that there was a small contingency in town that thought she might be a lesbian. She hadn't bothered to correct the misconception; she'd figured it would keep would-be suitors away—if there had been any.

Luc and Diego were the exception. They didn't have the same background information that her family and most everyone else in town did. They flirted with her, asked her out regularly and actually looked at her as if she were pretty, and not some shapeless plain Jane who wore her dirty-blonde hair in an out-of-date hairstyle and whose boring brown eyes were still hidden behind glasses.

"You realize we're going to keep asking until you give in." Luc was one of those dangerously handsome guys who used his looks to his advantage. It was no wonder every woman in town—including her aunts—had fallen under his spell. He'd flash those puppy-dog eyes and dimples until women were tripping over their own feet to get closer.

God. She really *was* feeling vulnerable. Because, for the first time ever, she was tempted to throw caution to the wind and say yes. Which would be utter insanity.

"What's holding you back?" Diego asked.

It was the first time they'd ever questioned her reasons for rejecting them. "Maybe the fact that you're just kidding?"

Luc reared back as if she'd struck him. "Kidding? This isn't a joke, Jeannette. Our invitation is sincere."

She wasn't sure how to reply to that. "Really?"

Diego threw his hands up, his eyes flying heavenward in exasperation. "Yes, really. Why in the hell would you think we were kidding?"

She shrugged, uncertain how she could explain that they were breaking an unwritten Maris code. The one that stated Jeannette Sparks was shy and standoffish and not on the market. She'd had her name jotted down in the Spinster for Life column since high school. If that had actually been a Who's Who category, she would have won it by a unanimous vote.

Finally, stupidly, she said, "Because no one ever asks me out."

"Why not?" Diego obviously had no intention of letting this go.

Her exhaustion gave way to an annoyance that quickly sparked to anger. "Because I don't want them to."

Diego opened his mouth, clearly planning to repeat the same question, and she snapped. "Why can't you guys just fall in line like everyone else around here and accept that this is who I am?"

Diego looked over his shoulder and she felt a brief moment of victory. He was looking for an escape.

Or that was what she thought—before he grabbed her hand and began tugging her away from her car.

She dug her feet in. "I'm parked right there," she said, pointing at her VW bug.

Luc followed behind, adding his own strength to Diego's, with his hand on her back. They propelled her across the street and into the park at the end of the block. They didn't stop dragging her until they'd found a quiet bench.

"Sit down."

She'd only heard Diego use that demanding tone a handful of times, most recently with Scott in the restaurant, but he'd never spoken like that to Jeannette. She should have been afraid, but that wasn't the response her body had. Again, she felt that annoying tingle between her legs. She pressed them together as she dropped to the bench heavily. Her anger evaporated as quickly as it had appeared.

Neither man joined her. So now they were *really* looming over her.

Diego crossed his arms. "You want to explain that last comment?"

She shook her head. "Not really."

Luc took pity on her, sitting down beside her. "What is it you think we're supposed to see?"

"Me. Nervous Nettie. The quiet Sparks girl. The awkward, shy one who doesn't date and doesn't have much personality. The woman most likely to grow up to be that horrible great aunt you have to invite to Christmas even though you'd rather not because she criticizes everyone and complains all the time and smells like mothballs."

Diego scowled. "You're joking about all of that, right?"

She shrugged. She wasn't. Not at all.

Luc looked seriously shell-shocked by her admission. "You're wrong, Jeannette. You're not awkward. You're pretty and sweet. And quiet isn't a sin, you know. There are a lot of folks in this town who could stand to shut up a lot more."

She laughed softly, and then she confessed something she'd never said aloud. "I don't think it's the town who hates me for who I am. It's me. I *want* to be different. I'm tired of worrying about stupid stuff, pushing people away and being lonely as a result. I'm sick of letting other people fight my battles for me, like you guys just did, because I'm too weak to stand up for myself."

Diego claimed the other side of her on the bench. "Then change."

She rolled her eyes. "Oh yeah. Because that's so simple. I've lived in Maris my whole life and I can tell you right now, everyone has their own pigeonholes and no one escapes them, especially not Nervous Nettie."

Diego twisted, resting his arm along the back on the bench. "Of course you can."

"No. I can't."

"Why not?"

She considered Diego's question and realized she didn't have much of an answer. "Sometimes I can't tell if people are reacting to my personality, or if my personality is driven by the way people treat me."

Luc grasped her hand. Her heart and stomach fluttered in unison at the touch. Ordinarily she would have pulled away, but she forced herself to accept the friendly gesture.

"So you start small," Luc suggested. "What's the most out-of-character thing you could do? Something that would shock the town, but wouldn't be impossible for you to carry out? Impromptu trip? New haircut? Wardrobe? Contacts?"

"A date with you guys." The words fell out before she could reconsider them. She rushed to recover. "I'm kidding!"

Diego shook his head. "No, you aren't. And you're right. That would catch everyone's attention. Shed a different light on you."

"We're doing it," Luc said, with complete confidence.

Panic began to set in. "Wait. I don't think—"

"Stop thinking. We're picking you up Saturday night and we're going dancing. Wear the tightest blue jeans you have, a silky blouse and leave your hair down." Diego used that damn deep voice against her once more. It was distractingly hot.

Hot? She didn't think of guys as hot or sexy or...anything.

Her mouth had gone dry, making it difficult to respond. "Okay."

Both men offered her breathtaking, blindingly beautiful smiles.

Luc leaned closer. "That wasn't so hard, was it?"

Self-preservation kicked in. "Just dancing. Nothing else."

Diego didn't acknowledge her request. "We're going with the flow, Jeannette. Nothing's going to be taken off the table or planned ahead of time."

"But—"

"But nothing," Diego said, grasping her other hand and helping her rise from the bench. "You want to change and we're going to help. You can fight us in the attempt or you can accept that it's going to happen."

His comment sparked a realization. "Why do you guys call me Jeannette? No one else does."

Diego shrugged. "Always got the impression you hate being called Nettie."

She did, but no one had ever noticed that before. "I do."

"So we'll make that part of the change. The good people of Maris aren't going to know what hit them when Jeannette Sparks comes to town."

* * *

Diego waved as Jeannette pulled away from the curb and out into traffic. Luc watched his friend, not bothering to hide his grin.

Diego didn't glance his way as he started walking toward the fire station. "Go ahead and say it. I can see you're busting a gut. Get it over with."

Luc laughed. "You've got it bad, brother."

Diego stopped walking and pinned Luc with a pointed stare. "And you don't?"

Luc lifted his shoulders casually. "I never pretended I don't have the hots for Jeannette. And you've been giving me shit for it since day one. What did you call it? My little crush on the pretty cook?"

"You fell too fast."

"Maybe I'm just a better judge of character than you."

Diego didn't take the bait. Instead, he started walking once more. "Yeah. Maybe you are. But I can't help thinking we're missing something. I don't think we've got the whole picture on Jeannette Sparks."

"Yeah. I'll admit I didn't realize she thought so poorly of herself. Even though she's quiet, she exudes this subtle strength. I know she believes she's shy, but sometimes I don't think she is. It's more like..." Luc struggled to find the word.

"Fear," Diego supplied. "She's afraid of something."

Until Diego spelled it out, Luc had missed it. Now, he realized his friend was right. "Yeah. She is."

"I'm not going to let her keep hiding."

Luc was very familiar with *this* Diego. The set of his jaw, the determination in his tone. When Diego put his mind to something, he didn't fail. Luc felt the unease and uncertainty he'd experienced ever since he'd first laid eyes on Jeannette fade.

Diego felt the same pull, the same desire.

Together, they'd do whatever it took to make her theirs.

CHAPTER TWO

Jeannette stared at her reflection in the mirror and cursed herself for being a fool. She'd given in to Diego and Luc in a moment of weakness and had spent every minute since agreeing to this ridiculous plan second-guessing it. She'd woken up last night in the midst of a full-blown panic attack so severe, she wondered if she was having heart attack.

She had called Luc this morning to cancel, expecting him to be the easier man to bail on. He'd simply told her to dress as Diego said, insisting they would be there to pick her up at eight. No amount of pleading or attempts to reason on her part would sway him. Then, it got worse when Diego had taken the phone from Luc. She shivered as she recalled him saying in that sexy voice, "Stop wasting your breath. And leave the top three buttons undone on that silky blouse you're wearing for us."

He'd disconnected before she could continue the argument. Not that she would have been able to after that command. Her nipples had gone tight and she'd actually felt lightheaded for a few minutes after hanging up.

Now it was five minutes to eight and the panic attack was back. Her breathing was thready, her chest tight and, despite the pains she'd taken with her makeup, she looked pale. And terrified.

She glanced at her blouse, extremely uncomfortable by how much skin she was showing. Ordinarily she wore shirts that covered her chest. All of it. With three buttons undone, she was revealing way too much cleavage. She buttoned one of the buttons, then a second, studying the result. While Nervous Nettie felt more at ease this way, tonight was about shedding that miserable skin.

She unfastened the buttons again.

And jumped when her doorbell rang. She hadn't heard their truck pull into the driveway.

"What the fuck are you doing, Jeannette?" she asked her reflection, making no move to answer the door.

A few seconds later, a loud knock came. They weren't going away.

She walked downstairs, fighting like the devil to calm her trembling. She hadn't gone out on a date in fifteen years. Had she really thought this feeling of utter terror would be better than the depression she'd suffered lately?

She stood behind the door, her hand on the knob, unable to turn it.

Somehow, Diego knew she was there. "Jeannette. Open the door, angel."

She twisted the knob, and then stood back as Diego and Luc stepped inside. "I, uh, I..."

Diego tilted his head. "Take it easy, baby. It's just me and Luc."

She felt like a fool, so she raced to recover, to escape his all-seeing gaze. "I just need to grab my purse from the living room."

They followed her into her tiny house. Penny lifted her head from her position on the back of the couch as a greeting, purring when Luc walked over to rub her head.

As she reached out to grab her bag, there was no hiding the trembling in her hand. Diego stepped beside her and clasped it, holding it to his chest. "You're safe with us, Jeannette."

Slowly, she felt the painful constriction in her lungs ease. And few moments later, her breathing had slowed. "What is that? Some sort of Jedi mind trick?"

She expected Diego to laugh, but a trace of concern still lingered in his gaze. Then his lips slowly tipped up. "You'll hear no complaints from me if you want to start calling me Master."

Jeannette shook her head, grinning. "Yeah. I don't see that happening. Ever."

Luc laughed, the pleasure of it surrounding them. "Never say never, Jeannette."

She rolled her eyes, picked up her purse and led them back to the front door. "Come on. The sooner we get there, the sooner you guys will see this was a mistake."

Diego twisted her toward him just as she reached for the doorknob. He slowly pressed her against the chilly wood. She tensed, her arms flying up in a defensive block, but it wasn't necessary. He took a big step back once she was facing him. "You're not going to sabotage the evening."

"What do you mean?"

"I'm sure you've spent the past few days convincing yourself this is just a game. It's not. It's a date. Luc and I are attracted to you. That's not a joke or a mistake. We want the Jeannette *you* seem to think is undesirable. Our intentions tonight are to prove to you that you're not. Nothing more, nothing less than that. You got it?"

She licked lips that had gone dry and nodded slowly. She heard his words, but her brain was struggling to comprehend them, to make them fit. They washed over her, warming and scalding at the same time.

They wanted her, found her desirable. To the shy, plain girl who'd always longed for love, those words felt like magic. To the woman who understood what that desire represented, she felt helpless, petrified.

She considered escaping. Flinging open her front door and running away as fast as her feet would carry her. Then Luc moved closer, his affable, friendly smile in place. "Tonight, you're brave, remember? You're Jeannette. Nettie's gone."

His faith in her was touching.

"Okay," she whispered. Somehow she'd find the strength to get through the night. If only to show these men how much their belief in her meant to her.

They each took a hand as they walked along the path from her front door to their truck. It was an older model, fire-engine red Ford F-150 jacked up on big-ass tires.

"I think I need a ladder," she joked when Luc opened the passenger door.

He didn't respond. "Nope. That's what you have me for."

Before she could question him, he lifted her off the ground and placed her on the front seat, then followed her in. She was forced to slide to the smaller center seat as Diego claimed the driver's side. Luc reached for her seat belt, buckling her in.

She glanced over her shoulder. "You realize there's a backseat. I don't mind sitting there."

Luc placed his arm around her shoulder, picking up a strand of her hair to play with. "You're fine here."

She'd grown up around a bunch of alpha men; her uncles—and her cousins Tyson and Evan—could give anyone a run for their money, so it wasn't as if she wasn't used to this type of heavy-handedness. The difference was, while it was annoying when her male relatives tried to control her life, with Diego and Luc, she found herself strangely turned-on by it.

Diego started the truck and pulled out of the driveway. On the way to the bar, they exchanged pleasantries, discussing the weather and tomorrow's lunch special at the restaurant. As they pulled into the parking lot, Jeannette made a face that Luc didn't miss.

"You don't like Cruisers?"

She shrugged. "I don't know. I've never been here."

Diego parked the truck near the front door and looked at her with surprise. "You're kidding?"

"Nope. This isn't really my scene. It's always seemed sort of shady."

Luc chuckled as he climbed out of the truck, and then reached in to help her down. "Oh, it's a dive, to be sure. But it's not danger-ous. Besides," he said, his hands lingering on her waist, "the only shady characters you need to worry about tonight are us."

She fought to keep her breathing steady, hoping Luc couldn't sense how much his hands on her waist were impacting her. Equal waves of nervousness and excitement clamored beneath the surface. There was no way she was going to make it through the night. Both men seemed intent on dragging her close, touching her. Even now, Diego was tugging her away from Luc, her hand held securely in his large, warm palm.

Before they made it to the front door, Jeannette was over-whelmed by the sheer noise of the place. Fast, ear-piercing music thumped out a heavy beat as people fought to be heard, laughing and talking loudly. There was a large crowd of people sitting in front of a long bar and the dance floor was packed, a huge mass of bodies stomping in time to some country music line dance.

Jeannette wasn't sure what Hell looked like, but she sort of imagined it would be a lot like this. Despite her large companions flanking her, no less than four people bumped into her, the last spilling beer on her boots before they made their way to a table.

"Hey, Diego, Luc, over here," a man called out. "We're just leaving. You want our spot?"

Diego smiled and nodded. As they got closer, Jeannette recog-nized Colby as the speaker. He grinned at the men, the smile freezing when he realized she was standing with them.

"Nettie?"

"Hey, thanks, Colby," Diego said, putting a proprietary arm around her shoulders and tugging her close. "I was afraid Jean-nette was going to be crushed there for a minute. This place is crazy tonight."

She noticed the way Diego stressed her name, and while she appreciated his efforts, she was still on the verge of freaking out. For one thing, she wasn't used to such large crowds, and secondly, she wasn't used to a man holding her so closely.

"Yeah. We got here early and Jeremiah sort of overdid it. Couple of my buddies took him outside to get sick while I settled up the tab." Colby looked at Jeannette again as if trying to convince himself it was really her. "Y'all have fun."

With that, Colby left. No doubt he and his friends would have a field day discussing the fact she was out with Diego and Luc. She estimated it would be less than ten minutes before the texts from her cousins and sister started arriving. She hadn't told anyone about her plans for the evening because she'd been ninety-nine percent sure she'd bail. She reached into her purse and muted her phone. Tonight was going to be hard enough without her phone chiming every ten seconds with another OMG, WTF text from a relative.

Luc pulled out one of the tall stools for her, and then claimed the one next to it, pushing it closer to hers. Diego followed suit on the other side until she felt caged in and sheltered. Every single thing about the evening was an experiment in insanity as opposite emotions battled within her. It was as if she was locked in a constant game of tug of war with herself.

Diego waved the waitress over and ordered three beers. For the first time since she'd entered the bar, Jeannette had a chance to really look around. There were a lot of familiar faces in the crowd, as well as quite a few people she'd never laid eyes on.

Cruisers was positioned just off Exit 57 on the highway, so she suspected it pulled in a lot of people from surroundings towns or tourists passing through. God knew the club spent a fortune on billboard signs, with advertising starting as much as fifty miles away in both directions. Clearly the promotion paid off.

Once again, Luc's arm found its way to the back of her seat, his fingers in her hair. "You look beautiful, Jeannette."

She smiled and thanked him. She'd spent an ungodly amount of time fussing and fretting in front of the mirror, not that she'd seen much difference, apart from a few more heat-created waves in her hair and heavier eye makeup—that she'd then hidden behind her glasses. "Saw the fire truck roar past the restaurant today. Was there a fire or a car accident?"

Diego took a sip of his beer. "Fire. That old abandoned shack at the corner of Route 26 and Poorhouse Road."

She tilted her head. "How on earth did that happen? There's no electricity in that thing. Kids playing around?"

Diego shook his head. "No. It didn't look like anyone had been there in a long time."

She considered the number of times she'd seen the fire truck answering calls in the past few weeks. "You guys have been sort of busy lately, haven't you?"

Luc continued to play with her hair, wrapping one strand around his finger. "Unfortunately. Today's was the third fire in that many weeks. The shack, plus two outbuildings—one at Buster Milligan's place and another at Roy Mathers' farm.

"Strange," she said.

Diego lifted his beer again and she watched as he took a long swig, the action drawing her attention to his full, extremely kiss-able lips.

She shoved *that* thought away. Even though Diego had insisted this was a date, kissing was not on her agenda. Just the thought of it made her blood run cold. And hot.

Fuck. She was getting seriously tired of all the contradictions.

"Glad you came out?" Luc asked, with a teasing gleam in his hazel eyes. "Starting to wonder why you ever turned us down to begin with?"

"Regardless of whether I'm having fun or not, I still say it's not normal for two guys to date the same woman at the same time."

Luc had been about to take a drink, but instead put the bottle down. "Who gets to decide what's normal?"

His question took her aback. Mainly because he sounded so serious. She was used to the easygoing banter between them. They were harmless guys who liked to tease. It wasn't as if they *really* wanted to date her. They were just trying to help her break out of her rut. Or at least, that was what she'd thought before Diego had laid down the law at her house earlier.

"I don't know who decides. Society?"

"Diego and I like going out with women together. To us and the women we date, it feels normal. So you're saying we should do something that wouldn't feel right, simply because what you view as polite society says we're wrong?"

"There are still those in society who say gay marriage is wrong. That interracial marriage is wrong," Diego added.

She raised her hand. "I don't feel that way."

"If you can accept those relationships, why can't you understand our preference?" Luc asked.

She blew out an exasperated sigh. "You guys are waging one hell of an effective argument. I don't like it."

Diego chuckled. "Sore loser."

It occurred to Jeannette that prior to this week, the three of them had never really had an opportunity to talk like this. Typically they were surrounded by lots of other people in the midst of the busy restaurant. "How long have you guys done this tag-team dating?"

Luc actually began to count. "Let's see. We met when we were fifteen. We're thirty now, so I'd say pretty much from the beginning."

"Seriously?" She was surprised. "You've never gone out with a woman without Diego there?"

Luc shook his head. "No. Never. Diego's always been with me."

The men exchanged a glance. It was just a fleeting look, but Jeannette saw something flow between them she hadn't seen before.

Genuine affection and...attraction?

She thought back to the gossip she'd heard about Luc and Diego's dating habits. There were a lot of satisfied women in town only too happy to spill the juicy details about their evening with the sexy firefighters. All of the rumors ran along the same vein. It was always a magical night where the woman walked away satisfied and ruined for all other men forever.

Jeannette had rolled her eyes at those comments more than once and chalked up the remarks to exaggeration and bragging. Even so, the legend surrounding Luc and Diego had grown, and more women had gotten in line for the hayride.

However, no one had ever gotten a chance for seconds.

And no one had ever mentioned there being more to Diego and Luc's relationship with each other. Perhaps she'd simply misinterpreted the look.

"Why do you prefer to go out with women together?"

Luc shrugged lightly. "It would probably take a few hundred hours on a shrink's couch to figure that out."

Jeannette and Diego laughed. She was surprised and touched when Luc still tried to give her an honest answer.

"We met in a foster home in Dallas."

Jeannette's gaze flew to Diego, but it appeared he wasn't uneasy with Luc sharing the details of their past.

"I didn't know that," she said. "Your parents?"

"My mom died. Never knew my dad. Diego's parents are in jail."

"Sold heroin to a guy who OD'ed. They got twenty years for it. I haven't seen them since. Don't have any plans to ever see them again," Diego added. "Believe me, the foster home was a big step up from where I'd been. Met Luc my first day there. He was pretty new to the place too. We just sort of clicked."

"We should have been born brothers." Luc smiled at Diego. "Destiny must have figured that out and found a way to get us into each other's lives. Anyway, we've been thick as thieves since then. And given our lack of family, we just decided to become that. Our own family."

"Brothers." Diego smiled at Luc, and again Jeannette got that sensation that told her there was more between them than just a shared past. Then she realized how little she knew about them. A wave of sadness washed through her. Not only did she suck at relationships, she was a terrible friend, superficial at best.

She was moved by their story, by their close bond, and their willingness to share it with her. Suddenly their reasons for dating together made sense to her.

While she was close to her sister and cousins, there was no denying she was lonely. Terribly lonely. And though she'd tried to pretend otherwise, she knew her constant exhaustion lately was driven by depression. It wouldn't be the first time she'd slipped into a dark place, but it had been long enough that she thought she'd found a way to control it.

Although...now that she thought about it...she wasn't feeling tired or sad at the moment.

She picked up her beer and took a drink. She'd anticipated needing the alcohol to help her relax, but the truth was her dates were easy to be with. The nerves she'd experienced at her house prior to their arrival had vanished completely during the ride here.

Luc leaned his elbows on the table. "I have to say *you* don't seem to be lacking for family. I have a hard time keeping all you Sparks kids straight. How many of you are there?"

Jeannette grinned. It was never a hardship for her to talk about her family. She loved them all. "There were five Sparks brothers, my dad and four uncles. They all grew up in Maris, working in Pop's diner, which was sort of the predecessor to Sparks Barbeque. Did you know the restaurant is one of the long-est-running and most successful barbeque joints in Texas? We've been featured on the Food Network twice."

Diego chuckled. "Yeah. I think we were only in town about three minutes before we heard all about Sparks Barbeque. And Sparks Bakery. And Sparks Hardware. Y'all sort of own the town, don't you?"

Jeannette laughed. "I guess we're obnoxiously devoted to and proud of Maris. No one in the family has moved away with the exceptions of Tyson and Paige, who went off to college. But even they came right back after graduation. All four of my uncles still live within ten miles of the home they grew up in."

Luc leaned closer. "You know, I never thought to ask, but where's your dad?"

Jeannette had anticipated the question. It was one she hadn't had to answer in a very long time. Most of the folks who lived in Maris had been there since God was a baby. They'd all been around when Jeannette lost her parents. "He and my mom were killed in a car crash."

Luc reached out and took her hand, giving it a comforting squeeze. "Oh Jeannette. I'm sorry."

It was a common response, but looking into Luc's eyes, she saw true understanding. He'd lost his mom. He knew what it meant to ache for that connection long after it was gone. "Thanks."

"How old were you?" Diego asked.

"I was sixteen and my baby sister, Gia, was only ten. It was okay. Like you said, I have lots of relatives. We went to live with my Uncle George and Aunt Stella."

Luc nodded slowly. "I'm familiar with your Uncle George. Judge Sparks, right? Serious guy. Does he ever smile?"

Jeannette laughed softly. "Actually, he does. I know he's kind of scary when he's sitting on the bench, but he's a teddy bear at home. He was really good to Gia and me after our folks died. He never blinked twice. Just took us in and raised us as his own alongside his two kids."

"He and Stella are Tyson's parents, right?"

Jeannette nodded. "Yep. They also had Paige."

Diego shook his head. "That's a hell of a lot of girls in one house."

"Tell me about it. Besides that crew, there's my cousin Sydney, who is Uncle Lynn's daughter. She's an only child, lucky bitch. Uncle Ronnie had Evan and Lacy, and Uncle TJ had Macie and Adele. Hope you were paying attention. There's a quiz later."

Luc leaned back as she wrapped up her recitation of the family tree. "I like Evan. He's a cool guy."

"Oh," Jeannette said. "Yeah, I guess you two probably see him a lot." Evan was a deputy on the Maris police force.

Luc nodded. "Yep. We usually run into him at car accidents and fires. He was with us today, along with Chuck, the district fire marshal. They were investigating the scene, looking for evidence of who might be starting the fires."

"Starting them?" she asked.

Diego drained his beer and sighed. "Yeah. It looks like we

have an arsonist in town. All three of the fires were purposely set, not accidental."

Jeannette considered that information. "Do you think it's someone's way of cleaning up the area? All three of the places that burned were sort of rundown, decrepit buildings. No one has lived in that shack for nearly thirty years."

Diego shrugged. "I don't know. But regardless of the usefulness of the buildings, setting fires is a crime."

"I'm sorry," Jeannette hastened to add. "I wasn't condoning it. Just wondering if someone had gotten tired of the eyesores and decided to take matters into their own hands. I know there have been some complaints about the shack over the years."

Luc drummed his fingers on the table as he chewed over what she'd said. "I hadn't considered that. And while that's true for the shack and that god-awful outbuilding of Buster's, that doesn't explain the fire at Roy's. The building that burned on his place was well off the road and at the edge of his property. I'm not sure anyone but Roy even remembered it was there."

Jeannette nodded slowly. "If not for the fire at the shack, I'd say it was a Hatfield-and-McCoy thing."

Luc gave her a questioning glance. "What do you mean?"

"You know how Buster and Roy are. They hate each other, and have for nearly forty years. Evan said the stack of complaints filed by those two against each other could fill its own drawer at the police station. If it was just Buster's and Roy's properties that burned, it would be a pretty simple case of somebody starting something and someone retaliating."

"Yeah. I'd agree with that. But now we've got this fire at the shack. Whoever is setting the fires is getting bolder, going for larger targets." Jeannette saw the genuine concern in Diego's eyes.

"You think they'll keep going?"

Diego rubbed his jaw, drawing her gaze to his freshly shaven face. Usually he was sporting a five o'clock shadow by this time of the day. He'd clearly taken some pains of his own in regards to his appearance for their date. "Yeah. If it's a serial arsonist, I'm afraid this is going to get worse before it gets better."

Jeannette started to respond, but she was distracted when she caught sight of Scott across the room. He was staring at her, scowling. She started to look away, but Diego and Luc noticed her attention had wavered.

"I don't like that guy," Luc said.

Jeannette agreed with his assessment. "He was never very nice. Always a bit of a bully."

"Damn," Diego muttered. She glanced over at him, and then realized he wasn't looking at Scott. Rather, something by the door had caught his eye. She followed his line of vision and understood the curse.

Billy was making his way to his brother's table. Scott wasn't happy to see him. They appeared to have words, and then Billy held out his hand. Scott slapped his keys into his brother's palm, staggering as he tried to rise.

Jeannette felt a false sense of hope when it appeared the two of them were leaving.

Then Scott lifted his hand and pointed at her.

Billy looked over, his face somber, his eyes unreadable as he saw her sitting with the two firefighters.

Her skin went cold and she resisted the urge to shiver. Nervously, her leg began bouncing beneath the table and she was overcome by the desire to go home. She'd stuck her neck out too far. Ordinarily, Jeannette would pull it back into her shell and hide. But this time, the idea of doing that rubbed her wrong.

She'd been having fun. For the first time in her life, she'd almost felt like a normal person. She resented Billy coming in here and taking that from her.

Diego's hand slipped beneath the table and rested on her knee, stilling the anxious bobbing. The action drew her gaze back to his face. "Are you okay?"

She blinked a couple times, trying to reorient herself. She couldn't keep doing shit like this every time Billy appeared. "Yeah."

"They're leaving."

Jeannette looked across the room at Luc's announcement and

watched Billy help his drunken brother out of the bar. The second the door closed behind them, she felt the pressure in her chest ease.

Diego's hand still rested on her leg, but Jeannette didn't mind. Typically, she recoiled from anyone touching her, but there was something very soothing about the way Diego's fingers were lightly stroking her knee.

"Why don't you like Billy Mathers?"

Jeannette worked overtime to school her features. When the silence drifted a second too long into the awkward range, she forced herself to speak. "Who said I don't like him?"

"I saw how you responded to him in the restaurant. You couldn't get away from that guy quick enough. And tonight..." Diego squeezed her knee to make his point.

She searched for some answer that might appease him, that might make sense. "I was just surprised to see him. It's been a long time."

It obviously hadn't been long enough. The response didn't convince either man. "Was it a bad breakup?" Luc asked.

She shook her head, laughing lightly. She hoped it sounded carefree and amused, rather than what it really was—desperation and panic. "It was high school. Aren't all breakups devastating when you're sixteen?"

Luc didn't smile. "Yeah. I guess so."

A new song came on. Apparently it was a popular one, as there was a roar of hoots from the surrounding tables and a bunch of people swarmed to the dance floor.

Luc must have been a fan as well because he grinned and stood. "Come on, Jeannette. We're dancing."

He took her hand, but she resisted. "I don't know how to dance to this."

"Lucky for you, I'm a good teacher."

Jeannette glanced at Diego, who made no move to join them. "I'll keep an eye on the table." She started to follow Luc, but Diego grabbed her free hand and tugged her back. "But I'm claiming the first slow dance." He sealed that pronouncement with a quick kiss on her cheek that sent flames to her face. This damn continual blushing made her feel like a schoolgirl instead of the woman of thirty-one she was.

Luc found a spot for them on the floor and that was the last cognizant thought she had as he took her in his arms and led her through a fast-paced, whirlwind of a dance. It was dizzying and a little bit terrifying as Luc spun her this way and that. She didn't have time to think about what she was doing, but she didn't need to. Luc hadn't lied. He was an amazing teacher. He led her through the motions with a strong hand on her back and easy instructions.

"Going for the spin, you ready?" he asked.

She nodded, loud laughter escaping her lips as he twirled her out, nothing but their hands keeping them connected for a split second. Then he drew her to him, his arm wrapped around her waist, her back snug against his chest. Twisting her to face him, he placed a strong hand just above her ass as he cupped her cheek with the other.

"You lied," he said as she continued to grin, breathless and sweaty, exhilarated and overwhelmed. "You're a great dancer."

"All I'm doing is holding on for dear life," she joked, delighted when Luc's loud, infectious laughter mingled with her own.

"Now are you ready to admit you're having a good time?"

She rolled her eyes, but gave him the compliment anyway. He deserved it. "I'm having a lot of fun."

"Enough to entice you to go out with us again?"

"You have enough women dangling on your hook. You don't need me."

Luc's face sobered. "You're the only one who matters."

She didn't know how to respond to such a serious—wonderful —comment.

Apparently he didn't expect an answer. "You're beautiful, Jeannette."

She tried to look away to hide the blush that accompanied *his* compliment, but he wouldn't let her escape.

"Don't," he murmured, tugging her even closer. The music

was pulsing at a frantic pace, but Luc was chiseling out his own rhythm. They swayed as people twirled around them. For a moment, it felt as if the rest of the world was playing on fast-forward as she and Luc moved in slow motion.

"Don't what?" she asked.

"Don't look away."

She couldn't have averted her eyes if her life depended on it. Luc lowered his lips to hers—and just like that, she was spinning again.

Jeannette hadn't been kissed much in her life, but she didn't need any past frame of reference to tell her this was one fucking incredible kiss. Luc cupped her face, the tips of his fingers stroking her cheeks gently as his lips brushed hers. It was a light touch at first, but when she didn't offer any resistance, he pressed harder.

Unfortunately, as quickly as the kiss began, it ended.

Luc gave her a crooked grin. "Been wanting to do that for a long damn time."

For years, she'd genuinely believed his and Diego's flirting was harmless teasing. Tonight they'd set her world on its ear, issuing compliments and sharing long-hidden desires as if it were the most natural thing in the world.

Her inexperience had her wondering if this was simply something guys did to get into a woman's pants. Was she falling for the oldest play in the world or were they really as sincere as she believed?

The music changed, the fast song giving way to a much slower melody. As promised, Diego was there, ready to claim his turn on the floor. Luc gave her a sexy wink as he relinquished her to his friend and returned to the table.

Throughout the dance she'd shared with Luc, she had been aware of Diego's eyes on them. Somehow knowing he'd been watching had excited her, though she was hard-pressed to understand why. It was as if she wanted Diego to know how Luc was making her feel...because she sensed that made Diego happy.

Which was bizarre, because she had no idea if that was true or not.

Diego took her into his arms, tugging her until her breasts were pressed firmly against his chest. He didn't ask, didn't hesitate. He simply took. While that idea should terrify her, it didn't. Instead, he had a way of making her feel cherished, safe, protected.

Like Luc, Diego was a skilled dancer. With subtle pushes and pulls, he guided them, taking over so that she could just enjoy the moment.

"You liked Luc's kiss."

It wasn't a question, but she answered anyway. "Yes."

"I liked watching it."

"I know," she whispered.

"Do you understand now?"

It was a vague question, but Jeannette didn't need clarification. She knew what he was alluding to. She nodded.

"You feel it to. I can see it in your eyes. Even though you're dancing with me, focused just on me, you know he's there watching us. It makes you hot and shivery inside, doesn't it?"

She swallowed, struggling to find her voice. "It does, but—" She tried to stop herself, tried to beat back the fears. It appeared Nettie refused to go down without a fight.

"But nothing." Diego tightened his grip. However, this time she couldn't sink into the embrace. Her back stiffened as self-preservation and years of running away ganged up on her.

He loosened his hold, tipping her chin up, forcing her to face him. "We're going to take this nice and slow, Jeannette. But we're not stopping."

"I can't...do..." Again, the words died. She couldn't go where they wanted to take her. But damn if she didn't want them to try anyway.

"You can't tonight. I can see that. But we're not going to stop trying. We've got as many nights as we need, all the time in the world."

She frowned and asked the question that had tormented her since they'd pulled her into the park and insisted on this date. "Why would you go to all that trouble?"

"If this weren't our first date, I'd take you home and turn you over my knee for that. Even now, I'm sorely tempted."

Had he seriously just threatened to spank her? And was she honestly disappointed he was resisting? God, this whole night was confusing. And maddening. And sexy as hell.

Regardless, her spine stiffened. "All I'm saying is, you and Luc could basically have your pick of women around here. I'm not sure why you'd want—"

Diego placed his finger over her lips. "I'm going to advise you to stop while you're ahead. If I hear one more self-deprecating comment come out of those pretty lips of yours tonight, I won't be held responsible for my actions. And believe me, angel, as much as you might want to tempt me on that, you aren't ready for it."

Jeannette wasn't sure how to reply. Diego's thumb stroked her lower lip, his gaze glued to her mouth like a starving man eyeing a steak.

Though the slow music continued to fill the air, couples swaying back and forth around them, neither of them moved. Instead, they stood there, on the edge of the floor, and looked at each other.

Diego didn't seek to close the distance between them. In fact, it seemed as if he were waiting for something. Waiting for *her*.

"Kiss me," she whispered.

He smiled at her request. He had been waiting for an invitation. "That wasn't so hard, was it?"

"Smartass," she murmured. She would have laughed, but Diego didn't give her a chance.

Unlike Luc's, there was no sweetness, no gentleness in Diego's kiss—not that she'd expected any. His lips were hard, hungry, demanding. When his tongue pressed against her lips, she opened her mouth, savoring the heat of his breath and the tang from the beer he'd drunk.

She wrapped her arms around his neck, holding on for dear life. While they were putting on quite a show, there was only one person in the audience she cared about. As she accepted Diego's kisses, she imagined Luc sitting at the table, his attention riveted.

Did he feel any jealousy at all or was this exciting for him? The concept of two men sharing a woman felt so foreign to her and yet, she felt the heart-thumping, pussy-pounding pull of it.

She gasped at the thought and jerked away. Diego frowned, but didn't try to force her back.

This was why she avoided these situations. She knew where this was leading. And it wasn't somewhere she'd ever go.

Diego's eyes narrowed, scrutinizing her face too closely. He was too adept at reading her expressions. It made it so much harder to hide.

She started to walk off the floor, toward the door and escape. She'd call Macie to come pick her up. She'd go home, crawl under the covers and stay there until she found a way to forget she'd ever thought this night was a good idea.

Diego gripped her upper arm, halting her before she managed to take three steps away from him.

Then Luc appeared in front of her. He *had* been watching. He'd seen it all. "Going somewhere?"

"I think we've accomplished our goal. Shattered the image of Nervous Nettie once and for all. I appreciate the help, but I really need to—"

"Stop." Diego's arm had snaked around her waist from behind, holding her tightly. His breath was hot in her ear.

Jeannette was fighting a strong impulse to stomp on his foot and run. She didn't want them to see her fall apart, but that was definitely where she was headed. Hot tears burned the back of her eyes and bile rose to her throat.

They wanted to have sex with her. She didn't do that. Couldn't do that.

"Luc, go settle up the tab and grab Jeannette's purse. We'll wait in the truck."

Luc nodded and walked off in search of the waitress.

"Slow and easy, angel." Diego stepped to her side, but he kept a firm grip on her waist as he propelled her toward the exit.

Somehow she made it to the truck on rubber legs. Once Diego

had her inside the vehicle, the doors closed, she realized she was panting loudly.

"It's okay, Jeannette."

She didn't look at him. She couldn't. She'd made a complete ass of herself. Had she really believed she could go out with them and remain detached? Unaffected? She had become a master at stifling her sexual urges for years, but the truth was, she'd never really been tempted. Men gave her a wide berth, so it was easy, untested.

She jumped when Luc opened the passenger door and climbed in. "Shit, Jeannette," he said, "I'm sorry. I didn't mean to scare you."

Jeannette kept her eyes forward, refusing to glance left or right. She couldn't bear to see the confusion—or worse, the pity—in their expressions. "Can you just take me home?"

Diego started the truck, but didn't put it in reverse. "Put on your seat belt, angel."

His words were gentle, as if he were speaking to a child or a lunatic, which wasn't too far from the truth. She buckled the belt, relieved when he shifted into gear and pulled out of the parking lot.

Mercifully, neither man attempted to make conversation. She could feel them both glancing at her from time to time and she could only imagine what was going through their heads. She kept herself calm by counting down the minutes until they would arrive at her house and she could get the hell away from them.

She had the seat belt unbuckled before Diego turned into her driveway and she was fully prepared to claw her way out of the truck if need be. Once Diego put the vehicle in park and shut off the engine, Luc opened the door and stepped down.

She intended to jump to the ground, but Luc was there, his hands lightly grasping her waist as he lifted her out and set her to her feet. She couldn't help but notice how quickly he released her. There was no lingering touch or hold this time.

She really had fucked up.

Jeannette walked to the front door hastily as they followed. Five more steps. Key in the door. Step inside. Freedom.

She made it as far as the key in the door before Diego's hand covered hers. Jeannette jerked away as if she'd touched a hot stove. "Thanks for tonight. I had fun."

Any normal guy would read the dismissal in her tone and get lost.

"Turn around, Jeannette." As always, Diego used that deep, commanding voice that had her body reacting before her brain could kick in. She turned, but she kept her eyes averted.

"I owe you an apology."

Her gaze flew up at his unexpected comment. "What?"

"I pushed too hard. Taking more than you were willing to give. It won't happen again."

Her heart fell. She'd accomplished her goal, shoved them away. So much for creating a new Jeannette. This old dog was way beyond the learning-new-tricks phase.

"It's okay. I understand." She truly did. She was hard work and she wouldn't wish herself on anyone. "Good night."

Diego slid the key from her door before she could twist it in the lock. She glanced back at him. "What are you doing?"

"I'm not finished talking."

Jeannette leaned against the front door, weary beyond words. The night had been one long roller-coaster of mixed emotions. She wanted off the ride.

"Diego—"

"I can see in your eyes that you don't understand a damn thing. So I'm going to spell it out. This isn't over."

She frowned, her gaze drifting from Diego to Luc and back again. A wall of sheer determination surrounded her. "I can't do what you—"

Luc reached for her hand. She forced herself not to react, not to pull away. "Aren't you tired of running, Jeannette?"

She nodded slowly.

"It's time to stop."

"I don't know how to do any of this," she admitted, giving voice to just one of her many fears.

Luc gave her that affable, crooked grin of his and she found herself returning it. "We'll teach you. It's as easy as dancing."

Strangely, his assertion comforted her. Dancing with them *had* been easy. Actually, the whole night had been. Until she'd freaked out.

Regardless, she offered them one more out. "I think it would be a lot easier if we just left it here."

Diego crossed his arms. "I'm not looking for easy."

She owed him some sort of olive branch. After all, he apologized for something that wasn't even his fault. "I'm sorry for walking away from you on the dance floor."

He smiled, and then he cupped her cheek. "We'll have plenty more chances to dance."

She wasn't sure she had any more dances in her.

"I can see you're not finished fighting this," Diego continued, "so let's go ahead and make plans for the next time. I don't intend to spend the next few days listening to your voice mail while you try to avoid us. When's your next night off?"

The damn man was pushy as hell, which didn't annoy her as much as it should. "Wednesday."

"Great. Luc and I will pick you up at six and take you out to dinner."

"Fine."

Luc chuckled. "That's it? No argument?"

She lifted one shoulder. "Would there be any point? Despite what I say now, you'll both be here at six on Wednesday, won't you?"

Luc winked. "Damn right."

"Then my answer is the same. Fine."

Luc leaned toward her and gave her a soft kiss on the cheek. "See you Wednesday."

He backed away as Diego stepped forward. He ran the backs of his fingers over her cheek. "Wear a dress for us?"

She'd never heard a question in one of his commands before. It touched her.

She rarely dressed up. In fact, she only owned two dresses, both Sunday dresses that were appropriate for church, but not very exciting for a date. Of course, the wholesome dresses would probably serve her purpose better.

Even as she thought it, she knew she was going shopping for a new dress. "Okay."

He didn't try to kiss her. She was grateful and disappointed. She was becoming accustomed to the contradictory emotions these men provoked.

Diego handed her the house key. "Good night, Jeannette."

She watched them drive away, no longer in such a hurry to escape. When they'd first arrived, she'd wanted nothing more than to crawl into bed and cry her eyes out. As she opened the front door now, she reached down to pick up Penny and headed to the living room. Finding repeats of *I Love Lucy* on TV, she sat in quiet solitude as a completely new emotion washed over her.

Hope.

DIEGO FOLLOWED Luc into their house, shutting the door and leaning against it. He'd almost let his overbearing need for control ruin things with Jeannette. Luc had been uncharacteristically quiet on the drive home. Diego could only assume he was pissed off.

Luc tugged off his jacket and hung it on the back of a chair. "You want to tell me what happened on that dance floor?"

Diego shrugged, trying to keep a rein on his temper. He'd been wrong to push Jeannette, but he resented Luc's tone. "I'm not going to lie to her about who I am. What I want."

Luc threw up his hands. "Jesus, D. It was the first fucking date. You can't at least try to hide some of that macho shit until we get our foot in the door?"

Diego stalked toward his friend. "Don't hear you bitching about that 'macho shit' when it's just you and me."

Luc held his ground even as Diego stepped close. "Don't try to intimidate me. Not now. It won't fucking work."

"You can act as pissed off as you want, but I think the person you're really mad at is yourself. I'm not hiding my true colors from her, Luc. What about you?"

"I want her. I've wanted her since the first time I saw her."

"And you're willing to pretend this," Diego pointed to himself, then Luc, "doesn't exist? For how long, Luc? How long will you keep her in the dark about your other lover?"

"As long as it takes," Luc replied through gritted teeth.

Diego snorted. "Yeah. That's obvious. Three fucking years, man. It's been three years since we've *really* been together with a woman. Don't you miss it?"

Luc looked away. He didn't need to reply. Diego could read the answer on his face. He was wrong to call Luc out for this. Especially considering they both wanted the same thing.

They'd walked into Sparks Barbeque two weeks after moving to Maris, deciding to try out the place so many people had raved about. Jeannette had been behind the counter and had taken their order.

Luc had been smitten from the start, not that Diego was surprised. Jeannette had a quiet, kind spirit. She was friendly, unassuming, and as tonight had proven, the woman didn't have a clue how damn pretty she was. They'd met more than their fair share of women who came on too strong, working overtime to gain their attention.

Instead, Jeannette had been the first to make them feel welcome in a close-knit town that tended to treat outsiders with cautious distance and sidelong glances. She'd asked about their new jobs, given them some advice on where to pick up affordable furniture for their house, and filled them in on a bunch of stuff she thought they needed to know in order to survive in Maris. She had whipped out her cell phone to share pictures of the cat she'd just taken in. The thing had been little more than skin and bones, but it was obvious Jeannette thought the cat hung the moon. And then she'd fed them the most delicious barbeque sandwiches they had ever eaten.

Luc had insisted they ask her out, so the next time they were in the restaurant, they issued the invitation. Jeannette had called them shameless teases and walked away quickly before they could press their suit.

Her dismissive response had confused Luc, but intrigued Diego. After that, he began to watch her more closely. There was something very sad lingering just below the surface that called to Diego's need to protect, to save.

They'd decided to bide their time, asking out other women, thinking perhaps it was the idea of a threesome that was holding her back. Jeannette was a Maris girl, through and through. They hoped she'd see the locals' acceptance of their unorthodox dating style and then feel okay about saying yes.

The plan hadn't worked. So for a while, they'd actually tried to move on. The attempts had been miserable failures as Luc insisted on hiding the true nature of their relationship.

For three long years, they'd hidden a huge part of who they were. Diego wanted to cast the blame solely at Luc's feet, but he couldn't. He'd gone along with it. Now, the harness was too tight and rubbing him raw.

His temper was frazzled. Luc was pushing him in the wrong direction.

"How do you think Jeannette is going to feel when she finds out about this?" Diego asked, reaching out, cupping Luc's cock. It was hard, thick. And he didn't bother to pretend Luc's current arousal had a damn thing to do with him. Like Luc, Diego had been walking around with a hard-on ever since Jeannette opened the door tonight in her tight jeans and silky blouse. He'd been hard-pressed to look away from her creamy white breasts.

Luc didn't pull away, didn't offer any resistance. Instead, he gave as good as he got, reaching over to unhook Diego's jeans. By the time Luc had freed his cock and tugged his jeans to mid-thigh, they were both panting, breathing heavily through their noses.

"Suck me," Diego demanded.

Luc narrowed his eyes, but didn't argue. Instead, he dropped to his knees, engulfing Diego's thick flesh in one deep thrust. Luc wrapped his fist tight around the base of Diego's dick, stroking him. Diego wasn't a small guy, and definitely more than a mouthful, but that didn't scare his lover away.

Luc worked him hard, sucking him deep and swallowing his head. Luc was still angry and he was taking it out in the blowjob. Diego would laugh at the foolish attempt if he weren't so fucking close to blowing. He liked the pain, and Luc knew it.

"Fucking suck it like you want it." Diego gripped Luc's hair roughly, making his demands known as he increased the pressure, shoved his dick deep and hard. Luc took it all, then gave back some of his own as he cupped Diego's balls and began to squeeze.

It was game over. Diego thrust in twice more, then let go, jet after jet of come filling Luc's mouth.

"Swallow it," he demanded, though the words weren't necessary. Luc had never spit in his life.

Slowly, Diego sank to his knees in front of Luc and pulled his lover, his best friend, his brother, closer for a kiss.

Their tongues tangled, but the previous heat from the argument had faded, giving way to exhaustion, anxiety.

"I'm sorry," Diego whispered.

For the first time since they'd returned home, Luc gave him his standard goofy, affable smile. "You're an overbearing bastard. Probably was a good idea to let the poor girl know what she's getting into."

Diego reached for Luc's cock. He was a firm believer in fair play, but Luc brushed his hand away. "No, man. It's alright."

Diego looked at him curiously until Luc explained.

"It might take the edge off, but it wouldn't make me less hungry."

Diego nodded. He knew that from experience. He had just come, but his cock still wasn't sated. It wouldn't be until he was buried deep in Jeannette's sweet pussy.

Luc rose and walked away from him, sinking down onto the

couch. "We came to Maris to make a fresh start, D. We agreed that we needed more and that we'd do whatever it took to get it. It's her. Jeannette is the piece that's missing. I just don't know how..."

Diego's chest tightened as he stood. His legs were a little less steady as he tried to recover from his climax. "We'll make it work, Luc. I think she needs us as much as we need her. We just have to figure out a way to prove that to her."

"You think we can?"

Diego sat next to Luc. "I don't think we have any other choice."

CHAPTER THREE

The after-church crowd at the restaurant was always a large one. As a result, Paige, who was in charge of scheduling, usually brought them all in to work. Jeannette and Sydney cooked quickly and efficiently in the kitchen, their routines in synch after so many years of preparing and serving up food side by side. Macie worked the counter while TJ, Adele, Gia, and Paige waited and bussed the tables. Lacy had gotten a bye this week because she was suffering from a terrible head cold.

Jeannette was grateful to be busy because it helped keep her mind off her worries—the main one being when one of her cousins would catch wind of her date last night. She didn't have a clue how any of them would react, considering she'd put on quite a production in the past, exclaiming that two men dating the same woman was appalling and not something to be condoned.

Talk about egg on your face.

She'd been at work less than an hour before the news broke.

Macie flung open the swinging door between the kitchen and the dining room, Gia in tow. "Where were you last night?"

Jeannette brushed a stray hair out of her face and shrugged. "Cruisers."

Sydney put down the knife she was using to chop tomatoes. "What? Seriously?"

Jeannette understood their outright shock, even though it did bug her. "Yes. You guys go there all the time, so I'm not so sure why it's such a big deal."

Macie knew why. "Who were you with?"

Jeannette scowled, tired of the third degree from a person who clearly already knew all the answers. "Who told you?"

"Colby."

"Then why do you need to hear it from me?" Jeannette asked haughtily.

Sydney took a step closer. "I'm tied to the damn stove back here. Someone give me the goods."

Gia shrugged. "I was restocking the paper towels in the women's bathroom. I'm as much in the dark as you."

Macie grinned. "You want *me* to tell them?"

Jeannette smirked at her cousin. "You're obviously dying to."

"Luc and Diego."

Gia's mouth fell open as Sydney's eyes widened.

"No way," Sydney exclaimed. "You've turned them down for years! Said it was despicable the way they dated women together."

Jeannette bit her lower lip. She'd said all that and more. "It wasn't exactly a date," she lied, trying to find a way out of this conversation. None of them would be satisfied until they'd squeezed every last gory detail out of her. She was still equal parts mortified by her actions and completely turned-on. She couldn't share either of those tidbits, so it was time for some serious deflection.

"Is that right?" Macie asked. "Hmmm. I wonder if Diego and Luc will say the same thing. Let's go ask them, Gia."

Jeannette stopped them before they could take a single step. "Wait. They're here?"

Macie nodded.

Jeannette didn't want them asking a bunch of questions, so she gave them as much of the story as she was able to. "Fine. It was a date. We went to Cruisers, drank a beer, danced a little and then they brought me home. That was it."

Gia smiled. "Really? Wow! That's the best news I've heard in forever."

Any annoyance Jeannette felt toward them vanished when she heard the sheer joy in her sister's voice. It was impossible to stay mad at Gia, considering all she'd ever wanted was for Jeannette to be happy.

"Did they kiss you good night?" Gia asked.

Jeannette shook her head. "No."

Gia looked disappointed by that information. If Jeannette was being completely honest, she felt the same way.

Adele popped her head into the kitchen. "Where did y'all go? We just had a bunch more customers come in. Looks like the preacher at Maris Baptist took mercy on them today. Short sermon."

They all laughed as Gia and Macie returned to take orders and pour coffee.

Jeannette pulled the cobblers she'd just made from the oven as Sydney used two forks to pull apart the tender pork she'd finished marinating.

They worked in quiet efficiency for several minutes. Though Jeannette would never say it aloud, Sydney had always been the cousin she felt closest to. They were the same age, so they'd gone all through school together. Then they'd spent their twenties honing their cooking skills in this kitchen. Unlike Macie, Sydney wasn't loud or excitable or prone to drama. Even now, she was giving Jeannette some space, not asking her a million questions about her date.

"Are you going out with them again?" Sydney asked after several busy minutes.

Jeannette nodded. "Wednesday. We're going to dinner."

Sydney smiled. "I'm glad. They're nice guys."

Jeannette agreed. "Yeah. I know."

"You think this is going anywhere?"

Jeannette shrugged and pushed her glasses up on her nose.

She wasn't sure how it could. She was fucked-up six ways to Sunday, but she didn't admit that. "I don't know. I think for now I'm just going to take it one day at a time."

"Wise decision."

Adele returned with a handful of orders, but instead of leaving, she leaned against the counter where Jeannette was stirring a fresh batch of coleslaw. "Heard about your date last night."

Jeannette rolled her eyes. "Am I going to be subjected to questions every time I go out with someone?"

Adele laughed and shook her head. "Nope. Macie filled me in on the details. And that's not why I'm here. I'm going to help Sydney for a few minutes. There are two hot firefighters out there who've asked to speak to you."

Jeannette swallowed nervously and ran a hand through her hair. A large hunk of it had escaped her ponytail, and after tossing and turning most of the night, replaying every minute of the date, she'd overslept and hadn't had time for makeup.

"You look fine," Adele reassured her. "I've always wished I was a natural beauty like you."

Jeannette snorted and said, "Yeah right," but she appreciated the compliment just the same.

She took off her apron and washed her hands. "I won't be long. Promise."

Adele waved her away. "Take your time. The other girls can handle the tables and I'm perfectly capable of filling these orders. We're cool."

When Jeannette entered the dining room, she was surprised to see Diego and Luc at a booth rather than their usual spots at the counter. She was also disappointed to see Evan with them. Obviously this wasn't going to be a social visit.

She was halfway across the room when her cousin Tyson stopped her. "Hey, hotshot," he said, reaching out for her. "There's some very interesting gossip flying around this morning about you."

"Oh my God. This town must be completely bored if my

Saturday plans were the most exciting thing that happened last night."

"So it's true?"

"Yeah."

She was surprised when Tyson gave her a quick kiss on the cheek. "Good."

Jeannette hadn't realized how much her family worried about her. She was more touched than she could say. "If you want details, apparently Macie is handing out some doozies."

Tyson chuckled. "I might let her regale me with that story while I drink my coffee." He looked up when the bell above the door rang and Billy walked in. Tyson lifted his hand to wave and called out, "Thought we'd grab a couple stools at the counter, Billy."

Billy stepped up and smiled, then looked at Jeannette. "Hey, Nettie."

"I go by Jeannette now," she said, not bothering to mask the hostility in her voice.

"Sorry, Jeannette. I'll just go grab a seat." Billy walked away quickly.

Jeannette looked at Tyson, trying very hard not to feel deeply hurt. Her cousin had no clue how she felt about Billy, or why.

He gave her a curious glance, but didn't take her to task for her rudeness. "Billy and I have some business to discuss." It was clear he felt as though he needed to offer an explanation, even if he didn't know why.

She nodded. "Okay."

Tyson studied her face a second longer, then he headed to the counter where Macie was holding court.

Jeannette caught more than a few sideways glances from the patrons in the restaurant. It was sort of unnerving, considering she was invisible most days.

Diego stood up when she got to the booth, gesturing for her to slide in. Before she could sit down, he grabbed her hand and gave her a quick kiss that had her blushing in record time.

"Everything okay?" he murmured.

"Yes," she whispered back.

"Then good morning." He gave her another, longer kiss.

"You realize Evan has a gun," she joked when he released her.

Evan didn't laugh. "She's right. I do."

They sat down, Jeannette, Luc and Diego grinning, while Evan appeared less than amused.

"We're really slammed. I can't stay long. You didn't call me out here to yell at me for last night's date, did you?" she asked Evan.

Evan tilted his head, his tone dripping in sarcasm. "Yeah, right. That's what this meeting is about. Because I have complete control of everything my cousins do."

She laughed at his sardonic tone. "Good point, but maybe you think you'd have a better chance with me?"

"I grew up with six girl cousins and a sister. I'm now married with a daughter. If I've learned anything in my life, it's simply this —shut up and nod."

Diego and Luc chuckled as Jeannette rolled her eyes.

"Then why the meeting?"

Evan reached for a little tub of creamer, adding it to his coffee. "We've been sitting here discussing the fires. Diego and Luc told me your thoughts about someone trying to rid the town of eyesores. It could be a good lead, but considering the two people who've always bitched the loudest are two of the victims who've lost property, I'm struggling for suspects."

Jeannette gave him a confused look. "You seriously don't think it was a game of tit for tat between Roy and Buster? Buster burns down Roy's shed, so Roy reciprocates?"

Evan shook his head. "No. I don't think that's it. Have you seen Roy lately?"

"No, but that's not unusual. Roy keeps to himself. Doesn't come into the restaurant more than a half-dozen times in any given year."

"When I went to talk to him about the fire, he could barely make it to the front door. Cancer," Evan added.

"Oh." Jeannette glanced back at Tyson and Billy sitting at the counter, speaking quietly, somberly. Suddenly she understood the reason behind Tyson's so-called business meeting. As a doctor, it was likely he was either playing a role in Roy's treatment or answering questions for Billy. "I didn't know that. Billy said he and Scott had come home because their uncle was sick, but he didn't mention cancer or how bad it was."

Jeannette would call her Aunt Louise after work. Knowing her aunts, they would want to take over dinner for the family.

"Can you think of anyone else who bitched about the shack and those outbuildings?" Evan asked. "Considering this is a gathering place and the hub for gossip about all things Maris, I figured you might have heard someone else complaining."

Jeannette pondered the question, but couldn't think of a single person who grumbled louder or more often than the rest. "Not really. I mean, that abandoned shack and Buster's rundown shed have been discussed from time to time and most people usually hop on the tear-'em-down bandwagon. Hell, Mayor Rock was in here a few weeks ago, promising to do something about them if he was reelected next month, but I wouldn't say anyone was overly annoyed by their presence."

Evan blew out a long breath.

"You still think it's a serial arsonist?" she asked.

Diego rubbed his chin. "Apparently the fire marshal is having trouble proving the fires are all connected."

"Really? I mean they have to be, don't they? To have so many fires in such a short time? What else could it be?"

"Oh, we're sure it's arson. And we're relatively sure it's the same person," Luc explained. "It's just going to be tough to prove that."

"Why?" she asked.

Evan took a sip of his coffee. "Because whoever is doing it is clearly an amateur, and it looks like they've made Maris their classroom."

She was confused. "What do you mean?"

Diego rested his arm along the back of the booth, leaning toward her. She wasn't sure if the action was his attempt to keep their conversation private or to pull her closer. "Whoever is setting the fires is using different accelerants, different ignition devices."

Luc stretched his leg out along the side of the booth and Jeannette finally understood why he and Diego preferred the stools at the counter. Both men were too large to sit comfortably in the booth. "Every fire was set differently. It's like the guy is trying out different things to see how everything works."

Evan tapped his fork on the table a couple of times, clearly frustrated at the lack of evidence. "And he's using common everyday items, so it's not like we can run down to the hardware store to see who'd bought some unusual wire. He set the first with rags and gasoline, the second with a cigarette in a trashcan, and he took the shack down paint thinners and a candle."

"You keep saying 'he'. Do you know it's a guy?"

Evan shrugged. "Most likely. That's the only lead that offers any hope."

Diego snorted. "You call that hope?"

Evan grimaced, silently acknowledging it clearly wasn't much. "We've found fresh footprints at all three scenes made from a man's boot."

"Can't you narrow down the suspects according to who has that type of boot and the size?"

Evan rubbed his forehead wearily. "It's been three *different* pairs of boots—all common brands—and in slightly differing sizes, each pair off by a half size."

Jeannette grimaced. "So the guy is smart enough to cover his tracks."

"Yep." Evan sighed. "Well, I guess I'm back at it. I'm going to head out to all three fire sites again today to see if there's something we missed."

Evan didn't bother to say what they were all thinking. Without more evidence, the arsonist would likely remain free to set another fire.

Evan tossed a few dollars on the table, and then slid out of the booth after Luc stood to let him out. Jeannette looked at Diego, expecting him to rise as well.

He kept her trapped.

"I really do need to get back to work."

Diego didn't budge. Instead he tucked his arm around her shoulder.

From the corner of her eye, Jeannette saw several heads turn in their direction.

"What are you doing?" she murmured.

"I've heard a lot tongues wagging around here this morning. Everyone seems pretty interested in our date."

That was an understatement. "Yeah. I know. I'm sorry if that makes you uncomfortable."

Luc laughed. "Seriously? Jeannette, how many Sunday mornings have we been the topic of conversation in here?"

She couldn't possibly tabulate that number. "A lot of them. God. Maybe all of them."

He nodded. "And how many Sundays have the good people of Maris discussed Jeannette Sparks?"

She didn't even have to think about it. "None."

"So maybe the question is, are *you* uncomfortable?" Luc asked.

Part of her wondered if she should be ashamed to be the subject of such speculation—all of it racy—but she couldn't summon a single ounce of embarrassment. She'd wanted to break out of her shell and, well, by God, she'd done it. At least for a little while, before she'd freaked out and ruined the whole damn thing. "I'm...sort of..." She sucked at playing it casual or coy, so she said what she felt. "It's slightly annoying, but if I'm being completely honest, it's kind of cool too," she confessed.

"So we're ready for phase two," Luc declared.

She frowned. "Phase two?"

Luc winked at her. "We're going to put Nervous Nettie to rest once and for all. Today, you're Jeannette again."

"I'd like that. Does it involve more dancing or...kissing?"

Diego looked at Luc. "I think we've created a monster."

Luc didn't appear concerned and, for a moment, Jeannette

thought she saw something pass between them, some unspoken desire.

"Maybe we should go for broke," Luc suggested.

Diego didn't respond immediately and when he did, Jeannette was certain he was answering a question she hadn't heard. "Yeah. Maybe we should."

Diego didn't give her a chance to ask what that meant. He bent his head and kissed her. This was no friendly, hey-how-you-doin' kiss. It was a big one. Lips, teeth, tongue, hands in her hair. It was so delicious—Diego's breath tasted like bacon and maple syrup—she didn't have time to consider the fact that most of her family was there witnessing it.

Finally, twelve years later, Diego released her. "I'm not sure that will hold me until Wednesday. Might have to stop in for a helping of that every day until then."

"I..." Jeannette couldn't have formed another word if someone was offering her a million dollars for it.

Diego rose from the booth and reached down to help her slide out. Luc was standing next to him. God, if he kissed her like that right now, she'd expire on the spot.

Mercifully, he gave her a sweet kiss on the cheek. She'd thought herself spared, but Luc gripped the nape of her neck as he whispered in her ear, "I'll be by later to collect mine when there are fewer people around."

She nodded her assent, unable to deny something she would spend the next few hours anxiously anticipating. "Okay."

Jeannette headed back to the kitchen, perfectly aware that everyone in the restaurant was looking at her. In the past, she would have hated every single step until she was out of view. Today, she simply threw her head back and forged straight ahead.

Her confidence didn't begin to waver until she reached the kitchen door.

Billy was staring straight at her, his expression unreadable.

She scowled at him, and then pushed through the swinging doors, refusing to think about him or what he thought. She wasn't the girl she used to be. He'd made sure of that. So he sure as hell didn't get to have an opinion about what she was doing to reinvent herself.

Once she was safely tucked away in the kitchen, she released a long breath and closed her eyes. Rome wasn't built in a day, so she couldn't reasonably expect that she'd become someone new overnight.

"You okay?" Sydney asked.

She wasn't. Not yet. But she was definitely getting there.

"Yeah. I am."

And for the first time in years, that answer didn't feel like a lie.

CHAPTER FOUR

Jeannette glanced out the front window for the tenth time in as many minutes. Luc had called a couple hours earlier to say they would be late. There had been a car accident on Merryman's Lane and they'd needed to respond.

She had offered to reschedule, almost grateful for the reprieve. She'd had too much time to think about tonight and her nerves were completely frazzled.

Luc had refused. Telling her they would be there as soon as they could.

Jeannette had been dressed and ready to go when they'd called, even though it was an hour before they'd originally intended to arrive. She suspected Gia would have teased her for that if she'd been around. Only a nerd was ready for a date an hour ahead of time.

She glanced down at her dress, hoping they liked it. She had walked around the department store for ages before picking it out. Prior to this week, she never would've worn a dress like this in a million years. It was red—the color reminding her of the guys' truck—and short. The flared skirt ended a few inches above her knees. The top part had a deep vee, showing off more cleavage than she'd ever bared in her life.

Jeannette had paced the floor for all of twenty minutes after Luc's call, then decided fuck it. She'd gone into the kitchen and started whipping up lasagna. Cooking helped soothe her and was a welcome distraction. Once she had the lasagna in the oven, she went to work on mixing a Caesar salad, taking the time to make homemade croutons.

When Diego had called ten minutes earlier to tell her they were on the way, she asked him how they would feel about staying in for dinner. He had been delighted. He'd sounded tired, so she was glad she'd made the decision to cook.

When she saw their headlights flash against the wall, she put the garlic bread in the oven, took off her apron and went to open the front door.

Luc lifted a bottle of red wine. "We made a quick pit stop when we found out we were staying in for dinner."

She accepted the bottle. "Thanks."

Both men inhaled upon clearing the threshold.

"Oh my God, that smells good," Luc declared.

She shut the door and led them to the dining room. "Hope you don't mind me changing the plans."

Diego took the bottle of wine from her hands and set it on the table before tugging her close to him. "I don't mind at all. This way we still owe you a dinner."

"Another date? You sure you don't want to see if this one ends as disastrously as the first before you tie yourself to that?" She'd meant her words as a joke, but they'd fallen very short. Jeannette had spent too much time this week worrying about her behavior at the bar.

Diego scowled, clearly displeased. He'd made it perfectly clear he didn't like it when she put herself down. Problem was that was something she'd become very adept at over the years. "I'm sure."

The timer beeped in the kitchen.

"Saved by the bell," Luc muttered.

She grinned ruefully. "You can say that again. There's a bottle opener in that drawer," she pointed to her corner cabinet, "and glasses in the hutch above. I'll grab the food if you pour the wine."

She returned with the salad and basket of bread, then the lasagna. Diego had poured them each a glass of wine while Luc lit the candles in the center of the table.

He noticed her looking at them when she returned. "Hope you don't mind."

Jeannette shook her head, not saying what she really thought. She'd lived in her little house seven years and she'd never, not once, lit those candles. Her practical, somewhat boring dining room actually looked romantic in the soft light.

They all took their seats as Jeannette scooped both men a healthy serving of lasagna. "Hope you're hungry."

Diego picked up his fork. "Starving."

She laughed. "One of you guys needs to learn how to cook. Or at least get a girlfriend who doesn't mind feeding you."

Luc winked at her. "I thought that's what you were."

She blushed, but didn't bother to correct him. The more time she spent with these men, the more she realized she wouldn't mind applying for that position.

Jeannette took a sip of her wine, hoping the alcohol would calm her nerves a bit. She hadn't really thought through her change of plans. Sitting with Diego and Luc in the quiet, romantic room, without the buffer of other people around, wasn't something she had considered. "So you said there was a car accident?"

Diego reached for a large slice of bread. "Yeah. One vehicle. It was Billy's brother, Scott."

"Oh," she said. "Is he okay?"

Diego nodded, scowling. "He was wasted. Took out a guardrail. Evan carted him off to the drunk tank. He could have killed somebody."

Jeannette understood Diego's anger. "He obviously has a drinking problem."

"The guy's an asshole," Luc said. "He raised holy hell when Evan tried to put him in the squad car. Seemed to think Evan should let him go with a warning. Not sure how he thought he was going to get home. Front axle of his car was bent in half."

"At least he'll lose his license for a while," she said.

Diego shrugged. "Hope so, but usually guys like that don't stop driving just because they don't have a license. Was he always a jerk?"

"Yeah." Jeannette nibbled on a small piece of bread as she tried to recall what she could of Scott Mathers. "He was the typical bully, but his brand of mean only worked on the smaller, weaker kids, you know. The guys who were his size or bigger never wanted much to do with him, so he was usually alone. Only person I ever knew who saw something good in him was Billy. Scott is his older brother and Billy always swore he was a decent guy."

Diego frowned. "Wonder if Billy still feels that way?"

Jeannette shrugged. She'd felt sorry for both Mathers boys back in school. Their mom was prone to quick marriages followed by even quicker divorces. As a result, they moved around a lot. Neither boy was particularly good at making friends or perhaps they just didn't see any use in bothering.

"I've only seen Billy a few times since he's come home and we haven't really spoken." Her answer was short, succinct, and as much as she was able to say without betraying feelings she didn't want to come to light. She resented that, once again, Billy Mathers had found a way to intrude on her time with these men.

"So what else is new?" she asked, desperate for a change of topic.

Luc grinned and it became apparent he had news to share. "We passed."

"Passed?" she asked, confused for only a moment before the light went on. Her eyes widened. "Ohmigosh. That's great!"

Since Diego and Luc had arrived in town, they'd become an integral part of the tight-knit Maris community. She supposed one of the reasons the locals turned a blind eye to their wild side was because they were hard workers constantly giving back, answering fire calls, filling swimming pools, chipping in whenever someone needed a hand. They'd spent the past six months raising money for a rescue squad and studying for their Emergency Medical Technician test, so they'd be qualified to transport patients to the hospital in a neighboring town.

Luc reached down to pet Penny, who was rubbing against his leg. "Long overdue. Makes me sick to think Mrs. Stevens most likely would have survived her heart attack last year if the squad could have gotten there sooner."

Diego grimaced. "Nearest rescue squad is all the way over in Douglas. Sometimes takes them forty, forty-five minutes to get to Maris. That's too damn long."

"You're right. It is." Jeannette was impressed by their convictions. "But now we'll have you guys."

Luc lifted the wine bottle and topped up each of their glasses. "We can cut that time in half, even more depending on the address."

She thanked him for the wine, though she debated the wisdom in drinking it. She rarely drank, so she was already feeling the effects of the first glass. "It's a wonderful thing you're doing for Maris."

They continued to chat as they ate. Despite her better judgment, Jeannette finished the second glass and got started on a third.

"That was the best dinner I've had in a long time," Luc said as he scraped the last bit of pasta from his plate.

"I owed you a dinner. I never properly thanked you for saving Penny. Figure the least I could do was give you some lousy lasagna."

"That was light years away from lousy," Diego said.

Luc laughed. "You know, Penny would have gotten hungry and come down from that tree eventually on her own."

"I know, but I'd only had her a few weeks and she was still pretty skittish. I can't believe anyone would dump such a sweet cat on the side of the highway."

"That's right," Diego said. "Evan found her, didn't he?"

Jeannette nodded. "He pulled his squad car over when she

sprinted across the road in front of him. The second he opened the door, she walked up to him and rubbed against his ankles." Jeannette bent over and picked up her dear cat, petting her head as Penny purred. "She was skin and bones and full of worms. Evan asked me to adopt her because his wife, Annie, is allergic to cats. I hadn't planned on taking in a pet, but I took one look at this pretty girl and fell hard."

"Better be careful, Jeannette, or people will start calling you a crazy cat lady," Luc teased.

"You have to own three cats for that designation. I only have Penny."

"Didn't realize there was a rule about that. Good to know." Diego rose from the table and picked up his plate. Luc followed suit. She watched as they carried them to the kitchen.

She trailed behind, touched when they started loading the dishwasher. "You don't have to do that."

Luc swished the plate under the water. "Got a rule in our apartment. If you cook, you don't clean. Of course, it's never a very fair deal, considering D sucks in the kitchen. Somehow he manages to go through every pan and invariably he burns the shit out of something. I end up spending half the night scrubbing scorch marks off aluminum."

Diego walked over to the sink where Luc stood. "You're hilarious."

Luc grinned, then bumped his hip against Diego's. It was a casual touch, more playful than affectionate, but it triggered that same suspicion.

No one had ever suggested Diego and Luc were anything more than roommates and best friends. Clearly Jeannette was seeing something that wasn't there. She chalked it up to nerves and wine. "I have one of those types in my family too," she said. "I spent the better part of two hours last weekend cleaning Macie's kitchen and living room with her. Didn't have time to tackle the bedroom."

"Why were you cleaning her apartment?" Diego asked.

Jeannette shrugged. "I have no idea, other than she called and asked for my help. I was so excited she actually wanted to clean, I got in my car and headed to her place before she could change her mind."

Luc winked at her. "You know, I could use a hand cleaning my bedroom."

She narrowed her gaze, though her grin gave her away. "I'm far too smart to fall into a trap like that."

Once the dishwasher was loaded and running, Jeannette put on a pot of coffee and reached for a box of fresh-baked cookies she'd brought home from the bakery. "You guys want to hang out in the living room for a little while?" She hadn't planned anything beyond dinner.

Diego placed his hand at the base of her spine, the touch evoking a shiver she was helpless to stem. "Hanging out sounds good." From the tone of his voice and the soft stroke of his fingers against her back, she didn't need to worry about what happened next. It appeared Diego had a plan.

"I really like your dress," he murmured as they walked to the living room. "Meant to tell you that as soon as you opened the door, but the smell of dinner distracted me."

She giggled nervously. "Guess it's true what they say about the way to a man's heart."

"Food is definitely one way," Diego said as he claimed the spot next to her on the couch. She was somewhat surprised when Luc opted for a chair across the room. She'd become accustomed to being surrounded by them, their close proximity no longer spooking her.

"Just one way?" she asked Diego, trying to keep the conversation going. If they stopped talking, she suspected they'd start kissing, and she wasn't sure she would manage to keep the demons at bay once that started.

"You would have found your way into my heart even if you couldn't boil water."

As always, his compliment left her blushing, speechless.

"I want to kiss you, Jeannette."

Diego didn't move toward her. He was giving her space to say yes or no. He hadn't forgotten her behavior at Cruisers. She hated the way she'd reacted, wanting desperately to regain some of the ground she'd lost.

The wine gave her more courage than she usually possessed. Regardless, she found it impossible to reply, her throat tight. So she merely nodded.

Diego didn't give her time to reconsider. Thank God.

He reached over to pull her glasses off, placing them carefully on the end table. Then he leaned forward, gripped the back of her neck with one firm, strong hand, and tugged her toward him. Their lips met somewhere in the middle, and just like the other night on the dance floor, Diego kissed her like she meant something to him.

She had no idea so much desire could be expressed through the simple melding of mouths. His lips were soft but firm, his grip on her neck caressing while unyielding. He'd release her if she asked, but until then, he clearly didn't plan on letting her go.

She felt wonderfully possessed as he pressed her lips apart, his tongue stroking hers.

Through it all, she felt Luc's gaze on them. The idea of being watched didn't feel the slightest bit strange; rather it was a pretty major turn-on.

Diego released her after several minutes, their hot, panting breaths the only sound in the room as he pressed his forehead to hers. "Jeannette," he murmured, so reverently tears burned the back of her eyes.

Luc rose from the chair, but made no move to approach them on the couch. Like Diego, he was awaiting permission, an invitation.

She turned to face him and smiled. "Come sit with us."

It was rare to see Luc without his usual affable, goofy grin, but as he approached, his face remained serious. Like Diego, he wasn't treating this moment as a joke or a lark. His expression revealed passion and something that looked a lot like pent-up desire. They'd told her they had wanted her for a long time. She no longer questioned the veracity of that statement.

Luc joined them on the couch and she turned, moving into his embrace as if it were the most natural thing on earth. Unlike Diego, Luc didn't go straight for the kill. He was better able to curb his baser desires, intent on seducing her slowly.

He wrapped his arms around her, hugging her tightly. She pressed her face against his neck, soaking in his scent—soap, wine, a hint of garlic and some light cologne that smelled wonderful.

"You smell good," she whispered.

Luc stroked her hair gently. "I think it's a good thing we all had the garlic bread. Otherwise, you might not feel that way."

She smiled, her face still burrowed against his neck. He was warm and, despite the powerful muscles that lay beneath his skin, he was soft, his body as comfortable as her bed.

"I love the smell and taste of garlic," she confessed.

"Benefit of hooking up with a cook," Luc teased.

She lifted her head as the slightest twinge of unease appeared. Hook up? Is that where this night was headed? For the first time in too many years, there was a small part of her that hoped for that end to the evening. Sadly, the desire wasn't quite big enough to snuff out the genuine panic the thought provoked.

Luc studied her face and she decided then and there she'd never play poker with the observant men. "Not tonight," he said, in response to fears she hadn't verbalized. "Tonight we're just cuddling. Getting to know each other. Okay?"

Again, she merely nodded, feeling like a complete idiot. She wore her inexperience like a rapper flashed his bling.

Luc responded to her quiet acquiescence the same way Diego had. He took it as if it were a gift. He placed his hands on her face and his lips against hers. Jeannette felt the gentle kiss all the way to her toes, her body tingling in an unfamiliar way. She was used to heat suffusing her face with blushes, but this time it felt as if every inch of her skin was flushing, on fire.

She wasn't sure how long their lips touched, his kisses soft, exploratory, but Jeannette could have happily remained on that couch forever.

Then she felt Diego's breath on the back of her neck as he

leaned closer. He pulled her hair to the side, tucking it over her shoulder as his mouth brushed against the nape.

She shivered, but didn't try to break the union. Luc continued to kiss her, his tongue tangling with hers playfully, his fingers stroking her face reverently.

Diego's hands drifted lower as he firmly gripped her waist. He ran his lips along the back of her neck, the simple contact firing off nerve endings she didn't know existed, electrical currents shimmering along her skin, causing her to quiver.

They moved slowly. There was a deliberateness to their motions. They were very much in control, neither man swept away by the intensity of the moment. Unlike her.

She was drowning in a sea of sensation, lightheaded, breathless. Air was overrated.

Jeannette's hands had remained unmoving on Luc's shoulders throughout it all, but now they itched for more. She ran her fingers along the front of his button-down shirt. She hated the barrier, so she slipped one of the buttons free. Then another. And another.

She was moving on instinct. Impulse.

Luc pulled away when she opened the last button. His shirt hung open, allowing her an unhindered view of his perfect chest, a chiseled six-pack with only the lightest smattering of hair between his dark-brown nipples.

"Like what you see?" Diego whispered in her ear.

It was only then that she realized he'd stopped kissing her neck—and was enjoying the same peep show she was.

"Very much." Jeannette glanced over her shoulder and spied Diego's eyes resting on Luc's chest. "You like it too," she said, no question in her tone.

Diego's forehead creased as he looked at her. "Jeannette…"

She wondered if he'd deny it. She had never heard any rumors about Luc and Diego being lovers because they'd apparently never shared that part of their relationship with anyone.

She held his gaze and let the silence linger. She wanted their trust more than she could even attempt to understand.

Finally, he nodded slowly. "Very much."

She tilted her head. "Just looking?"

Diego gave her a crooked grin that lacked humor. "Going for the jugular, aren't you?"

Luc cleared his throat, clueing her in to his discomfort with the direction the conversation had taken. "Tonight isn't about us, Jeannette. It's about you."

"No," she said, "it's not. It's about us. I'll be perfectly honest with you. I have no idea where this thing between the three of us is going, or even if it can go anywhere."

Diego scowled, his lips parting to disagree.

She cut him off before he could argue. Jeannette wasn't ready to delve into her own issues, so she drove the subject back to the one thing she could handle talking about. Them.

"It doesn't bother me," she said, quickly adding more to make her meaning clear. "Your relationship with each other, I mean. It's cool."

Her quick admission caught Diego off-guard. "Our relationship?"

He was testing the waters. She didn't blame him for treading carefully. She was a master at keeping the walls in place, never revealing every card in her hand. "The two of you are together, aren't you? Like a couple."

Diego shook his head. "No. We're not a couple."

She frowned, wondering how she could have misread things so badly. "Oh, I'm sorry. I thought—"

"We're together, Jeannette," Diego continued, breezing over her apology. "Luc is my best friend. We're closer than brothers. But it doesn't work with just us. We want...we *need* more than just each other."

"You need a woman," she whispered, her mind whirling over what it would be like to belong to these two men. Her foolish, heedless heart wanted that job.

"Yeah," Luc said, drawing her attention to him. "What we have right now isn't enough. There's something... someone...missing."

Jeannette swallowed, but it was difficult since her throat had constricted.

Luc's poker face wasn't any better than hers. There wasn't a doubt in her mind that they both believed she was the missing part.

Temptation warred with reality. Jeannette was far too aware of her limitations, and while the idea of what they were offering dangled in front of her like her favorite dessert, there was no way she could go there. No fucking way.

Diego ran a gentle finger along the scowl line between her brows. "Stop thinking so hard. This isn't going to move from zero to sixty. Tonight, we're just making out on the couch. It's not going to get any more complicated than that."

A breathy snort escaped despite her unease. They had her number. Had a knack for knowing exactly what to say to make her relax. "You think making out with two guys at the same time isn't complicated?"

Luc frowned. "You don't like it?"

She shook her head. "Oh no. That's not what I mean. The kisses are..." she flushed, then admitted, "really hot. It's just kind of overwhelming."

Luc and Diego shared a glance.

The wine she'd drunk with dinner hadn't just loosened her inhibitions; it had worked some magic on her mouth too. "Can I watch the two of you kiss?"

Luc's head reared back. "What?"

"I want to watch you. The way *you* watch when Diego kisses me."

Something sparked in Luc's eyes—and in Diego's.

Anticipation combined with desire when she twisted, turned and leaned back. Jeannette remained between them, but with her back pressed against the couch, she'd provided plenty of space for the men.

It was a simple matter of Diego reaching across her for Luc. She wasn't surprised that Diego took the lead. She'd been around them long enough to recognize Diego's dominance. While Luc was far from submissive, his laid-back personality came shining through in this encounter.

She'd never seen two men kiss like this. Not once.

Jeannette hadn't known what to expect or how it might make her feel, but her reaction to the embrace shook her to her very core.

The kiss was passionate, powerful, sexy as hell.

It triggered some very serious needs inside her. Her pussy was soaking, throbbing, and her nipples tightened. She struggled to take a deep breath, the air around them thick and humid. Part of her wanted to reach down to touch herself. Sexual need pulsed so intensely it was almost painful.

Somehow she managed to refrain. Embarrassment and fear were still the more powerful feelings.

Diego's large hand wrapped around the back of Luc's neck, holding him close as their lips devoured, their tongues stroked and twice Diego nipped at Luc's lower lip, evoking a groan—maybe of pain, but also desire.

It was the most beautiful kiss she'd ever witnessed and she was content to merely watch for several minutes. Then temptation—and too much wine—prodded, compelled her to lean forward.

The men had been so intent, so focused on each other, that she was surprised they'd seen her move. As one, they turned and somehow she was engulfed in their embrace, three faces sharing the close space.

Diego kissed her deeply as Luc dragged his tongue along the side of her neck. Then it was Luc's turn, his lips on hers, while Diego used those teasing teeth to nip at her earlobe. When that kiss ended, Diego and Luc kissed each other again, but this time Jeannette refused to just observe. She placed soft kisses on Diego's cheek, then Luc's.

Over and over, they changed the pattern, explored different combinations, the kisses alternating between soft and starving, hot and gentle. Neither man sought to advance the play, their hands never drifting from her waist or her face.

She'd given them far too many hands-off signals in the past.

They were clearly kind—and leery—enough to wait for an invitation. If only she could issue one.

After a thousand years, she pulled back, leaning against the couch in an effort to find some cooler air. Perspiration was trickling along her hairline and she was lightheaded from the lack of regular breathing.

Diego and Luc followed her lead, pulling away in need of a respite.

"Wow," she murmured when she finally had enough strength to speak.

Luc grinned. "That was fucking hot."

She laughed lightly. "Yeah. It was."

Diego didn't seem to share their mirth, concern in his eyes. "You're not freaked out?"

She raised one eyebrow. "Do I look freaked out?"

Luc rolled his eyes. "Diego has trouble accepting good things. I blame his fucked-up childhood. He always seems to think everything comes with a cost."

Diego tilted his head in annoyance. "Thanks so much for the psychoanalysis, Dr. Kovach. I'll be sure to pay your receptionist on my way out."

Jeannette understood Diego's concern. Hell, she'd suffered the same fear when she'd agreed to a date with both of them. Social norms made it difficult to accept something different as anything less than wrong or offensive. Polite society didn't view ménages as anything less than kinky or weird. And while the legal tide was definitely changing in terms of homosexuality, there were still too many people in the world unwilling to accept that love didn't see gender or color or—in their case—one too many people in the embrace.

"I think what you and Luc share is beautiful. I'm so touched that you were willing to show me. To include me."

Just like that, the clouds cleared and Diego smiled. "You're too good to be true."

She snorted—the sound completely unladylike. "Yeah, right. Give it some time and I suspect you'll reconsider that comment."

Diego narrowed his gaze. "You really don't want to put yourself down in front of me, Jeannette. It pisses me off."

Though his face was dark, his tone deep, she didn't feel a speck of fear. Neither of these men would ever hurt her. The longer she was in their presence, the deeper that conviction grew.

She reached up, cupping Diego's cheek and placing a soft kiss on his lips. Unlike their previous make-out session, this was more friendly than passionate. More thanks than desire.

"Tonight was..." She couldn't find a single word that would describe what the past few hours meant to her. "Perfect" didn't even come close.

Luc nuzzled her neck, and then he slowly rose from the couch. Diego followed suit as they prepared to leave.

Luc reached down and she accepted his hand, allowing him to help her stand as well. "Tonight was just the first of many."

Jeannette leaned against the front door after they left for a long time, letting herself consider something she'd never entertained before.

A future.

One that didn't consist of just her...and her cat.

CHAPTER FIVE

Jeannette stared at the book in her hand and realized she hadn't read a word since opening the damn thing. Instead she was daydreaming about two sexy firefighters.

Nope. "Daydreaming" was too mild a description. She was fantasizing. Dirty visions that were far too graphic and explicit for her usual PG—pathetically gloomy—lifestyle. It was making her hot and bothered and nervous as hell.

A week had passed since her second date with Luc and Diego. She'd seen them every single day since then as they stopped into the restaurant for a meal...or sometimes two. They'd sit at the counter and flirt with her, and several times they'd snuck back to the kitchen when she was cooking to steal a kiss or three—much to Sydney's delight.

Her cousins enjoyed teasing her and her sudden about-face in regards to dating two men at the same time. Their joking was all done in good fun. The girls were that she was dating. She hadn't realized how much they'd worried about her until this week, when they confessed delight over her new beaus.

"Forget it," she muttered to herself, pulling off her glasses and turning off the bedside lamp. She clearly wasn't reading tonight.

She lay down, but hadn't even found a comfortable position when there was a loud crash outside.

Even through her closed eyes, she could sense the quick flash of light. Her bedroom was at the front of the house, overlooking the street. Her eyes flew open and she realized something had sparked brightly then flickered away.

Car accident? No. She'd heard no squealing tires or engines.

Her tired mind thought lightning, but she dismissed that idea too. There hadn't been a cloud in the sky all day and what she'd heard was clearly glass breaking.

"What the hell was that?" she said to Penny. Not that the cat replied. Or even moved. When Jeannette had crawled into bed an hour earlier to read, Penny had claimed her usual spot, stretched out next to her above the covers. Jeannette referred to her as her own personal purring, electric blanket.

She was about to dismiss the flash when she smelled it.

Smoke.

A second later, one of her detectors downstairs began to beep loudly.

"Shit!"

Jeannette leapt from the bed, threw on her glasses, grabbed her cell phone, and dialed 911 as she dashed downstairs. Distressed by the amount of smoke filling her living room, she rattled off her address to the operator and begged her to send someone quickly. Racing around her house, she tried to find the source of the smoke.

Nothing appeared to be on fire, but the air was now thick and hot, clogging her lungs and burning her eyes. Her heart thudded loudly from her mad dash around the house and raced with fear.

Crossing the kitchen, she started to open the door that connected her house to the garage, but she reared back as she touched the blistering doorknob. She'd found her fire.

Sirens sounded in the distance, but they were too far away to offer much hope. She knew enough about fire to keep the door between the garage and kitchen closed, but she was filled with the need to find some way to douse the flames before her whole house was consumed.

"Oh my God," she cried out into the empty room as the blaze started to creep beneath the door. The words cost her and she coughed. She needed to get the hell out.

She darted back through the house in a panic. Should she put on clothes? Should she try to save some of her stuff?

Both thoughts vanished when she remembered Penny.

"Penny!" She yelled out for the cat, terror racing though her. She needed to find her kitty. She recalled the cat coming downstairs with her, but she'd lost sight of her after that. Jeannette dashed around the living room, coughing, her vision blurred by tears produced by the thick smoke. Crawling on her hands and knees, she looked under a cabinet in the corner. It was one of Penny's favorite hidey-holes and places to sleep. She thought she saw something move beneath, but it was too hard to tell in the dark.

The sirens were right outside now, but Jeannette didn't rise. She had to get Penny first.

"Penny," she choked out, her throat seizing, tight and sore. The bright lights of the fire truck brightened the room enough that she spotted Penny. The terrified cat burrowed deeper under the cabinet as the room was painted in an array of orange and red light from the fire. The blaze had reached the house and was spreading fast.

A loud bang distracted her as she glanced toward the front door. A firefighter in full regalia stood there. Jeannette wasn't sure how she knew who it was, the man's face was hidden behind the visor of his helmet, but she yelled out, "Diego!"

He spotted her in the corner and rushed over. "Goddammit, Jeannette. You have to get out of here."

"Penny!" she cried, not rising from the floor even though her lungs felt as if they were about to burst.

"Jesus Christ. Get her out of here!"

She looked around Diego to find Luc there as well.

Diego reached down to pick her up off the floor. She put up a fight, determined she wasn't leaving the house without Penny. "No!"

"I'll get the cat," Luc said. "Go!"

She stopped resisting. Her struggles hadn't done her any good anyway. Diego was strong as an ox and focused on getting her out of the house.

"Penny," she said between coughs. "Please. Penny."

"He'll get her, Jeannette. It'll be okay." Diego didn't stop carrying her until they reached the fire truck. Then he opened the front door and placed her on the passenger seat. He'd clearly thought to keep her warm in the vehicle. It was early spring and the night was more than a little chilly. Not that she could feel any of that, thanks to the bonfire raging nearby. She was sweating, her skin flushed. It felt as if she'd gotten a sunburn.

She belatedly realized she was only wearing a t-shirt and panties. In normal circumstances she would have been mortified, but these weren't normal circumstances.

She couldn't stop coughing and her hands shook roughly as she continued to call out for Penny.

"She's here," she heard Luc say and then, just like that, her cat was in her arms. She turned to thank him, but neither man remained. The passenger door was closed, sealing her and Penny inside, as Diego and Luc quickly joined the four volunteer fire-fighters who had pulled the hoses from the truck and begun to shoot powerful jets of water at her house.

For the first time since she'd seen the flash, the magnitude of what was happening washed over her. She'd been so focused on Penny, she hadn't even looked at the house. Now, she couldn't look away as flames erupted from the downstairs windows, which were shattered, gone.

A police car arrived, squealing its brakes as it slammed to a stop in front of the truck. Evan jumped out of the car and ran toward Diego. He stopped halfway across the yard when Diego pointed back toward the truck where she sat, and her cousin changed direction.

He opened the passenger door and reached in for her. Penny

was still in her arms, but the cat darted over to the driver's side as Evan grasped Jeannette and tugged her toward him.

"God, Nettie. When I heard your name and address come across the scanner…"

She wrapped her arms around him, grateful for the comfort. "I'm okay, Evan." However, speaking those few words cost her and she began to cough again.

"I'm taking you to the hospital."

She shook her head. "No. I'm fine. I don't want to leave."

Evan took a step away, clearly intent on arguing, but the words died on his lips when she turned back to her house. The blaze had lost some of its intensity, but she didn't need to be told she'd just lost everything. Whatever hadn't burned was going to be completely damaged by water and smoke.

Her gaze landed on Diego and Luc as they held the huge hose, working like the devil to save something that was already gone. Then she looked over to see Penny curled up on the driver's seat. The cat wasn't sleeping. Her eyes were wide, spooked. Jeannette reached over to stroke her soft fur. "It's okay now, Penny."

Luc and Diego had saved the most important thing. She was grateful for that. More than she'd ever be able to say. This silly, sweet cat had been the only thing keeping her from complete loneliness. Losing her would have been unbearable.

"You'll come home with me tonight," Evan said.

"No. Annie's allergic to cats."

Evan rolled his eyes. "Jesus, Nettie. She's not going to care about that. She'll take a Benadryl. You can stay with us as long as you need."

She considered the invitation. She was tired and numb. Her brain clearly wasn't firing on all cylinders and yet she knew she wouldn't go home with Evan.

"No. Thank you."

Evan fell silent for a moment. "Then I'll take you to Macie's."

Jeannette snorted. "Yeah. That's not happening either."

Diego and Luc returned to the truck, standing next to Evan. The fire was out for the most part, only smoldering ashes remaining. Her neighbors had come out of their houses in robes, standing on the sidewalk, looking equal parts shell-shocked and relieved. At least the flames hadn't claimed any of their homes, though Jeannette suspected the houses on either side would suffer a bit of damage from the heat and smoke.

The other volunteer firefighters had begun to roll up the hoses. Diego took off his helmet, the concern on his face not quite penetrating the shell that had slowly closed around her. She suspected she looked a lot like Penny right now, wide-eyed, confused, terrified. She found herself focusing on superficial stuff, like her neighbors' attire and the acrid smell of the smoke rising from the charred embers of her house.

Evan was still determined to get Jeannette away from the scene. "Fine. I'll take you to Uncle George's house."

She shook her head. "Not going there either."

Evan was trying to be gentle, but she could read the frustration her continual refusals sparked. "Where do you want to go?"

She didn't have a clue. Something inside her had cracked, splintered. She'd spent a lifetime nestled in the loving arms of her family. Buying this little house had been her first act of independence. Years had gone into making it her perfect refuge, a sanctuary, painting the walls, sewing the curtains, even sanding and refinishing the hardwood floors all by herself. Without it, she felt completely lost. "I don't know," she finally admitted.

Evan's forehead creased as he studied her face more closely. He clasped her hand. It wasn't until he touched her that she realized she wasn't hot anymore.

"You're freezing. Are you sure you don't want me to take you to the hospital?"

He thought she was in shock. Hell, maybe she was. But that didn't change the fact she wasn't going to the hospital.

"You're coming home with us," Diego said. He didn't ask, didn't offer. Simply proclaimed.

And Jeannette realized he was right. She was.

"Okay."

Evan frowned, unhappy with the plan. "What? No. Hell no."

Luc's face darkened. "What do you mean, 'hell no'? Jeannette is our friend and she needs a place to stay."

Evan shook his head. "She also has a thousand and twelve relatives who all live within spittin' distance. She has plenty of options."

"She's also sitting right here," she said sardonically, her voice tight and sore. It hurt to talk. Regardless, she plowed on. "And she's going home with Diego and Luc."

"Are you sure?" Evan asked.

Jeannette nodded. She didn't know why that invitation appealed to her while the others didn't. Perhaps because she'd just had her entire life uprooted. She longed for some sense of safety, security. It was something she'd spent a long time looking for. Lately, she thought she'd found it. With Diego and Luc. But she couldn't say all of that to her cousin, so she simply said, "Because I want to."

Clearly Evan could see she wasn't going to be reasonable, so he tried to appeal to Luc and Diego. "Listen, I appreciate the offer. And I'm grateful to you guys for all you've done here tonight, but—"

Diego crossed his arms. "But nothing. She's accepted our offer, so it's settled. Jeannette will stay with us for as long as she wants."

Any normal man would take one look at the fire flashing in Diego's eyes and back down. Of course, her cousin wasn't normal. The alpha dogs had come out and it looked as though it would be a fight to the death.

"Evan," she interjected, reaching for her cousin's arm when he took a step toward Diego. "Please. I'm cold and I'm tired and I just want to go to sleep. I'll be fine with Diego and Luc, and you know it."

While Jeannette was confident she would be well cared for, Evan looked far from convinced. Of course, knowing her older cousin, he was thinking of her virtue rather than her comfort.

Instead of continuing the fight in front of her, he jerked his head to the left and the three men stepped away from the truck.

While they were out of earshot, she could tell from Evan's face he was issuing a warning. She wanted to laugh at her cousin's attempts at protecting her. God, if he only knew how much breath he was wasting on that effort. Despite her unending fantasies of late, Evan's knight-in-shining-armor imitation was nothing compared to the walls she'd built around herself. She was in absolutely no danger in a sexual sense.

She wasn't sure what Diego and Luc said in reply, but their words must have worked. Evan's shoulders relaxed and he nodded. Then he returned to the fire truck. "I'm going to wait for the fire marshal, see if we can determine how this fire started. I'll talk to the neighbors to see if they saw anything. Luc and Diego will take you back to their place now."

She smiled weakly. "Thanks, Evan. For everything."

He pulled her into his arms for another bear hug, but the warmth of it didn't permeate her icy skin. It seemed ironic that she'd just escaped red-hot flames, yet she felt as if someone had dumped a bucket of ice water over her head.

"I'll call you in the morning."

She frowned. "I don't have my phone."

Evan sighed heavily. "I'll call Diego then. I'm glad you're okay." He gave her a quick kiss on the cheek, and then walked over to the other volunteers who were still cleaning up the equipment.

"Don't you guys need to stick around to help?" she asked.

"No." Luc lifted his hand to wave to the other men. "They can handle this. Let's get you back to our place."

***

Jeannette lay in Diego's bed, staring at the ceiling. She listened to the shower running as someone else rattled around in the kitchen down the hall. For years, she'd lived in a silent house. It felt strange to be here now, surrounded by sounds of life.

Penny climbed up on the bed, roaming around the unfamiliar space for a few minutes before finding a comfortable place near

Jeannette's feet. Within seconds, the small cat was purring, her eyes closed, sleeping peacefully.

"Oh, to be a cat."

Jeannette shivered and burrowed deeper under the blankets, wishing she could get warm. Part of her blamed the chill on the fact she'd been sitting outside in nothing but a t-shirt and panties the past couple of hours. The realistic part knew better. She was in shock.

I just lost everything.

She forced herself to think the words. Tried to make them soak in. The cold, hard truth was going to be there in the morning, so it was pointless to pretend otherwise.

Her thoughts whirled over the possessions that were now nothing more than ash. Her comfy couch and ottoman, the handmade quilt Aunt Louise had given her when she'd moved out, her computer, her autographed copy of *Outlander*, her parents' wedding album.

The moment she recalled the lost photos, a quiet sob escaped.

The door she'd left open just a crack, so Penny could make her way to the makeshift litter box Diego had put together for her, slid open.

Luc walked in, his hair still wet from the shower. She hadn't heard the water shut off. He'd thrown on lounge pants but his chest was bare.

"Jeannette." He padded across the room and sat on the edge of the bed. "You okay, angel?"

She swallowed against the lump in her throat, trying desperately to fight back the tears. It was a battle she couldn't win. Jeannette sat up slowly and shook her head.

With that, the floodgates opened as she fell into Luc's arms. He was there to catch her, hugging her tightly as she cried. She wasn't sure when Diego came into the room, but her sobs grew louder when he crawled onto the bed behind her, his hands stroking her hair.

"It's all gone," she choked out. "Everything."

"I know," Luc whispered, placing a soft kiss on the top of her head. "I know."

None of them said anything else as she mourned for all that she'd lost in a barrage of unending tears. Every time she managed to calm down, another precious possession would cross her mind and she'd fall apart again. Luc and Diego simply held her tighter until the painful sobs subsided. Time passed like the ebb and flow of waves crashing on the shore, fluctuating between gentle, soothing rocking and soul-shattering agony.

When the last tears evaporated, exhaustion and numbness took their place.

Luc released her, his large hand cupping her face. "You need to sleep."

She nodded slowly, letting them guide her down onto the mattress, plumping the pillow beneath her and tucking her in as if she were a child suffering a terrifying nightmare. The description seemed to fit.

They started to rise from the bed and she felt their absence instantly.

"Will you stay with me?"

Neither man hesitated. Luc crawled under the covers, tugging the blanket up to their necks as Diego leaned over to kiss her cheek. "Keep this side warm for me. I just need to get a shower."

She could smell the smoke on him. It was nearly three a.m. He and Luc had to be done in. Yet they didn't hesitate to take care of her, to give her what she needed. A place to stay, a litter box, consolation.

"Hurry back," she whispered.

He cupped her face, his thumb gently stroking her still-wet cheek, then he walked to the bathroom.

Luc wrapped his arm around her neck and tucked her against his firm chest. She hadn't expected it to make such a comfortable pillow. But there was no denying the warmth and quiet, steady beat of his heart lulled her into deep, dreamless sleep in a way her soft down pillow never had.

She didn't remember Diego coming back to the bed, but he

was there when she opened her eyes several hours later. Surprisingly, finding him there allowed her to close her eyes and fall back to sleep without any uneasy or sad thoughts creeping in to keep her awake.

They surrounded her, providing her with a sense of peace and wellbeing that went all the way to her bones. And she wasn't cold anymore.

CHAPTER SIX

Diego woke to a banging on the door that came far too early for his late night. Jeannette didn't stir. He wasn't surprised. It had been well after three before any of them had fallen asleep.

Luc rose clumsily, only half awake when his feet hit the floor. Diego stood as well. The knocking continued. Whoever was on the other side of the door clearly wasn't leaving.

Neither he nor Luc bothered to don shirts as they stumbled down the hall.

"It's eight o'clock in the goddamn morning. This better be an emergency or I may hurt this person," Luc said when they reached the front door.

They didn't have time to say hello before Macie, Sydney and Gia stormed into the house.

"Where is she?" Macie asked.

Clearly they'd gotten the news about the fire at Jeannette's house.

"She's asleep," Diego responded, his voice still gruff from lack of use and exhaustion.

"Is she okay?" Gia asked.

Luc nodded. His previous annoyance appeared to be gone.

Like Diego, he understood and appreciated their concern. "Yeah. I think it's going to take a little while for it to all sink in."

Macie's usual cheerful countenance was gone, replaced by a combination of worry and anger. "Do you know how the fire started?"

Diego had his suspicions, but he wasn't going to voice them to Jeannette's cousins and sister, especially not Macie, who looked ready to commit murder depending on his answer.

He shook his head. "No. We'll head over there this morning. And I'll put in a call to the fire marshal. He came out last night and poked around with Evan, though I'm not how much they could discover in the dark. It could have been anything, really. Faulty wiring or..."

Diego let the suppositions die there. Last night as they rode from her house to theirs, Jeannette said she'd heard something crash and then a bright flash of light. The fire had started in the garage. There had been too many arson fires lately for his mind not to lead him there. He prayed that answer was wrong, because it wouldn't be Macie committing a crime if that proved to be the case.

Diego felt Luc's gaze on him and knew his friend had the same suspicions he did.

"Paige and Lacy are out collecting clothes from our aunts and friends," Gia said. "In the meantime, we thought we'd take her to Uncle George and Aunt Stella's. They're getting her old room ready right now. It was really nice of you guys to take her in last night."

Diego understood her family would want to take her in, but he hoped to convince Jeannette to stay with them.

"Can we see her?" Sydney asked.

Luc frowned. "She's only gotten a few hours of sleep."

"We won't wake her," Gia was quick to interject. "I just want to see that she's okay."

Diego pointed down the hallway. "She's sleeping in my room."

Mercifully, none of them asked where *he* had slept. The three women walked down the hall quietly, and then peered into his bedroom. He and Luc followed.

Jeannette was lying on her side, facing the door, dead to the world. Penny lay curled up next to her, the cat's loud purring filling the room.

"Thank God you saved Penny," Gia whispered. "I don't know what Nettie would have done..." Her voice trailed off and it was obvious she was fighting back tears.

Luc reached out to take her hand, squeezing it kindly. "Jeannette is fine, Gia. Your sister is tough as nails. She's going to get through this. She has her cat, her family and..."

"And you guys," Gia finished for him, perfectly aware of what Luc had planned to say.

"Yeah. She has us," Diego confirmed.

Macie smiled. "Both of you?"

Luc laughed quietly. "Fishing, Mace?"

Jeannette's outrageous cousin didn't even feign pretense. "I'm just wondering what exactly it is Nettie has in you guys. Friendship or..."

"We're not falling into that trap," Diego said, crossing his arms. "We're offering whatever Jeannette is comfortable accepting."

Macie gave him a shit-eating grin. "Gotta admit I like the sound of that. Although I'm afraid Jeannette won't take full advantage of all the special features, bells and whistles."

Diego rolled his eyes. "We're not luxury cars, you lunatic. Do me a favor. Tell Paige to wait a few hours before delivering the clothes. I'd like Jeannette to sleep a lot longer. And hold off on the guest-room plans. Jeannette is welcome to stay here as long as she wants."

"But we're her family," Gia said.

"I know that." Diego didn't bother to say more. Apparently he didn't need to. All three women smiled, and then followed them back to the living room. They said goodbye, promising to return later in the afternoon when Jeannette was awake.

Luc closed the door and leaned against it. "Back to bed or breakfast?"

Diego rubbed his eyes as his stomach grumbled. "I'm equal parts hungry and tired. You decide."

Luc laughed, then headed for the kitchen. "I feel like bacon."

"You always feel like bacon."

Only a few minutes passed before they heard footsteps in the hallway, then Jeannette's sleepy face peering into the kitchen. "Smells good."

Diego reached out his hand, delighted when Jeannette took it without hesitation. She was much less skittish around them. He didn't release her until he'd tugged her into his arms completely, wrapping her up in a big bear hug. Her arms looped his waist and she sighed against his bare chest. "You okay?"

She nodded slowly. "Just feel sort of numb and groggy."

"You didn't get enough sleep. What do you say we eat a little bit, then crawl back into bed for a few more hours?"

"I'm supposed to work the dinner shift."

Luc rolled his eyes. "Jesus, Jeannette. I think your family can cover for you tonight. Your sister, Sydney and Macie were just here. Said they'll be back this afternoon with some clothes."

Jeannette slowly pulled away from Diego. "Shit. I forgot about clothes." She looked down at her bare legs peeking out beneath the t-shirt she had borrowed from Luc. Her shirt had reeked of smoke. "Guess I can't go to work like this."

She walked over to the kitchen table and dropped down heavily. "What the fuck am I going to do now?"

Luc took the pan of bacon off the burner before crossing the room. He knelt before her, taking her hand in his. "You're going to take it one day at a time. We'll do all the shit that needs to be done together and we're not going to let it overwhelm you. Today, we'll call the insurance company and get you some pretty new things to wear. Just those two things. Then tomorrow, we'll do a couple more things. And eventually, it'll all be okay."

She considered his list. "Alright. I can do that."

Luc smiled as he rose, leaning down to give her a quick,

friendly kiss on the cheek. Diego suspected that had been his friend's only intention, but Jeannette turned at the last second, her lips meeting Luc's.

The platonic-kiss plan evaporated in an instant. Instead, Luc grasped the back of Jeannette's head, his fingers threading through her hair as he held her in place for a much different kind of kiss. Their lips parted. Diego could just make out the hungry touch of their tongues. Jeannette's hands had been white-knuckling the seat of the chair, but as the kiss grew hotter, her fingers rose to Luc's arms, digging into muscle instead.

Diego made no move to join them, spellbound by the pure intensity of the moment. The shyness, the wariness that typically wrapped itself around Jeannette had vanished. Diego wasn't surprised. She'd lost everything last night. Desperation had her reaching out for anything she could lay her hands on.

Luc seemed to come to the same conclusion. His friend slowed the kiss, turning the heat down incrementally. Then he stood upright. It took a few seconds for the haze to clear, for Jeannette's focus to return.

"Why did you stop?" she asked.

"Because you're tired and upset and not thinking this through. I don't take advantage of women in weak moments."

She bit her lower lip. "I sort of wish you would. I wouldn't mind feeling something right now."

She glanced away from Luc, capturing Diego's eye. It took a bit of work for Diego to control his features, to keep his look stern. She was obviously hoping he'd be more susceptible to what she was offering and her sweet innocence made him want to grin. "Don't look at me," he said with a no-nonsense tone.

She threw up her hands. "You guys have been trying to seduce me for weeks—no, strike that. Years. Now, when I'm ready for what you're offering, you—"

"No." Diego cut her off gently. "You're not ready. You're hoping to escape, to forget. I understand that, Jeannette. But believe me, after the deed was done, you'd regret it. And you'd resent us for doing it."

"No, I wouldn't."

She looked so earnest, Diego couldn't resist touching her.

He pulled her up from the chair and cupped her cheeks in his hands, forcing her to hold his gaze. "I want you more than I've ever wanted any woman in my life. We're going to make love to you, Jeannette. We're going to take you to our bed and bury ourselves in that sweet, sexy body of yours. Over and over. That's inevitable. But it's not going to happen today. Not like this."

She closed her eyes and released a long breath. "I'm sorry. God, you're right. This isn't me. I don't throw myself at guys." She tugged away from him. Diego let her go with some reluctance. "I'm fucked-up, aren't I?"

Luc wrapped his arm around her neck, placing a quick kiss on her forehead. "You're not fucked-up. You're running on empty. That's all. Lucky for you, I have the cure."

She gave Luc an appreciative smile. "What's that?"

"Bacon. It makes everything better."

She laughed. "I can't disagree with that. You're right. It does."

The tightness that had been pressing on Diego's chest at her distress loosened. Leave it to Luc to dispel a tense moment with humor. It was one of the reasons he loved his best friend so much. Diego was always too serious. Luc never let him get away with that.

Luc returned to the stove and finished cooking the meat before splitting up the pound of bacon between three plates. Then he carried them to the table.

Jeannette giggled. "Just bacon?"

Luc shrugged. "I've never gotten the hang of cooking eggs."

"How about toast? That's not very complicated."

Diego got a kick out of watching her tease Luc.

"Burn it too."

"Wow. I'm starting to understand why you spend so much time at the restaurant. Part of me thinks I should offer to give you guys cooking lessons, but I'm not going to."

"Why not?" Luc asked.

"Because I'm afraid you might get the hang of it and stop coming to see me."

Luc grinned. "Careful, angel. That sounds a hell of a lot like flirting. You keep that up and we might start thinking you like us."

Her smile didn't fade, though it became a bit more serious. "I like you." Though she spoke very softly, the words more breath than sound, neither he nor Luc missed it.

Before Diego could respond, there was another knock on the door. "Dammit. It's like Grand Central Station here this morning."

Jeannette gave them a rueful smile. "I have a very big family."

"Yeah. I'm starting to understand just how big." Diego walked to the front door, Jeannette and Luc following.

Evan stood on the stoop. "Hey. You guys got a minute?"

Diego moved aside to allow Evan to enter. He saw the flash of a scowl when he discovered Jeannette standing there in nothing but a t-shirt, surrounded by he and Luc, both shirtless. He could imagine what was going through Evan's mind.

Luckily Jeannette's cousin was out of uniform, no gun in sight.

Luc gestured toward a chair in the living room. Evan took it as Jeannette sank down onto the couch. Diego joined her, while Luc stood nearby.

"Just got back from your house, Nettie. It was too dark to really determine anything about what caused the fire last night, so Chuck agreed to meet me this morning at first light."

Diego appreciated the fire marshal's kindness and willingness to get to the bottom of this so quickly. Chuck Kingston was a decent guy. Like Diego and Luc, he wasn't a lifetime Maris resident. He'd moved to town only a few years earlier after falling in love with and marrying a local lady, Gladys Harper.

"What did you come up with?" Luc asked.

Evan glanced at Jeannette. "Chuck's still there, digging around, but he thinks he found something that indicates arson."

Jeannette didn't move, didn't give the slightest inclination she'd even heard.

On the other hand, Luc was reacting enough for all of them. He exploded. "Goddammit! I knew it!"

Diego felt the same rage as his friend, though his anger turned inwards, heating his blood until it boiled. Neither he nor Luc said what they were really thinking. Jeannette could have been killed in that fire. She could have died.

Whoever was starting all these fires had crossed a very serious line from arsonist to attempted murderer.

Diego relaxed a bit when he saw the same cold determination to catch the motherfucker in Evan's gaze. Jeannette's cousin wouldn't rest until the criminal was made accountable for the crime.

Evan looked at Jeannette. "Can you walk me through what happened last night? How did you know the house was on fire?"

The shattered look in her eyes gutted Diego. Then Jeannette closed them, cleared her throat, and described the events in a steady, emotionless voice. "I'd just turned off the light to go to sleep when I heard a loud crash and saw a bright flash. I thought it was lightning or a storm or something. I was about to dismiss it when I smelled smoke and my detector started beeping. I ran through the house looking for the fire. When I got to the kitchen, I realized it was in the garage."

Evan's face turned to stone and Diego realized her story must have confirmed Chuck's suspicion.

"I'd called 911 immediately, so that was when I started looking for Penny." Her voice cracked when she said her cat's name, revealing the first trace of the horror she'd experienced.

Diego reached out and took her hand in his, squeezing it gently. She gave him an appreciative smile.

"Why would someone want to burn my house down?" she asked Evan. "I don't have any enemies."

"I don't know why, Jeannette," Evan said. "But you can be damn sure I'm going to figure it out."

"The house is—" she started before her voice gave out.

Evan didn't need to hear anything more. "It's a complete loss. I'm sorry. Jesus. I'm so fucking sorry."

Evan rose and reached out to her. Jeannette stood too and stepped into her older cousin's comforting arms, though no tears fell. It was as if she'd cried them all out the night before.

After several moments, Evan released her. "I'm going back to look around some more and to confer with Chuck about what you heard and saw. I'll let you know the second we find anything out."

She smiled. "Thanks, Evan."

"Aunt Stella is fixing up your old bedroom for you and the girls are running around getting you some clothes and toiletries and stuff."

Jeannette nodded. "I heard."

Diego swallowed heavily, hoping he could convince her to remain here over returning to her family's home. He felt better having her close. The idea of not being with her as she tried to deal with the aftermath of the fire bothered him more than he could say.

Luc had fallen quiet after his outburst, but there was no mistaking the anger radiating from his every pore. For now, his friend appeared to have managed to rein it in. Diego suspected that unlike himself, Luc would remain calm from now on. While Diego's temper was more like a simmering boil, Luc's flashed hot and fast before dying down just as quickly.

Evan saw himself out as the three of them struggled to deal with the information they'd just received.

"You okay?" Diego asked her after the door closed.

She started to nod, then changed direction, shaking her head. "I feel like I've been punched in the stomach."

It made sense. Someone had purposely tried to hurt her. Jeannette had spent her entire life surrounded by a loving family in a safe, friendly, small-town environment. Now that trust and comfort had been ripped away from her. Diego's heart ached. He couldn't look at her standing there so broken, so alone.

He reached for her, tugging her into his embrace. He wasn't surprised when Luc joined them, adding his own strength and warmth to the hug. The three of them remained there for several minutes, wrapped around each other.

"Stay here with us, Jeannette," Luc whispered. "Please."

"Okay." She didn't demur, didn't bother to pretend that she wanted to be anywhere else. For the first time since Evan had dropped his bomb, Diego felt capable of taking a deep breath. Jeannette began to go limp in their arms, her strength fading fast.

Diego was the first to step away, though it killed him to let her go. "Why don't you go back to bed, angel? Try to sleep and forget about all this shit for a few hours."

"I'd like to forget. Will you guys stay with me?"

Luc placed a comforting kiss to the top of her head. "Always."

CHAPTER SEVEN

Jeannette stirred, her eyes opening slowly, taking in the dark room. Since the fire, she hadn't managed to sleep without waking up several times each night, panic gripping her. The first few nights, she'd jerked awake roughly, crying out, her actions rousing Diego and Luc, who would hold her until she fell asleep again.

Tonight's panic attack was a quiet one. Her heart raced and a sharp pain pierced her chest. She hated feeling like this. Hated the utter desolation that swallowed her whole in the middle of the night. Hated that the things that never seemed bad during the daytime were completely unbearable at this hour. She tried to remind herself of that, but it didn't help.

Glancing to each side, she found her slumbering boyfriends. She'd given up pretending they were in the friend zone a few days ago. After all, they'd been living together for two weeks. They hadn't consummated the relationship or even really discussed the possibility of it, much to her relief. The idea of sex on top of everything else had the potential to push her over the edge.

True to their word, neither man pushed the issue. Instead, they offered only warm hugs, soft kisses and comforting words.

The night of the fire, she never would have imagined she'd be in their house fourteen days later. Initially she'd been numb and stressed out and not thinking clearly. Now, her thoughts were less jumbled, more coherent. And yet she was still here.

It had taken several days to convince each and every member of her family—sans Macie, who had been absolutely delighted by her current living situation—that she was fine at Diego and Luc's, and not budging.

But regardless of their kindness and their willingness to have her stay, it was time she started figuring out her next move. She couldn't keep sleepwalking through every day.

She'd gone on autopilot, moving through her days sluggishly—spending the time at work, filling out the mountain of paperwork associated with her insurance claim, replacing items she couldn't live without, like her phone, and hanging out with Luc and Diego. She hadn't returned to her house. Evan had told her there was nothing there to salvage. She didn't need to see a pile of ashes, didn't need to confirm it with her own eyes. She'd seen the destruction the night of the fire and it had torn her apart. She wasn't about to relive that anguish. If she stayed here, she could simply pretend everything was normal.

Evan and Chuck had declared the fire a result of arson. Apparently, someone had lobbed a Molotov cocktail at her garage. The device had crashed through one of the windows on her old garage door rather than smashing against the wood and landing outside. Whoever threw it had to have been close and on foot in order to get it inside. It landed next to and ignited a small gas can she used to fill up her lawn mower, which added enough fuel to produce a large, extremely hot fire that spread fast.

After Evan's explanation, she'd made some halfhearted joke about the jig being up and her secret life as a mobster revealed. It hadn't fooled anyone into thinking she was okay. Evan had been working day and night to catch the arsonist, while Luc and Diego had gone into full-time guard duty. They worked when she did and as soon as her shift was over, they were there to pick her up, never leaving her side until they dropped her off the next day.

She sat up slowly, trying to find some cool air, hoping it would calm her overwrought nerves. Sleeping between two giants some-times made her feel like newly molded clay placed in a kiln. She hadn't had five minutes to herself in two weeks. If she hadn't been so afraid, it probably would have bothered her. After all, she had lived alone most of her adult life.

However, the idea that there was someone out there who wanted to hurt her had taken root and, despite her belief that she was an independent, self-reliant woman, she'd clung to Luc and Diego as if they were a life preserver keeping her from drowning in the ocean.

"Jeannette? You okay?" Diego's quiet question caused Luc to rouse as well.

"Sorry. Didn't mean to wake you."

"Bad dream?" Luc asked.

She shook her head. "No. Just...same shit, different night."

"Another panic attack." Diego's words weren't a question. This wasn't new territory for any of them.

"Maybe I should start sleeping in Luc's bedroom. I hate that I'm constantly waking you guys up." She'd made the suggestion before.

Diego instantly rejected it, as always. "No. You're staying here with us and that's it."

She had become accustomed to his domineering comments. Every now and then, she'd call him on one; get after him for attempting to be so heavy-handed. Diego would apologize and try to rein it in, even though she knew it rubbed against the grain. He was a powerful man with the need to take control. Her situation was difficult for him because he couldn't fix what was wrong. She loved him for trying, so she cut him some slack when he started calling the shots.

She blew out an exasperated breath. "God. I'm so sick of feeling like this. It's like I'm stuck in fucking quicksand. I just want out."

Luc tugged on her shoulder, drawing her back down onto the bed. "Maybe you need some distraction."

She started to ask him what he had in mind, but the question was answered by his kiss. Unlike the gentle, platonic busses he'd offered lately, this one left no doubt in her mind what type of distraction he meant.

That thought was the last rational one she had as she let herself be swept away by Luc's kisses. She felt the bed shift next to her and, though her eyes were closed, she was aware of Diego moving closer. The second Luc released her, Diego was there, claiming his own kisses.

Jeannette offered no resistance. She had grown used to their touches, their close proximity. The fears that had consumed her in the past seemed a distant memory. For the first time in far too long, she felt a definite flicker of some pretty serious arousal.

Diego must have sensed her acquiescence. His hands drifted beneath her shirt, finding her breasts. They'd treated her with nothing but kid gloves since the beginning, so Diego's rough touch caught her unaware. He gripped one of her breasts with a firm hand and squeezed. She groaned against his mouth, the sound encouraging him. With strong fingers, he found her taut nipple, pinching it in a way that sent a lightning bolt of electricity straight to her pussy.

She gasped, then clenched her legs together tightly, trying to contain, to control the bone-shaking need ravaging her body.

What the hell was happening to her?

Diego continued to wreak havoc on her breasts and lips and, despite her best efforts, she couldn't still the steady thumping between her legs, no matter how hard she pressed them together.

Then, that effort was halted when Luc's hand drifted to her knee. She tried to resist his effort to tug her thighs apart, but he was stronger than her and her heart wasn't really in to keeping him out.

Like Diego, he wasted no time burrowing his fingers underneath her clothing. She turned her head away from Diego, gasping for air. She couldn't breathe. Her heart was racing once more, but suddenly she didn't mind the pounding beat.

Diego didn't attempt to reclaim her lips. Instead, he moved on, kissing her cheek, nipping at her earlobe, and then sucking gently on her neck as he continued to play with her nipples.

Jeannette's hips jerked roughly when Luc's finger grazed her clit. It had been a light touch, but the impact of it shook her hard.

Diego's lips left her neck and he studied her face. She was powerless to shield her emotions. Luc stroked her clit again, applying more force this time.

She cried out loudly. "Oh my God."

She could feel both men looking at her. Somewhere deep inside, she wondered why she wasn't embarrassed, wasn't uneasy with that intense scrutiny.

"Touch her again, Luc."

Jeannette sucked in a breath and held it, anticipating what the next touch would do to her. She was in a foreign country, looking at a landscape she'd never, ever seen before. It was beautiful.

"Please," she whispered. The words were a desperate plea, but she didn't have a clue what she was asking for.

Luc found her clit once more. This time it was no hit-and-run. He rubbed the sensitive flesh, took the distended nub and pinched it lightly. He worked that tiny place until her hips were rising, seeking more stimulation.

She was on the precipice of something that felt like the world's most powerful panic attack, yet this wasn't something she wanted to go away.

As Luc continued to stroke her clit with his wicked fingers, Diego held her gaze, forced her eyes to remain on his. Her eyelids started to slide shut, but he shook his head, his face determined, so strong. "Don't look away."

His tone was deep, commanding, sexy as fuck. Somehow the sound melded with Luc's touches and she disintegrated.

One minute she was static electricity, the next she was weightless, floating. The feeling was pure magic.

Until it wasn't.

As her orgasm started to waver, Luc upped the ante. Too much. He slid one finger inside her...

Ice water rushed through her veins, tamping out any fires still flickering after her climax. She jerked awkwardly, sitting up and sliding away from him until her back was pressed tightly against the headboard.

Her quick retreat startled both of them.

Jeannette was mortified by her behavior, but her head was swimming in a sea of utter terror and *Ohmyfuckinggod, that orgasm rocked*. The pieces didn't fit together. Not even close.

Diego narrowed his eyes and for a moment, she saw awareness.

No no no. Jesus. No.

"Wow," she said, forcing a lighthearted lilt to her tone. It fooled no one, but she forged on anyway. "That was...just wow. That was some serious distraction."

Diego scowled and Luc was visibly upset. Clearly he thought he'd hurt her. Or scared her. Which he had. Not that she was going to admit it.

"Can I ask you guys for something?" She was desperate to provide a bit of distraction herself.

Luc nodded. "You can ask us for anything."

For weeks, she'd studied Luc and Diego together, recalling the night she had watched them kiss. On nights when she struggled to find sleep, it was that image, that memory that soothed her, that helped her find peace.

"You haven't..." She swallowed heavily, trying to find the courage to give a voice to her thoughts.

"Haven't what?" Diego prodded.

"You haven't kissed each other or touched or..." There was no way she could say the last word.

She didn't need to. Diego wasn't shy. "Fucked?"

She nodded.

Diego gave her an exasperated look as Luc shook his head and said, "Jesus, Jeannette. Do you honestly think we can't control those impulses? You've been the victim of a crime. All that matters right now is you."

Now that Jeannette had managed to turn the focus away from

her foolish reaction, she realized there was something else she wanted. "I want to watch you."

Luc frowned. "You what?"

"I want to watch you. Together."

Luc's mouth opened then closed like a gaping fish. However, Diego appeared less surprised, less averse to the request.

"You want to watch me fuck Luc." It wasn't a question, though it certainly answered one of hers. Diego was the giver and Luc was the taker. No real surprise there.

"Is that how it usually works?" she asked.

Luc's eyes rolled toward the ceiling. "Are we seriously having this conversation?"

Again, Diego didn't hesitate. "Yes. That's how it works."

"Can you...? Would you...?"

Diego moved closer to her. She was still pressed tightly against the headboard, the position leaving her absolutely no room for retreat. He placed his palms against the smooth surface on either side of her head, but he didn't touch her.

"You're sure this is what you want?"

She nodded slowly.

"Fine. Tonight you get a reprieve. But I don't want you to think you've escaped. You're hiding something from us, Jeannette."

"I don't know what—"

He placed one finger on her lips. "You can keep your secret one more night. But tomorrow we're going to ask you for the truth. I hope you'll give it to us."

Jeannette didn't respond, didn't even bat an eye. She couldn't. She'd kept her personal hell buried too deep for too long. She wasn't sure she could give them what they wanted.

Diego didn't wait for her to answer. Instead, he turned around, gripped Luc by the neck and pulled him close for a kiss that was achingly beautiful.

Every conscious thought, all her anxiety, melted away as Jeannette watched Luc and Diego kiss. While it was apparent Diego was the more dominant of the two, Luc was by no means submissive. Both men made demands and concessions. They took and they gave. It was hot, incredible.

The kissing lasted longer than she would have expected. In her mind, she'd always assumed that guys weren't into foreplay. She pictured every guy on the planet with a Wham, Bam, Thank you, Ma'am mentality. At least that was how it had played out in her ridiculously limited experience. Guys undressed and fucked with reckless abandon. Everything was done simply for their own personal pleasure.

That wasn't how it was playing out between Luc and Diego. Their kisses, their touches were all designed to bring each other pleasure. Luc broke the union of their lips and leaned down, digging his teeth into Diego's pec. The bite looked painful to Jeannette, but the expression on Diego's face told a different story. Luc clearly knew what his lover liked and he was giving it to him.

Diego's working knowledge of Luc was just as vast. Diego reached for his friend's cock, cupping it through the thin layer of Luc's pajama pants, evoking a deep, hungry groan. Neither man held back anything.

At one point, they were gasping, their foreheads resting against each other's. Diego surprised her by speaking to her, not Luc.

"I swear to God, this is the last time, Jeannette."

"What?" she asked, her voice hoarse, throaty. Like the men, she was struggling to regulate her own breathing. The air in the room was thick, humid, heavy.

"The next time Luc and I are together, you're going to be with us. A part of this. It doesn't work without you."

Strangely, she didn't feel as if she was separated from them. If anything, she was in the midst of it all. Her body was tingling, her pussy wet. Maybe they weren't touching her, but damn if she didn't feel as though they were. She needed Diego to understand that. "I'm right here."

Both men turned to look at her and she saw awareness dawn.

"Jesus," Luc muttered. "You feel it, don't you? Everything."

She nodded.

Diego's eyes had grown darker, black than the darkest night. "Take off your clothes, Jeannette."

She hesitated. It was the wrong thing to do.

Diego's dominance reared.

"Goddammit. We're not going to touch you. But you're not going to be some passive observer either. Take off that fucking t-shirt. And the panties. I want to see you."

She'd never been naked in front of them. Hell, she actually couldn't recall the last time she'd been naked in front of anyone. It had been years.

Despite that, she found her hands drifting to the hem of her shirt, almost of their own volition. The material felt like a sexual caress as she drew the soft cotton over her head. Then she shifted to her knees and slid her panties down. Both pieces of clothing hit the floor in a quiet swish.

Neither man moved as she undressed, their eyes glued to body. Luc's nostrils flared as once more, his breathing accelerated.

"Beautiful," Luc murmured.

Diego didn't speak, but his gaze told her everything. He liked what he saw. He wanted her.

In the past, the sort of passionate, desire-filled looks she saw in their eyes would have terrified Jeannette. Tonight, they only fueled her own hunger.

"Don't stop," she finally prodded when Diego's hand fell away from Luc's cock.

Diego stood from the bed. "No one's stopping." With that reassurance, he gripped the elastic of his lounge pants and tugged them down.

Her mouth went dry as she got her first unobstructed view of his cock. "Oh fuck," she muttered, panting heavily. Here came the fear.

"Jeannette." Diego said her name loudly, firmly. "Listen to me," he added when she started to tremble. "We're not going to touch you tonight, angel. You have our promise on that."

Simple functions seemed to fail her. Her eyes had gone dry

from her sudden inability to blink, her lungs burned from a lack of air and her lips were actually numb.

"Do you hear me?" he repeated.

Somehow she found the strength to nod.

"Do you want us to go on?" Luc asked quietly.

She was tired of being paralyzed by fear. So she pushed the terror down, deep. She wanted this more than she wanted to escape. "I do."

Luc moved very slowly as he stood as well. No doubt he hadn't forgotten how he'd spooked her earlier. She forced herself to take a deep, steadying breath.

"I'm okay, Luc." Her tone sounded stronger than she felt, but it seemed to set the men's minds at ease.

Luc stripped off his pants, but he didn't give her much time to study what he'd unveiled. Clearly he didn't want her to panic again.

He reached out for Diego, who met him halfway. They stood at the foot of the bed, the kissing resuming. Both of them were holding, caressing, stroking each other's cocks. She was overwhelmed by the strength, the speed of their actions.

To her novice eye, it looked almost aggressive, rough, painful. Yet, they continued to groan and beg each other for more.

Diego reached the breaking point first. He broke off the kiss and turned Luc away from him, pressing on his lover's shoulders until Luc was bent over the end of the bed.

Jeannette still sat propped against the headboard. Luc's new position left his head close to her feet.

"Open your legs, Jeannette," Diego instructed.

This time, though the request was just as intimidating and frightening, she didn't hesitate to obey.

She spread her legs apart, perfectly aware that both men had a bird's-eye view of the whole kit and caboodle.

"Fuck me." Luc breathed out the words on a long sigh.

She started to grin, but was distracted when Diego walked to the side of the bed and opened the nightstand drawer. After he'd retrieved a tube of lubrication and a condom, he returned to his place at the foot of the bed, directly behind Luc.

The two had clearly been lovers a long time. Neither of them issued instructions or wavered. They knew their way around all of this. Diego squeezed the lube onto Luc's ass, working it in with his fingers. Luc's eyes drifted closed, his face the picture of utter bliss.

Once more, Diego took his time, used his fingers to drive his lover crazy while drawing out the anticipation, the moment. After several minutes, Jeannette began to feel, to share, Luc's impatience.

"Goddammit, D. Fuck me. Please."

Diego gave no indication that he'd heard. Instead, he said, "Jeannette."

Jeannette had been so spellbound by Luc's face, by the fast, deep motions of Diego's fingers, she hadn't looked up at him in several minutes.

Her gaze lifted.

"I'm going to fuck Luc now."

She nodded. "Yes," she whispered.

"I want you to touch yourself while I do it. Rub that pretty little clit just like Luc did earlier."

The second Diego issued the command, she felt the unbearable need to do just that. She wasn't much for masturbation. Jesus. She wasn't much for anything. For years, she'd simply thought of herself as asexual. She'd accepted that as fact and moved on.

The ache between her legs proved that theory wrong. Dead wrong.

Diego donned the condom, then placed the head of his cock at Luc's ass. However, he made no move to push in. His eyes rested firmly on her.

He was waiting for her to do as he'd instructed. Her hands shook slightly as she lifted them. Luc and Diego watched her actions.

With one finger she stroked her clit, the delicate touch incredibly powerful.

"Ah," she cried. Then, unwilling to resist, she moved in for more. Her touches became less tentative, faster. She applied more pressure and suddenly understood that rough didn't equate to pain. It meant pleasure. So much fucking pleasure.

Despite the waves of warmth gushing over her, through her, Jeannette didn't miss it when Diego tightened his grip on Luc's hips and slowly pushed his cock inside.

Luc wasn't a quiet lover. As Diego pumped his dick harder, faster, Luc's words mingled with sounds of the men's flesh slapping together and the cries Jeannette couldn't hold back as she moved her fingers over her tingling, pulsing clit.

"God, D. Yeah. Right there. Fucking right there." Luc pressed his forehead against the mattress for a moment before looking up at her. "You're so wet, Jeannette. Next time I'm going put my mouth on that pretty pussy of yours. Going to drive my tongue into all that sweet warmth."

Jeannette imagined Luc's lips on her clit and her arousal grew. His words felt like voodoo, a magic spell. She was so damn close to coming.

That last orgasm—her first ever—had taken her by surprise. This one was building slowly. She knew where she was going this time and she couldn't wait to get there.

"Can't. Stop." Luc beat his fist on the mattress as his climax raced toward him.

Diego didn't offer his lover a reprieve, didn't slow down his relentless, powerful pace. His fingers dug deeper into Luc's hips as he used his grip to drag him back.

Luc was the first of them to fall over. His voice was thick, hoarse as he cried out his release. Jeannette watched his reaction with wonder, then her gaze met Diego's.

Sometimes she felt as if she could get lost in Diego's eyes. The two of them continued their strokes—Diego's cock pounding into Luc's ass as her fingers flew over her clit. She recognized the moment Diego started to lose control. The image fired her own orgasm and she lost the ability to hold Diego's gaze. Her eyes drifted closed as lightning struck.

She was a trembling, sweaty mess, lying in a fetal position at the top of the bed when she finally drifted back down to earth. Luc was still facedown over the mattress and for a moment, she thought he was asleep. Diego had withdrawn from his friend's body and disposed of the condom somewhere. He was sitting on the edge of the bed. Luc chuckled when Diego slapped his ass.

Jeannette felt a bit like laughing herself. She'd spent the last couple of weeks in a haze, wondering if she'd ever manage to feel alive again. Then she reconsidered the timeline.

She'd been sleepwalking since the day her parents died.

Since the day Billy took her virginity.

She choked back a sob, unwilling to let the men see her sudden distress as a flood of painful memories crashed down on her head. She had thought there was peace in forgetting.

She'd been wrong.

Luc and Diego had taken her out of the dim coolness of her cocoon and exposed her pale, naked flesh to the bright sunshine.

There was no way she wasn't going to get burned.

CHAPTER EIGHT

Morning came too soon. Jeannette closed her eyes more tightly in an attempt to block out the sunlight streaming through the window. Diego had promised a day of reckoning. Today.

She owed these men the truth. They'd earned her trust, offered her friendship, a shoulder to cry on and a place to stay. More than that, they'd never given up on her and her unique brand of crazy.

No one in her life had ever looked beyond the surface or tried to find something more inside her until Luc and Diego.

Despite all of that, she was going to fuck this up. Going to shut them out because that was the only way she could keep her sanity in check. And they were going to resent that silence and leave. The ending to this twisted love story had been written before they'd made it past page one. She'd been a stupid fool to even entertain the hope that it could end another way.

She tried to escape the bed without waking Luc and Diego. Both men had dropped off to sleep almost immediately after last night's lovemaking.

Jeannette still couldn't believe the intensity, the beauty of what they'd done. Luc and Diego had opened her eyes to all that she had missed, all that she'd given up as she'd searched for safety.

She had just reached the edge of the bed when Luc rolled over and looked at her. "Mornin', angel."

She smiled at their pet name for her. Sure, it was a simple, common term of endearment, but it was the only nickname anyone had ever given her besides that damn Nervous Nettie one. She much preferred to be called angel.

"How about some breakfast?"

Luc perked up at the mention of food, but Diego didn't take the bait, didn't let her escape so easily.

Diego patted the mattress. "Why don't you come back to bed? I think we have a few things to talk about first."

Jeannette's stomach lurched. "I'm sort of hungry." It was a lie. She suspected any food she put in her mouth right now would taste like sawdust.

Diego sat up, determination rife in the lines on his face. "Jeannette, baby. You can't keep running away from us whenever things get too serious for you."

Actually, she could. She was a better escape artist than Harry Houdini. She feigned an easy-going grin and tried to minimalize the situation. "I'm only *running* to the kitchen, Diego. It's not like I'm packing a bag and racing off to Aruba or anything."

Luc didn't bother to intercede or join the debate. Regardless, she knew he was in Diego's camp. Both men wanted to know why she'd pulled away from them last night and it didn't look like they were going to give her any more byes.

"Please." With just one word, Diego managed to cut her to the core.

It was on the tip of her tongue to ask for more time, but she couldn't. She'd spent years trying to get these words out. They still wouldn't come. Wouldn't form or take shape.

She even opened her mouth just to see if any sound would come out. She thought the words in her head, over and over. Willing them to be heard.

Sex scares me.

Sex hurts.

And then she forced herself to think the truth.

He raped me.

She closed her eyes against the last, trying to drive it out once more. Neither man spoke as she had this entire insane conversation in her head. When she lifted her eyelids, she saw the concern on Luc's face. He was worried about her.

However, Diego's expression registered something more. Awareness. And anger.

Before she could respond to any of it, there was a knock on the door.

None of them moved. A few moments passed. Then the knock came again. This time, whatever spell they'd been under broke.

She stood slowly and tugged on the new pajamas and robe Macie had given her. Luc rose as well and pulled on his lounge pants.

Diego was the last to move. He threw on his pants, then headed out of the room with great reluctance. The three of them had just reached the living room when there was another knock. Diego halted at the front door, making no move to open it.

"This conversation isn't over, Jeannette."

"I know." Her reprieve would be short-lived. Maybe somewhere between now and the moment of truth, she'd find a way to speak over the roaring in her ears.

Diego answered the door, and then stepped aside as Evan and Tyson entered.

"Does anyone in the Sparks family own a clock?" Diego asked. "Because I have to tell you, where I'm from, nobody knocks on anyone else's door at this time of the morning unless it's an emergency."

Evan scowled, but Tyson chuckled. "The Sparks family is sort of prone to drama, so basically everything is an emergency."

Tyson stepped over and gave her a quick kiss on the cheek. "Morning, sleepyhead."

She grinned. "Why aren't you and Evan at the restaurant for your morning coffee?"

Tyson shrugged. "We started there, but a couple of things came up and we decided to move our morning meeting over here."

Tyson and Evan had a standing Thursday breakfast date at the restaurant. A tradition they'd upheld for years. Whatever had prompted them to break the routine clearly must've fallen into Diego's emergency column.

"What's up?" she asked.

"Any chance I can talk to you alone first?" Tyson asked quietly.

Now her curiosity was piqued. "Sure." She started to lead him to the kitchen, but Tyson placed his hand on her back and propelled her farther down the hall. Luc and Diego's house wasn't big. It was a small rancher positioned right next door to the fire-house. The house was part of their benefits package. As the only two full-time firefighters, they needed to be close to the station. To keep up the appearance of platonic roommates, they each had a bedroom, though Diego's was the only room that was used for sleep. Luc's doubled as an office, so Jeannette took Tyson there.

She tilted her head when he closed the door behind them.

"What's going on, Ty?"

"Before I say this, I'm just going to say I'm here at Macie and Sydney's request."

"Um...okay?" God. This couldn't be good. Tyson actually looked like he was blushing. Her cousin never got ruffled or embarrassed.

"And I only agreed because they assured me of two things. One, you wouldn't ask for this on your own and two, you might actually really want it."

She frowned. "What is it?"

Tyson walked over to the desk and opened the backpack he was carrying. When he turned around, she spotted the needle in his hand.

"A shot?" She tried to keep the alarm from her voice. She really hated getting shots. And Tyson knew it.

"It's birth control."

"Oh," Jeannette replied, flames licking her cheeks.

"I'm not trying to pry into your personal life and I don't want to know about your sex life. I *really* don't want to know about it," he stressed. "But the fact is you're living with two guys right now and...shit. This was a mistake. If it had just been Macie asking, I swear to God, I would have ignored her, but Sydney..."

He didn't finish the sentence. It wasn't necessary. They both knew Sydney would never make such a request lightly. He started to put the shot away.

"Wait." She raised her hand. "Give it to me."

"Seriously?" he asked.

She nodded. "Yeah."

Her unflappable cousin actually blushed. "Well, good."

She laughed. "Good?"

He shrugged. "I like Diego and Luc. And birth control is a smart way to go. I figure it's better than my dad's advice for safe sex."

"I'm afraid to ask. What did Uncle George say to you?"

Tyson lifted one shoulder. "Dad just looked at me and said, 'Son, if you're gonna tap it, wrap it,' then he handed me a couple condoms and walked away."

She giggled. "Oh my God. I think that would have traumatized me."

"Yeah. I should probably be in therapy."

Jeannette gritted his teeth as he walked closer. "I hate shots."

He rolled his eyes. "Yeah. I know. You're a big baby about it. Thought I was going to have to get my nurse to restrain you so I could give you that tetanus shot last year when you cut your foot on a nail at Evan's boat dock. Close your eyes and it'll be over with in no time."

She loved Tyson—for doing things that made him uncomfortable, for taking care of her, for being a completely cool guy.

Tyson had been nineteen and away at college when Jeannette's parents died. She'd actually been given his room, which meant Tyson had been relegated to sleeping on the pullout couch in the living room when he came home for visits. He'd never complained, never made her feel as if she was an imposition. When they were younger, he had always been her older, fun-loving, constantly teasing cousin, but once she moved in, he took on the role of big brother too.

"Thanks, Tyson."

Tyson laughed. "Just do me a favor. Don't tell Macie she was right. She's unbearable when she's right. Shove that robe off your arm and lift your sleeve."

She did as he asked, looking away and holding her breath as the needle pierced her skin. Once he'd given her the shot, Tyson slapped a Band-Aid on.

She rolled her eyes as she glanced at the sore spot and saw the colorful Band-Aid. "SpongeBob?"

Tyson winked mischievously. Then he lifted his hand to reveal yet another surprise.

A loud burst of laughter filled the room as he gave her a lollipop. She took it from him, and then tugged her robe back on. "Thanks."

"Anytime." Tyson put a cap on the used needle and tucked it back into his backpack. "For what it's worth, I'm glad you're here with Diego and Luc. I never liked you living in that house alone."

"I wasn't alone. I had Penny."

When he looked at her again, Jeannette was surprised to see such seriousness on his face. Tyson was rarely without a friendly smile. "I know things were hard for you after Uncle Doug and Aunt Katie died. Sixteen is a shitty age to lose your folks."

She shrugged. "Any age is shitty."

He nodded in agreement. "Sometimes I think having a big loving family is a curse."

Jeannette frowned. "What are you talking about?"

"I'm just saying we did a disservice to you, Jeannette."

She didn't agree. Hell, she didn't even understand. "How?"

"We let you retreat into your shell because we didn't want you to hurt anymore. We made excuses for your quiet nature. Said you needed time to get over your folks. Then, as more time went by, we stopped attributing your isolation to grief. We called it shyness. All we've ever wanted was to make sure you felt safe, felt our acceptance. Instead, what we did was leave you to deal with everything alone."

Crying wasn't an unusual occurrence for Jeannette these days. In fact, she had shed tears every single day since her house had burned down. The emotions she'd always been so good at suppressing weren't so easily contained anymore and they seemed to sneak up on her at odd, random times.

She swallowed hard against the thick lump in her throat, but she didn't bother to stem or hide the tears sliding down her cheeks. "You're wrong," she said, when she could finally force her voice to work. "I pushed you all away. If I'd reached out, even just once, and asked for help, you would have been there for me. I know that. None of this was your fault. It was mine."

Tyson shook his head, and then he reached out to hug her. As she soaked up the warmth of his embrace, she realized how many people had held her just like this in the past few weeks. Her cousins, her aunts and uncles, patrons in the restaurant, Luc and Diego. She'd been offered a million hugs and a ton of support. For most of her life, she'd thought of herself as being alone. She realized now she'd never been alone. Not once.

When Tyson released her, she didn't feel the pervasive heaviness that had been pressing down on her lately anymore. She felt...lighter. She wasn't entirely familiar with the concept, but she'd almost describe herself as carefree.

Tyson tilted his head and gave her a curious look. God only knew what he was thinking. "What's that goofy smile about?"

His description made her laugh. "I have no idea."

Tyson reached up and ruffled her hair the way he used to do when they were kids. She tried to push him away and for a minute it was like she was twelve again, her fifteen-year-old cousin Tyson trying to dunk her in the pool as they tussled and laughed.

"Truce," Tyson declared at last. "We better get back out to the living room. Evan has a lead in the case he wants to talk to you about. He's not the most patient of people these days."

Jeannette knew exactly what Tyson meant. "He's just determined to figure out who's setting the fires."

"Yeah. I know. I don't think he's slept more than a few hours at a time since the fire at your house. He's worried as hell. We all are."

She'd suffered that same terror right after the fire marshal had said arson, but she didn't feel quite as frightened these days. In fact, she felt safer than she had in a very long time.

Jeannette walked to the door. "Then let's see if we can put the clues together and catch the asshole."

Luc glanced down the hall when he heard the door to his bedroom open. Tyson and Jeannette were smiling when they returned to the living room. Luc found it difficult to take his eyes off the pure, unadulterated joy in her eyes. A quick glance to the right confirmed Diego was as spellbound by it as he was. Luc wasn't sure he'd ever seen Jeannette so happy.

What the hell did Tyson say to her?

Evan stood from the couch as they entered the room. "Finally."

He'd said he had some new information regarding the case, but he wouldn't say more than that, determined to wait until Jeannette returned so they could discuss it together.

Jeannette perched herself on the arm of the chair where Diego was sitting. "Tyson said you have a lead."

"Yeah. I was in the restaurant last night after my shift. Uncle TJ and Macie were working, holding court like they do."

Luc grinned. The fruit hadn't fallen far from the tree. Macie was as big a character as her dad. They were born storytellers with amazing memories. It wasn't unusual for quite a few regulars to make their way into Sparks for dessert and coffee or a beer, just to hang out with those two for a little while. He and Diego were guilty of doing just that more than a few times themselves.

"Jasper was there," Evan continued.

"Oh, he's back in town?" Jeannette asked. "How's Violet

doing? And the new baby? I've been meaning to send a gift, but I haven't had a chance with everything that's going on around here."

Jasper Bush was one of Jeannette's favorite neighbors and he had just become a first-time grandfather. He'd spoken of little else except the pending arrival of the baby since his daughter, Violet, announced she was pregnant. Violet had married and moved to San Antonio, and TJ had actually started a betting pool at the restaurant on how long it would take Jasper, a widower, to put his house on the market and move to be closer to the baby. Luc had money on two months and three weeks.

"For God's sake, everybody is fine," Evan said, somewhat impatiently. Luc suddenly spotted the dark circles under Evan's eyes. It didn't look like he'd been sleeping very well. Luc sympathized, but didn't care for the way Evan was talking to Jeannette. His tone couldn't be described as anything less that churlish, which was not normal for her typically kind cousin.

For a second, it looked as though Diego would call Evan on it, but then Evan said, "Sorry for snapping, Jeannette."

"It's okay," she said with a sweet smile. "I think it's safe to say we're all tired."

Evan nodded, but he wasn't deterred from the topic at hand. "Anyway, we were just sitting there, having a piece of apple pie, when the subject turned to you."

"Me?" Jeannette said. "Still? You would think people would be tired of rehashing the gory details of the fire."

Evan shook his head. "It's not the fire that has their tongues wagging. It's your current living situation."

"Oh."

Luc grinned at her carefree tone. He suspected that just a month ago, Jeannette would have been mortified to be the topic of such conversation. Nowadays, she didn't appear to give a shit.

Progress.

Evan studied her face and Luc could see that her nonchalance had taken her cousin by surprise too. Regardless, he continued with his story. "Jasper said he'd thought you had taken back up with Billy."

"Why would he think that?" Diego asked.

"Because he'd seen Roy's old truck sitting outside your house a couple of days before the fire."

"*What?*" Jeannette's face paled right before their eyes. Diego reached out and grasped her hand.

"You weren't home at the time, but Jasper just figured Billy was waiting for you to get off from work. Then Violet called to say she was in labor and he headed to San Antonio. I didn't question him about the fire because I knew he'd been out of town that night. I should have questioned him."

Luc could hear the guilt in Evan's voice, but Jeannette was clearly too preoccupied by the information he'd just dropped. "He saw *Billy* sitting outside my house?"

Evan shook his head. "I asked him that. He said it was definitely Roy's truck, but he never saw Billy's face. Just the back of his head. But he was pretty sure it was Billy just the same."

"That doesn't make any sense," she muttered. Despite her words, Luc wasn't so certain Jeannette was convinced of that.

Diego looked at Jeannette. "Was it a bad breakup? Did the two of you fight?"

The happiness that Luc had seen in her face only moments before had completely vanished and Jeannette's walls reappeared. She was an expert at building those fucking things.

"No. He just moved away."

Luc didn't need to glance at Diego to know his friend didn't believe that any more than he did. There was something in Jeannette's tone that told him whatever it was she was hiding from them, it had to do with Billy.

"I went around to Roy's house last night," Evan said.

Jeannette looked genuinely dismayed. "What? Why?"

Evan's brows furrowed. "What do you mean *why*? To question Billy. He's a suspect now."

Luc couldn't look away from Jeannette as she assimilated that fact. He hated always feeling in the dark with her. He was head over heels in love with the woman. Couldn't she see that?

"What did he say?" Jeannette's voice, like her face, had gone blank. She was a master at hiding her emotions.

"He wasn't there. Apparently his mother took a tumble down a couple of stairs and broke her foot. He's been in Oklahoma with her for a couple weeks."

"Roy tell you that?" Diego asked.

Evan shook his head. "No. Scott did. He stuck around to take care of Roy, while Billy went to care for their mom."

"Poor Roy," Jeannette muttered.

Evan shrugged. "Scott's actually not such a bad guy when he's sober, which he was last night. He was pretty helpful and obviously worried about his uncle. But damn if he isn't one mean-ass drunk."

"Did you take a look at Roy's truck?" Luc asked.

"No," Evan said. "Billy drove it to Oklahoma."

Diego stood, suddenly angry. "So if there was any evidence in the thing, he's had plenty of time to get rid of it."

Luc agreed. "Timeline on this fits, Evan."

"Yeah, I know." Luc was relieved to see Evan was on the same page they were.

"Timeline?" Jeannette asked.

"The fires started after Billy came back to town. And there haven't been any more since your house because he's been in Oklahoma. Did you take a look at the guy's criminal record?" Luc asked Evan.

Evan grimaced. "I've got a call into the state police. The ancient computer at the station finally gave up the fight to live a few days ago. Replacement doesn't come in until the day after tomorrow."

Luc never ceased to be amazed by the difference between big-city law enforcement and this small-town, Andy-Griffith style. He didn't know how Evan managed to do such good work with such limited resources.

Diego walked over to the window, his fingers tapping out an

angry rhythm against the glass. "You realize that 'mom falling' thing could be a lie and Billy skipped town."

Evan sank down on the couch with a long sigh. "I know, but I don't have enough evidence to justify putting out an APB on him."

"So we just have to sit here and hope that he comes back?" Luc asked hotly.

Evan nodded, defeat rife on his face. "Yeah."

The conversation died. Luc glanced over at Jeannette, who'd gone quiet. His heart ached at the desolation in her eyes. Luc longed for some way to put the happiness he'd just seen back on her face.

Tyson was the first to break the silence. "I think you guys are missing the point. You've spent two weeks looking for a lead and coming up empty. Today, you've got a place to start, something to dig your teeth into. Wait for the police report, Evan. Maybe there will be something in there that will help. Not all hope is lost, you know."

Luc appreciated Tyson's pep talk. Luc had always considered himself a glass-half-full guy, but he'd let his frustration get the better of him. Time to—like Tyson said—start focusing on the positive.

Jeannette was here with them and even though things were still touch-and-go, Luc felt like it was more touch than go. It gave him hope.

"You're right, Tyson," Luc said, when none of the others in the room reacted. "We're going to catch the asshole. We're the good guys, the Avengers. They always win in the end."

Luc was delighted when his joke put a grin back on Jeannette's face. "The Avengers, huh? Think pretty highly of yourself, don't you?"

Tyson laughed. "If we're the Avengers, I get to be Tony Stark. Iron Man is damn cool."

Evan rolled his eyes. "In what world are you Iron Man? If anybody is Iron Man, it's me. Tell him Jeannette."

Jeannette laughed. "Don't look at me. I'm the only girl in the room, which means I'm stuck with Black Widow."

Luc watched the three cousins continue to fight over which superheroes they wanted to be for a few minutes.

"God," Jeannette said at last. "The more things change, the more they stay the same. I seem to recall the two of you waging similar battles when we were kids. Back then it was a fight over who got to be Han Solo and who was stuck with Luke Skywalker."

Luc tried to imagine what it would have been like to grow up in the Sparks family. He'd been the only child of a workaholic mother. He'd been a latchkey kid from the time he was eight, which he was pretty sure had been illegal. How cool would it have been to have a whole gang of siblings and cousins to play with?

"Come on, Ty," Evan said at last. "I want to get back to the office to see if the state police have returned my call."

Tyson moved toward the front door with his cousin. "I'll see you guys soon." Then he gave Jeannette a quick wink and the two of them left.

As soon as the door closed, Diego turned to Jeannette. "What happened between you and Billy?"

Luc closed his eyes and sighed. His best friend had a bad habit of going for the jugular. While the rest of them had managed to shake off their concerns for a moment, Diego clearly had not.

Jeannette bit her lower lip. "I told you." The answer was succinct and drowning in stubbornness.

Before Diego made things even worse, Luc decided to call a time-out. "Aren't you supposed to be at work soon, Jeannette?"

Jeannette glanced at the clock and gasped. "Shit. Yeah. I was supposed to be there fifteen minutes ago." She dashed down the hallway to dress. She hadn't been out of their line of sight more than two seconds before Diego turned on him.

"What the fuck was that?"

Luc raised his hand. "You're going to have to give her some time to take in everything we just found out."

"You know as well as I do she's hiding something from us. Hell, from everybody."

Luc ran his hand through his hair, and then rubbed a palm over his stubbly face. "Yeah. I do. And I also know she's not ready to talk about it. You're gonna have to let her come to us on her own, D. You can't bully her into telling you a damn thing. You keep pushing her on this and you're going to push her away."

"So I'm just supposed to pretend that nothing's wrong?"

Luc nodded. "For now. I think that's exactly what we have to do."

Diego started to say something more, but Jeannette reappeared, dressed in her Sparks BBQ t-shirt and a tight pair of jeans that triggered a slew of dirty fantasies in Luc's mind.

She could tell they'd been fighting. "Listen," she started, "I know we still have a lot of things to talk about, but—"

Luc cut her off. "Not now, Jeannette. You're late for work. We've got lots of time to figure this all out. Weeks, months, years."

She grinned. "Years?"

There wasn't a drop of fear in her voice. It made Luc feel like a million bucks.

"Years," Diego replied, obviously as pleased as he was. Diego walked over to Jeannette, cupped her face and kissed her. "Sorry," he mumbled against her lips.

"Me too," she whispered.

Diego's hands dropped to her upper arms. "What's this?"

Luc watched him lift the sleeve of her shirt to reveal the Band-Aid.

"SpongeBob?" Luc asked with a chuckle.

At the same time Diego said, "Did you hurt yourself?"

Jeannette flushed. Luc was addicted to her innocent blushes. Sometimes the devil in him had him saying naughty things just to provoke that pretty color.

"Tyson gave me a shot." Her answer was vague at best.

"What kind of shot?" Diego asked.

She looked down, clearly embarrassed. "Birth control."

Luc's cock went from limp noodle to steel rod in two-point-seven seconds. "Oh, hell yeah."

She laughed. "You guys are incorrigible. And I'm really late for work." She offered them both a quick kiss on the cheek before darting out the door.

It wasn't until they heard her start the old car her Uncle Ronnie had loaned her, since hers had burned in the fire, that they realized they let her go without them.

"Shit. We usually drive her," Luc muttered.

Diego nodded. "I know. But it's not all that easy to walk with a boner the size of the Washington Monument in your pants."

Luc grimaced. "I feel your pain, brother. I *really* feel it."

CHAPTER NINE

J eannette ran a comb through her hair as she padded down the hallway to the bedroom she currently shared with Diego and Luc. It was funny how little time it had taken for this house to feel like her home. Diego had cleared out half of the closet and most of the drawers, making sure she had plenty of room for all her new things. Luc and Diego had emptied an entire shelf in the bathroom closet and bought a shower caddy to hold her shampoo and body wash. They'd made room on the desk for her new laptop and given her free rein to reorganize the whole kitchen to her liking.

And Penny had the run of the place. Sometimes Jeannette felt as if her cat had deserted her in favor of the guys. The shameless hussy was always rubbing against their legs, begging for treats, and it wasn't unusual for Jeannette to find Penny purring on either Luc's or Diego's lap as they watched hockey on TV.

She'd only gotten home from the restaurant an hour earlier. The place had been ridiculously busy after a tour bus had come through, so they'd been packed with tourists *and* regulars. Luc had taken one look at her tired face and run her a hot bath as Diego poured her a glass of wine.

A girl could get used to that kind of pampering.

Upon entering the bedroom, she found both guys in bed, her spot in the middle just waiting for her. Diego was reading a book, while Luc was playing some game on his phone. Both nighttime rituals were pretty standard.

"Feel better?" Luc asked.

"Yeah. Just tired. It was a long day." She'd anticipated Diego immediately bringing up the subject she had managed to dodge, so she was surprised when he simply pulled back the covers and patted the mattress.

"We kept your spot warm."

She grinned as she took off her robe and placed her glasses on the nightstand. Then, before she could talk herself out of it, she stripped off her pajamas as well. Her actions weren't lost on either man.

Last night was the first time they'd seen each other completely naked. The door had been opened and Jeannette couldn't see any reason to close it again. She wanted to lay next to them with nothing between them.

No clothing. No secrets.

Both men were watching as she crawled onto the bed. No one bothered to pull up the quilt. Instead, they kept their view of her body unconcealed.

Luc and Diego wasted no time in shifting closer. Luc gave her a soft kiss that soon turned into a scorcher. His hand drifted along her waist, caressing her sensitive skin.

From the corner of her eye, she could see Diego watching them. He'd propped himself up on his side, ensuring he saw everything.

Every now and then, the slightest trace of unease crept in, but Jeannette pushed it down. She wanted this. She had to find a way.

When Luc's hand brushed her pussy, she gasped and forced herself to hold still. She felt both men studying her reactions. She worked overtime to keep her face impassive.

Luc continued to kiss her, to stroke her body. There were very few places he didn't touch as Diego simply observed.

Then, Diego reached for her. As she twisted to face her other lover, Luc snuggled closer to her back, his hand wrapping around her to grip her breast as he kissed the nape of her neck.

She sucked in a calming breath as she tried to accept his closeness, hoping Luc couldn't feel her tensing up.

Diego was still looking at her, but she had her poker face firmly in place.

He ran his fingers along her cheek. "You're so beautiful, angel." He punctuated the compliment with the sweetest kiss she'd ever gotten from Diego. She was used to his passionate, hungry touches. God, she loved them. But she found this gentle side of his just as irresistible.

Jeannette relaxed.

Luc's chest was pressed to her back, his hand lightly caressing her breast, but the lethargic, lusty haze evaporated when he shifted closer, his erection brushing against her ass, through the material of his lounge pants. At the same time, Diego's hand found its way to her pussy.

She sighed with pleasure when the tip of his finger stroked her clit. She recalled touching herself there last night as Diego fucked Luc's ass. For such a small thing, that little button packed a wallop.

Diego pressed harder. She thrust her hips closer, wanting more of that magical touch.

"God, angel," Diego murmured when she began to move against him faster. Between Diego's wicked fingers and the constant nudge of Luc's covered cock against her ass, she couldn't decide which sensation was hotter.

Luc's hand left her breast, reaching down to cup her knee. He lifted her leg, guiding it over Diego's waist. The new position left her open, the cool air no match for the heat pulsing from her pussy.

Diego still stroked her clit, as Luc's hand caressed the cheek of her ass.

Jeannette felt as if she were floating on a cloud.

It took little more than one touch to send her plummeting back to reality.

On the next forward thrust of her hips, Diego moved his fingers, one of them penetrating her wet opening, gliding inside and straight to the hilt.

She gasped, then reared away, clamoring over Luc, tumbling off the mattress and crab crawling backwards along the floor until she hit the wall roughly.

Both men sat up rapidly, their hands out in surrender.

"Wait, Jeannette," Luc said. "Shit. Stop. Just stop. We shouldn't have done any of that without talking first."

Jeannette panted loudly, her breath coming out in painful gasps. "I, I can't..." She looked around the room, trying to figure out how to get out of there, out of the house as quickly as possible.

"Don't even think about it," Diego said, his deep voice leaving no doubt he wouldn't let her escape. "We're not going to touch you. Not going to force you to do anything you don't want to, but you're not going anywhere. Not like this."

Spots clouded her vision and she felt dizzy.

"Christ," she heard Luc exclaim. He gently tugged her off the floor and propelled her to the side of the bed, her legs dangling over the edge. "Put your head between your knees."

"W-what?"

"You're white as a ghost," he explained. "This will help. Keep you from passing out."

She did as he said, though she wanted to assure him she'd never fainted in her life.

Luc left the bed, kneeling in front of her. She saw him reach out to touch her. His hands hovered just an inch or so away from her before he reconsidered and pulled them back.

Instead, he just remained close, his soft tone comforting. "In through your nose. Out through your mouth." Over and over, he offered the simple instructions until she'd managed to get her breathing under control.

She lifted her head slowly, feeling like fifty different kinds of a fool. "I'm so sorry."

Luc gave her a sweet smile. "No apology necessary." His face sobered up slightly. "Jeannette, are you a virgin?"

She laughed mirthlessly and shook her head.

"Who did it?" Diego asked.

Though he'd been silent, she hadn't forgotten his presence behind her. She turned at his question. His expression was dark, thunderous.

She didn't answer.

"Billy?" he asked.

She'd never witnessed true anger until that moment. It should have scared the shit out of her, but instead, for the first time in years, she felt protected.

"Diego, please."

"Tell me the truth, Jeannette." Diego's jaw was clenched tightly.

"I think..." The words had been locked away so long. So fucking long. "I think he raped me."

"You *think*?"

"I don't...I don't really know..."

"Did he drug you?"

She shook her head. This is why she'd never talked about it. She had been a sixteen-year-old virgin with a dead mother and absolutely no knowledge of sex. Her first experience had been... terrifying and painful and so fucking confusing.

Luc ran his hand through his hair and sank down next to her on the mattress. "Jesus, Jeannette. You're killing me, baby. Please tell us what happened."

Bile rose in her throat. She swallowed heavily, praying she didn't get sick. She'd never told another living soul about that night. Not her sister or her aunt Stella or her cousins. Instead, she had locked it away and then retreated. Distance was safety.

"My parents died when I was sixteen."

Luc nodded. They knew that fact. Maybe that was why she started there. She prayed that once she started telling them everything, the hard stuff would come out with the rest. "I was dating Billy at the time. It was sort of typical, first-love kind of stuff. He was my first kiss, the first boy to touch my boobs—over my shirt, of course." She had hoped that comment would provoke a grin, but neither man made a move.

"Anyway, he was really sweet to me after I lost my parents. I cried nonstop for days and he was there for me. Then his mom got a new boyfriend and Billy told me they were moving away. Everything in my life was in upheaval. I'd lost my mom and dad, moved out of my childhood home and into Tyson's bedroom, complete with posters of sports stars and fashion models. I just felt sort of lost."

Luc reached out to take her hand. She clasped it, grateful for the support. Without words, he was letting her know he was there.

"Billy and I went out on a car date. My parents hadn't ever let me do that, but Aunt Stella knew it was our last date since Billy was moving the next day. And she knew he was a nice boy."

Luc's eyes narrowed, but Jeannette held up her hand. "He *was* a nice boy. Honest. We drove to the lake and sat there, watching the moon reflect off the water, talking about how much we were going to miss each other. We were both sixteen. Both virgins. We sort of felt like our world was ending."

Luc squeezed her hand. She was rambling. Avoiding.

"We started kissing, then more. Things escalated and Billy asked me to have sex with him. I should have said no because I didn't really want to. But he was leaving and I didn't want to hurt his feelings."

Diego growled at that. Jeannette smiled sadly. "I've never been overly assertive or very good at standing up for myself. Macie's always been my backbone."

Diego obviously didn't like that comment. "You're one of the strongest women I've ever met."

She appreciated his compliment, even if it was a lie. She was queen of the cowards and she knew it.

"I didn't give him an answer, but when he suggested that we move to the backseat, I did. I guess he took that as a yes. He pulled down my pants and then his. That was when I sort of started to panic. I told him I didn't think it was a very good idea. He said I was just nervous, which I was. He started moving quicker then. He pulled me down on the seat and he came over me. I told him I'd changed my mind, that I didn't want to do it."

Jeannette closed her eyes. She could still hear the fear in her voice, the way it got louder, higher. "He didn't seem to hear me. He started putting on a condom. I tried to sit up, but he held me down, kept saying it was okay, that it was right. I never realized how strong he was. I mean, I guess I should have known that. He worked on his uncle's farm. I kept trying to get away but he weighed me down, told me to relax. Promised me he'd make it feel good. I started crying then."

She felt the tears streaming down her face. She didn't bother to open her eyes. Now that she'd started, there was no turning back.

"He stopped talking to me. I pressed my legs together, but he just grabbed my knees and yanked them apart."

Jeannette felt the mattress shift. She lifted her eyelids and saw that Diego had risen from the bed. He was pacing the room, unadulterated fury flashing in his eyes. She hesitated until Luc cupped her cheek, drawing her gaze to his face.

"Finish it."

"It hurt. A lot. I cried. I begged him to stop. I tried to get away. He just kept going."

"Then what?"

"And then it was over. We got dressed and he drove me home. The whole way there he just kept saying that the first time always hurt for girls, that it would be better the next time." She snorted, a humorous, angry sound. "There wasn't a next time."

She recalled the rest of that night. How hard it had been for her to walk upstairs. How she'd gone to the bathroom and found her panties stained with tinges of blood. She had wrapped them up in a huge wad of toilet paper and thrown them away. She had crawled into bed and cried until there were no more tears left inside her.

At the time, she'd been embarrassed, ashamed. She didn't tell anyone what had happened. How could she? Aunt Stella had already opened her home to her, taken on the rearing of two more girls. Jeannette hadn't wanted to add to her stress, to make her aunt think less of her.

Besides, all she'd really wanted was her mom. Even now, she wished her mother were there.

So she crashed in on herself.

"He raped you." Diego broke the silence in the room.

She looked at him, feeling remarkably calm for the first time in…maybe forever. "What?"

"You said you thought he raped you. He *did*."

Jeannette nodded. "Yeah. He did."

"You've never been with anyone since then?" Diego asked.

"No. No one." She'd taken the pain associated with the rape and twisted it into a pretty serious phobia. Jeannette had never used a tampon, never masturbated, never gone to the gynecologist. Nothing.

Luc leaned forward and placed a soft kiss on her cheek. "What can we do, Jeannette? Anything. Ask for anything and it's yours."

There was only one thing she wanted, one thing she needed—and that was to move forward, to have a life, to feel normal. She was so tired of pushing people away.

Diego knelt on the floor by her feet. "*Anything.*"

She didn't like seeing so much pain on his face or hearing him sound so lost. Diego was strong, self-assured, confident. She'd come to rely on that strength. She'd fed from it, learned from it.

"Touch me," she whispered.

Diego frowned. "What?"

She didn't doubt for a moment that they'd both heard her request. For a moment, she feared they'd reject her.

"Touch me," she repeated, her voice stronger, more demanding.

"Lay down," Diego said, rising from the floor. She glanced to her right, relieved to see Luc's determination.

She crawled onto the bed and shifted onto her back. She became more aware of her nudity as she lay there before them.

"Take off your pants." She'd meant her words to come out as a question, but somehow it had turned into a command. Neither man refused.

Once they'd shed their pajama pants, they resumed their places on the mattress, surrounding her with their big bodies.

Diego was the first to reach for her. He turned her face toward his and kissed her. The passion was still there, but she felt him holding back.

One of the reasons she'd been so attracted to him and Luc was because they'd always treated her like a normal person. She didn't want that to change.

Reaching up, she gripped his wrist in her hand. "Kiss me like you mean it, Diego. Like you want me. I don't want you to treat me with kid gloves or act like I'm some broken porcelain doll."

Diego's eyes narrowed, but she welcomed the fire she saw there. "Regardless of what you think, Jeannette. You *are* a virgin, and I can't for the fucking life of me figure out a way not to hurt you physically. You just dropped a bomb on us, angel. We're only human. So you're just going have to give me a second to get my bearings, to find a way to make love to you that won't bring you pain."

She hadn't considered her request from their perspective. "I'm a selfish bitch, aren't I?"

Luc kissed her shoulder. "Nope. Not even a little. You've never asked anyone for anything. I'm flattered that you trust me and D enough to ask for this. Since Diego is freaking out over there, let's just cut to the chase. We've been touching, kissing and holding you for weeks. The problem has to do with penetration, right?"

From the corner of her eye, she saw Diego roll his eyes as he muttered, "Jesus."

She appreciated Luc's candor, his genuine desire to help her get past her fears. "Yes. That's what scares me. That's the part that hurt."

"So we just need to show you that it doesn't hurt, right?"

She nodded, even as her damn cowardly heart began to race. Luc didn't miss the change.

"Remember last night? What I promised to do?"

Jeannette hoped that one of these days she'd find a way not to blush.

Luc chuckled. "I guess you do. Good." With that, he sat up, moving lower until he knelt between her open legs. She reached out to grip his hair, the reaction purely an instinctive, protective one.

"Easy, angel," Diego whispered as he pried her fingers out of Luc's hair.

She turned to face him, searching for his lips. Diego kissed her once more, but this time there was no restraint, no holding back.

They wouldn't hurt her. Her heart, her head and her body were all in agreement on that.

She sucked in a deep breath when she felt Luc's fingers at the top of her thighs.

"Ohmigod!" she cried, when his tongue stroked her from opening to clit.

Diego moved slightly, his lips closing over her nipple. His tongue teased the sensitive nub before his teeth nipped. At the same time, Luc mimicked that sharp bite on her clit.

"Oh." Her back arched. "So good. Feels so good."

Jeannette struggled to keep up as her men, her lovers, continued their play. They were seducing her with all five senses, with their hungry looks, deep-throated groans, the light scent of sweat mingled with arousal, and the taste of their kisses working in tandem with their never-ending touches.

It was overwhelming. Amazing.

And then, it was the moment of truth. Luc lifted his head, his finger poised at the opening to her body. Her sudden stillness captured Diego's attention and he released her nipple with a pop.

None of them spoke, none of them dared to breathe, as Luc slowly slid his finger inside.

Her heart was racing, but it wasn't fear driving the pounding force.

"More," she demanded when he reached the hilt and held still. Simply having him inside wasn't enough. It felt...good. She wanted—needed—more.

Luc smiled. He pulled his finger out and returned with two. Jeannette's eyes closed, a blissful sigh escaping as Luc moved in and out. He curved his fingers on one inward thrust, finding a spot that had her hips jerking up in response.

"G-spot," Diego murmured. He was lying next to her, his hand cupping her breast as he studied her face. "Jesus, Jeannette. You're so beautiful."

She turned to kiss him, keeping the touch brief. "I want you too."

Diego didn't hesitate. The hand cupping her breast began its slow descent along her body, stroking her stomach, her hip. Luc pulled his fingers out of her, letting Diego take his place.

While Luc had touched her with care, finesse, Diego gave her what she'd asked for.

More.

He pressed three fingers inside. While they stretched her, it didn't hurt. Instead, she felt wicked, naughty, sexy.

Every inhibition fell away, revealing something even Jeannette hadn't realized lived beneath her skin. Speaking the words, releasing her fears had set her free. For the first time, she didn't feel alone or scared or judged.

She felt desired. Wanted.

And it made her want things she'd never wanted before.

"Harder," she demanded as Diego thrust inside. He didn't immediately comply, so she reached up, gripped his hair in her fingers and tugged it. He winced, but she knew about his penchant for pain. Knew he liked it rough.

Apparently she did too. "I'm tired of feeling nothing. Harder. Please."

Diego's eyes narrowed. "You can have control tonight, Jeannette, but don't think for one second I'm going to be some passive puppy dog waiting for your commands in bed. I have a few demands of my own for you."

His darkly sensual threat triggered a fresh round of arousal. She was soaking wet and that fact wasn't lost on her lover. He grinned slyly. "You like the idea of that."

She nodded.

Why the hell would she deny it?

Diego's fingers began to move faster, and every conscious thought was driven from her head. Especially when Luc added his fingers to the play, stroking her clit.

It was there in an instant. Bliss.

She splintered into a million pieces, only vaguely aware that she was screaming as she came.

"God, angel," Luc whispered in her ear, and then he started placing soft kisses on her cheek. "I'll never get tired of watching you come."

Jeannette smiled, and then realized they were both lying next to her, flanking her in their usual spots. They'd pulled the covers up.

"Wait. You guys didn't—"

"Shhh," Diego hushed her. "Not tonight."

"But..." There was no denying they were both still hard. Their cocks were brushing against her hips. "Doesn't that hurt?"

Luc chuckled. "We're fine, Jeannette. We're not going to rush this."

She knew he was being nice, but she couldn't help sulking. "But what if I want more?"

Diego twisted her away from him, spooning her from behind. His erection was nestled between her legs, but he made no move to put it anywhere else. "Go to sleep, baby. I was rougher with you than I should have been and there's a good chance you'll be sore in the morning. I promised not to hurt you, remember?"

"That didn't hurt." God, what they'd done to her was light-years away from hurt.

Luc grasped her arm and tucked it around his waist before

placing a soft kiss to her brow. "And we're going to make sure it stays that way."

Then, because Luc was sweet and always looking for ways to make her happy, he added, "We'll play more in the morning."

"Promise?" she asked, surprised by the sudden drowsiness in her voice.

"Promise," he whispered.

CHAPTER TEN

Diego was the first to rouse. The bright light in the room told him they'd slept later than normal. He grinned when he realized Jeannette hadn't woken up once during the night. For the first time since she had moved in with them, she'd slept through without any nightmares or panic attacks.

His mind replayed their conversation last night. It made him sick to think of everything she had suffered. To lose her parents was devastating enough, but to be raped only months later. To be left alone, without a mother to comfort her, to help her recover. He could only imagine the pain. The fact that she'd come through it at all was a testament to her strength, her courage.

Suddenly, her reasons for building such high, impenetrable walls made sense.

Which was why her trust in them left him in awe. Humbled. She was a good, kind person and sometimes he struggled to understand what she saw in him. He was Diego Rodriguez. He'd grown up on the wrong side of the tracks and he'd done some things to survive that he wasn't particularly proud of. Stolen money and food. Hustled people. Gotten into fights. Lied.

On top of that, he had a hot temper and a pushy, my-way-or-the-highway nature.

He lifted his head and spotted Luc lying on his stomach, his face turned toward them, snoring lightly. Diego smiled.

Luc was the first person to ever love him, to accept him for who he was, rough edges and all. Whenever he looked at Jeannette, he saw that same emotion, felt that same approval. They made him want to be a better man. There wasn't anything in the world he wouldn't do to keep this unusual, perfect family of three together.

"Good morning," Jeannette whispered, her voice thick with sleep.

He glanced down, surprised to find her awake and looking at him.

"Sorry," she said. "You were in the middle of a deep thought, weren't you?"

He nodded.

"Care to share?"

"I love you."

He hadn't meant to blurt the words out like that. If he had a romantic bone in his body, he would have taken her out for a special meal, bought her roses or something. Waited until they weren't naked between crumpled sheets with sleep-tousled hair and morning breath.

One look at her face told him Jeannette didn't give a damn about romance. "I love you too."

Luc stirred. "I'm going to pretend you two weren't just sharing a *moment* without me."

"I love you too, jackass." Diego had never said that to Luc. Not once. It had always seemed like a corny, wimpy thing to say. His best friend knew how he felt, so he didn't see the need to embarrass them with girlie sentiments.

Diego had expected his words to produce either a smile or a laugh from his never-too-serious friend, so he was surprised when Luc flipped to his back with a loud sigh.

"I can't believe I'm here," Luc admitted.

"What do you mean?" Jeannette asked.

"When I lost my mom, I guess I sort of thought that was it, you know? I mean, she was my only family and she was gone. Figured that meant I'd be alone for the rest of my life."

Jeannette reached over to hold Luc's hand. Diego listened, fascinated. Luc had never shared these feelings with him. He thought he knew everything about his best friend.

"Then I met D and I felt less lonely. He filled a big part of that void and for a while, it was enough."

Diego agreed. Trust didn't come easy to either of them. Once they'd earned each other's, they'd battened down the hatches and called it good enough. They hadn't sought to widen the circle because they'd both been hurt too much.

"Once we turned eighteen, we left the orphanage and got a place of our own. We were working two jobs each and it was rare when we got time off together. One night, we did. So we hit a bar, got a little tipsy and met a girl."

Diego grinned. "Donna."

Jeannette narrowed her eyes, though she didn't look angry. "Should I be jealous of Donna?"

"Hell no," Luc replied with a laugh. "She had bleached-blonde hair and the strongest Jersey accent I've ever heard. I'm still not sure I understood half of what she said that night."

"Why do I feel like there should be a 'but' at the end of that sentence?" she asked.

Luc winked at her. "But she had a cute butt and a great laugh and she was into us. Both of us. Said she'd always wanted to hook up with two guys at the same time. It's not like Diego and I hadn't seen each other naked, so we said yes. Went back to our place and realized we'd been too hasty in keeping other people out. We were both attracted to women and it was just...I don't know..."

Diego did. "Better. We were good as a couple, but with a woman, it was so much better."

"So you started going out with women...together?"

Diego nodded. "Yeah."

"Any serious girlfriends?"

Diego wanted to laugh at the slight tinge of jealousy in Jeannette's tone, but more than that, he wanted her to understand exactly what she meant to him. To them. "Not a single one. Until you."

"Oh." Her pleasure at his response was almost tangible. Then she turned back to Luc. "But I'm still confused. Why can't you believe you're here?"

"Everything I've ever wanted in my life is in this bed with me. It's going to take some time to get used to feeling this happy, for me to believe it's real and that it's going to last."

Jeannette's eyes misted with tears. "Me too."

"Me too. How do you feel this morning?" Diego asked, still worried that he'd hurt her.

"Horny," she confessed.

Luc laughed. "Me too."

Diego wished he could let go of his anxiety, but for all intents and purposes, this was Jeannette's first time. He wanted it to be special. "Jeannette…" he started.

She shook her head. "No. No more worrying, Diego. No more stress or fear. We turned that corner last night. Let's just keep moving forward."

Luc pulled the covers down and lightly slapped her bare ass. She giggled.

"What do you say we get a shower?" Luc suggested.

Jeannette sat up, her face excited. "All of us together?"

Diego rose from the bed. "That sounds good to me. We can do a little pre-gaming while we're there."

Jeannette rolled her eyes. "Is that your dude way of saying foreplay?"

Luc reached for Jeannette's hand, tugging her out of bed. "I don't care what anyone calls it. So long as we do it."

She gave both of them a saucy wink before rushing toward the bathroom. Diego was busting at the seams to be with her, but his desires didn't seem to hold a candle to Jeannette's.

She had the water running by the time he and Luc made it to the bathroom. None of them had bothered throwing on robes. Diego was pleased to see her unease, her shyness, had vanished.

Luc stepped beneath the steamy jets first, and then reached

out for Jeannette. Diego stepped in last, chuckling as he stood bone-dry at the end of the line. "I need to put in another shower-head on this side."

"We need a proper bathtub too. One of those big Jacuzzi types," Luc added.

Jeannette looked around. "I don't think you're going to be able to squeeze all of that into this tiny bathroom."

Diego shrugged as an idea niggled. "Then we'll move. Build ourselves a big house."

Jeannette glanced over her shoulder at him. "Wow. That was quite a leap. We haven't even had sex yet and you've got us all buying a house together."

"I know how this is going to end," he said as he placed a kiss at the nape of her neck.

"How's that?" she asked.

"Just like those fairy tales do. Happily ever after."

Jeannette turned to face him. As she did, a bit of the hot water found its way to his front. Then she made him even wetter as she rubbed her damp chest against his.

"I always was a sucker for *Beauty and the Beast*."

Diego kissed her, both of them jumping slightly when Luc's hands reached around her. His friend's hands were soapy and Luc lost no time rubbing the fresh-scent lather over Jeannette's breasts. Then he reached down to rub the soap along Diego's erection.

They each took turns scrubbing all the essentials. Diego suspected he'd never been so clean in his entire life. He was panting by the time Luc turned off the water. His balls were so full, they physically hurt.

"I don't think I can wait much longer," Luc said, voicing exactly what Diego was thinking.

"Me either," Jeannette confided. None of them reached for a towel. Instead, they walked back to the bedroom, heedless of the water dripping on the floor.

Once there, the three of them fell to the mattress in a pile of slick bodies, kissing, touching, licking. They were starving beggars set free at a feast. All semblance of control had vanished as they fought to consume and be consumed.

But despite the overwhelming need to take Jeannette, Diego still couldn't shake off his concerns about hurting her.

JEANNETTE COULD SENSE both of her lovers holding back. They were born protectors. If she didn't take matters into her own hands, they'd never get past this obstacle.

As always, the men had tucked her between them as they took turns kissing and touching. When Luc released her, the two of them coming up for air, she twisted quickly before Diego could move. She came over Diego, pinning him beneath her, her legs straddling his hips.

From his expression, she could see she'd surprised him. She also spotted the slightest trace of concern.

"Easy, angel," he urged, when she lifted her hips, intent on taking him inside her. He gripped her tightly, holding her back from her desired target.

"No, Diego. No more stalling."

He glanced to Luc, no doubt for support. She had apparently freaked-out the two strong, powerful, self-confident men. She didn't know whether to laugh or cry about that.

"Please," she added.

Diego released her hips, reaching to cup her face. He dragged her down for a sweet kiss. "I think you might have the right idea here, actually."

He stroked his fingers along the slit between her legs, grinning when he found her wet. "Lift up, angel. We're going to let you hold the reins for a little while."

From the corner of her eye, she saw Luc's brows fly up. "Damn, Jeannette. You did what I never thought possible. You made D submissive."

Diego scowled, but Jeannette wasn't interested in picking a fight. She understood what he was offering her, and why. By allowing her to be on top, she wouldn't feel overpowered. And she could decide how much she could take.

Before Diego could call Luc to task, she gripped his thick cock and placed the head at the opening to her body.

No one spoke as she moved. She suspected Diego *couldn't*. His breathing had grown rapid, his nostrils flaring with the effort to suck in air. Luc knelt beside them, his gaze never leaving the place where Jeannette's body joined with Diego's.

Despite her desire, Jeannette felt the same fears creep in. She braced herself for the pain.

However, as she slid lower, more and more of Diego's cock filling her, it became apparent there wasn't going to be any hurting this time.

When that knowledge hit, she gave up the fight and sank down in one final rough thrust.

Diego jerked a bit, his hands flying to her hips to hold her still, but it was too late. He was buried deep.

She closed her eyes and groaned. "Oh my God."

Luc placed a soft kiss on her shoulder. "Amazing, right?"

She didn't bother to open her eyes. Instead, she just nodded. "So good."

The mattress shifted slightly as Luc moved behind her. "Want me to make it even better?"

She glanced over her shoulder with one eyebrow lifted. "Think you can?"

It was a sexual dare—no, it was an outright taunt. Both men chuckled until Luc grasped her waist with his large, strong hands and lifted her. Strong men had always frightened her, but none of those fears emerged when Luc and Diego touched her. If anything, their power turned her on even more.

Luc raised her until just the tip of Diego's cock remained inside. "Time to take a ride, angel."

Then he pressed her back down—harder and faster than she would have attempted on her own. Stars flew behind her eyes, her hands reaching out for something to hold on to. She found Diego's chest, her fingers digging into the steel-like muscles there.

Luc didn't give her any chance to recover or assimilate to the new sensations pummeling her. He simply continued to take her on the ride of a lifetime—lifting and dropping, raising her up and pressing her back down.

Diego's hands found her breasts. She wouldn't have thought she'd notice anything besides the sheer electrical magic sparking between her legs, but she was wrong. When Diego pinched her nipples, her back arched as she screamed.

Her pussy clenched tightly around Diego's cock as she came. For a moment, it felt as if she'd been swept up in a cyclone, her body a limp ragdoll, at the mercy of the wind. It was an amazing flight.

Neither man seemed content to let her revel in the aftermath. Mere seconds had passed before she felt herself being propelled to her back, Diego coming over her.

His hands lay flat against the mattress by her head as his hips beat a beautiful rhythm inside her.

"Yes. Yes." The single word came out with each inward thrust, as she provided the lyrics to his song. She wrapped her legs around his waist tightly. The next climax came out of nowhere. Her body trembled with the glorious impact.

Before she could recover, the song changed. She opened her eyes to discover Luc above her. She reached up—a challenging effort, given her lack of strength—and cupped his cheek. "Come inside," she whispered when he remained there, hovering above her.

Unlike the rough tempo of Diego's lovemaking, Luc didn't use speed and force. Instead, he employed finesse. Somehow, he knew exactly where to stroke to set fireworks off.

"Holy shit," she whispered. "Right there."

Luc took care to find the spot again. And then again.

Jeannette's fingers fisted the sheets in a white-knuckle grip. She was staring orgasm number three right in the face. If she weren't so freaking happy to see it, she might have felt a bit of guilt over the fact neither of the men had come yet.

"Luc. I can't..." Her words turned into a cry as waves of white-hot bliss washed over her.

"I'm with you, angel. God. I'm right with you."

She came before he finished speaking—trembling, shaking. Had she seriously been afraid of this? *Of this?!*

Time passed without meaning. Hell, she wasn't entirely sure where she was. For several minutes, she simply laid there, her eyes closed as she focused on her breathing. In and out. In and out.

And the pounding of her heart. *Thump. Thump. Thump.* Neither of those processes had ever seemed so fascinating. Or obvious. They happened every single second of every day, yet they'd never been so loud.

She was just about to drift off to sleep when she felt something nudge her legs apart.

"Jeannette?"

Diego.

She and Luc had found their pleasure, but he hadn't. Exhaustion gave way to desire. It was incredible. She would have thought herself too tired, but the second she heard his voice, she wanted him. Desperately.

She opened her eyes as she spread her legs. "I need you."

Diego smiled at her admission. "You're the most amazing woman I've ever known."

She grinned, warmed by his compliment. "Come here."

Diego slid into her slower this time, his previous bat-out-of-hell approach gone. He moved in a way that calmed and stimulated at the same time. His motions were as gentle as a canoe floating on a lake. Soothing. Wonderful.

She wouldn't have thought she could come from such tender care, but when Diego added a soft stroke to her clit, his motions mimicking the way he was rocking in her body. She was a goner.

"I need—" she started.

"I know."

Diego gave up whatever grip he'd had on his own control and the two of them spiraled into orbit together, clinging to each other as they shook.

Jeannette lost all sense of reality after that. In fact, she blacked out. The next thing she recalled was waking up in a dim room, nestled between her two lovers. It occurred to her that Diego and Luc had made love only to her. While it had been the single most amazing moment in her life, there was part of her that longed for an even closer union. She wanted the three of them to truly be together. Equal partners in this unorthodox, but perfect relationship.

Then she glanced out the window and noticed the room had gone dark. Had they slept all day?

She grinned at the thought and decided she didn't care. Instead, she burrowed closer to Diego and closed her eyes again. Sleep didn't scare her so much anymore.

CHAPTER ELEVEN

"Who was that?" Jeannette asked when Luc hung up the phone.

"Evan. Apparently he caught wind that Billy is back in town. He's headed out to Roy's right now to question him."

Jeannette didn't like the identical looks of fury on her boyfriends' faces.

"Is that right?" Diego, who had been ready to sit down to breakfast, changed his course and headed for the living room. "Let me put my shoes on and I'll be ready."

"Ready for what?" Jeannette asked.

"Luc and I are going to go have a word with Billy."

She barked out a loud, "Yeah right."

They both stopped in the midst of getting ready to leave.

She put her hands on her hips. "Neither one of you is going anywhere *near* Billy."

Diego's brow furrowed as he somehow managed to take his six-foot-two frame up a few inches. "Excuse me?"

If his attempts at intimidation weren't so blatantly obvious, she might have been put out. As it was, she was tempted to laugh. "I mean it. The last thing I want or need is for the two of you to go over there half-cocked and get into a fight. You just said Evan was going to question him. You show up with fists flying and my cousin will have to arrest you both for assault. And I'm telling you right now, I won't bail your asses out."

"You don't seriously expect us to do nothing?" Luc's tone matched the utter disbelief on his face.

"Actually, I do. What happened between Billy and me is ancient history. I'm not about to keep digging it up. It was hard enough talking to you guys about it. I can't keep reliving it."

Diego walked over when her voice betrayed her, cracking despite her efforts to remain calm. "Angel. He's moving to Maris. He's going to live here."

"You're right. He is. Which means I'm..." She paused and reconsidered her wording. "*We're* going to have to find a way to deal with it. It happened fifteen years ago. It's not like I can press charges now."

Diego clenched his fists. "Which is why we have to utilize a different brand of justice."

She shook her head. "No. That's not justice. It's anger, revenge, violence. I don't want to be a part of that. For the first time in so damn long, I'm finally starting to feel at peace. If you go over there, if you start a fight, all of that is gone."

Diego rubbed his eyes wearily. "Shit, Jeannette. What you're asking...it's hard. We love you and that asshole hurt you. Asking us to pretend that didn't happen—"

"I'm not asking you to pretend. Or forget. I'm just asking you not to give in to that kind of hate. I'll held on to my pain for years and look what it cost me. So much wasted time. If I've learned anything in this past month, it's that sometimes you just have to let it go."

"You're not going to break into that freaking Disney song, are you?" Luc asked.

Jeannette laughed as she reached out to hug him. Luc found a way to make her laugh time after time, even during the heaviest moments. She loved him for that. "I'll try to restrain myself."

She glanced over her shoulder. She may have convinced Luc, but Diego was another story. "Diego—"

Before she could press her argument further, the loud blare from the fire station's alarm sounded, calling all the volunteers in the area to the station. It was an old-fashioned system, but it worked.

Luc and Diego both raced to put on their shoes when the call came across the scanner. The operator gave the address of a lake-front cabin.

Jeannette gasped.

"What's wrong?" Luc asked.

"That's Evan's cabin!"

Diego stood up and walked over to her, grasping her shoulders. "Go to the restaurant, Jeannette. Please. I don't want you here alone."

She nodded. "I will. Do you think Billy—"

"I don't know."

Luc stood by the open front door. "Diego. We gotta move."

Diego gave her a quick kiss. "Go now, Jeannette."

"I will."

"We'll call as soon as we can," Luc promised.

Jeannette finished dressing, and then headed to the restaurant. She was worried to death about Evan's wife, Annie, and their little daughter. She felt the need to be with the rest of the family.

She hadn't made it two steps inside the restaurant before Gia saw her and raced to hug her.

"You heard about the fire at Evan's?" Gia asked.

Jeannette nodded. "Are Annie and Eryn there?"

Gia shook her head. "No. Annie had dropped Eryn off at the sitter's and was nearly to work when she heard. She's headed back to the cabin now."

Jeannette was relieved to know they were safe, but she didn't wish anyone to experience the personal hell she'd just endured by losing their home. "And Evan?"

"He was almost to Roy's house when he heard."

Jeannette walked to the counter and sank down on one of the stools. "I hope to God Diego and Luc get there in time."

Gia sighed. "Yeah." Her sister went behind the counter to retrieve a coffeepot and started topping up the cups of their customers. Jeannette was just about to put on an apron and start pitching in when the bell above the restaurant door caught her attention.

Her chest tightened when Billy walked in. For a moment, she considered running away, but decided she was safer in the dining room surrounded by people. That feeling of security grew stronger when Uncle TJ and Tyson followed Billy into the restaurant.

Tyson made a beeline for her, murmuring in her ear. "I was next door in the bakery when I spotted Billy walking in here. You okay?"

She nodded.

"Jeannette?"

She jerked at the sound of Billy's voice, and then she forced herself to look at him.

"I was wondering if I could talk to you for a second."

Her mouth went dry at the thought. "I don't think that's such a good idea."

Tyson crossed his arms, giving Billy a look that warned him to back off.

Billy didn't take it. "I know y'all think I set those fires, but I didn't."

"Why was your truck parked outside Jeannette's house a couple of days before it burned down?" In Evan's absence, it appeared Tyson was prepared to issue the interrogation.

Billy's jaw twitched and he swallowed nervously. Tyson had asked the question, but Billy directed the answer toward Jeannette. "I wasn't the one parked outside your place."

"It was Roy's truck," she said.

"I know. Scott was driving it."

She frowned. "Why would he come to *my* house?"

Billy looked around the restaurant. Clearly news of the fire had begun to spread, and more and more locals had filed in, looking for some gossip. "Can we sit down? Somewhere more private?"

Jeannette was ready to say no, but Tyson pointed to a booth in the corner. "We can go over there."

Jeannette forced herself to remain calm. Tyson didn't know why she wouldn't want to be within fifty feet of Billy. How could he? As far as her cousin knew, he was questioning Billy about the arson, nothing more.

She followed both men, though it was difficult to concentrate on putting one foot in front of the other when sheer panic and fear were causing her entire system to shut down.

Tyson waited as she took a seat on the bench, then slid in next to her. Billy claimed the other side of the booth. Despite her large cousin's closeness, Jeannette didn't feel any less terrified.

"Why was Scott at Jeannette's house?" Tyson repeated her question. Which was a good thing. Jeannette's voice had deserted her.

"He heard about you dating those two firefighters. He didn't like it."

Tyson scowled. "Tough shit. It's none of his business who my cousin dates."

Billy threw his hands up in a sign of surrender. "I know that. I'm not saying it was right. It's just...Scott has some issues with alcohol."

Tyson nodded. "Yeah. I've heard."

"He's not a bad guy when he's sober."

Jeannette heard the earnestness in Billy's voice, and she recalled him saying similar things when they were in high school. Scott would get in trouble for bullying or fighting and Billy would hop to his brother's defense.

Billy looked weary, and though he was the same age as her, he looked closer to her Uncle TJ's age. Time hadn't been kind to him.

"Is Scott setting the fires, Billy?" she asked, though she already knew the answer.

Billy shrugged. "I don't know that for sure." Then he rubbed his eyes tiredly. "Yeah, I think he is."

Tyson stood. "I need to call Evan. Need to tell him." Within seconds, Tyson had his cell phone in hand as he walked back to the kitchen in search of a quiet place to break the news.

Jeannette started to slide out of the booth, anxious to put some distance between her and Billy, but he grabbed her hand

She jerked it out of his grip. "Don't touch me."

He reared back. "I'm sorry."

She turned to stand, but his words stopped her.

"I'm sorry for everything."

Jeannette looked at Billy and recognized true regret on his face.

"I'm sorry for that night," he added, when she didn't respond.

She didn't move. She couldn't. The restaurant was full of people—relatives, friends, tourists. The noise level had risen and yet, in that moment, everything had gone silent. The only thing she could hear was Billy's voice.

She didn't reply, but now that he'd started, Billy didn't seem able to stop.

"I know what I did to you. I know I hurt you."

Jeannette looked around the dining room slowly. Uncle TJ was sitting at the counter with Macie. Gia and Paige were flitting around, waiting tables. Sydney was standing just outside the kitchen door, talking to her boyfriend Chas.

It seemed surreal to be sitting here, in the midst of her loved ones, while facing down the man who had made her life a living hell.

"Okay," she whispered. It wasn't okay. Not by a long shot. She wanted to rage, to scream, to tear out his fucking eyes. The sudden onslaught of emotions after so many years of nothing was physically painful.

"You wanted me to stop and I didn't. I've replayed that night about a million times, wishing I had."

She forced herself to look at him, forced herself to truly see him. "Why didn't you?"

He shrugged. "You were the first girlfriend I'd ever had. Shit, you were my first friend. We moved all the time and a lot of the guys my mom hooked up with weren't very nice, so it wasn't like I could invite people over to our house. I was afraid I'd never... I was sixteen. Sex was pretty much an obsession."

She didn't reply. Didn't know how.

Billy shook his head. "I'm sorry. It sounds like I'm making excuses. I don't have any excuse. I was wrong. I hurt you. I'm going to carry the guilt of that with me until the day I die."

While the anger still raged inside her, it was now coupled with other emotions—pity, sadness.

"I'm selling Uncle Roy's farm."

She frowned. "What?"

"He's dying. Cancer. Hospice has been called in and they're saying he probably won't last the week."

"I'm sorry."

Billy shrugged. "I know I shouldn't speak ill of the dying, but he's not a very nice guy. Anyway, I came back here to take care of him and to try to get some of his affairs in order. After he's gone, I'm selling the land and moving back to Oklahoma. I know you can't forgive me for what I did and you sure as hell don't need a constant reminder of it."

So he was selling the farm in an attempt to be a decent guy. She could almost respect him for that. Until...

"I just shouldn't have made my brother come with me. I forced Scott to come here because..."

He clearly wasn't going to finish that statement, but Jeannette wouldn't let him get away with that. He owed her the rest. "Because?"

"He'd been getting into trouble with the law in Oklahoma. Vandalism, petty theft."

"Arson?"

Billy shook his head. "No. I swear to God, he never started a fire. At least not that I knew of."

"Did you suspect he was setting these?"

Billy looked down at the table. He'd shredded the paper napkin in front of him to bits. "Not at first."

"When did you figure it out?"

Billy didn't look at her.

"When?" she pressed, her voice cracking with rage.

"After the fire at the shack."

Jeannette struggled to breathe as an intense anger sent her blood boiling. When she spoke again, it was in a low, dangerous voice. "You knew and you didn't say anything?"

Billy swallowed heavily, but the fucking coward still wouldn't look at her. "He hadn't hurt anyone."

She exploded from the booth, slamming her hand down on the flat surface. "HE HURT *ME!*"

Conversation in the restaurant died instantly, the silence almost deafening. Despite that, Jeannette—the woman who had spent a lifetime being quiet and invisible—forged on. She was making one hell of a scene, but she didn't give a shit.

"He burned down my fucking house!"

From her peripheral vision, she saw Tyson return from the kitchen and move closer, Uncle TJ and Macie right behind him. Her family was gathering around, clearly ready to do battle for her if she gave them the slightest inclination she needed them.

Billy stood slowly, looking very small, very pathetic. All these years, she'd imagined him as this strong, strapping young man. A man with enough power to hold down a frightened girl and rape her. But he was nothing more than a coward, a weak-willed man. "I know, Nettie. I'm—"

"My name is *Jeannette*."

She took back her name; spoke it in such a way that she felt certain no one in Maris would ever call her Nervous Nettie again.

He looked at her and nodded. "I'm sorry."

She rolled her eyes. "Yeah. So you keep saying. That doesn't get my house back though, does it? Or my—" She stopped just short of saying "virginity". She'd shared that burden with the only two people whom she wanted—needed—to know. So instead she said, "Dignity." Billy would understand exactly what he'd taken from her.

His shoulders fell, his posture almost caving in on itself. And Jeannette realized she didn't feel a single bit better. In fact, she felt worse.

All she was doing was kicking a dog who was down. She'd given Diego and Luc a big speech this morning about moving on, being the bigger person, but when faced with that same decision, she'd struck out. Hard.

"I forgive you." The words came out on a whisper.

Billy's gaze was filled with confusion and wariness. "What?"

She cleared her throat and forced the words to come out with more conviction. She'd felt some of her anger and pain disperse. Maybe she could get rid of the rest. "I forgive you. For all of it."

Billy frowned. "You can't."

She snorted. "Of course I can. I can do whatever I want. And you can accept that forgiveness or not. It doesn't impact me one way or the other."

Billy didn't respond to that. She watched the words soak in. Then, slowly, some of the tension in his shoulders eased and he stood up a bit straighter.

Finally, he said, "Thank you."

She nodded, fighting hard not to cry.

Billy looked as though he were beating back some powerful emotions of his own. "I should leave." Then he added a quiet "goodbye" and walked out of the restaurant.

Jeannette let the awkward silence in the dining room linger for a minute more. The locals were going to have a field day with this for weeks. She turned around, and then announced to no one in particular, "Who needs more coffee?"

With that question, the floodgates opened and the chatter resumed, this time reaching rock-concert levels. In addition to the fire, everyone was now hot to discuss what they'd just witnessed.

They were all welcome to try to put the pieces together, but Jeannette knew none of them would ever have the whole picture.

Then she glanced at Tyson and reconsidered. The permanent

laugh lines by his eyes were gone, replaced by a scowl that spoke of concern and fury. She caught his gaze and gave him an infinitesimal shake of the head, warning him. She was finished talking about this.

He narrowed his eyes, his jaw set. Then he turned away.

She was wrong. She was only finished talking about it for now. He was giving her a reprieve, not a bye.

Macie, who had been talking on the phone, clicked off her cell and called her over.

"Was that Evan?" Jeannette asked.

Her cousin nodded. "Yeah. Apparently the fire was a false alarm."

"What?"

"They couldn't find anything burning. Not the cabin, not the woods. Nothing. Luc, Diego and Evan are heading back to town."

For some reason she couldn't understand, that information didn't relieve her. "Why would someone call in a false alarm?"

Her question was still hovering in the air when she heard a loud crash against the front window of the restaurant.

Jeannette recognized the sound and the flash of light in an instant.

It was the same thing she'd heard the night her house burned down.

The terror of that memory had only begun to resurface when she heard a woman yell, "Fire!"

Jeannette turned and watched as the Molotov cocktail burned on the sidewalk just outside. The flames flared high, smoke billowing and obscuring their view of the street.

Macie yelled for everyone to remain calm as patrons rose from their tables in a panic. She, Sydney and Chas started directing everyone through the kitchen door, so they could escape the building by the back.

Sheer panic kept Jeannette still. She couldn't look away from the flames that continued to flicker. Luc and Diego were too far away.

The false alarm.

Suddenly she understood. Luc and Diego had been called away to ensure *this* fire burned. The fire station was only a couple blocks away. If the truck and the guys had been there, very little harm would have come from this.

"Jeannette!" Gia yelled from the kitchen door. "What are you doing? Come on!"

Before she could respond, Tyson was there, his arm around her waist, propelling her toward her sister.

And then—she heard it. A siren. It was closer than she would have thought possible.

Hope emerged.

Jeannette joined the crowd in the back alley, and then made her away around the building to the front street, many people following her. As soon as she turned the corner, she spotted the fire truck squealing to a halt in front of the restaurant.

She was surprised to realize the fire wasn't as large as it had appeared from inside. It was running out of fuel fast. Whatever Scott had tossed this time, it hadn't been strong enough to break through the front glass of the restaurant. It had exploded on the sidewalk instead.

Within minutes, the flames had been doused and, aside from a huge scorch mark on the pavement and a crack in Sparks Barbeque's large window, there was nothing more to indicate what had just happened. Regardless, Jeannette appreciated exactly how bad things could have been if the firebomb had crashed through the window. The restaurant had been packed. People could have been seriously hurt. Killed even.

"Jeannette!"

She glanced around when she heard her name. She saw Diego searching for her in the crowd that had gathered, calling out.

She raised her hand. "Diego! I'm here."

He plowed his way through the people, Luc hot on his heels. He was dressed in his heavy fire jacket when he picked her up and hugged her tightly.

"Thank God," he murmured in her hair. "We heard there was a fire at Sparks and..."

"I'm okay," she reassured him.

Diego gave her a quick, hard kiss, and then released her as Luc took his place, holding her, obviously relieved to find her safe.

Luc rested his forehead against hers. "I didn't know that big-ass truck would go so fast. Pretty sure Diego had it on two wheels around a few corners."

She kissed him, her fingers tugging at his hair to keep his lips on hers when it was apparent he intended to pull back.

When she finally did release him, he grinned. "A guy could get addicted to this aggressive side of you."

She laughed lightly, though the kiss hadn't begun to satisfy her. "Where's Evan?"

Diego pointed to the police car. "Across the street. Apparently, Billy managed to tackle his brother in the alley over there just after he tossed that Molotov cocktail. He was pretty much beating the shit out of Scott when we rolled up. Evan saw them and headed over while we dealt with the fire."

Evan had a bleeding Scott facedown on the hood of the car, his hands cuffed behind his back. A visibly shaken Billy was standing next to them, talking to Evan.

"They should both be in cuffs," Luc murmured.

Jeannette shook her head. "No. They shouldn't."

Diego turned, intent on arguing, but Jeannette cut him off. "Later," she promised. "Right now, I need to report a fire."

Diego frowned. "Fire?"

"Yeah. I've got one raging inside me, most particularly between my legs. I need a couple of firefighters to help me put it out."

Luc grinned. "Well, as luck would have it..." He held out his arms, displaying his heavy coat, red suspenders and boots. "We're already dressed and ready to roll."

She gave him a flirty wink. "I'd prefer you *undressed* and ready to roll."

Diego groaned. "God, angel. You're killing me. Every busy-body in town is standing around here and now I'm sporting a boner."

She giggled. "I think you and Luc have already established yourselves as bad boys."

Luc shook his head. "Nope. Those days are over. From now on, we're off the market. Spoken for. Respectable men."

"Want to hear a joke?"

Both guys gave her a funny look, but Luc took the bait. "Oookay."

"Why do firemen wear red suspenders?"

Luc chuckled while Diego rolled his eyes good-naturedly and said, "To hold their pants up?"

Jeannette shook her head. "To tie their girlfriend up with in bed."

She laughed as both men fell speechless.

"I figure it's a good thing there are two of you. I have years of sexual fantasies to explore. You guys are bound to get tired while I make up for lost time."

Luc's eyes widened. "Jesus. We gotta get home. Now."

"You got that right." Diego moved so quickly, Jeannette didn't have time to react as he bent and tossed her over his shoulder, true firefighter style.

She laughed at the shocked expressions of her neighbors and relatives.

Macie let out a loud hoot, but Diego didn't give her a chance to hear anything else that was said. He and Luc had her in the fire truck within seconds. She laughed louder when Luc turned on the lights and the sirens, much to the delight of the crowd gathered around.

"Afraid your reputation is ruined forever," Luc teased.

Jeannette flashed him an incredulous look. "Are you kidding me? Ruined? For the first time in my life, I actually *have* a reputation. Drive faster."

CHAPTER TWELVE

They'd only just stepped through the door when Diego's cell phone rang. He was about to say fuck it and ignore it, but Evan's number flashed on the screen.

Jeannette looked over his shoulder. "Answer it."

Diego clicked on the button. "Hey Evan."

"Jeannette okay?" her cousin asked.

"Yeah. She's right here."

"Good. Scott confessed. He set all the fires. Told us what he used to set them. Even mentioned that he alternated between wearing his, Billy's and Roy's boots to try to throw us off the track. Said he hadn't intended to burn down Jeannette's house. He'd thought the device would bounce off the garage door and burn out in the yard. Apparently he was trying to teach Jeannette a lesson about screwing with two guys. Called it unnatural."

Diego relayed that information to Jeannette and Luc.

"We've got enough on the guy to put him away for a fucking long time. I really think today would have been much worse if Billy hadn't spotted his brother and tackled him mid-throw. That Molotav cocktail could have easily shattered that front window, if not for Billy intervening."

Diego digested that information, but it didn't change his attitude toward Billy. "I'm just glad it's finally over."

Evan sighed wearily. "Yeah. Me too. You might want to tell Jeannette. Roy Mathers died a couple of hours ago."

"Oh. Okay. I'll tell her."

"I'll touch base with y'all later. Right now I feel like going home and holding my wife and baby."

Diego grinned. "Yeah. I hear that. Talk to you later, Evan."

He hung up, and then told Jeannette about Roy.

Her response took him aback. "I'm not surprised. Billy said it was bad."

Luc, who had picked up Penny to rub her stomach, stopped mid-pet. "Billy? When?"

"He was at the restaurant just before the fire. I can only assume Scott had intended to move sooner, but hesitated with Billy inside. Sort of screwed up his time schedule with the false alarm because it gave y'all time to get back to town. He didn't throw the Molotov cocktail until Billy left."

Diego knew she was talking, but he struggled to hear, to understand the words. He took a step closer to Jeannette. "You talked to Billy?"

She nodded. "Yeah. I did. He apologized for..." She hesitated when he growled. The sound escaped before he could call it back. Then she finished, "He apologized for everything."

Diego scowled. "I don't give a shit if he said he's sorry. Is that supposed to make up for what he did to you?"

Jeannette had tried to convince him to let things with Billy go this morning, but he'd never agreed. He couldn't. That man had a day of reckoning coming. However, before he could explain that to Jeannette, she cut him off.

Jeannette lifted one shoulder. "I accepted the apology."

Diego's temper exploded. "You did *what?!*"

Luc placed Penny on the chair where she'd been sleeping and moved over to put his hand on Diego's arm. Diego shook it off. He didn't need Luc trying to placate him. This was fucking bullshit.

"Come on, D. Keep it together, man. Listen to what she has to say."

Jeannette gave Luc an appreciative smile, the look annoying Diego even more. He wasn't the bad guy in this. Billy Mathers was. "Jeannette—"

She shook her head, refused to allow him to speak. "No, Diego. It's done. It's over. Anger and fear take a lot of energy. I should know. I've been in a perpetual state of exhaustion for fifteen years."

Diego struggled to keep his tone quieter when he spoke again, but that didn't mean he wasn't still angry, still upset. "He raped you. I can't forgive that. You can't ask me to."

"You're right. I can't. All I can do is ask you to understand that I have. I'm tired of living in the past. He's moving."

He suspected she threw that last comment out like tossing a bone to a dog. "He is?"

"Yeah. He just came home to take care of his uncle, to get his affairs in order. He's selling the farm. Said he knew seeing him around town would only continue to remind me. To hurt me."

Despite his desire to remain angry, he had to admit he was glad the guy was leaving. "Good riddance," he said through gritted teeth.

Jeannette grinned sadly. "Besides, how much more bad karma can I wish on the guy? His uncle just died and he helped see his brother arrested for crimes that will put him behind bars for years, maybe the rest of his life."

Diego put his hands on his hips. "Are you saying he's suffered enough?"

Jeannette moved closer, wrapping her arms around his waist. "I'm not saying anything except I'm finished thinking about it. Right now, the only thing I care about is us. The present and maybe...a future?"

Diego didn't respond at first, and then he realized her words had come out uncertain. "Are you questioning our future? Because I'm pretty sure I mentioned that happily ever after thing already."

She kissed him. "Maybe so, but there's still the issue of that fire I need tending to."

Luc laughed. He'd been quiet during Diego and Jeannette's argument, but one look at his best friend's face told him Luc had been struggling with the same things he had. It appeared Jeannette's words had eased Luc's mind. Not surprising. Luc was better at letting things go. Diego was pretty sure he wouldn't relax until he saw the taillights of Billy Mathers' car as he drove out of town.

But for Jeannette's sake, he'd keep those feelings to himself. It had taken courage for her to confront her rapist and then to offer him forgiveness. Diego's love for her tripled at the thought.

"Bedroom," Diego said, pointing down the hallway. Today, the kid gloves were coming off.

Luc and Jeannette both grinned.

"Looks like the big chief is back in town," Luc joked.

Diego narrowed his eyes. Luc knew better than to taunt the bull. Then again, maybe his friend was doing it on purpose. Luc craved a rough touch.

But he wasn't sure Jeannette was ready to see just how much.

Of course, that concern was fleeting. Especially when Jeannette leaned closer to Diego. "Maybe you should punish him," she suggested.

Diego reached out to place a playful smack on her ass. "Or I could punish both of you."

She snapped his red suspenders, reminding him of her comment outside the restaurant.

Luc grabbed her hand and tugged her down the hallway impatiently. Diego followed, but he took his time, trying to get control of his own raging needs. His two lovers tested his stamina. He'd always sort of prided himself on his staying power, but with Luc and Jeannette in his bed, he felt like a fifteen-year-old boy, ready to blow within seconds.

As he entered the bedroom, he saw Jeannette helping unhook Luc's suspenders. When his friend dropped down on the edge of the mattress, she started tugging off Luc's boots as well. He imagined the two of them coming home in the middle of the night after running a call and Jeannette being there to take care of them.

Luc didn't bother waiting for either of them. He kept disrobing until he was completely naked. His cock was fully erect and ready for action. Diego wasn't sure he'd ever seen his friend so eager.

"In a hurry?" Diego teased.

Luc, the most peaceful man on the planet, narrowed his eyes. "You have no fucking idea. If you're planning some drawn-out fuckfest, I'm going to tell you right now, I'm not going to last that long. I figure it's a good thing the three of us have forever stretching out in front of us because it's going to take me some time to get a handle on how much I need both of you."

Leave it to Luc to sum up his feelings so perfectly.

"Jeannette," Diego said. "Baby, how would you feel about us tying you up later? Looks like Luc is hurting."

The cheeky minx laughed. "How chivalrous of you." She walked over and slid her hand down the front of his pants. Before Diego could react, she had her hand wrapped tightly around his hard cock. "You sure you aren't hurting too?"

Diego swallowed heavily. "I swear to God, one of these days I'm going to turn you over my knee and spank that pretty ass of yours."

She stroked his dick, applying just the right amount of pressure. She'd been paying attention.

Through gritted teeth, he finished his thought. "But right now...I just need to be inside somebody. Fucking them. Hard."

He expected Jeannette to giggle, but the hungry look in her eyes told him she wasn't faring any better.

"Take off your clothes, Jeannette." He used the deep-voiced, commanding tone she loved. It worked.

Jeannette's fingers flew to the task. Luc had risen from the bed to help both of them pull off their clothing. He snagged her glasses to place them on the nightstand before drawing Jeannette's t-shirt over her head, and then he turned to tug off Diego's boots. Only once they were all naked did they *really* start to touch each other.

By tacit agreement last night, he and Luc spent the evening focusing all their attention on Jeannette. It had been her first time and they both wanted to make sure it was special. Today, the game had changed.

When Luc kissed her, she reached out for Diego, pulling him into their circle. She pulled away briefly. "Kiss each other."

There was no hesitation. His lips met Luc's in a hungry, demanding touch that grew even hotter when Jeannette reached down and took both of them in her hands.

Luc reared back. "Fuck, Jeannette. That feels too good. I gotta be inside you."

While Diego had enjoyed the foreplay of last night's encounter, there was something very tempting about a quickie. He guided Jeannette to the bed, helping her scoot to the center.

"Open your legs, angel. Let Luc inside."

Luc and Jeannette moved into position in record time. So quickly that Diego realized he'd better move fast or he'd miss the train.

Luc had just seated himself to the hilt, his entrance provoking the sexiest gasp from Jeannette's pink lips. Her long blonde hair flowed over the fluffy white pillow and for a moment, he wondered if she really *was* an angel floating on a cloud, sent from Heaven just for them.

Diego placed his hand on Luc's ass, pressing down to halt his friend's movements. Luc gave him a quizzical look over his shoulder.

"Wait for me," Diego said.

Luc shuddered, pure, unadulterated need flashing in his eyes.

While they'd enjoyed each other's bodies, as well as those of the women they had taken to bed, Diego had never fucked Luc while he was inside their lover.

"Hurry," Jeannette pleaded, clearly unaware of the magnitude of what was about to happen. They'd explain it to her. After.

For now, Diego had two lovers to claim. He reached into the nightstand for the lubrication and a condom.

Luc groaned as he worked the gel into his ass with two fingers, then three. Every now and then, Luc's hips would lurch forward, driving him deeper into Jeannette. She would cry out and beg Diego to go faster. She was as turned-on as they were.

If there had been any doubts about her acceptance of his and Luc's relationship with each other, they were quashed in an instant.

Once Luc was ready, Diego knelt behind him on the bed. Slowly, he pressed into Luc's tight ass as his friend struggled to remain still. Diego could only imagine how intense this moment was for Luc. To take and be taken.

"Jesus," Luc muttered when Diego reached the hilt.

None of them moved. Or breathed.

Then Penny jumped up on the bed, startling them all.

Jeannette laughed as she shooed her cat away. And then, just like that, they were in motion. It took them a few attempts to find the rhythm. Luc rearing back as Diego moved forward. Then Luc pushed into Jeannette during Diego's outward motion.

The room was filled with a unique cacophony of sounds. Jeannette's lilting cry when Luc hit her G-spot. Luc's grunt when Diego came in harder or faster. Diego added his own groans when Luc reared back roughly, giving as good as he got.

Diego wasn't sure when he lost total control, but one of Luc's hard jerks sent him to another level. He gripped his lover's hips, pounding into Luc without heed or caution.

The flip switched the trigger on Luc, who took Jeannette with the same reckless abandon.

Red welts appeared on Luc's shoulders as Jeannette's nails raked his flesh. It was a strange thing to fixate on, but Diego couldn't pull his eyes away from the scratches or the look of utter bliss on Jeannette's face.

It was all too much. Diego thrust forward once more, his balls exploding as he came so hard it fucking hurt.

Luc and Jeannette were two beats behind him, both of them shaking as their own climaxes overtook them.

Luc was the first to fall, his body dropping to Jeannette's right. His eyes closed in a look that was the perfect mixture of pain and satiation.

Diego rose and tossed the condom into a trashcan, before claiming his place next to Jeannette, who turned and kissed him.

"I want to do that every single day."

He chuckled. "We'll be dead within a week."

"I don't care."

He could see she didn't. Hell, he didn't either. Diego placed a soft kiss on the tip of her nose. "Love you."

Diego would give every last penny he had just to see the way her face lit up when he told her that.

Luc rolled to his side, his arm coming around Jeannette, sighing. Diego grinned at the exhaustion in the sound. "Are we going to sleep today away too?"

"Sounds good to me," Jeannette said, just as Penny jumped back onto the bed. The cat found her way between Diego and Jeannette. She began to purr. "I think Penny is on board for that too."

Diego ran his hand along the cat's soft fur, which encouraged Penny to flip over onto her back. He rubbed her belly.

Luc reached over Jeannette to pet Penny as well. "I'm starting to think you guys are more into my cat than me."

Luc chuckled. "She is a pretty soft pussy."

Jeannette elbowed him, her expression going serious. "I'll never be able to thank you guys enough for saving her. And more than that...for saving me."

Luc pressed a kiss to her cheek. "You saved us too, Jeannette. There's a big difference between merely existing and living a life that's exciting."

Diego leaned as close as he could without disturbing Penny, who had already fallen asleep. "Happy ending?"

She nodded. "The happiest. We blew *Beauty and the Beast* out of the water."

They settled into their places, Diego and Luc surrounding Jeannette and her sweet cat, Penny.

Diego's last thought as he drifted to sleep was that they'd done it.

Created the perfect family.

EPILOGUE

Macie wiped up the counter. It was a Tuesday night and the dinner crowd had come and gone. Gia was bussing the last dirty table. She could hear Sydney and Jeannette closing down the kitchen for the evening. Her dad, TJ, had already gone home.

Luc and Diego were hanging out at the bar, while Chas was in a corner booth, chatting with Sydney's dad, Uncle Lynn.

The guys were there to pick up their girlfriends…just like they did every night. Macie tried not to roll her eyes at how annoyingly in love her older cousins were. Lately, all Jeannette and Sydney did was walk around in a continual state of just-had-amazing-sex. It was enough to drive her batty. Mainly because, for the first time since she'd lost her virginity in the backseat of Hank Watson's Buick back in tenth grade, Macie was suffering a dry spell.

She had decided early on that she didn't agree with the double standards attached to sex. Guys could fuck with reckless abandon and walk around like studs. If a woman did the same thing, she was labeled a slut. The whole thing pissed her off. She was a woman. And she liked sex. A lot. Whether she had that sex with a long-term boyfriend or if she hooked up the hot guy she'd just met at Cruisers didn't really matter to her.

However, lately, her attitude toward sex had changed. She suspected it was because of all the monogamous couples surrounding her. Macie had never had a problem separating sex and love. In her opinion, the two didn't necessarily have to go hand in hand. Or at least, that was what she used to believe.

Now, she was coming to the conclusion that she wanted to get married. Desperately.

That idea wouldn't have been quite so disturbing if it weren't attached to the realization that her Mr. Right wasn't in Maris.

Unfortunately, home is where the heart is, and her heart lived and breathed and flourished in this neck of the woods, and nowhere else.

"Earth to Macie. Hello?"

Macie blinked, then she realized Luc was talking to her. "Did you want something else?"

Luc tilted his head. "You okay, Mace? You've been quiet tonight. I'm not sure I've ever been in a room with you when your voice wasn't the constant white noise in the background."

"Asshole," she said in response to his teasing. She pitched a peanut at him, just narrowly missing his head as he dodged.

"Hey, I just finished sweeping the floor," Gia said, bending down to pick up the peanut.

"I asked what you thought was going on over there." Luc pointed to Chas, who'd just risen from the table. He shook Lynn's hand and they said good night as Lynn took his leave.

"No idea," Macie muttered, though she actually had a pretty good idea.

Chas joined them all at the bar.

"Everything good?" Diego asked Chas, fishing.

Chas merely nodded, but from the smug expression on his face, it was clear he was happy.

Before they could question him further, Sydney and Jeannette walked out of the kitchen and joined them.

"All clear in there," Jeannette said.

Sydney glanced around the room. "Did my dad leave?"

Chas nodded.

Macie tossed her dishcloth into the sink, her own cleaning finished as well. "Yeah, we were about to give Chas the third degree on the serious conversation they were having."

Chas narrowed his eyes at Macie.

"Serious conversation?" Sydney asked.

"We were just talking," Chas said. Then he looked around. Macie was surprised when he let loose a heavy sigh. "Dammit. I hate surprises. And waiting."

Sydney laughed and shook her head. "I know all about your issues with both of those things."

"You know I saw you for the very first time in this room. Gran had brought me here for lunch one day and you were sitting right there at the counter drinking a milkshake. You were giggling at something TJ said to you and I thought you looked really pretty. Isn't it funny how vividly I can remember that? I mean, I was only five years old."

Sydney blushed, and Macie could tell her cousin was touched by Chas' sweet memory. "You never told me that."

The room went completely silent when Chas dropped down to one knee in front of Sydney.

"I was going to do something romantic, take you out to eat, buy you flowers, but I can't wait for you, for *this* anymore, Syd."

Sydney's mouth had fallen open. "Chas," she whispered.

"I asked your dad if I could propose to you. He gave us his blessing."

Macie had never thought herself a romantic fool or someone who was particularly held up on such old-fashioned traditions, but suddenly she wanted to meet someone just like Chas. Someone who would remember the first time he saw her, who would ask her dad for her hand in marriage. Someone so excited to propose, he couldn't wait more than three minutes after getting the dad's permission.

"I love you, Sydney. You've been my best friend since kindergarten. I can't imagine how much my life would have sucked if you weren't in it."

Sydney laughed, though the sound came out half sob. There were happy tears in her eyes.

Chas reached into the pocket of his jeans and produced a beautiful ring. "Sydney Sparks, would you do me the honor of becoming my wife?"

Sydney had begun to nod before Chas even got the question out. "Yes."

Then Chas was up, hugging her.

Macie was relieved to realize she wasn't the only person in the room crying when she spotted Gia and Jeannette reaching for napkins to wipe their eyes.

Luc and Diego were quick to shake Chas' hand as Gia and Jeannette immediately started talking about dresses and summer weddings. Soon the guys were included in the conversation as they discussed honeymoon locations.

Macie, however, appeared to be the only person focused on the most important thing, the one thing that offered Macie an answer to her dilemma.

A change of scenery. A chance to break out of her damn rut.

Macie raised her hands, speaking above everyone. "I hate to interrupt all of you, but you're jumping the gun."

"How so?" Jeannette asked.

"There's not going to be a wedding..." she paused for dramatic effect, just because it was fun, and then she added, "without a bachelorette party. Vegas, here we come!"

WAITING FOR HIM

SPARKS IN TEXAS, BOOK 3

WAITING FOR HIM

According to the bro code, enacted by Evan and Logan years ago, sisters are out. However, Lacy isn't about to let a silly boyhood pact stand between her and the man she's wanted for twenty years.

She's waited for him long enough. Logan thinks she's too sweet to give him what he needs. He's about to learn as far as Lacy's concerned, in bed or out, nothing is off-limits.

To Liz Berry and M.J. Rose
For their belief in me and my stories

PROLOGUE

ne year earlier...

"Closing time," Lacy Sparks said, gently tapping on Logan's shoulder. He'd been looking down at his beer so long he had almost forgotten where he was.

"I thought maybe you'd found a way to sleep with your eyes open," she teased.

He glanced up at her, and then let his gaze wander around the restaurant. He was surprised to find the place empty. Where the hell did everyone go?

Her cousin, Macie was behind the bar, wiping the counter and he could hear Sydney in the kitchen, washing dishes. Lacy had already cleaned the dining area and he hadn't noticed them doing any of it.

"Sorry."

"No problem. I'll walk you home," she offered.

Logan wasn't drunk. Not even close. After all, he'd nursed the last still-full beer for over an hour. But he wasn't going to turn down the offer of company. Especially Lacy's. She was one of the reasons he'd returned to Sparks Barbeque tonight. He'd been here earlier with her brother, Evan. His best friend since first grade, Evan had picked him up after work and declared they were going out for happy hour. His friend had been hell-bent on cheering him up. After all, Logan had just gotten dumped. For the first time.

Logan had dated lots of girls, but in the end, he'd always been the heartbreaker because none of them had captured his affections. Until he met Jane.

He should consider himself lucky. Not many men made it too the ripe old age of thirty-three without ever having their hearts ripped out. Of course, the more he thought about it, the more he realized it wasn't his heart Jane had just tromped all over. It was his pride. His heart had walked out of the relationship about six months ago.

He and Evan had eaten dinner, kicked back a few beers and then Evan had dropped him off at his place. Logan had taken one look around the quiet apartment and then walked the two blocks back to the restaurant. He preferred noise to silence, and there was something very soothing about Lacy's Uncle TJ's off-color stories, Macie's boisterous laughter, and the sweet way Lacy kept stopping by to check on him. When you were with the Sparks family, it was easy to forget what ailed you. The pressure that had taken permanent residence on his chest since Jane moved out last week lifted when he was here.

"Logan?"

God. He shouldn't have bothered coming back. He was shitty company. "Sorry," he repeated.

Lacy reached out to clasp his hand, giving it a quick, comforting squeeze. "You ready to go?"

He nodded. "Yeah, but shouldn't I be offering to walk you home?"

She grinned. "I live five blocks from here and I walk myself home every night. Besides, your place is on my way."

Logan reached for his wallet, but she waved off his money when he tried to pay for the beer. "It's on me."

"Lace."

Rather than fight about it, she simply pulled her jacket on and walked to the front door leaving him no choice but to follow. "Night, Macie," she called out.

"Night, y'all," her cousin replied wearily. It had been a busy night at the restaurant and they were obviously pooped.

Once they stepped out onto the sidewalk, Lacy obviously decided to take the bull by the horns. "I know you're upset about Jane. If you ever need someone to talk to, I'm a pretty good listener."

There was no debating that. While he'd been Evan's friend growing up, once they became adults, Lacy had stopped being the kid sister and became a friend in her own right. She was one of the most upbeat people he'd ever met. An eternal optimist. Logan liked the humor and positive energy that seemed to surround her all the time.

"I'm not sure there's much to talk about. The breakup had been coming for a while. Not like it was a total shock."

"Another man?"

He didn't bother to lie. Logan nodded. "Yeah. Some old boyfriend from back home. Apparently they've been chatting on Facebook for nearly a year."

"Fucking Facebook," she said with a grin.

The joke worked. He laughed, but didn't bother to say Jane's flirting over social media had very little to do with what really broke up the relationship. And it certainly wasn't anything he could explain to Lacy. Not fully anyway. God only knew what she'd say if he went into all the gory details.

"This is probably one of those things that's best left alone. Rehashing it won't make it better. I just need to figure out where to go from here."

"So, I'll change my offer. If you ever want to hang out and *not* talk about it, you know where to find me."

"Thanks."

He appreciated her kindness, but he didn't see himself taking her up on the offer. Logan was getting out of a three-year relationship. He needed time to recover and to get his shit together. Looking at Lacy tonight, Logan felt something he didn't want to put a word to, simply because it would be too dangerous to acknowledge.

Once they reached the front of his apartment, he paused. "I really don't mind walking you home, Lacy."

She smiled, and then reached up on tiptoe to give him a quick kiss on the cheek. "It's Maris, Logan. I'll be fine. Night."

He watched as she walked away, not turning toward his front door until she was completely out of sight.

The second Lacy was gone, the heavy feeling he'd managed to keep at bay in the restaurant, returned, along with a new one.

Fuck it. He called it by name. He felt tempted. By Lacy Sparks. It was going to be a long night.

CHAPTER ONE

"This isn't Vegas."

Lacy rolled her eyes as Macie repeated the same sentiment she'd been muttering all night. Damn woman had been bemoaning the fact they were holding their cousin Sydney's bachelorette party in boring old Maris, Texas, instead of Las Vegas for about six weeks now.

"Yeah. That's totally not getting old, Mace," Lacy said with a sigh. "Besides, I think Sydney is handling the disappointment just fine." She lifted her chin toward the bar, where Sydney was giggling her fool head off while sporting a short white veil, jeans and a "Kiss Me, I'm the Bride" t-shirt covered with guys' signatures in Sharpie. She was drinking blowjob shots with three sexy ranch hands who were only too happy to celebrate with the tipsy bride-to-be.

"I bet she'd trade those three farm boys for male strippers any day of the week."

Lacy laughed. "This is Sydney's party, not yours. I suspect she's perfectly happy right here. We'll go to Vegas when you get married."

Macie tipped back her beer. "That's small comfort. I've done a thorough accounting of the stock around here and I'm fairly certain I'm never getting married."

Lacy found it difficult to argue with her cousin. Macie had cut a wide swath through most of the available men in Maris. Not that Macie was a slut. Quite the contrary. She was very discerning when it came to her lovers. However, she was an equal opportunity dater, which meant she didn't turn down many requests to go out. Only a handful had ever gotten a second date. "Maybe you should widen the search, check out some neighboring towns."

Macie simply rolled her eyes. "Already done that." Then, as so often happened with her cousin, Macie spotted a "squirrel" and changed topics. Shiny things constantly distracted her, too. "It's good to see Coop out tonight."

Lacy glanced toward where the rancher was sitting alone, nursing a beer. "Wonder how he's doing."

"Considering his wife died of breast cancer eleven months ago, I'm going to go out on a limb and say shitty." Macie rose from her seat. "And since the pickings around here are so slim, I'm going to give up on getting lucky and go buy that man a beer. Looks like he could use some cheering up."

Hank Cooper had always been a regular at Sparks Barbeque, the restaurant Lacy and her cousins operated, stopping in for lunch at least once a week. However, since his wife Sharon's death, he'd become even more regular, sitting at the bar with a sandwich, plate of fries and a beer nearly every single night as Macie held court.

While Macie was a terrible cook, she was one hell of a bartender. Lacy was pretty sure that, while people originally came for the delicious food Sydney and Jeannette prepared, they returned because of the fun Macie provided.

Lacy lifted her beer for a drink as her cousin walked away and took the opportunity to survey the bar. It was the first time she'd had five minutes to herself since they began this crazy adventure. Her boisterous cousins and several of their girlfriends had surrounded her all evening as they ran through the typical checklist of bachelorette insanity, complete with tequila shots and raunchy sex toy and negligee gifts. Then they started playing some silly game that Paige had found online, where Sydney had to find guys who fit certain characteristics to sign her t-shirt. She'd found men with tattoos, piercings and facial hair quickly, and had her pick of the litter on men wearing cowboy hats and boots. So far, she'd had no luck on finding a male prostitute or a transvestite—Macie's additions to the list, items she insisted Sydney would have found easily in Vegas.

With the exceptions of Sydney at the bar and Macie sitting with Coop, most of their party was now out on the dance floor, shaking their booties, completely oblivious to how many cowboys currently stalked them. Lacy didn't blame the guys. She'd always thought her cousins were beautiful women—inside and out. When they were out together in a pack, like they were now, they tended to turn more than a few heads.

Several men got bold and attempted to break into the circle, hoping to pick one of the women off and get her away from the others. It looked like one guy had just about managed to capture Adele's attention before she shimmied back into the fold. Obviously tonight's unspoken theme was *chicks before dicks*. Which suited Lacy fine, because there wasn't anyone here she was interested in hooking up with.

A slow song started playing and most of the girls headed back toward the table. Only four of them made land as the rest found dance partners and stayed on the floor.

"Damn. It's a total meat market out there," Amanda said as she and her girlfriend Brandi returned, along with Jeannette and Gia, who, unlike the rest of their cousins, had steady boyfriends.

"Tell me about it. I'm pretty sure at least three different guys tried to grope my ass during that last song," Gia added.

Amanda laughed. "Yeah. I saw that. One was my ex, Chuck, who's actually here with his girlfriend, Paula."

"Wait. You dated Chuck? Or Paula?" Jeannette asked, clearly thinking Amanda had misspoken.

Amanda waved away Jeannette's confusion with a grin. "Chuck, but that was way back in two thousand and straight. And believe me, if I hadn't already realized I was into girls way more than guys, Chuck would have pushed me into full-fledged lesbianism."

Gia tossed Chuck a dirty look as he did some sort of obscene bump-and-grind dance with Paula. "It's a dick move trying to feel up one woman when you're with another."

"It's late in the night." Brandi reached for a pretzel. "The drunker these rednecks get, the more hands they're going to grow."

"We should have gone to Vegas." Amanda wrapped her arm around Brandi's shoulders to tug her closer.

"Not you too," Lacy said. "I just managed to talk Macie off that ledge. Besides, you were both cool with this plan." Amanda, Macie's best friend all through school, and Brandi were currently saving up for their wedding. It was one of the reasons why they'd all elected to stay local for the bachelorette party rather than travel to Sin City.

Of course, the main reason was the restaurant. They would have had to close the place down this weekend if they had all ventured out of town, and that was something they only did on Thanksgiving and Christmas. They'd managed to get tonight off because Uncle TJ, along with Lacy's aunts and her mom, had volunteered to man the place during the dinner shift so they could go out.

Money was tight for all of them, so they had decided to stick with the tried-and-true bachelorette party, venturing to the only local nightclub in town, Cruisers. Given its close proximity to the highway, there was always a chance of meeting someone new, but tonight's crowd was nothing more than the usual faces.

Brandi pointed toward the front door. "That was before the guys decided to crash the party."

Lacy glanced up then scowled as her cousin Tyson and her big brother, Evan, made their way toward the table. As her Uncle TJ liked to joke, a person couldn't shake a stick in Maris without hitting a Sparks. That was certainly a true statement. Sometimes Lacy enjoyed having such a large, close-knit family.

Sometimes she felt like the only privacy she ever got was in the bathroom.

Then she realized Evan and Tyson weren't alone. Jeannette's boyfriends, Luc and Diego, as well as Evan's best friend, Logan, were there as well.

"Couldn't fit the groom in the car?" Gia asked sarcastically.

Sydney's soon-to-be husband, Chas, appeared to be the only fella who hadn't decided to crash the party.

Tyson looked unapologetic as he sat down next to Gia. He raised his hand to call the waitress over and asked for a round of beers as the other guys claimed the rest of the empty seats. Luc and Diego instantly flanked Jeannette, and she was clearly delighted to see them as they each took a turn kissing her.

"You gals have been here for three hours. We decided you were probably hitting the breaking point." Tyson looked around the bar as he spoke, no doubt doing a cousin head count.

"And what breaking point is that?" Gia asked.

"Either too drunk to make smart decisions or not drunk enough to deal with all the wasted cowboys. Figured it was time for reinforcements either way," Evan explained.

"It's a bachelorette party, Evan," Lacy said, all too familiar with her big brother's tendency to take overprotectiveness to new extremes. "You can't just barge in here like this. You're lucky Macie hasn't seen you yet. She'll flip out."

Lacy made sure to maintain eye contact with her brother as he studied her face, letting him see how much his presence annoyed her. Unfortunately, her anger was lost on him. The cop in him was trying to visually assess how much she'd had to drink. She was the first to look away in disgust. "You're pissing me off."

However, he wasn't. Not really. Lacy loved her brother more than words could say and in truth, she was sort of glad he was here. Not because she liked him hovering—that really did drive her up the wall—but because where there was Evan, there was Logan.

Lacy was delighted to see him out tonight. Since his breakup with Jane nearly a year earlier, he'd maintained the "stay-at-home" lifestyle he'd picked up with his ex, refusing to jump back into the dating scene.

Instead, he spent most of his time working. He owned his own furniture business and was a genius when it came to crafting beautiful things from wood or refurbishing precious antiques. He sold both in his store on Main Street, just two blocks away from the restaurant.

Glancing around the bar at the other men, Lacy realized that Logan would always be the yardstick by which she measured every man. So far, no one had ever come close to her ideal.

In addition to his creative talents in the woodshop, he used to play bass in Tyson's Collective, her cousin's bluegrass band. He could beat out one hell of a rhythm on the bass. What was it about musicians that made them so freaking irresistible and hot?

Plus Logan wasn't hard to look at. At all. He was six-one, with chestnut-brown hair that he wore just a touch too long, which gave him a permanent just-rolled-out-of-bed look that never failed to send her thoughts straight to sex. In addition to that—and his muscular arms and his chiseled jaw and his five o'clock shadow and his great ass—were his eyes. God. Logan had the most striking blue eyes she'd ever seen. They were ice blue, so light and piercing, she got lost in them.

Like now.

She blinked rapidly when she realized Logan was speaking to her. She hadn't heard a word he'd said.

"Lacy? Did you hear me?"

"Um. Sorry. Music is too loud," she lied.

"I said I finished fixing your chaise lounge. Wondered if you wanted me to deliver it to your place sometime next week."

She had found a gorgeous chaise at a flea market a month earlier. Picked the thing up for a song, but it had a couple loose legs and the upholstery had been torn. She'd driven it straight to Logan's store and asked him to fix it for her.

"That would be great, but I can come get it."

He chuckled as he leaned closer. "You were lucky you got the thing to me the first time. Still can't believe you managed to strap it to the roof of your car."

"It was too big for the trunk."

"I'll drop it by in my truck. It's not too heavy. Figure the two of us can get it up the stairs to your apartment on our own."

She nodded, delighted by the prospect of having Logan in her apartment alone. Not that it would make one iota of difference in the way he treated her.

To Logan, she would always be Evan's kid sister, which made her off-limits. The two idiots had actually made some sort of vow about it back when they were sophomores in high school. Evan called it their bro code, like that cliché wasn't old and tired.

Of course, Lacy knew their promise to not bang each other's sisters all those years ago had had absolutely nothing to do with her, and everything to do with Logan encouraging Evan to keep his hands off *his* sister, Rachel.

Rachel had been a year older than Logan and Evan, and growing up, she'd been the Maris High School It Girl. Every guy in the school—and Amanda—had been in love with her. And Rachel had been in love with at least half of them. Unlike Macie, Rachel had been a bit less discerning when it came to sex, and she'd gotten one hell of a reputation by the time she'd hit senior year.

Lacy suspected Logan initiated the bro code as his attempt at managing to keep at least one boy out of Rachel's pants. And Evan, because he was a good guy, had agreed to keep his hands off. Then he'd solicited the same promise from Logan.

She figured Logan hadn't even had to think twice before agreeing. After all, at the time, Lacy had been the annoying eight-year-old who hovered around them like a gnat that they constantly had to swat away. They had both been totally oblivious to the fact that even then she'd been in love with Logan.

Logan had eternal dibs on her heart. He had been her first crush, her first love, and the man to occupy every sex dream she'd ever had. When she'd kissed her pillow in eighth grade, she pretended it was him, and she had at least three notebooks she'd accumulated during middle and high school that were filled with her name and his.

Mr. and Mrs. Logan Grady. Logan and Lacy Grady. Logan + Lacy. LG heart LS.

And the worst part about all of it was, he didn't have a clue.

Logan looked at her and, rather than noticing she was now an available, attractive woman of twenty-seven, he still saw the kid sister.

Of course, it wasn't like Logan had been looking around much. He'd been happily shacked up with Jane for three years, then mourning her departure the last twelve months.

There had been very few people in Maris who hadn't expected to hear wedding bells in Jane and Logan's future, so everyone had been shocked when Jane moved out. And she hadn't just vacated their apartment, she'd left town. Packed up her stuff and hit the road.

Unfortunately, the rumor mill was precious low on details about the breakup, apart from her moving back home for another guy. Lacy suspected there was more. Evan, no doubt, knew what had gone down between the couple, but he would never betray a confidence and Lacy would never ask him to.

In the end, she realized she didn't really care why they broke up. She was just grateful as hell they had. For so many years, she feared she had missed her chance with him.

The table became too crowded for her to continue her conversation with Logan when the rest of the women returned from the dance floor. Then Macie dragged Coop over to join them.

Despite their protestations at the guys' presence, Lacy had to admit the party was more fun with them there. So much so, Sydney called Chas and asked him to come join them, which he did.

It was safe to say Lacy was having one of the best times of her life. She was surrounded by all of her favorite people in the world. Lacy's life was pretty simple, composed of work, flea markets and yard sales, and home. Occasionally she dated, but, like Macie, she wasn't having much luck on the boyfriend front. And since learning that Logan had broken up with Jane, she'd turned down every single guy who'd asked her out—all three of them—because in her foolish, stupid heart, she still hoped that Logan would finally notice her.

So they drank, ate, talked, laughed and danced the night away, and even the fact that Logan had headed to the dance floor a couple of times with other women hadn't dimmed her enjoyment of the evening.

Eventually, the couples began to peel off. Jeannette was the first to leave with her hot firefighters. Not that anyone could blame her for being in a hurry to get home with those two. While ménages were far from the norm, Lacy couldn't deny Jeannette, Luc and Diego fit together perfectly.

Sydney and Chas were the next to go. According to a very tipsy Sydney, they needed to start practicing for the honeymoon. Amanda and Brandi walked out with them.

Over the next hour, everyone else left, the sober ones offering rides to those who had over-imbibed until it was only Logan, Evan and Lacy left at the table.

"Slim pickings tonight, I'm afraid," Evan said as he slapped Logan on the back. It occurred to Lacy, her brother had brought his friend out tonight in hopes of finding him a girl. Or maybe just getting him laid.

It took all the strength she had not to jump up and down, wave her hands around and shout "Yoo-hoo! I'm right here."

Logan shrugged. "I wasn't really looking." He picked up his beer and took a swig, giving Evan a teasing grin as he winked at Lacy. "Let's face it. Hottest girls here tonight were all related to you."

Evan chuckled. "Bro code is still in effect. I know all about you, you kinky bastard. She's my sister."

Lacy felt like kicking her brother under the table. It was on the tip of her tongue to tell them she knew all about Logan's kinks, but both men would die if they realized everything she knew. If they found out she had followed Logan one afternoon about ten years ago and gotten one hell of a sex education...

Gladys Winthrop's granddaughter, Yvette, had traveled from New York to spend the summer with her. Every redneck in town had honed in on the city girl about ten seconds after she crossed the city line. Strangers in Maris were few and far between and when a gorgeous woman wandered into their midst, all the guys took notice.

However, it was Logan who had the distinct privilege of being the man to capture her attention. The two of them had been inseparable that summer—and Lacy had wanted to know why.

Then she'd found out. Oh man, had she found out.

She had followed the couple as they left the annual Fourth of July picnic at the public beach early and returned to Gladys' lake house. Peering through the bedroom window, Lacy had seen Yvette on her knees, her hands bound behind her as she gave Logan a blowjob. That ended when Logan picked her up, placed her facedown over his lap and started spanking her. She might have worried, if Yvette hadn't been begging for more, her expression one of total bliss.

Lacy had been equal parts horrified and turned on. At seventeen, she'd only just begun to truly discover her sexuality. That day had molded her fantasies, sparked feelings she had never had the opportunity to explore, and ignited cravings she had never wanted to indulge in with anyone other than Logan.

The deejay announced the last dance at the same time Evan's phone rang. "It's Annie. I need to take this." He stepped outside to take the call from his wife, leaving her alone with Logan.

"Want to dance?" she asked.

He shrugged good-naturedly. "Sure. Why not?"

She fought down her annoyance at the realization he was just humoring her.

Then she decided it was time to set the record straight.

Maybe he was determined to cast her in the role of little sister, and maybe he was determined to keep his hands off her because of some stupid teenage vow, and maybe he was still getting over his last girlfriend—but enough was enough.

There was no way Logan Grady was leaving here tonight

without the knowledge that she was an experienced, available and completely fuckable woman who was more than capable of keeping up with him in the bedroom. She refused to take one more second of his condescending pats on the head that made her feel eternally eight years old.

He took her in his arms, maintaining a polite distance that she instantly broached. He stiffened briefly as she pressed her breasts firmly against his chest. His hands rested lightly on her waist, the touch platonic, boring. She didn't follow suit as she wrapped her hands around his neck, letting her fingers play with his hair. It was even thicker than it looked.

Lifting up on her tiptoes, she lightly ran her lips along his neck. Logan's hands tightened, and for a moment, she expected him to push her away. Instead, he surprised her, letting his fingers drift around her back until he'd managed to split the difference between touching her waist and her ass.

Then he used his grip to tug her closer, letting her feel his erection pressed against her stomach—and it occurred to Lacy her plan was backfiring. She hadn't anticipated Logan returning her touches. In her mind, she would leave him hot and bothered, his punishment for failing to acknowledge her as a woman.

So much for that idea.

Her pussy clenched and her nipples tightened when his hands drifted even lower, his palms molding themselves to her ass.

Unable to resist, she glanced up and found him looking at her curiously.

"How much have you had to drink?" he asked.

"Not much."

Not enough.

She'd been relatively sober when they'd stepped on the dance floor, but now she felt wasted, her legs stumbling, barely able to hold herself upright under his sensual touches, and her brain was fuzzy from a system overload of arousal.

She kept one hand in his hair as the other traveled along his chest, her fingers digging into the muscles she found along the way. She didn't stop until her hand rested on the buckle of his belt, less than an inch away from his cock.

His hands tightened on her ass and she released a soft sigh.

"You know what you're doing?"

She nodded, though she wasn't so sure anymore. Originally, she'd thought she was seducing him. Now it felt like *he* was seducing *her*. And she was responding to it.

He left one hand on her ass as he lifted the other to the side of her neck. He lightly ran one fingertip along the neckline of her top. The shirt dipped low, revealing a healthy amount of cleavage. Macie had taken one look at her when she'd arrived at the party and wolf-whistled at what she'd jokingly referred to as Lacy's hootchie-mama shirt.

Logan paused when he hit the cleavage. "Nice shirt."

For the first time in her life, it felt like Logan was looking at her.

And really seeing her.

Reaching up, she grasped the hand still hovering above her breast and pressed his palm against it. She didn't have a clue where she'd found the outright boldness, but opportunities like this had been too few and far between. She couldn't run the risk of Logan finding another girlfriend and moving her in for three long-ass years before she took her shot.

He squeezed her breast roughly. The touch sent a jolt of electricity along her spine and straight to her pussy.

"Lacy," he whispered, his hot breath sweet from the soda he'd been drinking. "I—"

The song ended and another couple jostled against them as they left the dance floor. It forced them to break apart before he could finish his statement.

Rather than continue, he grasped her hand and led her back to the table. Mercifully, Evan hadn't returned. God only knew what her brother would have done if he'd caught sight of her and Logan fondling each other on the dance floor not three minutes after he'd reminded them of the bro code.

The waitress was at the table with their bill. Logan handed her his credit card. She resumed her seat, her legs still unsteady. It had only been a dance, but it had shaken Lacy to the core. She'd had sex before and she'd certainly experienced desire, but what she felt now seemed eons away from mere want. She was ravenous, predatory. Her whole body ached with a need so intense it took her breath away.

She searched for something to say, but her brain wouldn't function. Words wouldn't form.

Evan returned before she could gather her wits. "Hey, I gotta run. Eryn's got a fever."

"Is she okay?" Lacy asked, concerned about her adorable little niece.

"She was tugging at her ears earlier, so Annie thinks it's probably an ear infection. We're out of baby Tylenol and Annie asked me to pick some up on my way home. I need to get going. Do you mind driving Lacy home, Logan?"

Logan shook his head, but it seemed pretty clear that he wasn't exactly pleased by the prospect. "Not at all. I'll take her. You need to get home to your baby."

Logan's chilly expression went through her like a bucket of cold water. While his body had responded to her—and really, what guy's body didn't react when a woman threw herself at him? —it was obvious he didn't want to be alone with her.

Unfortunately, she was stuck without a car. She'd ridden to the party with Amanda and Brandi, but had elected to stay when Evan said he'd drop her off.

"Great. I'll catch you guys later," Evan said as he passed the waitress on her way back to the table.

"I can call a cab," she offered.

"Don't be silly." Logan signed the credit card slip, and then gestured toward the exit. "You ready?"

She nodded, draping the sweater she'd brought with her over her arm as they stood to leave. It was early spring in Texas, which meant warm days and chilly nights. When Logan placed his hand against her lower back lightly, she knew she wouldn't need the extra layer for warmth. He'd lit a fire inside of her that was going to take a few rounds with her vibrator to smother.

He helped her into his truck, the door panel plastered with the Grady Furniture logo, before circling to the driver's side.

She hadn't spoken a word to him since leaving the dance floor. Lacy feared she'd open her mouth and beg him to fuck her—right here, right now—in the parking lot of Cruisers. So she kept her lips pressed shut. Clearly he wasn't interested in following through on what they'd begun on the dance floor.

Logan fiddled with the radio as he turned onto the highway and stopped when he found a country station.

"Haven't heard this one in ages," he said as Glen Campbell's "Gentle on my Mind" played.

She loved the song too and tried to concentrate on the music, but all she could think about was Logan's hand on her ass, on her breast.

He lived in a studio apartment above his shop on Main Street, while she had a smaller place three streets over. For the past few years, she hadn't lived or worked more than a mile away from him. They saw each other almost daily, simply because they occupied the same small space and shared similar friends and interests. And while she fantasized about him a little bit too much, for so many years she'd never indulged the idea that they'd have anything more than a platonic relationship because, number one, he had been dating Jane, and number two, that stupid bro code thing was apparently still in effect.

Lacy had just about convinced herself that her actions on the dance floor had been ill-advised when Logan pulled up in front of her apartment building, parked and turned the truck off.

In fact, she opened her mouth to apologize to him for sending the mixed signals and for coming on so strong.

However, the words "I'm sorry" never came. Because the second her lips parted, Logan covered them with his own.

FIVE YEARS EARLIER...

"LACY? What the hell are you doing?"

"Walking home." She was still in a fury, and not even Logan's arrival was enough to calm her down.

He pulled over to the side of the road in front of her. "Get in the truck," he called out through the open passenger window.

"I'll get the seat wet."

"I don't give a damn about that. Get in."

She climbed into the front seat of his truck and gratefully accepted the jacket he handed her. Until that moment, her rage had been keeping her warm, helping her ignore the cold rain. Now that she was inside, she was struggling not to shiver.

"It's pissing down, getting darker by the minute and you're two miles out of town. I almost didn't see you. How the hell did you get out here?"

"I was on a date."

Logan hadn't put the truck back in drive. Hadn't bothered to start moving again. "A date?"

"With Bucky Largent. We got in a fight on the way home and I told him to let me out of the car. He did."

"That fucking asshole."

"Wasn't raining at the time."

"Doesn't matter. He knows he left you out here. Did he come back?"

She lifted her hands in a silent *duh*. "Would I be sitting here if he had?"

"Guess that depends on how pissed off you were."

"Not *that* damn mad." She sighed. "You're right. He's a fucking asshole."

"What happened?"

"We went to Cruisers together. I excused myself to go to the ladies' room and when I came back, the jackass was kissing someone else. I told him to take me home. We got in a big fight on the way to town and I decided I'd rather walk home than spend one more second with the idiot. He stopped. I got out. He spun tires when he pulled away. Big dramatic scene. And now *I* feel like the idiot."

"Didn't realize the two of you were a thing."

She shrugged. "We weren't really. We've gone out to dinner a few of times. Gotten pizza and watched movies at my place once. Tonight was our fifth date. And our last."

"I didn't think you liked the guy."

"When did I say that?" she asked.

"That day you were crying. When you told me that Missy kissed him."

She laughed. "Jesus. I was thirteen, Logan."

"Sounds like your first impression was the right one."

Lacy couldn't argue with that. "Yeah. I guess it was. Thanks for stopping."

He looked at her incredulously. "As if I'd right drive past you."

They chatted for a little while about the weather and a Christmas concert Ty's Collective was going to play. It took her a few minutes to realize Logan wasn't headed back into town.

"Where are we going?"

"Pit stop." She didn't question him. After all, he'd saved her from a very long, very wet walk home. It wasn't until they turned onto the lane to Bucky's house that she figured out what Logan intended.

"Uh, Logan—"

He raised his hand to cut her off. "Won't be a minute," he said as he put the truck in park outside Bucky's house.

Lacy watched as he got out of the vehicle, walked to the front door and knocked. The front porch light turned on as Bucky walked out. Though she couldn't hear a word that was said, she could read the body language just fine. Clearly Logan was explaining a few things to Bucky, who still seemed to think he was in the right. The conversation ended when Logan punched Bucky in the stomach. Bucky didn't bother to return the favor. Clever man just remained bent over at the waist as Logan walked away.

"You hit him?" Lacy said when Logan returned to the truck.

"I didn't like some of the things he was saying about you."

"Like what?"

"Like I'm not repeating them. Stay away from him. He's an asshole. Find yourself a nice guy."

Lacy smiled. She already had.

CHAPTER TWO

Logan hadn't planned to kiss her. That was his first thought the second his mouth pressed against hers. Her silence on the ride home had bothered him because Lacy was never quiet.

She'd been flirting on the dance floor. At first he'd assumed she was tipsy and feeling playful. So he'd given her a dose of her own medicine, teasing her back.

Then he realized she was relatively sober, and her touches took on a much different meaning.

It had been no secret that Lacy'd always had a crush on him. That idea had been cute when they were younger. He was eight years older than her and she'd only been a kid. Her doe-eyed devotion had fed his teenage pride, but that was all it had done.

Once she had grown up, she'd started looking in a different direction. She'd had a couple of serious boyfriends and she didn't seem to lack for dates. Whenever they ran into each other, they were cordial, friendly, and Logan had worked damn hard to make sure it was nothing else. He hadn't always succeeded, but for the most part, he'd kept his thoughts pure.

Sort of.

Somewhat.

He assumed Lacy had given up the crush after he'd gotten into a serious relationship and she'd lost interest. She had begun to simply view him as Evan's best friend, another brother figure, which was fine by him. It had helped him keep his hands off her this past year.

Because she was definitely off-limits.

For one thing, his needs would probably scare sweet Lacy Sparks spitless if he ever revealed them. And secondly, Evan would cut off his cock and feed it to him for breakfast if he touched her, because his best friend knew perfectly well all the things Logan liked to do with—and to—women in the bedroom. And they weren't things you did with your best friend's kid sister.

Hell, he'd spent the first couple hours of tonight drinking a beer in his workshop with Tyson and Evan, telling both men why he was finished with sweet, nice women, why he would never be happy in another vanilla relationship like the passionless existence he'd escaped with Jane.

He had probably gone into too much detail, talking about all the things he'd do to the next lover he took to bed. Evan and Tyson were likeminded guys—dominant lovers with a penchant for kink. However, neither of them held a candle to Logan. Which was why they'd been so surprised when he had eschewed that life-style and remained with Jane.

So when Lacy had opened her mouth to say goodbye, Logan should have let her. Instead, he reacted without thinking. Because he didn't want to let her go. Not yet.

He expected her to shove him away, to give him shit for the kiss, but she did neither. Instead, her arms tightened around his neck and her hands found his hair again. Lacy touched him like he mattered, like she wanted him. It was a heady, horny experience.

He twisted her body toward him while keeping his lips on hers. Lacy followed the direction, lifting and parting her legs as he tugged her onto his lap. Thank God he'd kept his old truck rather that opting for the new one with the bucket seats. The wide bench seat allowed him to drag her closer as she straddled his legs and press his dick against her.

He could feel the heat radiating from her even through the thick denim of his jeans. His cock was so hard it hurt. Logan raced through his memories, searching for a time when he'd wanted a woman this much.

The truth hit him like a two-by-four between the eyes. He'd never wanted anyone—not even Jane—as badly as he wanted Lacy right now.

"Want you," he said when she turned her face slightly, seeking air. He couldn't stop kissing her, so he ran his lips along her neck.

"Yes," she whispered.

The windows of the truck had fogged up, shielding them from the outside world, but that didn't change the fact they were still parked on the city street. Of course, this was Maris and it was three a.m. Most of Lacy's neighbors had no doubt turned in hours ago. He considered inviting himself up to her place, but realized he'd never make it that far.

So it was happening here.

Decision made, he rucked the miniskirt that had been riding high around her thighs to her waist.

Then he reached down and bit back a groan as he tugged her panties to one side and ran his fingers over her slit. She was hot and wet. She jerked when he ventured lower and thrust two fingers inside her pussy. Her body clenched around them tightly. Jesus. She was already close to coming. He wanted to see that. Wanted to watch her face.

But he needed to slow this party down or it would be over before it ever started.

Logan put a few inches between them, pulling his fingers out.

Lacy frowned and shook her head. "Don't—"

"Shh. Lift your shirt, Lace."

With clumsy, shaking fingers, she managed to tug the hem above her breasts. He'd had a hard time keeping his eyes above her neck all night. Somehow he had found a way. It probably helped that her overprotective brother and Tyson had been at the table.

Now, he took time to enjoy the feast. Logan had known Lacy her entire life, so he knew down to the day when she'd gotten boobs. However, back then, she'd been a kid while he had been a man, and the only thing he'd done with the knowledge that she was filling out was tease the fuck out of Evan with it, claiming he'd have to beat the boys away with a stick.

Logan shouldn't be here. Shouldn't be staring at Lacy's tits like a starving man eyeing a steak. But he couldn't look away. He reached out and tugged her silky bra down, cupping the bottom of her breasts to push them out and over the material. The second her pink nipples appeared, all bets were off.

He lowered his head, sucking one of her nipples into his mouth. Lacy's hands found his hair once more, and she used her grip to hold him in place. The effort was wasted. He wasn't going anywhere. He increased the suction, taking it to that place right on the borderline between pleasure and pain.

He was just about to ease off when Lacy groaned. "Harder."

Logan struggled with the request. He didn't want to hurt her, scare her. Rather than give in, he cupped her other breast with his hand, squeezing the generous flesh. She fidgeted on his lap, seeking relief as she tried to press her crotch against his.

He lifted his head, forced himself to look at her. This was Lacy. She didn't deserve for him to give her false hope or the impression that this would lead somewhere. Nothing could come from this because he couldn't be the kind of man she wanted, that she deserved.

What the fuck was he doing?

She didn't appear to notice his hesitance. Instead, she covered his hand on her breast and peered at him with sultry fuck-me eyes. "Pinch my nipple," she whispered.

His thumb and forefinger were there before his brain could engage. He applied pressure as he studied her face. Lacy never looked away as her cheeks flushed a deeper shade of red, not with embarrassment, but with longing.

Once again, he held back. It went against everything in his nature to stop, but he had to. He had sworn he wouldn't settle for another vanilla relationship. Wouldn't hide his dominant urges, his need for control. Lacy wasn't the woman he needed. She was sweet and loving. The kind of girl a man married. Not the kind you tied to your bed and fucked like a two-bit hooker.

"Please." Lacy bit her lip, her tone rife with frustration. "I need...I need..."

A light went on inside his brain. He increased the pressure and pinched her nipple hard.

He was rewarded by her loud moan as Lacy threw her head back in absolute bliss. She was responding to the pain.

Logan's cock thickened even more and he found it difficult to suck in a deep breath.

Fuck him.

This was bad. Really bad.

He needed to call a halt, to get out of here before he lost the battle.

Unfortunately, Lacy's actions sealed her fate. And his.

She reached down to stroke her clit, two of her fingers sliding into her own body. The damn woman intended to give herself an orgasm.

Hell no.

The Dom inside came roaring to the forefront. His women were not responsible for finding their own pleasure. Not unless he told them to so he could watch.

He gripped her wrist firmly, stopping her actions.

Lacy tried to shrug him off. She was too close and out of her mind with need to understand what she was doing.

"Stop, Lacy. Now!"

Her entire body froze as his deep-voiced command came out too forcefully, too loud.

"Logan—"

"Hush. I know what you need."

He leaned back slightly to watch her as he shoved three fingers between her legs.

She blinked rapidly, gasping loudly. Her hips thrust in time to the rhythm of his fingers. Lacy wasn't shy about taking what she needed. He liked that.

The last year they were together, Jane had become passive in bed, nonresponsive. Half the time, he never had a clue if she loved what he was doing or hated it.

He pushed the thought of his ex out of his mind. Fuck that. There was no place for Jane here.

Lacy continued to gyrate, moving faster. "God, yes," she groaned. "Harder. Do it harder."

Logan had been worried about hurting her, but her request set that concern to rest. He moved his fingers deeper. She was so fucking tight. He couldn't wait to get his cock inside her.

But first...

He rubbed her clit with his thumb and Lacy started to scream. Logan gripped the back of her head and covered her mouth with his, capturing the sound. The last thing he needed was for someone to call the cops. He could see it now. Evan roaring down the street in his patrol car with the lights flashing and siren blasting only to discover his best friend with his fingers buried deep inside his little sister.

He wouldn't have to worry about being arrested. Evan would simply pull out his gun and shoot him.

Lacy was the one to break the kiss as her orgasm began to wane. She panted, her eyes resting on his face unseeingly. He wasn't sure where her climax had taken her, but she wasn't back yet.

It gave him some time to consider what had just happened. He'd just finger-fucked Lacy to an orgasm. And he hadn't been gentle about it.

This was Evan's sister. Not only did the promise they'd made to each other all those years ago hover in the air like a swarm of killer bees, but so did the fact that Evan knew him, knew what he liked in the bedroom too well. He'd never approve of this.

He shouldn't do this.

No. He *couldn't* do this.

He slowly dragged his fingers out of her, her pussy walls fluttering against them. She would feel like heaven on his dick. They sat in silence for a few moments as he gave her time to recover.

And himself time to figure out how to end this without hurting her feelings.

"Lacy—"

She shook her head and placed a quick kiss on his lips. "No. Don't say it. We both know the reasons we shouldn't do this. There's no need to list them."

"I shouldn't have started it. Shouldn't have kissed you like that."

Lacy grinned and gave him a friendly shrug. "You don't really expect me to complain, do you? I'm still sort of flying high from that orgasm."

He chuckled. Leave it to Lacy to take what should have been a damn awkward situation and make it funny.

"My relationship with Jane...it ended badly."

"Okay." The word belied the tone. Lacy didn't understand. "So...the timing is bad?"

He shook his head. He was over Jane before she'd pulled away from the curb. Maybe he should feel guilty about that, but she hadn't shed any tears either. As far as breakups went, theirs had been as lackluster as the last year of the relationship. If anything, she'd fucked up his head more than his heart.

"No. Not really. After she left, I took some time to reevaluate my life, my priorities. To decide what I want and need."

Jane was everything he'd always thought he wanted in a woman. Sophisticated, stylish, elegant, educated. She wasn't from Maris. She was big city. Prep school. And a far cry from every woman in town.

Evan claimed Logan had been attracted to her because she reminded him of Yvette. Yvette had been the first woman to expose his penchant for BDSM. While their affections hadn't been engaged, their sexual attraction had been off the charts. Yvette and Jane had many similar attributes and, looking back, Logan figured his friend had probably been right. He probably *had* homed in on Jane and thought she was the complete package. Sexual attraction and love. He thought he'd found both in her.

Jane was an artist, a sculptor, and they'd spent hours together following their creative endeavors and sharing their love for the work. She had been attentive, intellectual, interesting. He'd fallen for her hard.

However, the chemistry they shared initially had morphed into something much less chemical—although it was certainly toxic—over the years. He had believed her the perfect submissive to his dominant tendencies because in the beginning, she had let him believe that she shared the same interests.

As more time passed, Jane began to balk at his sexual requests until finally, at the end, she acted as if he were a monster anytime he suggested bondage or a sensual spanking or wax play. That was when he'd discovered she had started a long-distance, online flirtation with an old boyfriend. Apparently, the guy convinced her BDSM was something enjoyed by sociopaths, so she packed her bags.

"And I don't fit the bill?" Lacy asked. "As far as these needs go?"

Logan was worried if they took these explorations much further, he'd discover that she fit perfectly. But what would happen a few years down the road? Would she still feel the same? He never wanted to be a monster in Lacy's eyes.

"Evan." He merely spoke her brother's name. More for himself than her.

She rolled her eyes. "I can't believe that stupid bro code thing is still in effect. You guys made that silly promise when you were in high school. We're all adults now."

He needed to explain, needed her to understand why, though the promise they'd made back then had been based on something childish and immature, it still remained today. Because of the man he'd become, because of his need for control. Evan knew way too much about Logan's bedroom habits. He wouldn't like the idea of his sister on the receiving end of them, even if she did enjoy them.

And given Lacy's responses to him tonight, Logan was pretty sure she'd love submitting to him. For now.

"I'm not an easy man to be with, Lacy. Evan knows that."

She frowned, obviously confused. "Evan is your best friend.

He loves you, Logan. I hardly think that would be the case if you were an asshole or something."

"I just got out of a relationship where I basically had to shut away a big part of who I was. I spent years denying my needs in the name of love. When Jane left, I swore I wouldn't do that again. Wouldn't pretend to be anything other than the man I am."

"I'm not asking you to change. I would never do that. I'm not even asking for a relationship, Logan. Just a hookup."

Her words were a lie. He knew her well enough to understand that. But Lacy knew him, too, which was why she knew exactly what to say right now to diffuse the situation. She thought that by convincing him the stakes were low, he'd give in.

Logan forced himself to look at Lacy and he recognized something that he should have seen right from the start. Something that had been there for years.

Lacy loved him. She had always loved him.

And he'd ignored it. First because she'd been too young and because she'd been Evan's sister, and then because he'd been in love with Jane. Seeing it now only drove home exactly how high the stakes were.

That realization gave him the strength to say the hardest words he'd ever uttered. "It's not going to happen, Lacy. Ever."

Her eyes narrowed with anger and frustration. "Because of that stupid promise?"

He shook his head. He owed her the truth. Total honesty. Even if it did shock her.

His sex drive was too strong for her. And right now, it was on system overload. He'd spent the last few years of his life playing Missionary Man and feeling like an ogre for wanting more. He couldn't go back to that. Not even for Lacy. He'd explode.

"No. Because I'm not going to lay you down on my bed and make love to you like I'm Prince fucking Charming. If I took you to my bed, I'd fuck you hard, Lacy. Tie you down. Clamp your nipples. Gag you. Spank your ass with my hand, my belt. Take your mouth, your pussy, your ass. I'd make demands I would expect you to obey and if you didn't, I'd punish you. I couldn't just love you, Lacy. I'd claim you. Body and soul. That's what I would want from you."

Her mouth gaped, but no sound emerged.

"I need to leave, Lacy. Now."

"But—"

"Have you ever been tied up?"

She shook her head.

"Fucked in the ass?" His question was deliberately crude. He needed to make her see reason.

Again, she shook her head. "But I—"

"You need to get out of this truck while you still can. While I can still let you."

"Logan—"

"Now!" he shouted.

Lacy jerked at the anger in his voice, then slowly slid across the seat and reached for the door handle. Her chest rose and fell rapidly, no doubt with fear.

Maybe now she'd give up on this schoolgirl crush and turn her attention toward a nice man who could give her everything she needed, who would put her on a pedestal and treat her the way she deserved.

He couldn't be that man. He had tried for Jane and it had nearly killed him.

She slammed the truck door behind her. Logan started the engine, ignoring the way his hands trembled. He waited until she'd entered her building and then he pulled away from the curb.

In the past, it hadn't been difficult to say goodbye to her, to watch Lacy walk away. Now, it took every ounce of strength he had not to follow her inside.

NINE YEARS EARLIER...

. . .

"Y'ALL PLAYED REALLY GOOD TONIGHT," Lacy said, leaning against Logan's truck.

Logan lifted an amp and placed it in the truck bed. "Thanks. What are you doing out here?"

"Waiting for my cousin, Paige. She's my ride. She's inside flirting with some guy. Thought I'd give her space to work."

Logan laughed. "That's real nice of you."

"Was sweet of y'all to play a song for my birthday." Lacy hadn't been able to take her eyes off him all night. She loved watching him knock out a deep beat on the bass.

"Not every day our girl turns eighteen."

She sighed. The older Logan got, the more he treated her like a kid sister. It was starting to get annoying. "So, I was thinking maybe you could give me my other present."

Logan's forehead crinkled. "I'm sorry, Lace, but I didn't buy you anything."

She grinned and stepped closer. "No, nothing like that. You said you'd kiss me when I turned eighteen."

His confusion grew. "I did? When?"

"That day on my back porch when I was crying because Missy had kissed Bucky."

The light went on. "That's not exactly what I said."

"You said you'd kiss me on my eighteenth birthday if nobody else had. Well, I'm here to tell you I've been kissed by a bunch of nobodies."

"Forget it. That's not what I meant and you know it."

She crossed her arms. "I don't want to forget it. You promised."

"Be reasonable, Lacy."

"It's my birthday. Please?"

Logan glanced around the dark parking lot. The community dance had wound down. Most people had gone home, and now there were only a few folks left inside, cleaning up the mess.

"Fine." He leaned forward and placed a quick buss to her forehead. "There. Happy birthday."

She lifted one shoulder in a dismissive shrug, not bothering to hide her disappointment. "Whatever, Logan. I was hoping to finally get a kiss from someone who knew what he was doing, but obviously, you're as clueless as every other guy I've ever kissed."

He moved toward her, caging her against his truck as his hands rested on the roof of the Chevy. "You think taunting me will get you your kiss, little girl?"

She hadn't really expected it to work until he moved. Now, she wasn't so sure. "Yeah. I do."

"Your brother is going to kick my ass for this."

"I won't tell," she whispered a mere second before his lips touched hers.

Lacy didn't possess blinders when it came to Logan. She had watched him far too closely her entire life. She'd seen him kiss other girls, seen the way he cupped their faces, pulled them close and took control. Hell, she'd seen him do a lot more than kiss them, though she certainly wasn't going to tell him about that.

He didn't do any of that with her. The kiss was sweet, gentle, and excruciatingly boring. His tongue touched hers only once, a brief stroke, and then he pushed away.

Then he practically dared her to complain with serious eyes that said she wouldn't get anything else from him tonight. Her heart refused to add the word "ever" to that thought.

Logan didn't think she was ready for him. But one day, he would change his mind about that. She'd make sure he did.

CHAPTER THREE

"You look like shit, man."

Logan glanced up from the paperwork on his desk to find Evan leaning against the doorjamb in his police uniform. He'd been sitting in his office for the past three hours and he'd managed to accomplish nothing.

Instead, he replayed the scene with Lacy from Saturday night over and over, torn between whether he should kick his own ass for kissing her or for driving away without fucking her. Now it was Friday and he was no closer to putting her out of his mind than he had been when he'd climbed into bed that night. He'd been sporting an almost constant erection; his dick pissed at him for denying it the treat of sliding into Lacy's hot, tight—

He shoved the fantasy away as Evan frowned.

He should not be thinking about fucking Lacy while her brother was there. Shit, he shouldn't be thinking of fucking her, period.

"I didn't think you were all that torn up over Jane leaving."

Mercifully, his friend had misinterpreted his expression. God help him if Evan ever found out what he was really thinking about.

"You should have taken my advice," Evan continued. "Found yourself a pretty girl and gotten laid Saturday."

"I'm not ready."

"Jesus, man. It's been a year." Evan leaned forward. "You know there's a woman out there for you, right? One who is better suited to you than Jane was. She fucked you up, man. Made you think things that aren't true. There's nothing wrong with liking your sex rough. Even Annie and I have been known to do some kinky role playing." Evan wiggled the handcuffs that were hanging from his belt. "These aren't just for bad guys."

Logan shrugged. "Spare me the details about your unnaturally happy marriage. You found a good one. And yeah, I know that old adage there's someone for everyone, so I don't need the clichés. I'm not pining over Jane. I'm simply being a realist. The chances of me finding that woman in Maris is…"

Logan's words drifted away as he struggled to finish a sentence that no longer felt true. So much of his thoughts this week had been consumed by the idea that Lacy actually might be exactly what he was looking for. He shut the idea down when he recalled the look in her eyes as she'd climbed out of his truck.

"You'll find her," Evan reassured him. "But hiding in your office isn't going to help. You haven't met me for lunch or happy hour once this week."

He hadn't met Evan because both of those weekly events took place at Sparks Barbeque. Logan wasn't ready to see Lacy yet. And he was sure as shit she didn't want to see him.

"I'm not hiding. I'm just…busy. I've got a lot of work piling up. I guess the stress is getting to me."

Evan accepted the excuse easily. "Busy is a good problem to have. Means money. You'll come through. You always do."

"Yeah. Thanks. Hey, did you need something in particular or did you just stop by to nag me?"

He expected Evan to laugh. Instead, the man stepped into the office and plopped down in the chair opposite his, the desk between them. "Actually, I'm on patrol. Thought I'd take a second to stop in and thank you for taking Lacy home the other night."

Logan swallowed heavily, forcing a casual tone to his voice. "No problem."

"Did she seem okay to you after the party?"

Logan wasn't sure how to respond. Did Evan know something? Lacy sure as hell wouldn't have talked to her brother about what had happened. Had one of her neighbors seen them?

"Yeah. Why?"

Evan shrugged. "She's been really quiet since then. I thought maybe she was getting sick, but it's going on too long. She's got dark circles under her eyes and Macie said she's been snapping at them at work. You know as well as I do Mary Sunshine is never in a bad mood, so I'm worried. Wondered if she said something to you, if something happened at the bar that pissed her off or if someone bothered her."

Logan shook his head. "She didn't say anything. I'm not sure what could have happened," he lied. He knew what was ailing Lacy. It was the same thing that was making him irritable as fuck.

"Yeah, okay. I might talk to Tyson, see if he can talk her into going in for a checkup. Maybe she does just have a touch of something."

There wasn't a damn thing Dr. Sparks could do for her, but Logan nodded as if it was a solid suggestion. He'd avoided the restaurant since Saturday because he suspected he was the last person Lacy wanted to see. As such, he'd holed up here, moving between his apartment upstairs, down to work, and then back again. Unfortunately, he was starting to run low on food. He would have to venture beyond the front door eventually.

Evan's walkie-talkie crackled. "Guess I better get back out on the road. Call me this weekend if you want to meet up for a couple of beers."

"Will do." Logan rose as Evan left, debating what to do now. He hated knowing exactly how much he'd upset Lacy, but he was at a loss over how to help her. The best thing he could do for her was to keep his distance.

His phone beeped and he glanced at the screen to find a text from Lacy.

Coming by in a few. Bringing lunch.

He considered texting back and telling her to stay away. However, as always, his gut overrode his brain when it came to Lacy.

He simply tapped in two letters.

OK

His cock thickened at the thought of her arrival, so he forced himself away from the desk. Time to hit the workshop and start working on a new piece. Hopefully he'd manage to lose himself in the project enough to ward off this fucking erection. His brain needed all the blood it could get if she was coming by to talk.

Work was always a good distraction for him.

Logan closed his eyes and sighed. Work hadn't distracted him once since Saturday night.

He closed his eyes and recalled his first kiss with Lacy. She'd been eighteen, beautiful, vivacious and just discovering her sexuality. She'd dared him to kiss her and he'd been just weak enough to give in. Somehow, he'd managed to keep the kiss fairly platonic and push her away that night, but it had been a damn close call.

Great. Now, he wasn't just obsessing over Saturday night, he was recalling things he'd managed—just barely—to forget.

He was fucked.

Lacy stood outside Grady's Furniture with her bag of takeout and tried to calm down. She'd spent the entire week in a state of constant horniness.

After Logan kicked her out of his truck, she had spent two days in a fury. He'd pushed every hot button in her body, told her in no uncertain terms all the ways he wanted her—ways she wanted to be taken—and then gone into that frustrating, protect-ing-you-for-your-own-good mode that drove her insane.

He had pissed her off enough that she'd actually decided she was finished with him. She wasn't going to keep begging the dumbass to acknowledge that she was fucking perfect for him. If he couldn't figure it out on his own, then screw him.

The anger waned around Monday afternoon, at which point, her hormones kicked back in. She was lightheaded and dizzy from the never-ending, pussy-pulsing arousal she felt every time she thought about Logan's assertion that he would claim her.

This morning, she managed to fight her way out of the haze of horniness enough to make a plan. Logan thought she was off-limits, thought his needs were too much for her. So she had to find a way to get him to take that first step toward her without feeling guilty about breaking his vow to Evan or fear that he'd hurt her—physically or emotionally.

That thought produced a mental eye roll.

Yeah. Like he'd hurt me in any way I don't totally want.

Overcoming his reticence was a tall order to fill, but she was determined to make it happen.

A tiny bell rang as she opened the front door. The showroom was empty. Then she heard the buzz of an electric saw from the workroom. Turning, she flipped the sign that hung on the front door that said "Be back in one hour" and locked the bolt.

She made her way around his handmade furniture, mentally reorganizing the place as she went. It was a good thing Logan made such beautiful pieces they sold themselves, because his ability to show them off sucked. It was a damn maze in here. Total chaos.

She paused at the door to the workroom. His back was to her as he guided a piece of wood through the jigsaw. She had never had the opportunity to watch him work. The muscles of his back and arms flexed as he pushed the cedar plank through the blade, moving it in a waving pattern.

Once the cut was complete, he turned the saw off.

"What are you making?"

He turned at the sound of her voice, and then glanced back down at the wood. "A hope chest."

She lifted the bag she carried. "Lunch. Hope you're in the mood for barbeque. Haven't seen you at the restaurant this week, so I figured you were ready for a fix." Logan usually made it to Sparks Barbeque at least a couple times a week. She'd felt his absence intensely, her gaze traveling to the entrance every single time another patron entered. Searing disappointment followed each arrival when he never bothered to show up.

"I thought you'd prefer some distance from me."

So, he was going right for the jugular. She was relieved. Lacy didn't have the patience to pussyfoot around the issue either. "You thought wrong."

"Lace—"

"No." She cut him off the second she heard that condescending tone in his voice that made her see red. "Hear me out first."

He lifted his hand, inviting her to speak. "Fine."

"I'm off-limits, right?"

He frowned. "What?"

"I'm off-limits. Because I'm Evan's sister and because you think I can't handle what you want from me."

He nodded slowly.

"So we won't have sex. You can keep your stupid promise to my brother. No bro codes will be broken. But I want the chance to disprove the second part of your argument."

Logan crossed his arms. "How do you propose we do that without having sex?"

"For the sake of argument, we're going to call sex actual penetration. Your dick in my vagina."

"That's a pretty narrow interpretation."

She grinned. "And it leaves plenty of wiggle room...so to speak."

He shook his head. "Please don't do this, Lacy. I'm trying to do the right thing."

"How is this right? You want me and I want you."

Logan rubbed his forehead, his expression incredulous. "Even after everything I said last weekend?"

"Especially after that."

He chuckled at her quick response. "God. You're going to be the death of me. You don't have a clue what you're saying. What you're inviting."

She scowled. "You're wrong. I know exactly what I want. And you're the man to give it to me."

He didn't respond, but she didn't fool herself into believing he was wavering. He wasn't. The asshole was stubborn. Which sucked for him because she was too.

"I can't do what you're asking."

She took a step closer to him, relieved when Logan didn't back away. She didn't fancy the idea of chasing him around the workshop like some lovesick Pepé Le Pew. "Yes. You can. In fact, I think you're the only man who can give me what I want."

"You're too young to know—"

"Finish that statement and I'll stab you in the heart with that screwdriver over there. I'm twenty-seven, Logan. I'm not a virgin and I'm not stupid. I've done my research on BDSM because the idea of it turns me on. A lot. I need someone experienced to teach me about it. Someone I trust."

Lacy had him on the ropes, so she decided to go for broke. "Besides, Evan made out with your sister the summer after you guys graduated, so we're entitled to bend the rules a little too."

"He what? No way."

"I caught them."

"That son of a bitch."

She grinned. "So the bro code has already been broken."

"Making out is a far cry from what you're proposing we do, Lacy. It doesn't mean that you and I—"

Lacy tugged her t-shirt over her head, tossing it to the floor. Logan's gaze landed on her breasts within an instant.

"What are you doing?"

She tilted her head. "I thought I was making it pretty clear. I'm seducing you."

"Put your shirt back on." His heated look didn't match his request. He hadn't looked away from her tits yet.

She shook her head. "No."

"I need you to be sensible."

She scoffed, then reached behind her back and unhooked her bra. She dropped it on top of her shirt.

Logan's jaw clenched. She had to give him credit. His powers of resistance were stronger than she'd anticipated. Which only pushed her to up the ante.

Her fingers started to work loose the button on her jeans.

"Stop!"

Logan used that same commanding voice he'd unleashed in the truck, the one that had her panties going damp.

His gaze captured hers and held. "Put your shirt back on, or..."

"Or what?" she taunted.

"Or I'm going to tug down your jeans and beat that cute little ass of yours."

She gave him a coy smile. "You think my ass is cute?"

Logan closed his eyes and she wondered if he was praying for patience. When he opened them again, she shuddered at the intensity, the hunger laid bare on his face. He had clearly turned a corner.

The friendly, safe, hands-off Logan she'd always known was gone. In his place was this new Logan, dangerous, sexy, demanding.

"You have three seconds to do as I said."

She didn't move. Instead, she counted. "Three, two—"

One minute she was facing him down, the next she was face-down. Over his lap.

Logan rubbed her ass through the denim of her jeans. She hated the barrier, wanted his hands on her bare skin.

She started to shift, hoping to find a way to work the jeans over her hips, but he caught her hands, dragging them behind her and holding them together at the base of her back.

"Not so fast. Ground rules."

Lacy growled. "I don't want rules. I want sex."

He tightened his grip on her wrists. "That's the first rule. No penetration."

She *had* made that suggestion. And she was already regretting it. "We already determined that," she said impatiently, wondering if she could change his mind.

Logan smacked her ass, but her jeans dulled the impact. It wasn't even close to enough for her. "Three times. That's it."

"What?"

"There has to be a deadline to this, Lacy. We'll get together no more than three times, each meeting one week apart, during which I'm going to show you exactly what kind of man I am. I'll expose you to BDSM and you can see if you like it. If you want to call it off before that, you can. But we're not doing this more than three times."

She wanted to argue, but it was clear he didn't intend to be swayed. It didn't matter. She planned to use every single second of those meetings proving to him why they should extend the deadline indefinitely. "Fine."

"Your safe word is chaise. Say that anytime it's too much for you or you get scared and we'll stop, talk it out. Okay?"

She nodded.

"Say okay."

"Okay," she said, her voice betraying her shortness of breath. She was worried he'd misinterpret it as fear when the truth was she was so turned on, her whole body hurt.

He released her hands and she instantly missed the restraint. Then she was disappointed even further when he helped her stand.

Logan took her hand. "Not in here. Too much sawdust, too many wood shavings. I don't want you to get cut." He led her toward his office, but stopped just as they reached the threshold and glanced toward the front. "I need to—"

"I already locked the door and flipped the sign."

He gave her a crooked smile and reached down to pinch one of her nipples. She gasped as moisture pooled between her thighs. "Pretty sure of yourself, aren't you?"

"I think the word is determined."

He shook his head. "No. It's stubborn. Something the Sparks family has in abundance."

"Remember that in three weeks."

Logan twisted her, guiding her into his office. "I'm not

changing my mind, Lace. I'm already crossing too many lines by agreeing to this."

Once they entered the room, he closed the door and locked it as well.

"Take off your jeans."

Lacy lost no time kicking off her shoes and tugging the denim —and her panties—off. Within sixty seconds, she stood before him completely naked. Meanwhile, Logan was still dressed.

"What about you?"

He didn't reply. Instead, his gaze traveled over her nude form like a caress. She held her ground and let him look his fill. She liked the look in his eyes, the genuine appreciation there. He thought she was pretty and it made her feel that way.

"Beautiful," he whispered when his eyes met hers once more.

She flushed at the compliment and lifted one shoulder timidly. She wasn't sure she'd go that far, but she was touched that *he* had.

"Turn around and bend over the desk. I owe you a punishment."

Lacy did as he said without question, her pussy clenching in anticipation. She had seen him do this to Yvette all those summers ago and since then, her imagination had run wild with the fantasy.

Logan stepped behind her as she assumed the position, his hand cupping the back of her neck, pressing her more firmly against the smooth surface of his desk. "Open your legs."

Again, she responded to his request. It was so easy to do. With Logan, she didn't have to think, to consider. She wasn't worried about her safety because he would never hurt her. At least not more than she would enjoy.

He ran his fingers along her slit and she shivered as one hand held her tight to the desk. She started to reassure him she wouldn't move, but she liked that extra restraint, liked the feeling of being his captive.

One of his wet fingers circled the rim to her anus. Lacy realized she'd forgotten to breathe. She sucked in as much air as she could, releasing it in short pants through her nose as he fondled her ass.

Logan didn't speak as he explored. She longed to end the silence, but her chest was too tight to utter a single word. A million questions flew through her head. She wasn't used to being *apart* while a part of something like this. In the past, her lovers had been equal partners and everything was discussed and voted on in committee meetings.

Logan was clearly the CEO, CFO, and dictator rolled into one. He'd do what he wanted and he didn't ask permission beforehand.

God. The quiet was maddening. What was he thinking? What would he do next? When was he going to spank her? Could she convince him to forget that stupid thing she'd said about not fucking her? Why had she said that? She needed—

"Shh." Logan bent over her back, his soft hush blowing hot against her ear. "Shut it all down, Lace."

His words washed through her like a gentle wave and just like that, she relaxed.

"Say your safe word," he commanded.

"No." She panicked. There was no way she was going to call this off. "I don't want to."

"I just want to hear you say it. Want to make sure you remember."

"You won't stop?"

She half expected him to laugh at her childlike pleading, but instead he pressed a warm kiss against her cheek.

"I won't stop. Right now, I'm worried that I can't." A tinge of pain seemed to lace his tone. He felt it too. She had never experienced desire so strong that it hurt, but the only thing she was sure of right now was that her body physically ached for him. It was agonizing.

"I'm glad."

He shook his head, a motion she felt more than saw. "No. That's not good. Say the word. I need to hear, need to..."

"Chaise," she whispered.

She wasn't sure why that word set him free, but whatever harness held him tethered and kept him from giving in to his baser instincts, broke.

He pushed himself upright and his hand landed against her ass in a solid smack. The loud cracking noise filled the room.

Reflex took over as Lacy tried to escape. It was a futile effort. His large, strong hand had returned to the back of her neck, holding her down. The second and third blows fell as she still struggled.

When the fourth came, the pain and heat mingled. Transformed.

Lacy's back arched and she went up on her toes to meet the fifth and sixth smacks.

"Logan," she cried out, her voice tight with unshed tears. The spanking hurt, but not in a way that she longed to end. Instead, she wanted more.

Logan's fingers found the opening to her body and before she could assimilate to the change, he had two buried deep, pounding roughly inside her.

This. God. Yes. This.

She tried to thrust back against his hand, but he still held her to the desk. She couldn't move, couldn't steal any extra stimulation. It was as hot as it was frustrating.

"Let me go." She clenched her fists and beat them against the surface.

"No." His reply was firm, unyielding.

"I need to move!"

He tightened his grip, added a third finger to the other two and increased his pace.

Lacy gasped at the increased tension, the beautifully brutal way he took her.

No. Claimed.

He promised to claim her. And now he was.

She wanted more. Wanted him to take everything she had to offer and then demand more from her. God. She'd give it all to him. Every. Fucking. Thing.

Lacy's orgasm hit her like a bullet, arriving out of nowhere. One second she was grasping for harder, faster, deeper. The next, her body was writhing like a rag doll in a storm, shaking almost painfully as she came harder than she ever had before.

Logan didn't give way. Didn't stop the powerful thrusting. Instead, he rung out every drop of sensation he could. It seemed to last for hours. And when it began to wane, Lacy finally stopped fighting.

She wasn't sure how long she lay there, draped over his desk, how many breaths she'd taken in and blown out before his fingers slowly withdrew.

Her pussy clenched greedily, trying to hold them in, but as always, Logan did as he pleased.

Lacy lifted her head and glanced at him over her shoulder. She shuddered at the hungry, almost feral look in his eyes.

Though she had known Logan her entire life, his beloved face as recognizable to her as her own, she had never seen *this* man. And yet she seemed to know him just the same. In some ways, it felt as if she knew this man better than the other.

She pushed herself from the desk as he took a step away. The connection of their gazes never broke as she twisted to face him, and then dropped to her knees.

Logan issued no complaint as she worked to free his erection from his jeans. She dragged the denim to his knees and then took his cock in her hands.

He didn't say a word as she stroked the thick, hard flesh. God help her if she thought three of his fingers stretched her. He'd tear her apart with this baseball bat. And she'd love every second of it.

She ran her tongue along the bottom of his cock, her eyes studying his face. She'd never been very sure of her abilities when it came to blowjobs. She'd gone down on a few guys and while they made all the right noises, sometimes she felt like those sounds were similar to her grunts when the guys fucked her. They were based more on encouragement than actual excitement.

Logan didn't make any sounds, but his face and the way his hand cupped her cheek told her he liked what she was doing.

It gave her the confidence and courage to continue. Parting her lips, she sucked the head into her mouth, enjoying the way Logan's hand flew from her face to her hair.

She closed her mouth around it and applied a bit of suction. Then, recalling the way Logan had suckled her nipples in his truck, she sucked harder.

His fingers gripped her hair tightly, tugging it. As she lessened the pressure on his cock, he softened his hold on her hair. She repeated the suction and his hands gripped her hair almost uncomfortably. The burning in her scalp traveled straight to her pussy, her own arousal returning with a vengeance.

Lacy held on to the base of his dick as she moved her mouth lower, trying to take more of him inside. She hadn't even hit the halfway point before his head brushed the back of her throat.

While Logan's hands remained in her hair, he didn't seek to drive her actions. Instead, he let her continue to explore, to play, to figure it out. He was a very well-endowed guy, so she had to improvise. Lacy was desperate to give him the same pleasure he'd just offered her.

Soon, she found her pace, moving her lips and her hand in unison along his erection, trying to keep the pressure tight, hoping it was enough to push him into climax.

Whenever his fingers tugged her hair roughly, she knew she'd hit a sweet spot and she catalogued the information, returning there over and over.

For several minutes, she worked her mouth on his hard flesh, losing herself in the quiet magic of the moment as Logan rocked gently toward her.

When Logan's fingers tightened on her head more roughly than before, she thought he'd made it to the brink. She started to move faster, but he halted her motions.

Tipping her face up until her eyes met his, he held her there, his cock still in her mouth.

"You ready?"

Her brows creased, slightly confused. She assumed he meant

for his climax, but he didn't look like a man on the verge of blowing.

She nodded slightly—and then everything she ever thought she'd known about blowjobs was blown out of the water.

Logan gripped her cheeks as he took the reins from her. Lacy's fingers flew to his thighs, seeking purchase when he tripled their previous pace.

He fucked her mouth, pressing deeper than she'd dared to take him on her own. All she could do was hold on as he took. Her eyes began to water and she gagged a couple of times, but Logan didn't cease the movement.

Once again she was overwhelmed by the sensation of being taken. Claimed. When he'd spoken that word in the truck, she'd thought it sounded hot. It triggered all those sexual fantasies she'd never shared with anyone before, the ones where she was captured by a stranger and used roughly. She had always felt slightly ashamed of those dreams, like they were wrong, like she shouldn't feel arousal over such things.

Then Logan had promised to claim her, and it had brought all those shameful fantasies to the surface.

She couldn't find a damn thing wrong with what she wanted now. Instead, she struggled with the realization that she was close to coming as well. How was that possible? He wasn't touching her.

"Fuck yourself, Lacy. Put your fingers in that hot pussy of yours and fuck it. Hard."

Her fingers tightened in the hard muscle of his thighs, her nails scratching his skin. However, she wasn't sure if his loud grunt was due to pain or a precursor to his climax.

Then she obeyed his command, pressing two fingers inside herself as he continued to pound inside her mouth.

"How many?"

He tugged his cock out of her mouth briefly and she cried out in frustration.

"How many fingers are you using?"

"Two," she gasped.

He shook his head almost angrily. "Not enough. Four. Shove

four in there." He punctuated his command with a rough return, his cock trying to slide all the way in. She panicked for a moment before her throat opened and he slid deeper.

"Fuck," he murmured.

Lacy added two more fingers to her pussy, curling them to find that special place that never failed to set her off.

Stars exploded as she came. Logan was mere seconds behind her.

One moment he was pounding into her mouth, the next he was jerking roughly as he came, jets of hot come splashing against the back of her throat.

She swallowed several times, but didn't seek to pull away. Even as his cock softened in her mouth, she held him there.

Wanted him there.

She was his. Completely.

But more than that, he was hers. And she was never going to let him go.

Off-limits or not.

Eleven years earlier...

Logan tilted his head, confused when Lacy opened the door, wearing a tatty old t-shirt and jeans. "What are you doing here? Thought you were going to prom tonight."

She shrugged casually, though her painted-on smile looked fake. "My date got chicken pox."

"Oh man. I'm sorry."

She stepped aside so he could come inside. "It's okay. It's not like he did it on purpose." She paused for a second, and then looked at him, concerned. "You don't think he got them on purpose, do you?"

Logan chuckled. "I'm one hundred percent sure Tommy didn't get chicken pox just to get out of going to prom."

"Yeah. I guess not."

"You could always go stag," he suggested.

She looked at him like he'd sprung a second head. "That's social suicide. No thanks."

Logan figured she was probably right. He'd been out of high school for too many years to remember all the silly rules.

Lacy's mom, Beverly, walked into the room before he could devise a way to cheer her up.

"There you are, Logan. I just finished wrapping the tray of cookies for you. Lacy, will you go grab it for me?"

Lacy nodded and headed for the kitchen.

"Tough break on prom," Logan said when Beverly's gaze followed her daughter's retreating form.

"I absolutely hate this. You know Lacy. She smiles and pretends it's okay, but she's devastated. She worked every single day after school in the bakery with me for six months, saving the money for that dress."

Beverly quickly dashed a tear. Logan couldn't stand the thought of Evan's mom and sister upset. They were two of the sweetest women he knew. "Mrs. Sparks. What if Lacy comes to the barn dance with me tonight? Evan's heading over there in a couple hours, once his shift ends. Tyson and I will keep an eye on her until then."

"Are you sure?"

Ordinarily, Beverly would never have consented to let her sixteen-year-old daughter hang out with them, but the fact that she so quickly agreed proved how much she wanted to see Lacy happy. It wasn't that they hung with a rough crowd. Hell, half the people there tonight would be Lacy's older cousins. She'd be surrounded by friendly faces and Logan didn't doubt for a second they'd all make sure she had a prom night to remember.

"We just play music and dance. I'll make sure she stays out of the spiked punch and Evan will get her home at a decent hour. We won't let her out of our sight. Promise."

"Oh, Logan. How can I ever thank you for this? She'll be delighted."

Lacy entered the room with the cookies Beverly had made for the barn dance.

"Hey, Lace," he said, taking the tray from her. "Go upstairs and put on your prom dress. You're going to the barn dance with me."

Lacy's eyes widened in sheer joy. "Seriously?"

She glanced at her mom for confirmation, who grinned. "Logan and Evan will keep an eye on you."

Lacy dashed toward the stairs excitedly. "Five minutes. Give me five minutes." With that, she raced up, with Beverly hot on her heels.

"Better give us fifteen, Logan. I have the cutest idea for her hair."

Logan waved, grinning. Surprisingly, he was kind of looking forward to taking Lacy to her first barn dance. God knew the kid had been begging him and Evan to let her tag along with them for years.

Beverly and Lacy split the difference on the time it took to get ready. Lacy descended the stairs ten minutes later.

She looked absolutely gorgeous—and Logan suddenly regretted the offer. It would have been easier to keep an eye on her when she was still dressed like a gangly sixteen-year-old girl. Right now, she would pass for much older in her form-fitting dress. It was way too fancy for the barn, but no one there would care when they heard about her sick prom date.

"You look amazing, Lacy."

Her smile lit her entire face.

"Here," Beverly said. "You two stand there real quick and let me snap a picture."

"Mom. It's not like Logan is my date." From her blush, it was clear she was embarrassed.

"I don't mind." Logan set the cookies down and put a friendly arm around her shoulder. They both said, "cheese" and then, somehow, Logan found himself taking Lacy to "prom."

CHAPTER FOUR

Logan stood outside Sparks Barbeque and cursed himself for being the world's biggest jackass. It had been a week since Lacy had shown up at his shop and seduced the fuck out of him.

And for seven days, he'd done nothing but think about how he wanted her to do it again. After her mind-blowing blowjob, he had helped her dress and cuddled her on his lap as they sat in his desk chair for nearly an hour. He *cuddled* her, for God's sake.

Then, he told her to take a week to decide if she wanted another round. Damn woman had said yes before he had finished speaking, but he'd rejected the response and insisted she really think about it.

Now, it wasn't her at his doorstep, but him at hers. He tried to reassure himself he wasn't here because of the sex—yeah, right—but because of business. He had to get her chaise lounge out of his shop. It was driving him insane. He'd been a fool to make that her safe word. Every time he looked at the thing, he recalled Lacy bent over his desk as he spanked her.

It was way past time to get Lacy Sparks out of his head. He hoped that by engaging her here—amongst her family—he'd remember why it was a very bad idea for him to become involved with his best friend's sister.

Lacy homed in on him the second he crossed the threshold, her too-pleased grin doing funny things to his insides. It occurred to him she had always lit up like that whenever he walked into a room, even when she was just a kid. And it had always made him feel good. Made him want to be a good man, a positive role model, the kind of person who was worthy of her admiration.

Now it just made him want to push her into the nearest broom closet and have his wicked way with her.

"Hey," she said as she approached him.

"Hi, Lace." His fingers itched to pull her close to him, to hug her tightly. That impulse seemed odd. He would have expected to feel desire—and he did—but the urge to simply embrace her and soak up the smell of her perfume was even stronger.

"Did you come for dinner? I'm off the clock in about ten minutes. I worked the breakfast and lunch shifts today. I could join you."

He shook his head. "No. I'm not here for food." He pointed to where his truck was parked out front. "I've got your chaise. Thought I'd see if you could take a few minutes to pop over to your place and unload it. Looks like I picked a good time."

She leaned closer and murmured, "It's been a week."

Logan sighed. "I know."

"Hey, Logan," Tyson called out from his seat at the end of the bar. "Come have a beer with me."

Logan nodded. "Go finish your shift. I'll wait for you."

He crossed the crowded room, stopping to say hello to a few people. One of the best—and worst—things about living in the same small town your whole life was that everybody knew every-body else. And not just in a "passing acquaintance" way, but in a "remember you when you were knee-high to a grasshopper" way.

As such, Mrs. Higgins had no compunction about asking him for the millionth time how he could have let that lovely girlfriend of his go. He politely told her the breakup had been Jane's deci-sion, not his.

TJ didn't mind slapping him on the back and joking he'd been smart to avoid putting on the ball and chain. Then he'd not-too-subtly reminded him that his daughter Macie was still single.

Logan simply raised one eyebrow. "I think Macie is too much woman for me."

TJ laughed loudly, the sound booming across the room. "Yeah. She probably is. What about my baby girl, Adele, then?"

TJ was always trying to play matchmaker for his daughters. Something that drove Macie and Adele nuts, since all those efforts were made right in front of them.

"Ignore him, Logan. We suspect dementia is setting in," Macie called out from behind the bar. "And dear God, Dad. Why are you still here? You're not even on the schedule to work today."

"It's happy hour," TJ called out, lifting his beer and clinking glasses with the two old cronies at his table.

Sparks Barbeque was actually TJ's restaurant, but he left the cooking, waitressing, management, basically everything to the girls. And between the seven of them, they had put the restaurant —and by extension, Maris, Texas—on the map. The place had been featured in several national magazines as one of the best barbeque joints in the country, and just last month, Paige had received a call from the Food Network about filming a show there. For several days, the local gossips had been all abuzz about the possibility of their little town appearing on TV.

Finally, Logan made it to the bar, claiming the stool next to Tyson. "Busy in here tonight."

Tyson shrugged. "It's Friday in Maris." He let the comment stand as if that explained it all, which it did. With the exception of Cruisers, which was on the outskirts of town and catered more to the party crowd, Sparks Barbeque was the only other option for social drinking. It was quieter, and it attracted the older men who liked to toss back a few with TJ, and the established couples out on dates, looking for a place where they didn't have to yell to be heard over the loud music.

"Budweiser?" Macie asked him, even though she was already pouring the draft.

Logan nodded his thanks as Macie went back to the other end of the bar, continuing the story she'd been telling Coop without missing a beat.

"You know," Tyson said, "I've been thinking. Maybe we should get the band back together."

Logan laughed as he shook his head. He, Tyson, and their friends Harley and Caleb had formed Ty's Collective back in high school. When Caleb and Tyson went off to college, they'd do local gigs whenever the guys were home over holidays and then they had resurrected it fulltime after Tyson graduated from med school and returned to Maris. "Hell no."

"Why not?"

Logan lifted his hand as he ticked off his reasons. "For one thing, Cal's too busy running his father's Feed and Seed while he recovers from his heart attack, and Harley moved away. Band wouldn't sound the same without her killing it on the banjo."

Harley Mills had been an integral part of their group of friends for the past thirty or so years, but that changed when she took off to Florida a year ago after her brother's death. They all felt her absence. With her departure, the band had dissolved. Logan missed the music and the camaraderie, but he also knew Ty's Collective only worked with Harley on the stage with them.

"I can be the lead singer," Macie interjected.

"Jesus, Mace. How do you do that?" Tyson asked. "You're in the middle of a conversation with Coop, yet you're listening in on ours."

Macie shrugged. "It's not that hard. Besides, I don't like to miss stuff. Like Mrs. Higgins over there bitching about the new sign outside the Baptist church. Let it go, Agnes."

"I'm not bitching," Agnes called out. "I just said it was hard to read."

Macie ignored the woman's outburst and pointed to TJ. "And Dad's over there making a bet on next week's Rangers game with Earl, even though he promised my mom he wouldn't gamble anymore."

TJ frowned, hotly denying what everyone in the place knew

was true. "I am not. And don't be feeding your mother those stories either."

Macie rolled her eyes and turned her attention back to Logan and Tyson. "So I can be lead singer."

Tyson shook his head vehemently. "No way. Never. Not in a million years. I've heard you sing, Mace. It's bad. Really bad."

Macie was infamous for her extraordinarily awful singing voice, a fact she drove home when she took it upon herself to sing "The National Anthem" at the annual Fourth of July picnic by the lake a few years earlier. Patriotism hit a new low as everyone in attendance burst out in hoots and hollers, laughing until their sides hurt at the painful performance. Which, of course, only encouraged an unoffended Macie to sign louder and to draw out the high notes longer.

"You're tone deaf," Logan added.

"I've been practicing in the shower. I really think I'm getting it. Tell them, Coop. You were here last week when I sang 'Happy Birthday' to Paige. Nailed it, didn't I?"

Coop looked at her, frowning. "You were singing? I thought you'd burned yourself on one of the candles."

Macie chucked a peanut at Coop's head, which he deftly dodged. "To hell with all of you." Then she launched right back into whatever story she'd been telling Coop before interrupting them. She was impossible to keep up with, but funny as hell.

Logan had avoided the restaurant for two weeks, trying to hide from Lacy. Now, he realized he'd missed it.

"Maybe we can find another banjo player, and I can do most of the lead vocals," Tyson offered. "We all took turns at the mic anyway."

"Tyson, I know you'll probably find this hard to believe, but we weren't that good." It was a boldfaced lie. They were awesome. More than once, it had been suggested that they all quit their day jobs and pursue the music career fulltime. None of them had been tempted. It was a passion that they all shared—on a hobby level.

Tyson chuckled. "Bullshit."

"Why the big need to start it all up again? Aren't you pretty busy these days?"

Dr. Tyson Sparks was the one who'd suggested they take a hiatus after Harley left. He was one of only two general practitioners who lived in Maris, while the nearest hospital resided nearly forty minutes away in the neighboring town of Douglas. As such, he was in constant demand, treating everything from cut fingers to the more serious medical concerns.

"I thought you might like the distraction," Tyson explained.

"Distraction?" The only thing Logan needed to be distracted from was Lacy, but God help him if Tyson knew that. He was as overprotective of his cousins and sister, Paige, as Evan was.

"It was just a thought."

It occurred to Logan that perhaps it was Tyson who needed the distraction. Logan had been walking around with his head up his ass for so many months, he'd failed to see Tyson was facing his own struggles as well.

"You miss Harley?"

"Is that really a question?"

"I'm sorry, man. Didn't realize how rough it was on you. I miss her too." He really did. Though her departure had been easier for him. He'd always hung out more with Evan than Caleb, Harley, and Tyson—who had been inseparable for most of their lives.

"It's alright. Let's face it. You took a double hit. I mean, Jane took off just a few weeks after Harley."

"Yeah, I guess I did."

Tyson placed a friendly, comforting hand on Logan's shoulder. "Believe me, there are plenty of other women out there who would be lucky to have you. Jane didn't deserve you."

"Uh. Am I interrupting?"

Logan glanced over his shoulder to find Lacy standing next to him with her purse over her arm.

Great. From the look on her face, it was clear she'd heard Tyson's comments and now she thought he'd been sitting here crying in his beer over Jane.

"No. You're not," Logan said, standing. He needed to get her out of here. Set things straight. "You ready?"

"You two going somewhere?" Tyson asked curiously.

"He fixed my chaise. We're taking it back to my place," Lacy replied. The happiness she'd shown when he had first arrived at the restaurant was gone, replaced by uncertainty.

"Need any help?" Tyson started to stand.

"No," Logan said quickly. "It's light. We can manage."

He placed his hand at the base of Lacy's spine and guided her to the door before Tyson could insist.

He continued to propel her toward his truck even though she appeared to be dragging her feet. When he opened the door, she paused. "If you'd rather do this another time…"

Logan shook his head. "Get in the truck." He didn't make it a request and he didn't bother to make it sound nice. He'd spent a week waiting for the moment when he'd get her alone again, and he wasn't wasting the opportunity on misunderstandings.

As always, Lacy responded to his commanding tone, which didn't help his already painful erection. He'd stopped trying to beat the fucking thing down the second they got out of the restaurant. Now he was wondering how the hell he could walk around to the driver's side without limping. God help him if anyone in the restaurant was looking his way. It was bound to be obvious what was troubling him.

Logan climbed behind the steering wheel, adjusting his dick before he did himself an injury. Lacy's eyes twinkled briefly and she opened her mouth—no doubt to give him shit for his condition —before she sobered up again and remained quiet. He hated seeing her upset.

"Don't."

She tilted her head, confused. "Don't what?"

"Don't think what you're thinking. I'm not still hung up on Jane."

"No one would blame you if—"

"I don't miss her."

Lacy didn't appear to believe him. "Logan—"

"I don't miss her, Lacy," he said more resolutely. "The breakup was long overdue and I think I'd mourned the end of that relationship before it was even over. She and I were wrong for each other. It's over. I swear."

"Really?"

He could read the doubt in her tone and he didn't blame her. Three years was a long time to live with someone. And he hadn't helped himself by holing up inside his shop for a year after it ended, not bothering to date anyone else.

"She has nothing to do with us."

Her smile grew. "There's an us?"

He closed his eyes, wishing she didn't befuddle him so. She had him talking in circles, saying everything wrong. "For now."

His response didn't dim her enthusiasm. "Now works for me."

His lids opened at the sound of her shifting on the seat. She was wearing a short skirt that she lifted just enough to show him that she wasn't wearing panties.

Logan had never considered himself the jealous type, but knowing she'd been flitting around that restaurant all day like that had his vision going red. "You worked like that all day?"

She laughed. "Good God, no. My Uncle TJ was in there. How awkward would that be? I took them off and stashed them in my purse just before I came to meet you at the bar."

She was too adorable for his own good. "I like the idea of you dropping your panties whenever I show up."

"Logan?"

"Yeah."

"Can we go now?"

He made no move to start the truck. "In a hurry?"

The dirty girl reached between her thighs and ran her finger along her slit. Logan watched, spellbound, as she raised one very shiny finger to him. "Yes."

He started the truck, using the five minutes it took for them to get from the restaurant to her front door to control himself. Foolishly, he'd agreed to the no-penetration rule, as if that somehow kept him true to his promise to Evan. He hadn't just broken the damn vow to his friend; he'd shattered it and was currently dancing barefoot on the shards.

When they arrived at her place, he took a steadying breath and forced himself to calm down. He'd sworn to himself when he loaded up the chaise and left his shop, he wouldn't touch her tonight. He'd slowly extricate himself from whatever this was.

Lacy was halfway to her front door before he could find the voice to call out, "Forgetting something?"

She looked over her shoulder, finding him standing at the end of his truck bed. "Oh. Yeah. The chaise."

From her heavy-lidded eyes, Lacy had expected him to drag her upstairs and let the games begin again. He was sorely tempted.

Logan lowered the back of the truck and slid the chaise out. It wasn't that heavy. Lacy helped him guide it down then held on to the light end, leading him to her door and up the stairs to her apartment.

He'd been in her place once before three years earlier, when he, Tyson and Evan had helped her move in. He had spent the day lugging furniture, placing it here, there, and then back to here as she directed their movements and changed her mind every five seconds. Logan hadn't been back since.

Once she opened the door to her apartment, he followed her in and whistled. Damn. The place had been nothing more than white walls and a few hand-me-down pieces of furniture last time.

"You like it?" she asked, setting the chaise down just inside the door. He followed suit, letting his gaze travel around the space. Logan knew she had an eye for decorating and a knack for taking someone else's trash and uncovering hidden treasures. But seeing all her efforts put together like this...

"It's beautiful, Lace. So homey."

Her apartment looked like the kind of place where a man could come home, kick off his work boots and sink into the comfy couch with a beer. He could spend hours just looking around at all the cool pieces she'd found. While he knew most of the decorations in the place were flea market and yard sale castoffs, every-thing worked together. More than that, it looked damned elegant.

Lacy was clearly pleased by his praise. "Thanks. You know, if you ever want to redesign your showroom, I'd be happy to help."

"Is that your subtle way of telling me the place looks like hell?"

"Well..."

He chuckled. "I'd love your help. Keep intending to work on it, but I never manage to shift around more than a couple pieces before I get overwhelmed and give up."

"I was thinking that if you added some funky artwork to the walls and maybe set it up like a house layout, it would show off your furniture better. Plus, I could add a few vases, knick-knacks, stuff like that, to add some color and some visual interest. I think it would make the whole place pop."

He nodded. "Yeah. I'd really like that."

"Awesome. I'll come by next week on my day off and we can draw up a layout. And then I'll start hitting the sales looking for the pieces I'm envisioning. It won't cost much. Promise."

"Money's not an issue. I suspect the investment will be worth it in the long run."

"And you'd be helping me out too."

"How's that?"

She grinned as she waved around the room. "I'm sort of at maximum capacity for crap in here. This way I can still fuel my bargain-shopping addiction without crowding up my apartment."

"I see. Speaking of, where's this going?" he asked, pointing at the chaise. There didn't seem to be a spot for it in the living room.

"My bedroom."

Of course.

Logan blew out a long sigh. "Listen, Lace. I think—"

She stepped closer and placed her finger over his mouth. "You promised me three times." She smelled like flowers and French fries; the combination was ridiculously appealing.

"We need to be practical about this."

"Okay. So be practical. You said Jane wasn't an issue. Is that true?"

He nodded though he wasn't sure that answer was entirely accurate. While he wasn't still hung up on his ex, he was struggling with the fallout, trying to find a way back to normal.

"And what do you think Evan would say if he found out?"

Logan knew the answer to that. "He wouldn't say anything. He'd beat the shit out of me very quietly."

"You're best friends, Logan. He loves you like a brother. What makes you think he'd disapprove of us as a couple? Is it the age difference?"

He shook his head. "No. It has nothing to do with your age. We're both consenting adults."

"Then it's the sex. I mean...the way we like to have sex."

Logan didn't reply for a long time. He had been terrified of scaring Lacy away with his sexual appetite, but rather than run, she'd responded to it. With Jane, he'd worn the kid gloves at the beginning, introducing her to his desires slowly. That technique had blown up in his face. By the time he figured out they weren't compatible lovers, he was in love with her, so he adapted, tried to hold back some of his stronger urges.

When the silence stretched too long, Lacy filled it. "You didn't seem to have these hang-ups when it came to Yvette. What makes me different from her?"

He reared back. "Yvette?"

Lacy flushed. "I followed you one day. Watched you take her when her grandmother was out of the house."

"That was nearly ten years ago."

She shrugged. "I know."

"You were just a kid."

She scowled at his comment. The woman was touchy about him referring to her youth, but he'd spent too many years of his life seeing her as a kid. While that certainly wasn't true now, the fact remained that she had no business spying on him at that age.

"I was seventeen and not entirely innocent." Then she seemed to recall what she'd seen. "Of course, after that, I wasn't innocent at all." She laughed, but Logan didn't find the humor.

"Jesus. You were too young to see that."

"Maybe I was, but I'm not going to pretend it didn't turn me on. A lot. Like *a lot* a lot."

Logan ran a hand through his hair and forced himself to recall all the things he had done with Yvette. He had no idea which day she'd followed them, but any of them would have provided her with a fairly substantial education in kinky sex.

The knowledge certainly explained her interest in pursuing him, in her research on BDSM. He'd unwittingly exposed her to his true nature and the spark had ignited. Years ago.

He had no business being here.

"Let's put this chaise in your bedroom. Then I need to head home."

"What? Why? Are you pissed off I followed you and Yvette? Because—"

"No, Lace. I'm not pissed. I'm just coming to my senses."

She fell silent for several moments. He let her sort through her thoughts, taking the time to get his own settled.

"I'm getting tired of chasing you, Logan. Sick of trying to force you to see something that's standing right in front of you. You want to be blind? Fine. Be blind. I'm not in the mood to beg."

She bent over and picked up her half of the chaise. He lifted his side and followed her to the bedroom, her words racing through his brain. Why couldn't she see that he was trying to do the right thing?

They were halfway across the room when something on the bed captured his attention.

He put the chaise down and walked over to the mattress. "What the hell?"

Lacy followed him, picking up a thick butt plug and waving it around as if it was nothing more scandalous than a hairbrush. "I did some online shopping after the last time we were together. I was sort of hoping you'd educate me on all of this."

"That was one hell of a shopping trip."

In addition to the plug, there was a vibrator, a large dildo, nipple clamps, a crop and a jumbo-size tube of lubrication.

He'd met the woman of his dreams. And he'd known her his entire life.

Lacy sank down on her bed, letting her skirt ride up high on her thighs. "Guess I'll have to find someone else to introduce me to—"

"Lacy," he said through gritted teeth.

"Yeah?"

"Get undressed. Now."

CHAPTER FIVE

Lacy fought hard to hide her grin as she tugged her t-shirt over her head. It was simply a stroke of luck that her new toys had arrived that morning and she'd decided to unpack them to take a peek. After that, she'd lost track of time, fantasizing about Logan using all the toys on her until she'd been late for work and had left them lying on the bed.

Logan was still resistant to a relationship, but Lacy wasn't sure why. Whatever was holding him back wasn't something he was ready to talk to her about. So she needed to find ways to keep him returning to her bed until he was. She didn't intend to give up on him. Especially not now, when it was obvious they were so perfect for each other.

Once she was naked, she waited, curious about what he would ask her to do next. He was looking at her treasure trove of naughty toys intently.

"You really want to try all of this?"

"Yes." She was taken aback by his uncharacteristic hesitance. She wasn't used to seeing Logan unsure of himself. Typically, he was the king of confidence. "Of course I do."

"You're not doing this just to please me, because you think it's what *I* want?"

Lacy frowned, wondering where his questions were coming from. This was the first time he'd shown this touch of reticence. "I love what we do together. It doesn't just please *you*, Logan. God, you're giving me orgasms that make my teeth rattle. It's amazing."

He considered that, and then—finally—the dominant lover she'd come to adore reemerged. His gaze swept over her naked form.

"Get on the bed. Lay down on your back in the center."

As she moved into position, Logan swept the toys to one side of the bed.

"You forgot something," he said as he walked toward her closet.

"What's that?"

"Handcuffs."

Lacy squeezed her legs together and cursed herself for the oversight. "I'll steal some from Evan's house tomorrow."

He chuckled. "I'd prefer to buy you some. Last thing we need is Evan arresting his kinky kid sister for stealing his cuffs." He opened the closet door. "Scarves?"

"They're in a box right there on the floor."

He followed her direction and tugged the box out. Opening it, he searched until he found several long scarves that apparently suited his purpose.

Lacy squirmed on the bed, wishing for the millionth time she hadn't taken sex off the table. As fun as the toys looked, she would never be fully sated until Logan was buried deep inside her.

She watched as he approached the bed. He looked so large, so serious, so powerful. A sane woman would probably be terrified. Lacy felt nothing but excitement.

"Lift your hands above your head."

Lacy obeyed, directing her hands toward opposite sides of the headboard.

He shook his head. "No. Cross your wrists."

She moved them together. In her fantasies, she was always spread eagle. The idea that he would tie her up some other way had her heart racing at a dangerous pace.

Logan rested one knee on the mattress by her side as he reached up, tying her wrists together and then securing them to the headboard. Her arms were stretched taut, and she didn't bother to test the knots for more than a second or two. Those suckers weren't coming loose.

Logan rose from the bed and pulled his t-shirt over his head. She was treated to a visual feast of muscular arms, six-pack abs and smooth, tanned skin she longed to lick like an ice cream cone. She hoped the striptease would continue, but Logan stopped with just the shirt.

"Pants," she suggested hopefully.

His eyes narrowed and she knew she'd made some sort of faux pas. "I won't gag you this time because it's all new to you and I want you to be able to say your safe word. So here's your only warning. We're doing this my way."

"So...in other words, no suggestions from the peanut gallery. Got it."

His stern expression slipped for just a moment, his lips tipping up in a smile he was trying to hide. He recovered quickly, but the twinkle in his eyes told her he wasn't really annoyed with her.

"Don't make me regret the gag decision."

She bit her lip, trying to look chastised. In truth, the action was helping her to not laugh. It wasn't that she wasn't taking this seriously. She was. It was just that she was so happy. God, her joy was seeping out of her and it was hard to keep inside, contained.

She had loved Logan Grady her entire life and now, being here with him like this, she felt as if she'd come home. As if every dream she'd ever had was coming true.

Logan returned to the bed, crawling between her legs as he pushed them apart. The man certainly liked having her on display. She didn't mind her nudity with him. He looked at her as if she were the most beautiful piece of artwork in the museum. It warmed her up, made her feel cherished. Sexy.

He ran his fingers along her slit. This time, she did flush. She was dripping wet. To the point where it was slightly embarrassing.

"Guess we won't need that lube," she said, jokingly.

Logan moved one finger lower and pressed just the tip into her anus. The move was unexpected, the penetration tight. It pinched slightly and she gasped.

"We're going to need it."

Suddenly, Lacy was reconsidering the size of the butt plug she'd purchased. In her overheated, horny mind, she had selected one that would be approximately the same size as his dick. She hadn't fully considered the ramifications of putting something that big in such a small hole.

"Relax, Lacy."

The man read her like a book. "I'm cool," she lied.

This time he didn't bother to hide his grin. "No. You're not, but you're worrying about the wrong things."

As always, his words calmed her down. She assumed it all came back to that trust thing. He wouldn't hurt her, wouldn't abuse her or force her to do anything she didn't want to do. She knew that as sure as she knew tomorrow was Saturday.

Logan lifted her legs, resting them on his shoulders as he bent forward to suck on her nipples. She was suddenly grateful she'd started taking those yoga classes at the gym. Logan was definitely going to stretch her flexibility limits.

When his teeth bit into her nipple, her mind went blank. She longed to grip his head, to run her fingers through his thick dark hair, but the scarf held firm.

She'd never had anyone pay so much attention to her breasts. Or to just one nipple. Logan spent ages laving the distended flesh, licking, sucking, biting. Every sting of pain he produced was followed by softness. He hurt. He soothed. Over and over. Her body trembled with the conflicting sensations, her pussy clenching resentfully on empty air.

Lacy needed to be filled. Needed him to fuck her.

"Please," she gasped after several minutes. "God. I need you, Logan."

He lifted his head, letting her see the pain etched on his face. He was suffering too. Strangely that idea comforted her. She wasn't alone in this.

She was so distracted by his expression, she never saw him pick up the nipple clamp. She didn't realize he had it in his hand until the sharp teeth of the wicked contraption snapped down.

"Ahh," she cried. "Shit. That hurts."

Logan didn't remove it, but he didn't put the other on either. Instead, he studied her expression. "Focus on your breathing, Lace."

She did as he said, sucking in as much air as she could muster, which wasn't much.

He shook his head. "No. Like this."

She followed his lead, her chest rising and falling in time with his, in slow inhalations followed by long exhalations. Lacy had just adjusted to the sting of the clamp when he snapped the second one on.

"Fuck!"

He waited again, leading her through the breathing exercises. This time, it took fewer seconds to regulate, to adapt. Mainly because Logan had distracted her. Two fingers slammed inside her pussy and Lacy jerked roughly.

God. She was going to come. Like...right now.

She screamed and thrashed her head on the pillow as every nerve ending in her body exploded. What the fuck was happening?

It was several minutes before she realized Logan's fingers were no longer inside her. Instead, he was hovering over her, caging her beneath him as his elbows rested by her shoulders. He kissed her gently, the touch in direct opposition to the pleasurable pain he'd just produced.

"Okay?" he asked quietly when she finally managed to gather her wits.

She nodded. "I don't understand how..."

"You're submissive."

Lacy would have argued that point. She'd chop off any guy's dick if he tried to control her life, tell her what to wear or how to behave. The Sparks women had more than their fair share of independent and authoritative streaks.

But that wasn't what he meant. She understood that.

And whether he realized it or not, Logan had molded her desires when she was seventeen, unwittingly revealing a part of her that she might never have known existed.

"I want you, Logan."

The moment she uttered the words, she wished she could take them back. They seemed to break whatever spell had settled over them.

He pushed himself up and glanced at the pile of toys that still rested next to her on the bed. "We're not finished with the lessons yet."

The affection she'd just seen in his eyes was shuttered away. Logan would play with her, broaden her horizons, indulge her curiosity about BDSM. But he wouldn't give her what she truly wanted. Him. All of him. Heart, soul and body.

Unfortunately he didn't give her the chance to mourn that fact. Instead, he uncapped the lube and threw her back into a maelstrom of sensation.

Logan squeezed some of the lubrication onto his finger, and then slowly worked it inside her ass. She struggled to adapt to the pinch. It didn't hurt, but it wasn't entirely comfortable. She recalled his declaration about fucking her there. The masochist in her wanted that, even knowing it was likely to hurt like hell.

She had to hand it to him. Logan seemed to have the patience of Job. One finger eventually became two, and two became three. Hours could have passed for all Lacy knew as he took his time to stretch her. All the while he added even more lubrication.

Finally, seventy-two years later, she felt the tip of the plug against her ass.

"Shit," she breathed out on a whisper as he pressed the wicked toy deeper. She really should have picked a smaller size.

"Logan," she gasped as he continued to breach the tight portal.

He captured her gaze and then, with a wink, he pushed the fat end completely inside as her anus clenched around the base.

"Ohmigod." Once again, he led her through the breathing

exercises and then, just like before, he distracted her. This time with the dildo.

He grinned as he rimmed the opening of her body with the toy. "We won't need lube for this one. You're soaking wet."

"You can't put..."

That was as far as she got before Logan shoved the dildo in to the hilt.

Her back arched off the bed as her second orgasm rumbled along her spine, ravaging her. That orgasm was followed immediately by a third, more powerful one when Logan removed one of the nipple clamps and then the other.

Her cries were hoarse as her body trembled in the aftermath. Logan laved her sensitive nipples with hot, wet, soothing kisses. He'd done no more than push the dildo inside. He hadn't even fucked her with it. She had come three times tonight and it had only taken him one little thrust to do so.

A trickle of sweat tickled her cheek as it slid along her damp skin. The room had been chilly when they'd first walked in. Now, it was like a sauna, the air thick and humid.

Logan untied her wrists, slowly drawing her arms down as he massaged her shoulders. He had just given her three earth-shattering orgasms. It felt as if she should be the one worshiping at his feet, taking care of him and giving him the moon on a silver platter.

However, it was Logan who gave as she lay there with no more strength than a newborn kitten. He ran his fingers along the valley between her breasts, over her stomach and back to her pussy. Her inner muscles fluttered against the thick plastic as he pulled the dildo out.

When his fingers drifted lower, to the plug, she sucked in a deep breath and held it.

"Ready?"

It was the first time he'd asked permission to do anything tonight. The fact that, ready or not, the damn big thing needed to come out, wasn't lost on her.

Logan placed a quick kiss on her cheek as he gripped the base of the plug and pulled it free. She closed her eyes tightly as the thickest part passed, sighing in relief—and disappointment—as he dropped it to the floor by the bed.

She felt...empty.

"That was..." Lacy couldn't find the words.

Logan simply nodded, looking at her so intently she had to fight the urge to glance away. He could see too much and she didn't have the strength to hide, to shelter her emotions.

"You're incredible, Lacy."

She closed her eyes and pretended there wasn't going to be a "but" added to the end of that statement. She could read him too. Whatever he'd just seen in her face—and she was pretty sure it was pure, unadulterated, undying love—had helped him batten down his hatches.

He was going to break her heart.

"We can't do this again."

She tried to push herself upright, but her arms were still weak so it took some effort. "Why not?"

"You've had a crush on me since you were a kid."

She blushed and glanced down. "I wasn't sure you knew that."

He cupped her cheek, forcing her gaze to meet his. "It was pretty hard to miss. I didn't know you knew about Yvette, that you'd followed us. God, Lacy. How much of what you're feeling right now is based on what you know about me and my needs? How do you know this is really what you want?"

She scowled. "Um...maybe because I'm a fucking adult and I know what I like."

"Jane pretended she liked BDSM at first too. We fell in love with each other and when those emotions were new it was easy for her to go along with my desires because she wanted to make me happy. In the end, she wound up resenting me for what I wanted."

"I'm not pretending."

"How can you be sure?"

She snapped. Her temper flaring red-hot. "I can!"

"I don't want to hurt you. You're the last person on earth I'd *ever* want to hurt."

The anger that had flashed dissolved into heartbreak. "You're hurting me now."

"And that's why I need to leave."

FOURTEEN YEARS EARLIER…

"I THINK it's on the back porch," Evan yelled from the kitchen.

Lacy glanced up, surprised when Logan stepped outside. She turned her head away from him quickly, not wanting him to see her cry. She'd had a crush on Logan her entire life, so it was just her luck he'd show up and catch her ugly crying.

"Hey, Lace." He walked over to retrieve a cooler. Logan and Evan were going camping with a bunch of their friends for the weekend. Needless to say, once again, she had been deemed too young to tag along.

"Hey," she said, not looking his direction.

She was used to being invisible to her brother's friends. They were eight years older and there was precious little a gang of twenty-somethings had in common with a thirteen-year-old. So she hadn't expected Logan to walk over to where she was slowly rocking on her mom's loveseat glider.

"You crying?"

She shook her head, refusing to face him. Of course, she didn't help her lie by reaching up to wipe away her tears.

"What's wrong?"

"Missy Martin kissed Bucky Largent."

"Oh. And you like Bucky?"

Lacy crinkled her nose in disgust as she looked at Logan. "Eww. No. Gross."

"You like Missy?"

She rolled her eyes. "No. But now I'm the only girl in my class who hasn't kissed a boy."

Logan chuckled. She expected him to walk away, as he clearly didn't find her reason for crying very important.

Once again, he did the unexpected. He put the cooler down and sat next to her on the loveseat. "I wouldn't worry about that too much. You're going to kiss lots of guys in your life. Doesn't matter if you're last or not."

"Nobody likes me like that."

"They will."

Lacy had her doubts. The boys in her class tended to flock toward the girls with the big boobs. Hers had yet to make an appearance. "Pretty sure I'm going to die alone."

Logan laughed and stood up. "Tell you what. If nobody's kissed you by the time you're eighteen, I'll kiss you." With that, he picked up the cooler and headed back into the house, while Lacy did some math.

In five years, Logan Grady was going to kiss her. Lacy had waited this long. She could wait five more years.

CHAPTER SIX

acie stood with her hands on her hips. "Alright. Let's have it."

Lacy looked at her cousin, wondering what she'd forgotten. "Have what?"

"Who is he?"

Lacy bit her lower lip, especially when Evan's head popped up as he dipped one of his fries in ketchup.

"He?" Evan asked.

Lacy shook her head and fought like the devil not to cry. "There is no he."

She was able to say the words with confidence because they were true. Logan hadn't returned a single one of her calls in five days and, despite her efforts to get him alone, the man somehow always managed to have customers in his shop.

She'd stopped by his place after hours the last two nights, but he either wasn't in or he wasn't answering the door.

He had told her when he left Friday that it was over. He'd blown her world away with his clamps, plug and dildo. Given her the greatest sexual experience of her life and then, at the end, he'd simply walked away.

Once he said he was leaving, she hadn't bothered to beg or

plead. One look at his determined face told her all she needed to know. He wouldn't be swayed.

As a result, he'd left her with a big freaking hole in her chest where he had ripped her heart out.

"There's no one."

Her cousin studied her face too closely for Lacy's comfort, so she worked hard to keep her expression impassive.

"Only guy troubles would explain your behavior the last few weeks."

Lacy rolled her eyes. "I'm behaving like I always do."

Macie made an annoying buzzer sound, as if Lacy had given the wrong answer on a game show. "Nope. You've been all over the charts. Testy as hell one day, then the next you're walking on air. Spent the better part of a week yelling your name until you finally managed to pull your head out of your daydreaming ass long enough to answer me. During that phase, I had to brush my teeth twelve times a day while trying not to get a toothache looking at that sappy, sweet, can't-wipe-the-grin-off-your-face look. Now you've spent the last few days moping around here like you lost your best friend. If that's not some man fucking with your head, then I don't know what else it could be. You've got all the classic symptoms."

"Lace?" Evan asked. She hated seeing the worry in his eyes.

"No one is jerking me around, Evan." Logan had been a straight shooter from the start, telling her they could only have a short-lived affair. She was the one who'd pushed for more than he was willing to give.

Her brother nodded and she was relieved that he appeared to accept her words. "Maybe what you have is catching."

"What do you mean?"

"Logan's down in the dumps too."

Lacy was very careful not to look too interested in that tidbit, but Macie picked it up like it was a hundred dollar bill on the ground. "Really?"

Though she was responding to Evan's comment, Macie's gaze had zoomed in on Lacy—big time. The last thing she needed was for Macie to put two and two together. That wouldn't be good for anyone.

Lacy needed to get out of here. Her head was pounding, her throat closing and she was in serious danger of falling apart in the middle of the restaurant.

"Listen, Mace. Things are slow around here tonight. Do you mind covering for me? I've got a wicked headache."

Macie nodded slowly, still studying her face too intently. "Sure. If things get busy, I'll call Gia or Adele to come in and help out."

"Thanks." Lacy grabbed her purse from the storage closet then gave Evan a quick kiss on the cheek on her way out.

"You're sure you're okay?"

She nodded. "Pinkie swear."

He smiled and said goodbye.

Lacy waved then rushed outside. Glancing toward the sky, she saw a dark cloud forming in the distance. Looked like they were in for a storm tonight. Strangely, Lacy found some comfort in that thought. She wasn't in the mood for sunshine.

Besides, maybe a good old-fashioned, noisy thunderstorm would drown out her crying. Because she had every intention of throwing one hell of a temper tantrum the second she got home. For days, she'd walked around in a haze of pent-up sorrow. She'd held her depression in, afraid to let it out. Now her skin felt as if it would crack from the pressure.

She stared at her feet as she pounded the pavement, walking the five blocks from the restaurant to her apartment in record time. She'd been so focused on the ground, she hadn't noticed Logan's truck parked on the street out front until she'd passed it. Then she glanced from the vehicle to the door.

Logan sat on the front stoop, his face stoic, unemotional. She hated the way he could tuck away his feelings so easily. It took all the strength she had not to go over and punch him in the stomach the way he had Bucky.

She felt a tear slide down her cheek, but she didn't bother to dash it away. Ordinarily, she'd rather eat dirt than let someone see her cry. That didn't apply this time. She wanted Logan to see her pain, to understand exactly how bad he'd hurt her.

Logan stood as she approached him. "Lacy."

She simply stared at him as another tear fell. She was unable to speak, too afraid she'd rain down a torrent of horrible words on his head.

"Please don't cry."

Her jaw tightened, her teeth clenched. It was on the tip of her tongue to scream the words "Fuck you!" He didn't get to tell her what to do. How to feel. "What are you doing here?"

"I'm going to break my promise to Evan."

She frowned. "What?"

"Get upstairs."

Her body responded before her brain could engage. She started upstairs. She hesitated briefly, but Logan was there, urging her to keep moving.

Lacy's tears evaporated, her head whirling over what he'd said.

Broken promise.

She allowed him to propel her forward as she struggled to figure out what the hell was going on. Why was he here? Was he collecting on the last night? Did he still intend for this to be the end? Maybe his hormones had finally gotten the better of him.

God knew she'd been fighting some seriously hardcore sexual needs, employing her vibrator far more than was probably healthy. What was worse was the whole time she sought to assuage her needs, her heart was shattered. She missed him even as she cursed his name, and then screamed it during her self-inflicted orgasms.

She was a fucking mess.

If he'd simply come here to use her for sex, she'd...what?

Kick him out?

She wouldn't do that. All he'd had to do was tell her to move and she was all but running to her bedroom. She should hate him for that.

Or maybe she should hate herself.

Once she unlocked her door and entered, Logan was right behind her.

"Bedroom."

"Logan—"

"We're going to talk, Lace. We're going to say every single fucking thing that needs to be said. I promise. But if I'm not inside you in the next five minutes, I can't be held responsible for my own actions."

Every ounce of pain she'd felt in the past five days vanished. She wasn't going to let him leave again without that conversation. But he was right. The physical aches needed to be quenched first or she wouldn't be able to say anything coherent.

"Fine." She grabbed his hand and led him to her bedroom quickly. It sounded as if he had turned the corner on whatever had been holding him back.

At least she hoped he had.

If not, she was making the mother of all mistakes.

Not that it mattered. She was diving into this fire feet first, aching for the burn, because as much as her heart ached, her body was currently suffering more.

As they entered the room, she lost no time. She turned to face him and unbuckled his belt, her fingers grazing his erection as she worked. He was rock hard. How long had he been suffering with that condition? The petty part of her that was still pissed he'd made her wait hoped it had been a while.

She unbuttoned his jeans, slid the zipper down, wrapped her hands around his cock and stroked it slowly. She shuddered as she considered how full she would feel with him inside her.

"I want you so much, Lace."

She smiled and placed a soft kiss on his cheek. "I'm right here."

"I'm sorry," he said. "For the way things ended last time."

He had promised her they would talk. After. She wrapped her arms around his waist and hugged him. "It's okay."

He shook his head as if to disagree, so she forced him to look at her. His apology had gone a long way toward soothing her anger, her pain. So had the fact he'd shown up here tonight. They would discuss whatever had compelled him to leave, but not right now.

"I mean it. It's okay."

Logan gripped her cheeks in his large palms and gave her a kiss so passionate it took her breath away. This was what she'd hoped for on her eighteen birthday. There was nothing on earth so magical as being kissed by someone who clearly adored you.

"God, I missed you."

She grinned at his confession. "Ditto."

He was obviously trying to hold back, giving her the chance to tell him to take a hike.

"It's time."

His jeans hung on his hips, so he reached back, trying to dig out his wallet. Lacy gripped his upper arm to stop him.

"Don't. I'm on the Pill."

"Lacy—"

She pressed her cheek against his. "Please. I want you to come inside me."

He didn't respond for several moments. Then he cupped her cheek affectionately. "I find it impossible to say no to you."

She laughed softly. "That's good. That's *very* good. Hold on to that thought and we'll always be happy."

He twisted her away from him with one quick motion and swatted her ass. "Minx."

"Wait," she said, unfastening her own pants. "Let me get these silly jeans out of the way and you can try that again properly."

"If I wasn't in agony, I'd gag you for trying to run the show, but as it is..."

Together, they got each other out of their clothing. When Lacy climbed onto the mattress, Logan was right there behind her.

She turned, lying down on her back as he came over her.

Her legs were parted in invitation and Logan took no time accepting. He placed the head of this dick against her pussy and pushed in. One hard, deep thrust.

Lacy gasped, her fingers gripping his arms. Her pussy muscles tightened around him. Her head swam. She was close. Again. It typically took her ages to reach her orgasms, but Logan found them within seconds.

He hadn't sought to move. Instead, he remained buried deep. When he lifted his face to look at her, she was blinded by the emotion she saw there.

He loved her. Thank God.

He loved her.

"Logan," she whispered. "I'm not afraid. I'm yours."

Her words set him free. After that, any semblance of control vanished. They came at each other like animals in heat, taking what they wanted with a ferocity that should have been painful. Hell, it was.

Logan beat a power rhythm inside her, crashing up and down like a jackhammer as she cried out. She came, but Logan never stopped moving.

Then she pressed on his shoulder, forcing him to his back as she straddled his hips. Lacy rode his cock like it was a stallion as he kept hold of her hips, pounding her against him roughly.

"Lacy." His hands tightened as she continued to bounce.

She was going to have bruises on her hips from his fingers. She reveled in that thought. Then decided she wanted to mark him as well.

Her fingers were in his hair, so she pulled it. Hard.

He groaned. "Goddammit."

It was the greatest sex of her life, but it still wasn't enough. He twisted once more, pressing her to her back as he came over her again, and he took her even harder, even faster.

Lacy lifted her legs, wrapping her ankles around his back. She didn't shy away, didn't try to stop him. She'd never been fucked with such force. She loved it, begged him for more. She dug her fingers into his shoulders and tilted her hips so he could stake a deeper claim.

Then Logan hit that magic spot inside her and she went off like a bottle rocket. This time, he did too.

"Jesus, Lacy. So. Fucking. Good." Jets of come erupted, filling her.

For several moments, the only sound in the room was the two of them, panting loudly, her heart pounding in her ears.

Logan had Lacy caged beneath him, his dick still inside her. He studied her flushed face and she wondered what he was thinking.

She decided to break the silence first, despite the tiny fear that he'd retreat again. "That was amazing."

He nodded. "It was."

She tightened her legs around his waist. "You're inside me."

"Yeah. I am." His cock stirred as she grinned.

"Are you getting hard again?"

Logan's lips tipped up in a sexy grin. "I've been in misery since we started this game. I'm fairly certain it's going to take me a long damn time to get this need for you out of my system."

She didn't ever want him to get her out of his system. But she didn't say that aloud. They still hadn't sorted through the mess, so she decided to hold off on declaring her undying love for him until he confessed his first. She'd been wearing her heart on her sleeve her entire life. It was his turn to open himself up to her.

"Where's that lube?"

She pointed toward the nightstand drawer. "Not sure that's necessary. I'm more than ready for round two."

He grabbed the tube anyway, his cock still buried inside her. As far as recoveries went, she wondered if this was some sort of world record. The man was rock hard and as thick as ever.

"That's good to know. But I think we're going to give this sweet pussy of yours a rest this time around." As he spoke, he withdrew.

Lacy's pussy clenched hungrily as she realized his plan. She hadn't touched the plug since the last time he'd been in her bed. And as large as the thing was, it was no match for what he was proposing to put inside her this time.

"I..."

"What's your safe word?"

"Chaise," she whispered.

Logan gave her a quick kiss on the lips. "Good girl."

She had expected him to get right down to business, but Logan never did anything the way she anticipated. He reached back into the nightstand drawer and pulled out the vibrator.

"We didn't get to use this last time."

She didn't bother to mention that particular toy had become her favorite over the last week and a half. Hell, she'd even started calling the stupid thing Logan.

He slid the thin vibrator into her pussy with ease. She was still wet from her arousal and his come.

He turned the toy on low and she groaned at the sudden sensation against her well-used, uber-sensitive tissues.

Logan narrowed his eyes when she started swaying her hips, working the vibrations against her G-spot. "Don't even think about coming."

She froze. "What?"

"I've let you grab those orgasms of yours whenever you want. No more. Next time you come, it's going to be with me, while I'm buried in that tight little ass of yours."

"But I'm close."

His expression was stern, though his eyes gave him away. He was amused, even if he was trying to act all big and bad. "You're always close. Hold it off."

She started to shake her head. The truth was she had absolutely no control over her orgasms with him. Hell, half the time they hit when she wasn't even expecting them. "I can't—"

Logan gripped her chin and forced her to look at him. "If you come without my permission, I'm going to tie you to this bed so that you can't move a fucking muscle and keep that vibrator on low all night until you *do* learn how to control it."

"You wouldn't dare. That would only hurt you too."

The smile he gave her was pure danger, especially when his gaze traveled to her mouth. He ran his thumb over her lower lip before he pushed inside. Her lips closed around it instinctively. "I don't intend to suffer."

She closed her eyes, trying to ward off the impact of his words.

His dirty talk was as detrimental to her self-control as his actions. This was not going to end well.

"I'll try," she said begrudgingly.

"Just remember that I'm a man of my word. I will do exactly what I've said if you don't succeed."

She didn't have time to respond before he flipped her onto her stomach. He stroked her ass cheeks with calloused hands. She loved the rough feel of them against her soft skin. It was incredible to her that he could use those hands either to spank or caress and produce the same heart-pounding effect.

"Lift your ass in the air."

She did as he said, the vibrator still buried inside her. She was fighting like the devil to ignore the thing, but as she shifted, it hit one of her happy places. She gripped the sheets in her fists and winced, batting back the urge to come.

"God. I think I might hate you."

He chuckled, completely unconcerned by her confession. "That's good."

Logan squeezed some lube in her ass. Lacy shivered when the cold gel hit her.

He slowly worked it inside her, adding lube and fingers over the course of the next several minutes. Lacy forgot to be nervous about what was coming as she worked overtime not to come. Somewhere in the midst of Logan stretching her ass, he bumped the vibrator up to the next speed.

She called him a long string of unsavory, rude names, but he ignored her and kept going.

Lacy was so focused on not coming, she jumped slightly when she felt the head of Logan's cock pressing against her ass. At some point, he'd covered it with a condom.

"Oh!"

"Shh," he soothed, running his hand along her back. "Say your safe word if you hate it."

He'd only pushed the head in before she decided she wasn't going to hate it. He was so much bigger than the plug and his fingers, not just in width, but in length.

"How much more?" she gasped as he continued to work his way inside with short, easy thrusts.

"Halfway there."

"Fuck me," she groaned, prompting him to laugh a little.

"That's not the safe word."

She glanced at him over her shoulder. "Keep going, asshole."

He slapped her ass lightly. "That's not it either."

During their previous sexual encounters, she had been so focused on how fucking good the sex was and on finding a way to get him back in her bed, that she hadn't had a chance to consider what it would be like to truly date Logan.

Words like fun and playful floated to the surface. Even as he dominated their play, taking her to places she'd never imagined in all her twisted, kinky fantasies, she couldn't deny that being with him was as much fun as it was hot.

When he was fully lodged, he paused. "That's it." His words sounded almost pained, which seemed weird to her. She was the one being practically split in two. Then she considered how much control it must have taken for him to move so slowly, to give her this experience with as little pain as possible.

She took a second to adjust, marveling over how freaking much she loved everything they'd done together. Something told her a hundred years with the man wouldn't be enough to get him out of *her* system.

"Lacy," he murmured. He was holding on for her. "Baby..."

"Can I come now?"

A short burst of laughter filled the room. "God. You're all kinds of perfect. Yeah. Come at will, gorgeous."

With that, he began to fuck her. He kept his motions slow, easy. She appreciated his efforts at not hurting her, but it wasn't enough.

"Logan," she gasped. "Please. More."

"As you wish." He reached down and found the control to the vibrator. He cranked the thing on high and then it was game over.

He took her hard, driving deep into her ass, as Lacy came violently. One orgasm stretched into a second before Logan joined her. His fingers tightened on her hips as he jerked once, twice more. Then he fell to her side as she turned to face him. She shuddered when he reached between her legs to turn off the vibrator and pull it out.

"I think you killed me."

He took her hand in his and gave it a squeeze. "I was going to say the same thing to you."

"Logan."

"Hmm," he murmured sleepily, his eyes drifting closed.

"Can we do that again?"

He chuckled, his lids lifting briefly. "Sure. Give me a few minutes."

She laughed softly. They hadn't talked yet, but at least he wasn't sprinting for the door. They had time to get into the heavy stuff. Later.

She sighed happily at the thought of what else they'd do later before giving in to her own need for sleep.

NINETEEN YEARS EARLIER...

LOGAN STUDIED the lake until he found his sister. Sure enough, Rachel was boob-deep in the water, wrapped around Rodney and kissing him like the guy was going off to war or something. He wouldn't mind so much, but last week she'd been doing the exact same thing with Lee.

"We need to make a pact," he said, glancing over at Evan. The two of them were sitting in the sand, chowing down on hot dogs they'd bought at the concession stand. He knew a lot of his friends were looking forward to growing up, becoming adults, but Logan figured they had it made. They were fifteen, out of school on summer break and their biggest decision each day was whether to hit the beach at the lake or head over to the park to play baseball.

"What kind of pact?" Evan asked.

"We don't hook up with each other's sisters."

Evan glanced at Rachel and Logan spotted the reticence on his friend's face. He knew. Knew Evan had been looking a little too often in Rachel's direction. What Evan didn't realize was that Logan was putting the pact in place for his friend more than his sister. Rachel was a man-eater.

"I don't see what the big deal is if—"

"I mean it, man. I don't want you hooking up with Rachel."

Evan frowned and then, because he really was a good friend, he shrugged and agreed. "Fine. But same goes for my sister."

Logan looked across the sand and spotted Lacy building a sandcastle with her little friend, Bucky. "You got it," he said with a grin.

Evan rolled his eyes. "You realize I'm getting the bad end of this deal."

"It's a bro code," Logan said, reaching out for the traditional handshake to seal the deal. "And it's binding. Forever."

CHAPTER SEVEN

Logan stirred as a roar of thunder pierced the quiet of the evening. He and Lacy had been dozing in bed for nearly an hour, both of them physically exhausted.

Then he recalled the thunder. "Damn."

"What's wrong?"

"I left the windows rolled down on my truck."

"I don't understand why you drove here. You only live a few blocks away."

He reluctantly disentangled from her embrace. "Made a furniture delivery, and then came straight here."

"In a hurry to see me?" she teased.

Logan tickled her, enjoying her giggle. "Yeah. I held out as long as I could, and then realized I was being a first-class tool. Turned the truck toward your place and decided it was time to set things right."

He reached for his jeans and tugged them on.

The two of them still needed to have a serious talk. Logan had spent the past five days trying to come to grips with everything that had happened. Lacy had come into his life—and his bedroom—and she'd saved him.

He had let Jane mess with his head, let her convince him that his needs were wrong if he wanted a long-lasting, normal relationship. Which he had finally been able to admit to himself that he wanted this morning. He wanted what Evan and Annie had. A loving, kinky, forever relationship. And there wasn't a doubt in Logan's mind he was going to find that—and more—with Lacy. She was perfect for him.

He'd accused her of pretending to please him. He owed her an apology for that. Lacy didn't lie. She was the most genuine, honest person he'd ever known, yet he'd foolishly let his insecurities cast her into shadows that simply weren't there. There wasn't an insincere bone in her body.

"Tell you what. Why don't you order a pizza while I run out to take care of the windows?"

"Sounds good," she said, lazily stretching. The sheet drifted lower, giving him a perfect view of her breasts.

"Do me a favor and get dressed before I get back. You and I need to talk, but there's not a snowball's chance in hell of accomplishing that with you looking so sexy."

A glimmer of nervousness crept onto her face. He hated that he'd left her so uncertain. She'd just given him the best—and worst—three weeks of his life. When he was with her, everything felt right, but spending the past five days without her had been brutal. Jane had left after a three-year relationship and he'd gone to work the next day as if she'd never been there. For the last five days, he hadn't been able to work, eat, or sleep. He had been miserable.

"Hey," he said, grabbing her hand and tugging her to her knees at the edge of the mattress. "It's nothing bad. Okay?"

She smiled, though he could read the doubt in her expression. He had a lot to make up for.

Logan gave her a quick kiss. "Won't be a minute."

He didn't bother with a shirt as he walked out of her front door and downstairs. There were three floors in the building and each one contained two apartments. It was unlikely he'd run into any of her neighbors, but the more time he spent with her, the less he gave a shit who saw them. It was a dangerous mindset to have until he came clean to her brother, but he was currently too happy, too sexually sated to give it much more than a passing care.

He was halfway to his truck when he realized Evan was standing next to it. His best friend's gaze drifted from him to the truck and back again, his expression going as dark as the cloud-ridden sky as he took in Logan's half-dressed state.

"What are you doing here?" Logan asked.

"Thought I'd swing by, see if I could figure out who Lacy's new boyfriend is."

"Boyfriend?"

It was the absolute worst thing he could have said, but Evan's comment caught him off guard. Had Lacy told her brother she had a boyfriend?

Evan was in front of him after three long strides, which he followed with a hard right to the face.

Logan stumbled at the impact of the punch and it took him a couple of seconds to shake off the pain, and then regain his vision. When he did, he stood there with fists clenched, ready to defend himself if Evan came at him again.

"The first one is free. I probably had it coming. But you hit me again and I'm going to punch back."

"You *probably* had it coming? You're questioning that?" Evan shouted.

"Alright. I definitely had it coming, but you're not much better than me. I know about you and Rachel."

"How?"

"So you *did* make out with my sister."

Evan looked slightly chagrined, but it was clear any guilt he felt was struggling to outweigh his anger at finding out Logan was sleeping with Lacy. "How did—"

"Lacy saw you."

Evan dismissed the accusation as insignificant—which it really was. "Who gives a shit? We were teenagers and all we did was make out one time. Is that all you're doing with Lacy?"

He shook his head.

Evan's fists were still clenched. "That goddamn bro code thing was *your* idea."

Logan shrugged. "I know. We were just kids, Evan."

Evan ran his hand through his hair as Logan braced himself for another blow. Instead, his friend hit him with something much harder to deflect. "I don't give a shit about the stupid vow. Never did. I thought you weren't doing vanilla again."

Logan didn't reply. What the hell could he say? He'd fucked Evan's sister six ways to Sunday, introduced her to bondage, clamps, butt plugs and spankings.

Evan's jaw clenched as the silence lingered too long. "She's my fucking sister, Logan!"

"And she's a grown woman," Lacy said, rushing out of her apartment.

She was barefoot, but at least she'd had the good sense to throw on a t-shirt and jeans. Evan really would have beaten him to a pulp if she'd come outside in just a robe or something. It was one thing to know your best friend was fucking your little sister and another to have it slammed in your face.

Lacy stepped between them, clearly concerned the fistfight was going to continue. "My sex life is none of your business."

"Dammit, Lacy. I'm always going to worry about you. You can't ask me to stop that."

"Then worry about shit that matters. How Logan and I have sex doesn't qualify."

Evan winced, but he rallied quicker than Logan would have. "Please don't say the word sex to me. I prefer to think of you as my sweet, innocent sister. Pure as freshly fallen snow."

Lacy rolled her eyes and snorted. "Yeah. That snow was plowed a decade ago."

Evan groaned and shook his head. "You're killing me."

"Serves you right for hitting Logan."

"He had that coming, and he knows it. So what is this? A relationship? Are you two dating?"

Lacy looked at Logan and shrugged, taking her time to reply. "I don't..."

Evan's face turned murderous. "Don't say you don't know. I swear to God, if this is just a hookup, if you're just using her to get your rocks off, I'll fucking kill you."

Raindrops began to fall. Logan looked at Lacy, even as he spoke to Evan. "I'm in love with her."

Lacy's eyes widened. "You're in love with me?"

"Of course I am. How could I not be? You're everything I've ever wanted."

"Took you long enough to figure that out," she teased.

He pulled her into his arms. "I mean it, Lacy. You're perfect for me."

"Then why did you leave last time?"

The rain started to come down harder. He hadn't intended to have the conversation with her outside, in front of her brother and —he glanced around—the seven people who'd opened their front doors in hopes of catching a fistfight.

"Looks like the two of you have a few things to discuss." Evan was giving them a chance to escape back inside.

Logan nodded. "Evan—"

"Later, man. We'll talk it out later. Make things right with her first."

"Okay."

Evan sighed. "And do me a favor. Never, under any circumstances, talk to me about your sex life again. Promise?"

"New bro code?"

Evan's eyebrows lifted as he considered that question. "If you fix things the way I hope, maybe the 'bro' part of that code could become a legal, binding, official thing."

Lacy interjected. "Dear God. It's only been three weeks, Evan. Go away before you screw everything up."

Logan wrapped his arm more tightly around her shoulder. None of them bothered to seek shelter from the steadily pouring rain. "Technically, it's been three weeks, plus a lifetime."

She twisted out of his arms and narrowed her eyes. "This better not be a proposal, Logan. I haven't even had a chance to yell at you properly for breaking my heart."

"You broke her heart?" Evan asked, his scowl returning.

Lacy threw her hands up in exasperation. "Go home, Evan. Turn that annoying overprotective nonsense of yours on Eryn. Poor girl."

Evan glanced at Logan, hesitant to leave.

Logan reached out to put his hand on Evan's shoulder. "I won't hurt her."

Evan's expression cleared. "Yeah. I know you won't." And with that, he walked back to his patrol car and climbed in.

Lacy turned to look at him. "You told Evan you loved me before you told me."

He grinned. "He forced my hand. Guy packs one hell of a punch."

His words sent Lacy's gaze to his left cheek. "I think you're going to have a black eye."

"Great," he said with a grimace.

"Why did you leave last time?"

He looked up at the dark sky. "It's raining, Lace. Do we have to do this here?" They were both drenched.

"Come on." She accepted the hand he proffered and the two of them returned to her apartment. Once they were inside, Lacy went to the bathroom to grab them a couple of towels. He wiped off his chest as she used hers to dry her hair.

"Here. You'll catch a cold if you don't get out of those wet things." Logan drew her wet t-shirt over her head, forcing himself to keep his eyes on her face. Her breasts were his kryptonite, and they needed to talk before they continued with anything else.

She peeled off her jeans as he did the same. They threw their wet clothing in a heap on the floor of her laundry room, and then returned to the living room.

Lacy grabbed a fleece blanket and tossed it to him before getting a second one for herself. They curled under them on the couch. Lacy didn't resist when he tugged her legs over his thighs so he could rub her feet.

"Jane did a number on me."

She nodded slowly. "Yeah, I figured that much out. It's just... you said you weren't brokenhearted about her leaving."

"I'm not. That's not what I mean. When we first started dating, I thought the two of us were compatible lovers. She seemed to enjoy my rough edge, although I'll admit I didn't..." He paused, trying to find the right words.

"Unleash the Full Monty?" she supplied helpfully.

Logan laughed. "Something like that. I didn't want to scare her right out of the gate, so I took things slowly. However, the more I tried to introduce BDSM into our sexual relationship, the more she resisted. I was in love with her, Lace. So I held back."

"I'm not afraid of what we do, Logan."

"I know."

"Have you been holding back with me?"

He shook his head and chuckled. "No. Not at all."

"Phew." She pretended to wipe her brow. "That's a relief. I'd hate to have to deal with twenty or thirty more orgasms every time we crawled between the sheets."

He playfully messed up her hair. "Smartass. You realize that's just daring me."

"Good. That was my intention."

Logan took a deep breath and said what had been keeping him from her, though even as he said the words, he knew exactly how stupid he'd been. "I can't do vanilla. It's not in my nature."

"It's not in mine either. Not anymore. Maybe not ever. You ruined me when I was seventeen."

"Do me a favor, Lace. Don't tell your brother about that peeping Tom escapade of yours. He'll punch me again."

She leaned closer and pressed a kiss against his cheek. "I love you too, Logan. I didn't get a chance to say that outside." She blushed and he wondered what she was thinking. "Of course, I probably didn't need to say it. I haven't exactly hidden my feelings from you all these years."

"I know it's only been three weeks, but when I look at you, Lacy, I see a very long future."

"Forever?"

He nodded. "I hope so."

"I'd like that, but I'm going to need a promise from you."

"In addition to the 'I Do' one?"

She rose from the couch and grasped his hand, pulling him to his feet as well. "Yep. I want you to promise me that nothing...and I mean nothing...is ever off-limits between us again."

He laughed, shook her hand. "Deal."

TWENTY YEARS EARLIER...

LOGAN LOOKED over and caught sight of Lacy sitting in the stands with one of her little friends playing with dolls. Her hair was pulled up in pigtails and she gave him a toothless grin. She waved, so he waved back.

"SEE THAT BOY OVER THERE?" Lacy pointed to a fourteen-year-old Logan, currently standing on first base.

Justine Matthews laid her Barbie doll on the bleachers and looked. "Yeah."

"His name is Logan Grady, and I'm going to marry him one day."

ISN'T it time for Dr. Tyson Sparks to find his happy ending in the Sparks in Texas series? And what better way than with a sexy ménage! Pick up *Waiting for Them*, available now.

And be sure to check out other books in the Sparks in Texas series.
Waiting for Us (prequel)
Waiting for You
Waiting for Her

Waiting for Him
Waiting for Them
Waiting for Love
Waiting for Snow

0.

ABOUT THE AUTHOR

Virginia native Mari Carr is a New York Times and USA TODAY bestseller of contemporary romance novels. With over two million copies of her books sold, Mari was the winner of the Romance Writers of America's Passionate Plume award for her novella, Erotic Research. She has over a hundred published works, including her popular Wild Irish and Compass books, along with the Trinity Masters series she writes with Lila Dubois.

Follow Mari:
www.maricarr.com
mari@maricarr.com

Join her newsletter so you don't miss new releases and for exclusive subscriber-only content.